THE
OTHER
BROTHER

THE OTHER BROTHER

TIERNEY PAGE

FOREVER

New York   Boston

Copyright © 2025 by Tierney Page

Cover design by Emily Wittig
Cover copyright © 2025 by Hachette Book Group, Inc.

Forever
Hachette Book Group
1290 Avenue of the Americas, New York, NY 10104
read-forever.com
@readforeverpub

Originally published in 2025 in Australia and New Zealand by Hachette Australia (an imprint of Hachette Australia Pty Limited)
First Forever trade paperback edition: July 2025

Forever is an imprint of Grand Central Publishing. The Forever name and logo are registered trademarks of Hachette Book Group, Inc.

The publisher is not responsible for websites (or their content) that are not owned by the publisher.

The Hachette Speakers Bureau provides a wide range of authors for speaking events. To find out more, go to hachettespeakersbureau.com or email HachetteSpeakers@hbgusa.com.

Forever books may be purchased in bulk for business, educational, or promotional use. For information, please contact your local bookseller or the Hachette Book Group Special Markets Department at special.markets@hbgusa.com.

Library of Congress Control Number: 2025936391

ISBNs: 9781538778364 (trade paperback), 9781538778371 (ebook)

Printed in the United States of America

LSC-C

Printing 1, 2025

For all the people out there who just want to be run through like a sewing machine.
Banger.
Happy reading.

Disciaimer

This book contains graphic language and sexually explicit content and is intended for mature audiences. These scenes involve mild bondage, as well as breath, spit, and anal play. There is mention of parent death, and there is an instance of infidelity involving secondary characters—not the main characters. If any of these are a sensitive topic for you, please proceed with care.

Chapter 1

April

I glance down, admiring my ring as it glimmers under the soft amber glow of my bedroom light. A simple, classic two-carat round solitaire set in a yellow gold band, timeless and elegant. The exact ring I would have picked for myself. Four months have passed since Lucas asked me to be his wife, and since then, I've lived in a bubble of pure bliss. Every aspect of my life finally feels like it's falling into place.

Releasing a breath, a flutter of butterflies erupts in my stomach as I reach to pull the zipper of my dress. Turning to face the mirror, I study my reflection. Auburn curls cascade over one shoulder, skimming down to my ribs. For tonight, large gold hoop earrings are the only jewelry I opted for, aside from my ring, of course. Completing my ensemble, I matched my earrings with a pair of stunning gold strapped heels, which cost far more than I'm willing to admit. It's my engagement party, so I decided there was no harm in splurging on some niceties.

My fitted silken midnight dress stops mid-calf, hugging my curves like a second skin. I feel sultry and feminine.

The gentle material falls off the shoulder to reveal a golden-champagne highlight dusted across my collarbones, shimmering softly when it catches under the light. My make-up is natural, just the way I like it. A swipe of deep berry lipstick adds color to my lips, while a few layers of black mascara make the lighter shades of my blue eyes stand out.

I finish with a spritz of my favorite Chanel perfume—delicious notes of vanilla and musk. I know black isn't exactly the most cheerful choice for my own engagement party, but it's the color that always makes me feel the most confident and sexy. Plus, there's the practical side to it: Black hides spills, and given my track record, wearing white is a disaster waiting to happen.

I hear the bedroom door creak open, and my smile widens. I turn to find Lucas standing at the threshold, and my breath stalls. Standing at six five, he commands attention. His chestnut hair is perfectly styled, a little shorter on the sides and slightly longer on top. He's clad in a black suit and white shirt, pressed and tailored flawlessly, which accentuates his muscular torso. A pair of patent dress shoes add a finishing touch to his clean and polished appearance. I try to gauge his reaction as he drinks me in.

His gaze lingers on me as I attempt to read the emotion behind his dark eyes—wondering what he's thinking. I clasp my hands together in front of me to keep from fidgeting. Silent, his eyes slowly travel from my red-tipped toes up to my nervous smile. Blowing out a long exhale, he palms the back of his neck and shakes his head in response. "Fuck, April. You look . . . You're so beautiful."

My cheeks heat, and I duck my chin, feeling exposed and shy. I adore getting dressed up, but I don't think I'll ever get used to being the center of attention. I would much rather bleed into the background.

He steps forward, closing the distance between us. Towering over me, he tenderly cups my face in his large hands, lowering himself until our foreheads and the tips of our noses meet in a gentle press. The gesture feels so safe and intimate. I close my eyes and breathe in his familiar Ted Baker cologne—citrus and pepper—my favorite scent in the world.

"I can't believe my luck," he murmurs, softly sealing our lips together. My breath catches and I fist the lapels of his jacket, deepening the kiss. He sucks my bottom lip into his mouth, biting it gently before pulling back. Releasing my face, he traces his hands over my bare shoulders and down my sides, barely touching, and my flesh erupts in goose bumps as he reaches my ass. Squeezing, he pulls us together so my hips meet his. A soft moan escapes my lips as I arch into him, desire surging through me, rushing to my core and dampening the thin fabric between my thighs. Wary of my dark lipstick making a mess, I pull back and giggle.

"Berry is a great color on you," I say, using my thumb to wipe away the stain left on his mouth. He smiles softly in response. With lips swollen and adoration in his eyes, I melt at the sight of him.

Heavy footsteps echo down the hall, breaking our spell. "Okay, lovers, if you could stop making out and tell me where the champagne bucket is, that would be great."

Anna marches in, snapping her fingers as if she could conjure a bucket from thin air, her phone gripped firmly in her other hand.

I can't help but beam back at her. She is a few inches shorter than me, even in her taupe two-inch heels. Her natural, sun-kissed complexion pays homage to her Italian heritage. We may be chalk and cheese, but somehow, we couldn't be a more perfect match. Her dark hair, streaked with blond highlights, is fashioned into an effortlessly messy up-do. Her eyes are lined with black kohl, accentuating their golden hazel, and her lips are painted peony pink. She wears a blush pink floral A-line dress with a sweetheart neckline, which suits her perfectly, a fun and playful vibe to match her bubbly personality.

Anna has been one of my best friends for over twenty-five years. We met in Year 1 when we were both the new kids at school. Her family had returned home to London from living in Fiji, and I had recently switched schools after moving to West London. Being the two new kids at school, we were seated next to each other, and we've been inseparable since. Now, at thirty-one, it's incredibly special to share this moment with her.

"It's under the staircase. I'll get it," Lucas says, shooting me a wink before disappearing through the door.

Anna waits until he's left before letting out a low whistle. "Girl, if he hadn't already put a ring on it, I'd lock that shit down myself. Look at you! You look amazing!"

"Thank you," I murmur, lowering my eyes to the carpet.

"Don't be shy. Turn around," Anna instructs, waving her finger in a circular motion.

I turn slowly, offering her a complete 360-degree view.

"Ass looks great, good for you," she says, giving a chef's-kiss gesture.

"And what about you? That dress is gorgeous! You look so beautiful."

"I know," she states, punctuating her words with a curtsey.

I roll my eyes, chuckling.

"Picture time! We need to get a few snaps in before everyone starts arriving."

"Oh, good idea. I'm so bad at remembering to take photos."

"Don't worry, I've got it covered." Stepping beside me, Anna unlocks her phone, switches it to selfie mode, and holds it in front of us to snap a few photos. After studying and selecting the best, Anna sashays out of the room and heads downstairs to assist with the final touches for the party.

We opted to have our engagement fête at home. It's where we love to be, enjoying time with friends and family. We cook, drink wine, play board games, watch movies, and talk endlessly until the early-morning hours. Our home isn't big, but it's inviting. Hosting the party here felt right; anything lavish or fancy just wouldn't be *us*. I prepared most of the food myself with help from my other dearest friend, Gemma.

My heels click along the hardwood floors as I walk down the stairs and through the lounge. The scent of warm pastry and desserts envelops me, and I take a deep breath.

Champagne buckets, hors d'oeuvres, cheese platters, and charcuterie boards are neatly arranged across the island bench and coffee table, while the oven fills the space with the delicious aroma of hot food. Two large glass doors reveal a deck and fenced-in courtyard beyond, with an outdoor heater, chairs and neatly arranged potted plants adding vivid pops of color. Fairy lights are strung from the deck, weaving along the fences like twinkling fireflies. It's late winter here in London, so we leave the doors closed to ward off the biting cold.

I spot Anna in the kitchen fiddling with a champagne cork until the distinctive pop sounds. "Cheers!" Anna yells, extending her hand and offering me a filled flute. I accept and clink it against hers before bringing it to my lips. A hint of liquid courage to calm my nerves. Anna pours another glass.

"Where's Lucas?" She peers over my shoulder just as Lucas sidles up beside me.

He playfully bumps my shoulder with his, smirking down at me before reaching for his glass and tipping it toward mine in silent cheers. "To us," he says, lifting it to his lips.

"To us," I say, smiling.

The front door bursts open, hitting the wall with a loud bang, causing Gemma to wince as she makes her grand entrance.

"Crap! Sorry about your wall! Am I late? What can I do to help?" she asks as she sheds her coat and unwinds her scarf, revealing a short, black leather skirt and laced bodysuit. She's paired the outfit with black pumps and cherry-red lips. Her blond hair is slicked back into a low bun, and her usual quirky glasses are perched on her nose. She looks sleek and sophisticated. I all but skip toward her with excitement, wrapping her in my arms for a tight hug.

"You aren't late. You're just in time for a drink! Anna opened the champagne."

"Oh my God, April...wow. Luc, you better watch yourself because I'm Mrs. Gonna Steal Yo' Girl!" Gemma exclaims as she holds my hands, taking me in.

"I know. I'm going to have to watch her this evening," Lucas says with a smile.

"You clean up pretty good yourself," I say to Gemma. She beams at me as we approach Anna, who offers her a glass of bubbly.

"Gemma, are you wearing a lingerie bodysuit to our best friend's engagement party?" Anna questions.

"Anna, come on. Do I wear anything else?" she asks, as if the answer is obvious.

"She's in her ho era," I reply, taking another sip.

"Ah yes, the best era. I remember it well." Anna nods.

Gemma turns her attention to Lucas. "Speaking of ho, is James coming?" she asks, wiggling her eyebrows.

"That's way too close to home, Gemma," I say, my voice laced with disapproval.

I quickly avert my gaze, scrunching my nose in confusion. Why do I feel so protective of James? The thought of him with Gemma doesn't sit right.

I take a long pull of my champagne. I don't want to explore why it bothers me.

James is Lucas's younger brother, but the two are cut from different cloths. Lucas is romantic and light-hearted—the kind of man who favors crisp shirts, listens to '80s hits, and fills notebooks with poetry. James, however, is broody and dark, wears ripped jeans and band T-shirts, listens to metal and rock, and plays the bass guitar. Even though the brothers aren't the closest of friends, due to their differing tastes and five-year age gap, I've always got along reasonably well with James, despite his reserved nature.

Admittedly, there's something alluring about his mysterious vibe, and I know I'm not the only one drawn to his dark charm.

Lucas strolls over to the sound system, fiddling with buttons and his phone until the first few notes of a song start to play. As the familiar tune fills the room, Anna, Gemma, and I exchange excited glances—we all love this song. Giggling, we finish our champagne and bustle around, belting out lyrics while setting up food and drinks before the guests arrive.

Chapter 2

April

As our nearest and dearest pour in, the room comes to life with laughter and celebration. Lucas and I circle the space, ensuring we spend time with every guest. Now and then, we're separated to make sure drinks are refilled, food is stocked, and everyone is having a good time.

With relief, Lucas's parents, Caroline and Peter, arrive and take over the role of hosts, and I couldn't be more grateful for the reprieve. Caroline has been incredibly kind to me since her son and I have been together, treating me as if I were her own daughter. She's nurturing and sweet, and I feel privileged to have such a wonderful female role model in my life, after my own mother.

Caroline approaches me as I pluck a packet of dried apricots out of the pantry and tear it open to refill the charcuterie board.

"You shouldn't be working at your engagement party, honey. Let me worry about the food. Here," she says, extending her hand for the packet, "you go and enjoy yourself."

"It's no trouble, I'm happy to," I reply.

"My dear, I promise you no one is worrying about the apricots," she says as she grabs the packet. She makes a gentle shooing motion with her hands. "Go on."

I smile, shooting her a grateful look before rounding the kitchen island.

As I slip away to the upstairs bathroom, I huff a sigh as I catch a lonely reflection of myself in the mirror. Even though my own parents passed away ten years ago, I still carry the weight of their loss with me; the burden is hard to bear in times of celebration. Lucas and I have been together for three years. I was twenty-eight when we met, so they never got the chance to meet him. It's so bittersweet.

My father is supposed to be the man walking me down the aisle.

My mother is supposed to shop with me for my wedding dress.

My parents were killed in a car accident when I was twenty-one. The money I inherited from their estate, along with the sale of their flat in Notting Hill, helped me buy our townhouse in Fulham, securing a future I never thought I'd have so soon. I think about them often, wondering if they'd be proud of the life I'm building and the choices I've made. I know they'd love Lucas; they'd recognize in him the qualities they always valued—kindness, loyalty, and a quiet appreciation for life's simple pleasures.

I've always wanted what my parents had—the kind of love that knows no bounds, free of expectations, where joy is found in the little things. My father adored my mother in every way that mattered, and growing up surrounded by that kind of love made me long for a happily ever after of my own.

I'm fortunate to carry those memories with me—precious morsels I'll treasure forever. And I know how lucky I am to have grown up the way I did, in a way not everyone gets to experience. I'm incredibly grateful for that. We never left the house without saying, *"I love you."* It wasn't just a habit—it was a promise, a way of ensuring no moment passed without reminding one another how much we mattered. Christmas Eve was always spent huddled together in their king-size bed, watching Christmas films on the old telly we refused to upgrade. Our joined laughter filling the room felt like the best gift of all.

Even though I grew up without siblings, I never felt like I was missing out, because they were more than just my parents—they were my best friends. The kind of friends who made even the simplest things feel extraordinary.

My mother was an art teacher, so we spent hours every weekend painting in watercolors and making ceramics. Throwing clay was always my favorite. I still hold on to a pair of mugs we sculpted and decorated with vibrant tulips. Since they passed, I haven't been able to touch my pottery wheel, but I keep it with me, just in case. I know she would be devastated if I ever got rid of it.

And now, when the house is quiet and the lights are low, I can almost feel them here with me, tucked away in the corners, watching over the life I'm building and reminding me that love like theirs never truly leaves.

The inheritance gave us more than a roof over our heads; it gave us freedom. We don't live extravagantly—no designer clothes and furniture or exotic holidays—but we live comfortably, and that's enough for me. I've never needed much to be happy, just the little things: the smell of freshly brewed coffee, the warmth of Lucas's hand resting on my leg during a lazy Sunday afternoon, the way sunlight filters through the bedroom window on a quiet morning. Those small, fleeting moments mean more to me than any grand gesture or luxury ever could.

And though Lucas doesn't earn as much as he'd like working in administration at the local university, that's never mattered to me. It's never been about the money. He has his love for helping students and his hobby of writing on the odd occasion too. What we have is simple but good—bills split evenly, a home we made together, with enough left over to indulge now and then. It's solid, the kind of life I used to dream about when everything felt uncertain. I treasure that stability. It's not perfect, but it's ours.

Celebrating this pivotal moment in the house their loss provided feels surreal.

Opening the top drawer of the bathroom counter, I pluck out my lipstick, snapping it open to swipe a fresh layer across my lips. I'm tousling my hair, running my fingers through the waved strands as Lucas steps in. I turn to face him as he places a large hand on my hip.

"Is everything okay?" he asks.

"Yeah, everything's fine. I was just freshening up."

"Are you sure?"

I sigh. "It's times like these when I can't help but think about my parents. I'm so happy, really, I am . . . But I wish they were here to share my happiness. I wish they could have met you."

"I'm so sorry, baby. How can I make you feel better?" he asks, pulling me in closer.

I pause, contemplating momentarily. "I can think of something," I reply, a hint of mischief in my tone.

"Oh yeah? What's that?" he asks, pressing his index finger underneath my chin to tip my head up.

"We have guests downstairs . . ." I say softly.

"They won't even notice we're gone." He pulls up his trouser legs before dropping to his knees before me. A surge of excitement and heat courses through my body, pooling at my center. Lucas delicately presses the fingertips of both hands to my ankles, the touch sending shivers up my spine as he slowly trails along my calf, gathering the silk of my dress. His palms flatten against the backs of my thighs, drawing me closer to him as he continues to push the material of my dress toward my hips.

I part my legs slightly to grant him better access, my heart thundering. He grunts his approval when he sees the wet fabric of my thong before spreading me wider. He hooks his thumb underneath the lace, pushing the flimsy fabric aside and exposing me.

"Fuck, April," he breathes, running his fingers through my arousal, collecting my wetness. "Look at you."

Leaning in, he swipes his tongue along me in a single, firm stroke. I arch my back. "Luc."

His gaze shifts from my core, rising to meet mine. "What do you need?"

A desperate whimper escapes me.

"Have I rendered you speechless?"

Meeting his hungry look, I straighten my posture and say, "I need more, Luc."

That's all it takes before his restraint snaps and he turns feral. He dips his head, gripping my thighs possessively as he indulges. His tongue flicks across my clit before he releases my thigh to circle my entrance with his fingers. He slides two thick digits knuckle-deep, eliciting a heady moan from me. Curling his fingers in a beckoning gesture, he expertly rubs the precise spot I crave, over and over, as I mewl above him.

He increases his pace, and his mouth latches onto my clit, sucking as he continues to stroke me. I rock my hips back and forth, riding his face. I throw one hand behind me, gripping the counter tightly to support myself; the other instinctively tangles in his hair. He inserts a third finger, stretching and filling me more, and I can't hold off any longer. Throwing my head back, I squeeze my eyes closed, releasing a muffled cry of ecstasy as my release courses through me.

Groaning, Lucas slows his pace, softly moving his fingers inside me as I ride out the wave. Releasing me, we lock eyes, cheeks flushed, our chests rising up and falling with breathless pants.

Lucas delicately presses a kiss to the inside of my thigh before readjusting my soaked thong and smoothing my dress. I run my hands down the soft fabric, ensuring no creases.

"I love seeing you come undone for me, baby," he says, rising to his full height.

A sudden knock on the door startles us.

"Luc? Mum sent me to check on you. Is everything okay? Have you seen April?"

Oh God. I recognize the gruff voice immediately—James.

Lucas and I exchange a glance, panic flickering in my widened eyes. He shrugs his shoulders, adjusting his jacket, and I mouth, "*Shit.*"

Swiping the back of his hand over his wet mouth to remove the glistening evidence of my orgasm, he turns toward the door.

"James? Is that you? Give me a second."

Lucas shoots me a nod before he clears his throat and reaches for the knob, pulling the door open. James pauses in surprise, leaning one arm into the frame as he eyes me, standing sheepishly beside his brother. He's wearing a band T-shirt under his distressed leather jacket; his sandy blond waves fall perfectly out of place, shorter on the sides and longer on top, giving him a rugged look. He's donning his usual scuffed, black combat boots. He reaches into his pocket, pulling out a black guitar pick, and brings it to his mouth to nibble on as he considers us with an arrogant, knowing smirk.

Was he always this handsome?

I cast my eyes downward, feeling sheepish under his scrutinizing gaze.

Where Lucas is soft and clean-shaven, James has sharp edges and prominent cheekbones, his jaw dusted with stubble and a dimple in his left cheek. Seeing the two of them standing side by side is striking. Lucas has an imposing presence, but James, just an inch shorter at six four, matches him in intensity.

Yes, Caroline birthed two monsters.

Her poor, poor vagina.

"You couldn't wait until the party ended?" James asks, his tone dry.

"You couldn't put on a suit?"

James blows out a breath. "Give me a break, Luc. I came straight from practice. This is what I'm comfortable in. We have that audition coming up and I lost track of time, so I came straight here. Suits are *your* thing, not mine."

"Whatever, the Golden Child does what he wants. Always has."

Lucas has always referred to James as the Golden Child, and I've never understood why. Despite their lack of closeness, they've managed to remain relatively amicable, given their differences.

I give him a small, awkward wave. "Hey, James."

His brows crease slightly. "Hey, April."

As if drawn to each other, our eyes lock. My breath catches as I take in the vibrant green. His eyes are captivating, almost unreal—flecks of gold encircle his pupils, making them even more mesmerizing.

There's curiosity in his stare, a flicker of amusement too, and just the barest hint of a smile. The air between us crackles, and my pulse quickens.

There's no denying what just happened between Lucas and me—no pretending we're innocent. The realization makes my cheeks burn hotter with the shame of being caught by my fiancé's younger brother.

After a beat, James awkwardly looks away, his eyes skimming everything but me.

What was that?

Removing the pick from his mouth, he simply says, "Your mascara's smudged," before stepping away from the door-frame, turning, and disappearing down the hallway. His words hang in the air, and my mouth pops open, mortified, as I swivel to face the mirror. I do, in fact, look like a panda. I begin swiping madly underneath my eyes, desperate to fix the smudged mascara before rejoining the party.

"Don't worry, he's just being a dick," Lucas says, stepping closer. He places a hand on my shoulder, pressing a soft kiss to the crown of my head before turning toward the door. His phone pings, and he pulls it from his back pocket, typing furiously as he walks down the hall.

I wait a few minutes to allow the flush of my face to settle before rejoining the party.

Chapter 3

James

"All right, good job, lads," Oliver calls, clapping me on the shoulder. I give him a brief nod, slipping the strap of my bass over my head and settling it back into its case. The latches click shut, and I straighten, turning to pack up the rest of my gear.

During the week and on most weekends, I work as a construction laborer. Most of my time is spent digging, preparing worksites, mixing concrete and assisting other trades. But my side hustle, and my main focus, is playing bass in a band, Atlas Veil, with my best mates. We mainly play progressive rock, but sometimes we throw in a classic rock or punk cover when we gig at local venues. While I also play the electric guitar, the bass is where my heart really lies.

We've just wrapped up another long day of rehearsal at Tom's house and I'm exhausted. Oliver, Tom, Will, and I have been grinding nonstop for months—working twice as hard ever since we found out that our favorite band, Bound to Oblivion, one of the biggest names in rock, is holding auditions for an opening act on their European tour. The second we caught wind of it, we were all in—no hesitation.

This is the chance of a lifetime—playing for fans who love progressive rock and sharing the stage with our heroes. It's our shot at recognition. We've paid our dues with pub gigs, weddings, and festivals; now we're ready for the next step. We want to be signed by a major label, perform in stadiums around the world, in front of tens of thousands of people. If we nail this audition, we could be on the fast track to the big time. We submitted the audition application two months ago, and as soon as we got the approval, we dove into work, putting in the hours, day in, day out.

"You lot fancy a pint?" Tom asks, his eyes flitting between us, eager for takers. A cold lager sounds perfect right now. But no—I've got to show up at my brother's engagement party. The problem isn't the party or even April. It's the fact that I have to celebrate my bloody brother.

"As much as I'd love to, I've got Lucas's thing tonight," I tell them.

"You mean his engagement party," Oliver clarifies.

I grunt in response.

"Ah," Tom says in an amused tone, "my condolences, mate."

"Have one for me, yeah? I'll see you next week," I say, nodding at the boys as I grab my gear and head for the door. Oliver follows close behind me toward my car. London's great for public transport, but I wouldn't risk jumping on the tube with my bass. She's my baby.

"I think I can manage that. Try to enjoy the evening," Oliver says as I place my gear into the back seat.

"Yeah, man, I will," I reply, turning to bump his fist before swinging open the car door and dropping into the seat.

Turning the key in the ignition, the speakers roar to life, blasting Bound to Oblivion's latest album through the small space. I press the accelerator, reluctantly heading to my brother's party.

It's not a great distance from Tom's place to Lucas and April's townhouse in Fulham, but Friday night traffic in London is always a bitch. Not that I'm complaining about running late. In fact, I'm grateful for the delay.

I take a deep breath, letting the bass wash over me. My shoulders and fingers ache from hours of playing. Already ninety minutes late, I skip going home to change. Lucas can deal with me turning up as I am—he'll give me shit for it, uptight prick, but fuck it.

As I pull up to Lucas and April's, a groan threatens to slip from my lips. I can't believe I'm doing this. The last thing I want is to pretend everything's fine while my brother gets to play happy couple with his fiancée. I'd rather be anywhere else, but no—I'm stuck playing the part of the dutiful little brother, making small talk and enduring insipid conversations Lucas decides to drag me into.

Reaching across the center console, I toss a couple of stray sweaters and dirty work vests over my guitar case, hoping to hide it. Stepping out of the car, I adjust my jacket and start walking.

I've got a party to get through, a smile to wear, and a brother to appease.

* * *

"Oh! Look, Peter, he's here!" I hear my mum's excited voice as soon as I step through the door. My eyes immediately find her as she hurries over. I spot Dad standing and chatting with a young blond woman as I bend to kiss Mum's cheek and shoot him a nod in greeting before pulling her in for a firm hug.

Christ, I love this woman.

"Hey, Mum," I say, offering a smile. I let her go and take in the room. The lively music fills the space, and the buzz of conversation surrounds me. There are plenty of people here, most of whom I don't recognize except for April's close friends—Gemma, Anna, and Anna's husband, Mason, I think. I'm sure most of these guests belong to April. Lucas has never really had many friends—he's always been a bit too wrapped up in himself to bother with other people. It's not like he's short on charm; he just prefers things to be about him.

My brow furrows. Is Gemma wearing lingerie?

I shake the thought away as the delicious smell of party food wafts through the air. The house looks gorgeous—April's doing, no doubt.

"You're a bit late, hon," Mum gently chides, glancing at her wristwatch to make her point.

I roll my eyes. "We had practice. Got caught up. Sorry, I'm here now."

Her eyes rake over me, from my messy hair to my scuffed shoes, and she purses her lips before leaning in. "You couldn't have thrown on a shirt?" she teases.

"It was this, or I'd have been even later. It's fine. Lucas won't care," I say, and she scoffs playfully. We both know damn well that Lucas will notice and not approve.

"Do me a favor, will you?" Mum asks, snapping me back to attention.

Oh God, what now?

I raise an eyebrow, bracing for her request.

"Go and find Lucas and April. More guests have arrived, and I have no idea where they've gone. I'm sure people are looking for them," she says.

19

I let out a long breath, nodding before stepping around her and heading straight for the stairs. Ducking my head through doorways, I search the rooms for the happy couple. I reach their bedroom and stop mid-step, noticing their bathroom door is closed. Rolling my eyes, I knock.

"Luc? Mum sent me to check on you. Is everything okay? Have you seen April?" I ask.

I hear gasps and hushed whispers.

"James? Is that you? Give me a second," Lucas replies.

For fuck's sake.

I know exactly who's in there. And I'm sure I can guess exactly what they're doing.

I lean against the door-frame just as the door swings open, revealing the newly engaged pair, both looking rather sheepish. I can't help but smirk, knowing I've caught them in the act. I reach into my pocket, pulling out my guitar pick to nibble on. Old habit I can't seem to kick.

My gaze darts from Lucas to April, who is staring intently at the floor, heat searing her cheeks. "You couldn't wait until the party ended?" I ask, fixing Lucas with an amused look.

"You couldn't put on a suit?"

I pluck the pick from my teeth, roll my eyes, and blow out a breath. "Give me a break, Luc. I came straight from practice. This is what I'm comfortable in. We have that audition coming up and I lost track of time, so I came straight here. Suits are *your* thing, not mine."

"Whatever, the Golden Child does what he wants. Always has," Lucas replies in a condescending tone.

His use of *Golden Child* doesn't escape me, but I know it's his favorite dig, thrown at me because of my close bond with my parents—particularly Mum. My closeness with Mum has nothing to do with favoritism, but he'll use anything to try to knock me down and make himself feel better. I shake it off, ignoring his jab, as April finally meets my gaze and offers me an awkward wave.

"Hey, James," she says in a soft, shy voice.

My brow creases. "Hey, April."

It's only now that I have the chance to take in what she's wearing. Her off-the-shoulder dress reveals smooth, creamy skin, with a pink flush spreading from her collarbones to her neck. Her chest rises and falls as if she's just caught her breath. And even though she's wearing minimal makeup—she's never needed much—her blush stands out.

I'm not sure if it's the color in her cheeks, the glow in her eyes, or the way her hair falls in untamed waves over her naked shoulders, but it's like I'm seeing her for the first time.

She's radiant, undeniably. And it's obvious—she's just come. But the fact that it was my *brother* who brought her to this state sends a sharp, unexpected pang through me.

What the hell is wrong with me?

I've never looked at April like this.

Because I can't.

Because I *shouldn't*.

Not until now.

Sure, I've always known she's a beautiful woman. But right now? She's superb. And I can't look away.

Shaking off the thought, I tuck my pick back into my pocket. Unsure of what else to say, my brain supplies the most idiotic line possible: "Your mascara's smudged."

Before she can respond, I step back, turn on my heel, and rejoin the party.

I don't know what just happened, but one thing's certain—it's going to be a *long* night.

Chapter 4

April

No one notices as I slip downstairs on wobbly legs, a dull throb between my thighs. The thought of what we just did sends a wave of heat through me—I want more. I want his tongue teasing me and his fingers buried deep inside me. My cheeks burn again at the memory, knowing that while everyone else was caught up in the party, I was completely consumed by him.

As I step off the last stair, I glance up, only to lock eyes with James. We stand, suspended in time, his gaze holding mine for a beat too long before he blinks, turning away and taking a slow pull from his beer. The way his jaw shifts sends a prickle of unease through me. He knows exactly what Lucas and I were doing. The fact that he caught us twists something inside me.

"There she is!" Anna's voice slices through the moment as she weaves through the crowd with two sparkling flutes of bubbly. I wrench my eyes from James, accepting the glass from Anna. The condensation kisses my skin, tracing a path along my hand as the droplets slip down my fingers. I shift my focus to Anna, and we clink our flutes before both taking a sip. I'm still hot and flushed from my orgasm, so the wave of bubbles cools me down.

I catch sight of Lucas standing alone beside the outdoor heater in the courtyard, glued to his phone screen. Anna tracks my line of sight and nudges me, dipping her chin toward him. "Go on," she says. "I'll catch up with you later."

I return her smile, giving her arm a gentle squeeze before slipping through the crowd. As I approach, Lucas glances up and slips his phone into his back pocket, stepping forward. His eyes latch onto mine, and before I can say a word, he wraps a thick arm around my waist, drawing me in close. "You really do look beautiful, baby," he murmurs in my ear. I crane my neck to meet his gaze.

God, I love this man.

"I love you," I whisper.

His hand drifts lower, sliding from my waist to my ass, giving it a firm squeeze. "Oh yeah?" he asks. "How much?"

"I'll show you how much later."

One of his eyebrows arches as he tilts his head. "Well, I can't wait for everyone to fuck off, then," he says, and I lean into him, giggling.

Rising onto my tiptoes, I press my lips to his; he parts them instantly, opening for me. The kiss is unhurried, and as his tongue works against mine, I press my hips into him, and he groans in response.

I pull back just enough to whisper, "I can taste myself."

His eyes darken. "You're my favorite flavor."

The faint buzz of his phone vibrates between us. He steps back and pulls it from his pocket. The absence of his touch feels like water lapping at my skin, cold and slipping away too quickly.

"Everything okay, babe?" I ask, keeping my voice light.

"Yeah, why wouldn't it be?" he replies, glancing up briefly before slipping the phone back into his pocket.

"Oh, nothing. You've just been on your phone a lot lately. You seem a little distracted," I say, hoping not to push too hard. I've noticed that he's been on his phone more and more. From the moment he wakes up until he leaves for work, and then again the second he walks through the door. It's not that he's distant—he's still sweet and affectionate— but I can't seem to shake the feeling that there's something he isn't sharing with me.

I don't like to pry. I never have. I've told myself again and again that if something was wrong, he'd tell me. But lately, that nagging doubt has started to fester, and it's becoming difficult to ignore. I mentioned it to Gemma recently, and she reassured me that I shouldn't take it personally. He's probably nervous or busy with work. And she's right—if Lucas didn't want me, he wouldn't still be here. If there was something going on, I'm certain he'd tell me.

His smile is easy. "It's just a mate from work," he says, rubbing his hand affectionately up and down my arm.

"Oh, okay." A flicker of unease nestles into the shadows of my thoughts. His focus rests on me for a moment, then he tilts his chin toward the living room. "It's cold, baby. You go on inside. I'll be in shortly," he says.

"Sure," I say, offering a forced smile before turning away and heading back into the party. As I thread through the crowd, I can't resist glancing over my shoulder one last time. He's already back on his bloody phone, tapping away. My brows furrow as I try to figure out what's going on with him, and by the time I turn back toward our guests, I spot James.

His height makes him stick out like a sore thumb. He's standing with his parents chatting with my colleague

Bridget. Bridget is famously single and clearly not wasting a second cozying up to James, and to be honest, I can hardly blame her. I watch as she leans in to speak to him, brushing her enormous cleavage against his arm.

She's tall, with long, sleek blond hair that tumbles over her shoulders, and she's wearing a red minidress that hugs her hourglass figure, showing off her toned legs. She's in her mid-twenties and totally gorgeous—the kind of woman all the doctors in my office fawn over. But James doesn't seem remotely interested, despite the opportunity for a good tit-wank. I know this because he's fixated on me, as if he's barely registered Bridget. His expression is cool and unbothered, but the way his eyes keep flitting from Lucas to me—and then back again—makes me feel a little unsettled, like he's figured something out before I have.

I push the feeling aside, willing myself to let it go as I slip into the kitchen, joining Gemma, Anna, and Mason, Anna's husband. They've been married for three years, and he is completely besotted with her, as he should be. She's fantastic. "Mason! You made it!" I say, a big smile spreading across my face as I open my arms wide for a hug.

He grins—one of those infectious grins that lights up his whole face—and steps forward, scooping me up in a bear hug. "Of course I did! You think I'd miss this?" he says, pulling me close and lifting me just enough to make me laugh. When he sets me back down, he keeps his hands on my shoulders, holding me at arm's length. His brown eyes twinkle as he takes me in. "You look amazing, April," he says, "and happy."

"Do I?" I ask, tilting my head, but his compliment makes me smile. "Thanks. I feel happy."

"Good," he replies with a wink, giving my arms a final squeeze before letting go.

Anna sidles up beside him, looping her arm through his with a playful smirk. "So smooth," she says, resting her head dramatically on his shoulder. "That's how he got me."

Mason looks at her adoringly, tucking a stray hair behind her ear. I smile seeing them together. They make it look so easy.

"You've got a good one, Anna."

"I know," she says, grinning up at him.

Gemma scrunches her nose in mock disgust. "Ew. Go be cute somewhere else—you're making me queasy."

I sip my drink, staying quiet as Anna and Mason flirt and giggle. They're so wrapped up in each other, it's genuinely sweet. That's what I want—what I've always wanted, really—a love that's all-consuming. And the fact that I've found it with Lucas, that our life together is unfolding for real, fills me with so much hope. I really want this to be *it*.

Gemma catches my silence and narrows her eyes at me. "You good?" she asks, leaning in a little closer.

I nod, forcing a smile. "Yeah, I'm fine."

She gives me a skeptical look but doesn't push—at least, not directly. "Lucas glued to his phone again?" she asks, raising an eyebrow.

I wave it off, trying to sound casual. "It's nothing. He's fine, Gem."

She raises her hands in surrender. "All right, I won't say another word about it. By the way, we saw Bridget making a move on James. She didn't waste any time, did she?"

I swallow, keeping my tone as even as possible. "Yeah. She's persistent, I'll give her that."

"Jealous?"

"Of course not," I say too quickly, earning a smirk from her. Why on earth would she think I was jealous of James and Bridget? This is *my* engagement party with Lucas, for crying out loud. She taps a manicured nail against the rim of her glass. "He didn't seem too interested, though. Did you notice the way he looked at you? It was like Bridget wasn't even there."

"Gem, really not appropriate," I scold, shooting her a warning look.

"Fine, fine," she says, rolling her eyes and setting her glass on the counter. The sharp crack of shattering glass snaps my attention back to the living room. Bridget stands frozen with a hand over her mouth as everyone stares. Her eyes lift to meet mine. "*I'm so sorry*," she mouths.

I offer a reassuring smile and wave it off. "*I've got it*," I mouth back, hoping to ease her embarrassment. I scan the courtyard and living room quickly, but there's no sign of Lucas. What the fuck is he doing?

James sets his beer on the coffee table before making a beeline for the utility room. I follow him, watching as he pulls open cupboard doors. I step in, reaching up to open the top cupboard next to him where the dustpan and brush are kept, standing on my tiptoes to grab them.

"Here, let me," he says. Warmth encases me as James steps in close, pressing his chest lightly against my back. His woodsy scent drifts between us, and with an easy stretch, he snags the items from the shelf above, brushing my arm in the process. I quickly pull my hands away and pivot to face him, but he doesn't step away. Instead, he stays close, his eyes trained on mine.

My skin burns at his proximity, and, for reasons I can't quite determine, I feel . . . nervous. The fact that he's been watching me all evening has been distracting, not to mention hard to avoid, and being this close to him feels like a slow burn—a heat builds in the pit of my stomach that I can't control. For a moment, I lose track of everything around us.

It's just me and his commanding presence, looming like a shadow.

Blinking, I shake myself out of my daze and try to focus on the task at hand. Clean the broken glass. Because being this close to James feels like standing on the edge of something I'm too afraid to acknowledge, let alone dive into.

"I've got it," I say, holding out my hand for the items. "Thank you."

"Where's my brother?"

"I'm sure he's just using the bathroom upstairs," I say, attempting to sound unaffected.

"Mmm." He opens his mouth to say something when—

"Oh, James, there you are!" Caroline says as she sweeps into the room, startling us both. James exhales, as if he's frustrated, before he steps back, creating a sliver of space between us. "Good, you're helping," Caroline adds with a bright smile. She steps forward, reaching for the dustpan and brush in his hands. "Here, honey, I'll take care of the glass. You both go enjoy yourselves." She nods toward me. "Go and spend time with that fiancé of yours."

If I can find him.

James hesitates, handing the dustpan and brush to his mother. He doesn't spare me a glance or utter a word before striding out. Caroline turns and follows close behind, her heels clicking against the floor as she hurries to the scene of the crime.

I need another drink.

Clearing my throat, I smooth my dress and make my way back to the party, pasting on a smile, pretending this night is exactly as I imagined. Even though it isn't. Even though, deep down, it feels like everything is starting to unravel at the edges. I just can't figure out why.

Chapter 5

James

As the last of the partygoers clear out, I rap my knuckles against the downstairs powder room door. "I'm in here!" someone yells from the other side. From the slurry sound of it, it's Bridget, April's colleague, who's been hovering around me like a bad bloody smell since I arrived.

Don't get me wrong—she's pretty. And daft. But right now, I don't have the energy to give a fuck. I'm too focused on the woman standing in front of her sink with a distant look on her face, scrubbing a pile of dishes. Alone.

After her own fucking engagement party. No fiancé in sight.

I roll my eyes and head upstairs to use Lucas's bathroom. I step through the door and stop short. Lucas is sitting at the end of his bed, tapping furiously at his phone screen.

"Hey, sorry to interrupt. You cool if I use your bathroom? Downstairs is occupied."

He looks up at me, blank-faced. "Huh?"

"I asked if I could use your bathroom."

He shrugs, not even looking at me. "Whatever."

After handling things, I wash and dry my hands, then swing the door open to find him still glued to his phone.

"Is everything all right with you?" I ask.

He lowers the phone to his lap and groans in frustration. "Jesus, James. What is it? What do you want?"

Tosser.

"You seem distracted. I was just—"

"Well, don't. I'm fine. I'm just busy."

"Seems like you've been busy all night." I slip my hands into my pockets and rock back on my heels.

He scoffs. "Hardly."

I frown. "You realize your fiancée is helping Mum and Dad clean up, right?"

He tosses his phone on the bed and twists toward me. "Leave it, would you? You should be more concerned about whether you're going to end up with a shovel in your hand for the rest of your life."

What. A. Prick.

His words land precisely where he intended, the jab cutting through me like a blade.

"Unbelievable," I mutter under my breath, shaking my head as I make my way downstairs.

I step off the staircase to find Dad trailing Mum, a large bag in hand as she tosses used napkins and paper plates inside. April is still at the sink, working away at the dishes, while Gemma wraps up the leftover food on the coffee table, organizing it into containers, and Anna sweeps the floors, blowing out candles as she goes.

The door to the powder room swings open and a very wobbly, very drunk Bridget stumbles out. She makes her way over to me, pushing her tits out as she moves her hips with more sway than is natural. Her eyes latch onto me like leeches.

Usually, I'm up for an easy lay. But no thanks. I'm into enthusiastic consent, which I highly doubt Bridget is capable of right now. And after seeing April tonight, I'm not sure anyone could compare.

Fuck, I don't want to entertain that thought.

Bitterness rears its ugly head, planting deep in my gut and spreading its roots. Something about this doesn't sit right. I suddenly feel this protectiveness, this urge to tell her she deserves more. Lucas has given her the cold shoulder all night, and as much as I don't care about him, I'd be a dick not to notice how it affects her. It's glaringly obvious. Her movements and facial expressions have seemed robotic. Unnatural.

The house looks amazing. The effort that's gone into the food and decorations, which have made the night what it is, leaves a sour taste in my mouth. Because I don't think Lucas appreciated any of it. Or her, for that matter.

I catch a whiff of Bridget's sickeningly sweet perfume as she approaches.

"James, there you are. I was wondering if I could—"

"No."

"Oh, but I just thought—"

"You thought wrong." I can smell the alcohol wafting off her.

"But I just—"

I whirl around to face her. She crosses one leg over the other, stumbling to stand upright.

I blow out a breath. "I'm not interested."

She pulls her head back, eyes dazed.

Jesus Christ. "Do you have a way home?" I ask.

Her lips quirk to the side. "Why, is that an invitation?" she asks, waggling her eyebrows.

I rub my forehead. "No. It wasn't. Do you need me to call you a cab?"

She pouts, her tone sulky. "No, it's fine. I'll sort it myself."

I watch as she wobbles out the front door, gripping the railing for dear life as she descends the front steps. When I focus back on April, she's scrubbing an oven dish with a scouring pad, rubbing with force as she worries her lip between her teeth. My legs spring into action before I even register that I'm moving. Sliding up to her, I place my hand over her forearm as she reaches for the next dish. Her skin is wet and sudsy from the water, and she pauses, tipping her head toward me.

"Let me help."

"It's fine, I've got this," she says, blowing a stray hair that's fallen across her face out of the way.

"Then I'll dry," I say, reaching for a tea towel.

"Thank you."

We fall into a production line. She scrubs while I dry. "So, did you have fun tonight?"

She hesitates before answering, like she's not sure whether to be truthful. "Yes."

I don't believe her.

I remain silent, unsure of how to respond.

"I saw you made quite the impression on Bridget," she says.

I chuckle. "I don't think so."

"Why?"

I shrug. "Not sure, just don't."

She chews the inside of her cheek. "I think she was interested in you."

"Why do you say that?"

"She couldn't stay away from you."

"How do you know that?" I say, my lips tipping up at the corners. "Were you watching me, April?"

She blinks, floundering for words. "No, I just—"

"I'm kidding," I say, nudging her with my elbow. She offers me a soft smile and hands me another plate. We rarely have the chance to talk, just the two of us, so I'm not sure why she's focusing on Bridget. I couldn't care less about the woman.

"I'm not interested in her."

She glances at me.

"Bridget—I'm not interested in Bridget," I clarify.

"Why not? She's gorgeous."

Because I couldn't take my eyes off you.

"I just don't fancy her," I say, struggling to find the right words.

"Hmm," she murmurs. "She does have those supermodel legs that go on for miles." Her hands slow over the dish.

I swallow, shaking my head *no.*

"Really?" she asks, releasing the dish to float in the sink. She plucks the tea towel off my shoulder to dry her hands, then turns to lean against the counter, tossing the towel back over my shoulder. Her smile is cheeky as she says, "What about any of my other friends? You could have any woman you want. You know that, right?"

I know she's just being playful, that there's no deeper meaning behind her words, but still, I hold her gaze. "I wouldn't say that. Not *any* woman."

Her smile falters, her brows pulling together slightly as her lips part. "Well, do you have a type?"

"Yes."

"And what is it?"

I open my mouth to respond, but Lucas's footsteps thunder down the stairs. He grabs the banister, swinging himself into the kitchen. "Sorry about that, love. I was just changing." He nods at the tea towel over my shoulder. "Cheers for doing that."

33

Lucas strides over, wrapping an arm around April's waist and kissing the top of her head. Without waiting for a response, he dashes into the utility room, grabs something, and disappears upstairs without so much as a backward glance at her.

I lower the plate in my hand, placing it carefully on the drying rack. April's gaze drops to the floor, defeated.

I grind my teeth. I need to leave before I cross the line. Before I tell her she deserves more. Before I tell her he doesn't appreciate her. Doesn't see her, not really.

"You look really beautiful tonight, April."

Before she can respond, I turn and step out into the frigid night air. I can't risk looking into those somber, bluebell eyes.

If I did, her sadness would undo me.

Chapter 6

April

The week after the engagement party unfolds like any other. Lucas and I follow the same rhythm: work during the day, then back home to our usual routine. While he showers and changes, I make dinner. We eat together and chat about our days before settling into our own worlds for the night.

Most evenings, I lose myself in a book—usually an erotic romance. Lately, I've been devouring one about a single father of two and his younger colleague. I love snuggling up in bed with my cat, Basil. He's been my loyal companion since I was seventeen. My parents and I adopted him when he was just a year old. Back then, he'd curl up in their bed while we watched films or sit with us during dinner, hoping for the inevitable scraps my dad would sneak him under the table. It's memories like these that make me treasure how Basil still curls up with me and Lucas now. It's as if Basil still carries a little piece of them with him.

Sharing that connection with Lucas means everything to me.

Lucas, on the other hand, alternates between his devices, a secondhand book, writing or lounging in front of the TV with a glass of full-bodied red in hand. More often than not, he falls asleep on the sofa before the night is over.

I'm good at switching off from work when I get home. My job ends the moment I step out of the office—no stray thoughts tugging at me, no stress weighing on my shoulders. My time is mine to enjoy. I adore my job as a personal assistant to one of London's leading vitreoretinal surgeons. Sure, it's not the highest-paying job, but the lifestyle balance makes up for it. It gives me the freedom to indulge in life's little pleasures—buying the occasional book or slipping into a pair of sparkly heels to enjoy a night out with the girls when the moment calls for it.

It's Saturday morning and my period has me firmly committed to a date with my sofa, TV show, and a bag of truffle crisps.

"Bye, baby," Lucas murmurs, leaning in to press a soft kiss to my lips.

"Bye, babe. Have a good hike," I reply.

"Are you sure you don't want to come with me?" he asks, a hint of hope in his voice.

"I'm sure. It's freezing and these cramps are killing me."

He frowns slightly but gives a small nod. "Rest up."

"I love you," I say, managing a tired smile.

"Love you too," he calls over his shoulder, striding toward the door. I turn to watch as he grabs his rucksack, slinging the straps over his shoulders.

The door slams shut behind him, and the sound echoes through the quiet room, startling poor Basil curled up next to me. I take the last sip of my drink, setting the mug down on the coffee table. My hand drifts toward the open packet of crisps, and I pluck one from the top and pop it into my mouth with a satisfying *crunch.*

I'm totally enraptured in the latest episode of my TV show when a sound cuts through the air. *Ping...*

Ping...

I groan, abandoning the half-eaten bag of crisps as I push myself off the sofa and head toward the kitchen counter.

Crap.

Lucas forgot his phone.

Ping...

I pick it up, intending to silence it, but my eyes catch on the notification banner at the top of the screen: *"I love this one* ♥*"*

A strange tightness grips my stomach, and I lurch back slightly. I feel a flush of redness bloom across my chest as heat prickles up my neck. I set the phone down momentarily, only to pick it back up again seconds later.

I never go through Lucas's phone. I've never had a reason to. I trust him... don't I?

Lucas is glued to his phone and every time it chimes, he's on it instantly, like it's magnetized to his hand. He never leaves it unattended, always checking it. And I've caught him smiling at it a few times—the same smile he usually gives me. I've told myself to believe him, that it's just work, but deep down, I know better.

There's something more going on here, and I can't ignore it anymore.

Swallowing thickly, I swipe the lock screen and open Instagram. The app loads to a profile I've never seen before, and my heart begins to pound.

It's not Lucas's usual account.

My fingers hover above the screen, uncertain of whether to snoop, but curiosity wins out.

Giving in, I scroll through the feed and find images of women in lingerie, models, poems, and women talking about books. It's then that I spot the profile picture. It's a black-and-white photograph of his hand holding a pen. The sleek, black Montblanc I gave him on our first anniversary.

I tap to view the profile grid, and the account name beneath the profile picture reads: *GhostWriter*. I feel myself changing shape inside. With each flick of my thumb, I notice his posts becoming more sexual: faceless photos of Lucas—his back, arms, torso. Sometimes dressed, sometimes not. Among them are random pictures, like the odd poem here and there, as well as pictures of Basil curled up on the bed, or pictures of hiking trails. Considering the number of posts, he's clearly had this account for a while.

I tap on a random post—a photo of his body from the neck down, his abs and muscular arms on full display. Below it, a caption reads:

"For someone who's on my mind more than she knows."

I scroll to the comments—there are dozens, all from women. Complimenting him, admiring him—some are just outright flirting.

Why does he have this?

What the fuck is he doing?

The questions come thick and fast.

I exhale a ragged breath and glance at the clock. Half past noon. Deciding that he's not returning for his phone, I figure Lucas won't be back from his hike for at least another hour. My legs feel weak as I stumble to the sofa, pulling a thick, fluffy blanket over my lap as I try to steady my trembling hands.

I take my time as I continue to scroll through every post, every caption, and every comment. The way he writes his captions and the occasional post about desire, beauty, and lust—it feels as though he's whispering these thoughts to someone else. *Thinking* of someone else. And I can't shake the gnawing feeling that these words aren't just harmless musings—they seem too real, *too* personal.

I tap on his *following* list, and it becomes painfully clear. Every account he follows belongs to a woman—random women, models, and bloggers. Not a man among them.

The truth sears my skin.

This isn't just some harmless Instagram page.

These are thirst traps.

He's using this account to lure women in.

Chapter 7

April

Heat surges through my body in a crushing wave of panic as a new notification pings at the top of the screen.

"Hey, baby. Just wanted you to know I'm thinking of you . . ."

"What the fuck?" I whisper. My fingers grip the blanket as I adjust it over my lap, seeking comfort as my heart races. I swipe back to his main feed and tap on the *Messages* icon. The air leaves my lungs when conversations with dozens of women flood the screen, each more intimate than the last. I open the top message, a thread with a woman named Katelyn.

"Hey, baby. I just wanted you to know that I'm thinking of you. Work has been so busy this morning, but I've managed to sneak a break and thought I'd check in. How's your day going? Did you manage to get out for a hike this morning? Love you xxx."

Love?

I slap a hand over my mouth to keep the sob from spilling out. Every word feels like a dagger to the heart, the ache seizing my throat. I push past the pain, desperate to find out when this all started. The date on the messages stops me cold: six months ago. Scrolling through their conversation, I find images of her. She's beautiful, with soft freckles, fiery red waves, and feminine curves. The further I look, the photos she's exchanged become more explicit, along with videos and voice notes.

And then I find them.

The inevitable photos and videos Lucas has sent her—naked, and he's either hard or touching himself in every one.

Tears spill freely now, sliding down my cheeks in hot, bitter streams. The flirting, the explicit language, the way he talks to these women—it's the same sweet words he's whispered to *me*, the same promises he's made to *me*. Words that once made me feel cherished, adored, and special have been recycled and fed to strange women like lines from a script.

"I really like you. I've fallen for you."

"I can't just view you as someone I'm sexually attracted to anymore. You're beyond that."

"You're the only one who has my heart."

"What we have is so special. I know it's not going to happen with anyone else."

The man I love is a stranger.

Oh God, I'm going to be sick.

Dropping his phone to the couch, I stagger to the bathroom and collapse in front of the toilet. My body shakes as I retch violently. Everything inside me comes up in painful heaves until there's nothing left. My palms sweat, and my pulse thunders in my ears. A scream lodges in my throat, but I swallow it down.

I curl into myself as fresh tears blur my vision. I cry on the cold, biting tiles until there's only emptiness in the brutal knowledge that everything I ever wanted is slipping away.

Chapter 8

April

I slump against the bathroom wall, completely spent. It feels as if my skin has been peeled away, leaving nothing but raw muscle and nerves exposed.

What am I supposed to do?

Lucas will be home soon, but I can't possibly face him. Not like this. I'm too emotional, too reactive. If I see him now, I'll fall apart all over again.

The thought alone gives me just enough strength to move. I drag myself to my feet, gripping the edge of the sink for balance. I smooth my shaky hands over my hair as I try to gather my thoughts. Deciding it's best to keep myself busy, I wrench open the bathroom cupboard and grab a bottle of bleach. Twisting off the cap, I pour it into the toilet bowl. I scrub until the fumes sting my throat and tears prick my eyes, forcing me to stop.

I need to get out of here.

Once the bleach is put away, I move back to the lounge.

Lucas's phone sits on the sofa, where I left it. My hands tremble madly, but I manage to pick it up, unlock it, and open the messages. I scroll through the DMs, using my phone to take photos and screen recordings of everything—photos, messages, videos, voice notes—and return Lucas's phone to the kitchen counter.

Basil follows close behind as I take the stairs, two at a time, to our bedroom where I rummage through drawers, tossing clothing and toiletries into an overnight bag. A faint meow pulls me from my frantic packing. Basil's sweet, inquisitive eyes meet mine, and his beautiful little face threatens to break me all over again. I crouch and thread my fingers through his lush coat, scratching under his chin. He purrs contentedly, leaning into my touch. Pressing a kiss to his tiny forehead, I whisper, "I have to go, baby. I'll be back when I'm ready, I promise." His gentle nudge almost undoes me. I'm leaving Basil with Lucas—also an avid cat lover—and that, at least, brings me some comfort.

I grab my toiletries, zip up the bag, and sling it over my shoulder. Downstairs, I snatch my car keys from the counter, shove my arms into my mohair cardigan, and slide my feet into the nearest pair of shoes. I fling open the front door and step into the icy afternoon air, marching to my car without a second thought.

I finally pull up outside Gemma's flat. I unbuckle my seat belt and round the car. I lift a wobbly hand to the buzzer. A moment later, Gemma's voice crackles through the intercom.

"April?"

"Hey, Gem," I whisper. "Can I . . . Can I come up?"

"Of course."

The door clicks open, and I push it wide, stepping into the foyer. I climb the staircase, reaching her flat on unsteady legs. It feels like I'm made of jelly. I reach the top to find Gemma waiting at the door, concern marring her face.

The moment I step inside, her arms wrap around me and it's as though the last thread holding me together snaps. I collapse into her embrace, my body wracked with exhaustion and uncontrollable sobs.

"It's okay, I've got you," she murmurs, tightening her hold.

I try to speak, my words coming out strangled. "He's . . . cheating."

She pulls back slightly, just enough to look me in the eye. "Lucas?"

My body locks up as I try to keep the sobs at bay, but they spill over, anyway.

"Oh, April . . ." Her voice is soft and full of sympathy as she brushes a tear from my face. "Come inside. Sit down and I'll get you something to drink."

I sink onto Gemma's sofa while she busies herself in the kitchen. "Would you like a tea?" she calls out.

"Do you have anything stronger?" I ask.

"Does a bear shit in the woods?"

I hear the fridge door, then the sound of a bottle being twisted open. A minute later, Gemma returns, placing two glasses of chilled wine and a block of milk chocolate on the coffee table. She sits beside me with her legs folded under her. She pulls out her phone, tapping away madly at the screen as I ready myself. When she's finished, she drops her phone to her lap and fixes her attention on me.

"Sorry, I was just messaging Anna. Right," she says, shifting in her seat. "Tell me everything. What happened?"

I suck in an unsteady breath and rub my hands over my thighs. My voice thins to a wisp as I spill the details of my morning. Gemma shares in my disbelief and horror as I explain the Instagram account, showing her the messages, voice notes, screen recordings, and photos from Lucas's interactions with Katelyn and the other women, choking out the details through a mess of tears and snot.

The intercom buzzes through the flat, making us both jump. "Are you expecting someone?" I ask.

"Gemma, open the door! I'm about to commit murder in the first degree, and I really need someone to stop me!" Anna's voice screeches through the speaker.

"Shit," Gemma says, leaping up from her seat to buzz Anna in.

A second later, Anna barges through the door, rattling the frame as she enters. "That *cunt*," she spits, storming inside.

"Well, that's one name for him," Gemma says dryly, trailing behind her.

"I take it Gemma's filled you in?" I choke out, staring at the phone clutched firmly in Gemma's grip. Anna rushes toward me, pulling me into a tight hug, and I surrender in her hold. Then, with a determined expression, she glides into the kitchen, returning moments later juggling three shot glasses, a few lime wedges, a shaker of salt, and a bottle of tequila. Once she's settled, and we're all armed with our shots, I bring her up to speed. Then, we do what any normal group of women would do in this situation: We sign Lucas up for a Scientology welcome kit, a membership for the Flat Earth Society and, of course, we get sufficiently drunk.

* * *

I wake with a stiff neck and a thumping headache. I'm half draped across Gemma's lap, and my feet are tangled over Anna's legs. A groan slips from my lips as I shift, noticing the uncomfortable positions they're both in—propped awkwardly against the couch, their expressions serene in sleep.

Reaching for my phone, I'm met with a flood of notifications. Lucas's missed calls and unread messages fill the screen.

Baby, where are you?

Are you okay?

Seriously, where are you?

Please call me when you get this.

I'm starting to worry. I love you.

The words swirl in my stomach as I read them over and over, bitter and nauseating. "Bullshit," I mutter, tossing my phone onto the table with more force than necessary, wincing at the loud *thud.* The sound startles Anna from her sleep.

"Morning," she says through a yawn, rubbing at her eyes. But the moment she sees me, her expression sharpens, and she sits up rod-straight. "April. You okay?"

"No," I whisper, dropping my head and curling into myself. My voice cracks, and the tears are there before I can stop them. Anna is quick to scoot closer and pull me in, her arms enveloping me. I lose the battle, my will completely breaking. My body shakes as she holds me tighter. Gemma stirs beside us as her eyes blink open. Her gaze widens in concern before she leans over, wrapping her arms around both of us.

We sit there, huddled together in a tight embrace. No matter what happens, I know that as long as I have these two women, I'll survive this.

* * *

We sit around Gemma's kitchen table, each nursing a mug of much-needed coffee.

"Have you responded to him?" Gemma asks.

I set my mug down with a sigh, combing my fingers through my tangled hair.

"Yeah," I murmur. "I told him I'm here and we need to talk."

46

Just then, another message from Lucas lights up my phone.

Is everything okay?

I nibble the inside of my cheek, unsure of how to respond. The girls lean in eagerly as I turn the screen to show them his latest message.

"Are you going to tell him you know?" Anna asks.

I take a deep breath, contemplating my next actions. "I think I should...At least he'll have time to process before I get home. But I don't know what to say." I shrug my weary shoulders.

Gemma's chair creaks as she scoots toward me. "I think you should send him the screenshots and recordings. Let him see the truth."

God, this is beyond horrible. My stomach lurches at the mere mention of the messages.

Anna nods in agreement, her eyes lighting up. "Yes! Good one," she says, snapping her fingers. "He won't be able to talk his way out of *that*."

I swallow hard. The mix of nerves and caffeine causes me to tremble as I send the evidence. My heart gallops when the *delivered* notification appears. I drop the phone to the table, exhaling a shaky breath. Not even a minute passes before my phone rings. I don't answer. Instead, I turn it screen down, letting it buzz again and again while I cradle my hands around the warm mug, fiddling with the handle as I try to ground myself.

Gemma reaches for me, brushing her fingers gently over mine. "We're here, no matter what," she says.

I manage a watery smile.

Anna moves closer, her hand gently resting on my back as she rubs soothing circles.

These women will be my way through this.

47

It's done.

He knows.

I squeeze my eyes shut as the past twenty-four hours haunt me. I keep seeing us together, his arms wrapped around me, and it makes me sick.

Were those moments real? Or was I just another woman to him?

After a long moment of silence, I summon what courage I can, rising from the seat and gathering my things.

It's time.

I have to end it.

It's time to break up with my fiancé.

Chapter 9

April

I cross the threshold to find Lucas slumped on the couch, gripping his hair tightly. The soft click of the door sounds through the quiet room, startling him. His head snaps up, his eyes meeting mine. I drop my bag and kick off my shoes.

"Hey," he grits out.

"Hey," I whisper.

Frozen by the doorway, I watch him carefully.

"I just boiled the kettle. Would you like a tea?" he offers.

"No, thanks."

He nods sharply. Silence stretches between us until he rubs the back of his neck, exhaling in defeat.

"Are you just going to stand there?" he asks impatiently, snapping me out of my trance.

His words prompt me to move, so I walk over to the sofa and sink into the seat farthest away from him. His short hair is disheveled, he fidgets with the material of his tracksuit pants, and his eyes are bloodshot. Faint stubble peppers his face, looking so unlike the clean, put-together Lucas I'm used to.

My eyes fall to my hands resting in my lap, and I pick at my nails uncomfortably.

"Please say something, baby."

"I don't know what you want me to say."

He nods in response, releasing a long breath before speaking. "I don't fully understand what happened. But I feel I should at least clarify a few things."

I raise my eyebrows, waiting for him to continue.

He shifts in his seat, leaning forward to rest his elbows on his knees, his eyes fixed on the floor as he continues. "I know I've been distant lately, and I'm sorry for that. It's not about you—it's me. I've been dealing with some personal stuff, and I haven't handled it well. I felt like my depression was returning, and I shut down, and I know it's hurt you."

I stay silent, unsure of what to say.

He continues, his voice strained with emotion. "I thought I could work through it on my own, but I was wrong. I should have leaned on you more, should have let you in. But I couldn't. And I see now how much that hurt you."

I temper the anger that's now bubbling, trying to keep my composure.

"This isn't about being distant, Lucas. Your personal issues, which I'm surprised I'm only hearing about now, have nothing to do with that Instagram account and those women. That's a separate issue. You told me there were problems at work, you *lied* to me. What you've done is *cheating*."

"It's not what you think."

"It's exactly what I think. I saw it, Lucas. I read the messages, I heard the voice notes. I..." I trail off, a lump forming in my throat. "I saw the photos." My voice cracks as I continue. "Were they your way of sorting through your personal issues?"

His eyes glaze over as he desperately searches my face, but I continue. "I trusted you. I've never lied. I've shared *everything* with you." Tears stream down my cheeks, and my chest heaves as I begin to cry.

"Baby—" He leans over and reaches for my hand, I pull away, shaking my head, unable to withstand his touch.

"Don't. Please don't touch me," I say.

"I messaged those women when I was at a low point," he urges, and his voice wobbles. "I'm so sorry," he says as he closes his eyes.

This time when he reaches for me, I give in. I have no strength left to fight it. He gently cradles my head in his hands and presses his forehead to mine. Our breaths mingle, our tears mirroring each other.

"I'm so sorry," he repeats, as if it's a mantra. "I'm so sorry, baby. I'm so sorry."

I squeeze my eyes shut. "I know you are."

"I've been selfish," he admits, barely above a whisper. "I've taken you for granted, and I hate myself for it. You deserve better than this. Better than me."

A sob escapes and I turn away as he continues. "I want you to know that there's nobody on that account who I care about, even as a good friend."

"Months, Lucas. This has been going on for *months*. You told this Katelyn that you *loved* her—love. And not just once, you said it a lot. You called her *baby*." I place my hand over my heart, hoping it could somehow keep the shattered pieces together. "That's what you call me."

I wait for his response, but nothing comes. We remain in deafening silence.

I finally look at him, seeing the pain and guilt reflected in his gaze.

"April," he whispers as his eyes glisten with unshed tears, "I don't know where we go from here."

I feel a deep, overwhelming ache in my chest, a sense of heartbreak that threatens to consume me. Every fiber of my being longs to lash out at him, to seek answers, and demand he tell me what went wrong, where *we* went wrong. I want to scream, to plead with him to explain why he turned to those women, strangers on the internet, for solace instead of confiding in me, or seeking professional help. What did they offer him that I couldn't? What void did they fill that I failed to? But I know, deep down, that even if I did scream, even if he did offer explanations, it wouldn't bring me the peace I crave. It wouldn't undo the hurt, or the lies.

His actions have irreversibly altered our relationship, shattering the trust I once held so dear. No words could erase this pain. I fear his betrayal is stitched into my soul. And so, I hold back my screams, I stifle my pleas, and I resign myself to the truth: Some fractures are too deep to mend.

Rather than reducing myself to begging, I give up.

Instead, I ask the question that has haunted me for the past twenty-four hours. The question that has been stuck in my throat, squeezing my chest. The question I never thought I would have to ask my fiancé. "Do you still love me?"

His anguished gaze searches mine, darting back and forth, before he slowly closes his eyes in defeat.

"I do love you, April. But I can't return the depth of affection you have for me. I don't deserve you. You deserve someone far better than me, someone who can be everything you want and need."

I close my eyes and bring a shaky hand to my mouth to stifle my sob.

"You are one of my dearest friends, and I am so honored to know you," he whispers.

And that's it. My heart cracks open and bleeds.

"We can't fix this," I say softly.

He doesn't say anything back to me—he doesn't have to.

At that moment, I realize that this is the end. The end of us.

And finally, once he's packed his bag and the front door clicks shut, I climb into bed, fully clothed, and pull the duvet over myself.

The silence settles, and I let go, allowing myself to fall apart.

Chapter 10

April

One week later...

As the days drag on, I manage to extract myself from bed and fix a cup of breakfast tea before taking a long shower. I haven't washed my hair in days, leaving it in a messy topknot, but at least my body feels clean.

Little wins, right?

I glance over at the kitchen counter, which is littered with food delivery bags and empty coffee cups—remnants of my daily attempts to feel human—and I release a sigh. I know it's a dump, but I just don't have the energy. My diet has consisted exclusively of tea, coffee, takeaway, and dry crackers. The fruit in my bowl has gone bad, the milk in my fridge is likely spoiled, and the whole place is a mess.

My phone vibrates on the counter, but I don't even bother looking at it. It won't be the person I want it to be, and I *really* don't feel like talking to anyone, anyway. What would I even say? *Oh, I'm fine. Honestly. Don't worry about me, just going through the motions.*

How awkward. The last thing I want is to dump my problems on the people I love. They don't need to carry that burden around with them.

I take a slow sip of my hot tea, savoring the warmth as it spreads through me, when a sudden buzz cuts through the quiet. Basil, startled, legs it upstairs in a fluffy blur.

Of course I kept Basil. That wasn't even a question after Lucas and I split. He's seen me through the worst of days. He's my little anchor—we've been through everything together. Now, with just the two of us, I find comfort in dropping food to him under the table, smiling at the thought of Dad laughing beside me.

"Shit," I mutter as the tea sloshes over the rim of my mug, scalding my hand. I wince at the sting and quickly grab a tea towel to mop up the mess.

Buzz.

The doorbell buzzes again, longer this time, forcing me into action. I roll my eyes and make my way to the door. As I open it, I'm met with two familiar concerned faces staring back at me—Anna and Gemma. Anna stands with her arms crossed, tapping her foot impatiently. Gemma's eyes widen as she takes me in, her gaze traveling from my face down to my dirty, rumpled clothes. I pull my cardigan tighter across my chest, trying to cover the stained shirt. Embarrassment flushes through me—I obviously wasn't expecting to be seen like this.

Anna cocks an eyebrow. "You look fucking awful," she says, scrunching her nose.

"Well, I wasn't expecting guests," I mutter, turning on my heel and flopping onto the sofa. Gemma and Anna follow close behind.

"Clearly," Anna whispers to Gemma, who stifles a laugh behind her hand.

My gaze flits to Gemma and my eyes narrow in on the large bruised spot on her neck. "And what about you? Nice hickey," I remark.

"Oh," Anna interrupts, elbowing Gemma's side, "you *have* to tell her."

"Tell me what?" I ask.

"Thanks a lot, Anna," Gemma says, shooting her a pointed look and rolling her eyes. "So, I went on a date with this guy I met at the coffee shop. He was cute, so I thought, why not? Things started off great—he took me to this incredible Turkish place, the food was amazing, ten out of ten. Then he asked if I wanted to keep the night going, and I thought, sure? So, we went back to his. When we got there...he refused to turn the lights on. His flat was basically empty—like, *zero furniture*—but I figured, whatever, I can roll with it. Everything was going fine *until*..." She pauses for dramatic effect. "He leans in close and, dead serious, asks me to lick his face and *bark like a dog.*"

"Excuse me?" I say, disgusted.

Anna lets out an evil laugh. "How fucked is that?"

"But that's not why we're here." She waves her hand dismissively. "Why haven't you been answering your phone?" she asks, settling beside me on the sofa.

"Because I don't want to," I reply flatly.

"We were worried about you," Anna says, her tone softening as she exchanges a look of concern with Gemma.

"I'm fine," I say, but the words sound hollow, even to me.

Anna scans the kitchen, taking in the cluttered countertops and takeaway containers. "I can see that," she says, arching a brow. I follow her eyes, embarrassment prickling at the back of my neck.

"I haven't felt up to cooking," I reply, shrinking under the weight of their observation.

Gemma's hand rests gently on my knee. "We heard you haven't been at work all week?"

My bottom lip wobbles as I fight to hold back the emotions. But it's no use—the cracks are forming, and I can feel the tears about to spill over.

"I can't," I whisper. The dam breaks, and tears slip down my cheeks, hot and unstoppable.

"Tell you what," Anna says, her voice hopeful. "We spoke to your boss—" I shoot them both a look of absolute horror, but Anna holds up her hand. "Let me finish." I slump back into the sofa, bracing myself for whatever comes next.

"He's fine with you taking more time off," she says. "And guess what? Gemma's been following this TikTok creator who's running a retreat this weekend, and guess who bagged us three spots?" Anna's eyebrows dance a little jig.

"What kind of retreat?" I ask, wiping my face with the sleeve of my cardigan.

Anna and Gemma exchange a glance that screams guilt.

"Oh, bloody hell," I mutter. "Please tell me this isn't another disaster like Bali. I was shitting through the eye of a needle for a *week*, Gemma!" I groan, clutching my stomach at the thought.

"No," Gemma says with an unsettling grin. "It's way better—we'll help you pack!"

I've got no idea what they have in store for me, but I don't have the energy to argue.

"Wait—" I ask, panic creeping in. "What about Basil?"

Gemma and Anna exchange another suspicious look, one I do *not* like.

"What?" I press, narrowing my eyes.

"Umm ... well," Gemma says, shifting uncomfortably. "We kind of didn't know who else to call ..."

My stomach falls out of my ass. "Who did you call?" I ask.

Before they can answer, the doorbell buzzes again. I shoot to my feet, scanning the train wreck around me. I frantically begin brushing down my clothes like that'll somehow make me look less of a disaster. "Who's here?" I demand.

Anna blows out a long breath before finally answering, "James."

"*What?!*" I gape at her in horror. "You couldn't find *anyone* else? You had to ask my ex's *brother?*" I throw my hands in the air.

They both flinch guiltily.

"Oh my God," I groan, looking down at my rumpled clothes. "He can't see me like this!" I'm bolting toward the staircase before either of them can open the door.

"April!" Anna shouts after me.

"What?" I spin halfway up the stairs, gripping the railing as if my life depends on it.

"Please, for the love of all things holy, *wash your hair!* You could host a family of birds in there."

I shoot her a murderous glare but know she's right.

* * *

I jump into the shower and scrub my hair with extra vigor—it's amazing what a little panic-induced motivation can do. I still can't believe they invited James. *Here.* To *my* house. To take care of *my* cat. The thought sends me spiraling. I have no idea how I'm supposed to face him, but at least I won't be alone. Small mercies, I guess.

Then my brain shifts gears, landing on the clutter downstairs. The sheets on my bed are only a week old—thank God—but the rest of the place is an absolute disaster. Normally, I keep everything spotless. I'm proud of my space. But this week? It's been chaos. Just dragging myself out of bed has felt like climbing Everest, and cleaning the kitchen or keeping the place in order hasn't even been a consideration.

I turn off the water and step out of the shower. After pulling on a pair of clean trousers and a fluffy hoodie, I slip into some white sneakers and tell myself I look presentable enough. I grab my toothbrush, running it over my teeth twice for good measure, then swish with mouthwash.

I tug a brush through the wet strands of my hair, wincing as I comb through the knots. I work quickly, untangling my long tresses as best I can before wrapping them in a towel and rubbing furiously, trying to dry them out. I don't have time for perfection—just *not looking like a complete mess* will have to do.

I lean closer to the mirror, studying my reflection. Dark shadows frame my eyes, and my skin looks sallow and lifeless, as if all the light had been drained from me. Anna's right. *I look awful.*

Letting out a long breath, I open the top drawer and rummage through it until I find my fruity lip mask. I swipe it on, smacking my lips together. Then, I quickly pinch my cheeks, hoping to coax some color into them. I look more put together than I did before, and I have to admit—it feels considerably better to have clean, fresh hair.

Now, all that's left is to face my ex-fiancé's brother.

Basil saunters into the bathroom, brushing himself lazily against my leg. I crouch down, running my fingers over his soft fur, and he purrs like an MG under my touch.

"You be a good boy for James," I murmur, scratching behind his ears. He closes his eyes slowly. "I love you too," I tell him. I press a firm kiss to Basil's forehead before straightening up. I pull open the wardrobe doors and grab my overnight bag, not caring what goes in there. The faster I get packed, the less time I have to dwell on what's waiting downstairs.

Their chatter drifts into the room, and I catch the distinct low, raspy timbre of James's voice. My anxiety rapidly returns. I wonder what Lucas told him—what version of events he spun. I wonder what James knows, what he thinks. Do his parents know the full story? Or just Lucas's version? Which, I'm sure, he edited carefully.

James and I barely exchanged more than a few words when Lucas and I were together, and whenever we were in the same room alone ... well, I don't even know *how* to describe it. It was tense, maybe. Charged. Like there was always something simmering beneath the surface that I could never quite put my finger on. Like at the engagement party—he kept looking at me in a way I couldn't decipher, as if he was studying me. Even when I caught him watching, he'd never look away. He'd never look *interested*, but still, he never looked away. James has always been a bit of a mystery; I've never been able to read him.

I straighten my sheets and scoop up any stray clothes, tossing them into the washing basket. Satisfied that things look somewhat tidy—or at least not entirely disastrous—I gather myself and head downstairs on shaky legs.

I hear laughter as I reach the landing. James spots me and clears his throat. The girls spin around, and Gemma gives me a soft smile. "You ready?" she asks.

I open my mouth to respond, but no words come out. My attention settles on James, and it feels like the air's been knocked out of me. He's arresting. His hair is tousled in that annoyingly perfect way, like he's run his hand through it a dozen times, and it's just fallen into place without effort. Thick lashes frame his emerald eyes, which appear a deeper green in the soft light. He has a spot of dirt on his cheek, and a smattering of chest hair peeks over the top of his sweaty work vest, which he's wearing under a thick jacket. It's clear he's been on-site.

He doesn't smile.

He doesn't speak.

His jaw tightens, the muscle flexing as he just . . . regards me.

I drop my head to stare at the floor, feeling suddenly nervous, and my heart thuds against my rib cage. "Hi, James," I say, giving him a small wave.

"Hi, April," he replies, his voice low and gravelly.

I look up to see Anna's eyes bouncing between the two of us, her expression barely contained. She mashes her lips together, clearly trying—and failing—not to grin.

"Thank you for agreeing to look after Basil," I say finally. "I'm sorry about the state of the house. I . . ." I trail off, fumbling for the right words.

James crooks a small, sympathetic smile. "It's fine, I'm working in the area this weekend anyway," he says. "And don't worry about the house, I get it."

I catch him studying my left hand, where my engagement ring used to be, before I quickly slip it behind my back. I gave the ring back to Lucas before he moved out. I couldn't stomach looking at it.

His lips press into a thin line, but he doesn't say anything—just blinks, angrily almost, for a second. The moment is so fleeting I might have imagined it. I fiddle with the strap of my bag, not quite knowing what to say next.

Anna claps her hands, snapping both James and me out of whatever weird daze we'd fallen into. I blink, suddenly hyperaware that we have an audience.

I clear my throat. "Do you need me to run through where everything is?"

He steps closer. His voice is calm, and his touch is warm as he reaches out and squeezes my bicep gently. "I know where everything is. I've got this." He nods toward the front door. "Just go and enjoy your weekend."

The ferocity in his tone makes it clear—no more fussing.

"April," Gemma interrupts softly, glancing down at her watch. "We'd better get going—it's a three-hour drive."

"Oh," I say, my eyes flicking back to James.

He takes another step toward me, close enough that I catch the faint scent of him—sweaty and masculine. He tilts his chin toward the front door. "Go. Have fun. We'll be fine," he says.

"Thanks," I whisper, hesitating for a moment, unsure if I should hug him. We've never hugged before—it would feel strange, but maybe not entirely wrong. I take a half step forward, but before I can decide, he steps back, slipping his hands into his pockets. Guess not.

He pulls out a familiar guitar pick and starts spinning it between his fingers. I catch myself staring at his hand longer than I probably should, distracted by the veins working as he deftly moves his fingers.

"All right, well, thanks, James. You're a lifesaver," Anna says, awkwardly clapping him on the shoulder. Then, she quickly adds, "Oh yeah, I don't know if you know—April, have you told him? Basil sometimes shits on the floor."

I gape at her, mortified. "Anna!"

James grins, the first hint of amusement flickering across his face. "Good to know," he says, lips twitching as he slips the pick back into his pocket.

I close my eyes, humiliated.

"What? He does," Anna says with a shrug as we shuffle toward the door. I shoot her a glare, my cheeks burning.

"Not all the time," I mutter defensively. But yes, he definitely shits on the floor.

James trails behind us, leaning casually against the door-frame with his arms crossed, the worn leather of his jacket pulling snugly across his broad chest. A subtle smirk plays at the corner of his mouth, like he's thoroughly enjoying this.

As we step outside, Anna glances at me over her shoulder with a cheeky smile. "Now you don't have to worry—he's prepared."

Gemma laughs and I groan quietly, fighting the overwhelming urge to bury my face in my hands. The last thing I need to be thinking about is this gorgeous man cleaning up my cat's wayward poos.

Chapter 11

April

Gemma pulls up in the middle of nowhere—proper bumfuck territory—just outside Hereford, a small town about three hours northwest of London. I've barely said a word the entire drive, letting the hum of the engine and Gemma and Anna's conversation fill the space. And, as happy as they sounded, I couldn't bring myself to join in. My mind kept going back to Lucas and how his younger brother was just in my house. I tried to focus on the scenery, the Tudor-style buildings, winding canals, and postcard-perfect gardens, but none of it registers. There was no flicker of joy or any sense of appreciation, when usually I enjoy road trips.

Now we're parked in the middle of a muddy patch, surrounded by sad, drooping trees and a dodgy-looking dam—where I wouldn't be surprised if a body or two had been dumped. A few weathered tin cabins dot the area and, to be honest, the place gives off an unsettling vibe that screams *horror movie.*

"Well, if I wasn't depressed before, I sure as hell am now," I mutter, eyeing the bleak landscape.

"Excuse me," Anna says. "Positivity only, please." She throws me an encouraging look.

"Seriously, what *is* this place?" I ask as I scan the grim, wet surroundings. Before Gemma can respond, the faint rhythm of bongo drums drifts through the air, growing louder and louder. I frown. *Where the fuck are we?*

"Where the fuck is that drumming coming from?" I ask as I look around. I'm starting to wonder if I've accidentally signed up for a cult retreat instead of whatever this is supposed to be.

Suddenly, a man emerges from behind one of the cabins, catching all three of us off guard. We gasp in unison, and Gemma clutches her chest as if she might keel over from a heart attack. He's brandishing what I assume is a smudge stick.

"Welcome!" he booms, far too enthusiastically for this depressing setting.

Is he missing teeth? Jesus Christ.

He's tall, has leathery tanned skin, and is worryingly thin. He's draped in a set of moonstone beads and a feather tied to a leather strap around his neck. His arms are covered in tribal tattoos, and his clothes are threadbare. I know Gemma found him through TikTok, but he doesn't look like he can even afford a phone. Nor does he seem the type to believe in 5G. I half expect him to communicate through an empty can and a piece of string.

Before we can react, he steps in front of us and waves the sage stick in wide circles, wafting smoke over us. I glance at Anna and Gemma, silently pleading for one of them to explain what fresh hell they've dragged me into.

"Hi!" Gemma says brightly as a short, voluptuous woman steps into view. She's dressed in a flowing boho-style dress with a blue paisley pattern. She's wearing Jesus sandals and rhythmically banging a small cowhide drum.

"What's with the drum?" I ask, nodding my head toward the woman.

"It's for your energy," the skinny man replies, as if it's obvious.

"Of course," I deadpan.

I shoot Gemma a look, wondering how she's this enthusiastic.

"Where *are* we?" I whisper-shout at Anna.

"Welcome to our Solstice Retreat," the woman announces. At least she's finally stopped banging the bloody drum. "Your friend Gemma here has told me *someone's* in need of healing."

"I think I might start crying again," I say.

Anna loops an arm over my shoulders, pulling me into a side hug. "Ignore her. She's just a little fragile at the moment."

"Come, I'll show you to your cabin, and then we can join the rest of the guests. We're so pleased to have you here," the woman continues, gesturing to herself with a smile. "I'm Rose, and this," she says, nodding toward the hippy beanpole who is now spinning in circles with his smudge stick, "is my husband, Gary."

We're led to our cabin, which features a linoleum kitchen, laminate flooring, and a shared bedroom with three single beds squeezed together. The bathroom, however, is surprisingly large, with a full-size bathtub, a single sink, and a spacious shower.

"I hope you didn't pay too much for this," I say to the girls, dropping my bag onto one of the beds.

"Just try to enjoy it. At least we're together," Gemma says, hopeful.

I nod, forcing a small smile. She's right. This is a thoughtful gesture—they meant well. I shouldn't be ungrateful. If it weren't for them, I'd be at home, alone, crying into a carton of ice cream. They've gone to the effort of organizing and paying for this weekend, so the least I can do is try to appreciate it.

If this were any other time, I'd probably be laughing with them, enjoying the absurdity of it all. But I can't. My mind is trapped in a constant state of missing Lucas. My heart is so broken, it physically hurts. No matter how much I sleep, I remain exhausted. I'm not sure I remember feeling anything but this anymore.

"Come on, we better meet with the others," Gemma says, holding my hand and leading me to the central deck.

Twelve other guests are seated around a large, square table, chatting amongst themselves. Eleven women, all older, and one man who, from what I can tell, has a thick Canadian accent. Friendly chatter fills the air as Gary emerges from a nearby cabin, balancing three large mugs on a tray. He hands each of us a cup of tea and I offer him a polite smile in return, reluctantly accepting the mug.

Please, for the love of God, let this not be laced with LSD.

As I sip the tea quietly, the others begin introducing themselves to the group. Their voices blur together as I half listen, not quite ready to engage.

I'm extracted from my thoughts when the space falls silent. I blink, realizing the everyone is expectantly staring at me.

Anna nudges me with her elbow. "This is April," she announces. I force a small smile and give a brief nod. That's all they're getting from me.

A small, pale, middle-aged woman leans over to me.

"Hi, I'm Moira," she offers with a sprightly smile. "Is this your first time?"

I nod silently.

"This is my third retreat with Rose and Gary. They're amazing. It's a real awakening journey . . ."

I nod along, feigning interest while my mind drifts. Her words fade into background noise, just like everything else around me.

Rose joins us at the table, clapping her hands and rubbing them excitedly. "All right, team! We're going to start with some sound healing before giving you a short break. Tonight, we'll commence the fire ritual, and tomorrow morning we'll dive into breathwork. Who's excited?"

What the fuck is a fire ritual?

The guests nod and murmur their enthusiasm, offering optimistic smiles. Moira looks like she's about to come in her pants. I glance sideways at Anna and Gemma, both of whom are beaming. Without excusing myself, I stand and slip away. I head inside the cabin where I crawl into the small bed, pulling the covers over me. As soon as my head hits the pillow, I fade into sleep.

* * *

I wake to wan daylight. Rolling over, I tap my phone screen, checking Instagram, DMs, message requests, emails—anything. Desperately hoping that somehow, Lucas has sent me a message, some small sign that he's thinking of me. But nothing.

Needing to distract myself, I decide on a long soak while the girls are still at their sound healing. I trudge into the bathroom, open a pink bath bomb, and fill the tub. Dropping it in, I watch as it fizzes, releasing ripples of pink and glitter across the surface. I strip off my clothes, the scent of raspberry floating through the warm room. I dip my toe in to check the temperature before I immerse myself.

Reaching over to my phone, I press play on the audiobook I started weeks ago, hoping the soothing voices will drown out any loitering thoughts of Lucas. I close my eyes and tip my head back to let the audiobook lull me into relaxation, when suddenly, the front sliding door flies open, groaning on its tracks as a metallic hiss reverberates through the cabin.

The girls are back.

Anna strides into the bathroom, unfazed by the fact I'm naked and covered in pink glitter. She raises her eyebrows at me, surprised. "Hey! You're out of bed."

"Obviously," I say, pulling the bubbles higher over my chest so I don't flash her my nipples.

"I've seen your tits, April. Don't be shy. They're great," she says, waving her hand in front of her. I stare at her, waiting for her to explain why she's barged in, but she just stands there as a few seconds pass before she speaks again.

"How did you sleep?"

"Well. I think," I say.

"Good." She nods. "So, sound healing was fucked."

"What?" I sit up a bit too fast, sending bubbles sliding off me, nipples now making their grand appearance.

Before I can cover myself, Gemma barges in, leaning against the door-frame with a grin. "You're up!" she says.

"I was just telling April about sound healing," Anna says.

"Oh God. That was *not* sound healing," Gemma replies, rolling her eyes.

Curiosity gets the better of me. "Why? What happened?"

My audiobook pipes up in the background.

"Oh, Damian. Yes. Right there. Fuck, I love it when you fuck my tits with your big, throbbing cock."

The three of us freeze.

"Nice choice in relaxation material," Anna says, raising an eyebrow and looking impressed.

"Please continue," I say, face burning.

"So," Anna says, "they had us lying on freezing bloody tiles for two fucking hours! There was this woman making sounds with a bunch of bowls, and at first, the music was all right, quite relaxing even. But then, out of nowhere, I felt this sharp jab in the middle of my forehead."

"What was it?" I ask, eyes wide.

"Gary skewered me with a bloody acupuncture stick. Right in the middle of my forehead!" she says. "I'm *certain* that wasn't to code. But that's not the worst of it. Just as I'm starting to get over the whole unsolicited acupuncture trauma, the woman playing the bowls starts screaming hymns right into my ear. *Screaming!*"

"That's not even the half of it," Gemma says, crossing her arms. "I had that Moira woman lying next to me bawling her eyes out, and I'm pretty sure someone farted. It stank."

"I assumed that was you," Anna says, looking at Gemma.

"I don't fart!"

Gemma definitely farts.

Anna scoffs, then looks at me. "Oh, by the way, Rose said you need to get out of the bath. We're doing the fire ritual."

"Right now?"

"Like, right now. She sounded *pissed.*"

I glance down at my naked, glitter-covered self, and just as I'm about to argue, there's a knock at the door. *Jesus Christ*, can't a heartbroken woman just take a fucking bath? My eyes widen as Rose ducks her head through the doorway.

"The fire ritual is about to start. It would be nice if you *actually* participated in this activity, April." She shoots me a scolding look. She's waiting for my response when the

70

audiobook pipes up again, *"Yeah, baby, you like me fucking these juicy tits? I'm gonna come all over them. Then I'm going to rub it all over you before I fuck your mouth and come in there as well."*

Rose's mouth pops open, horrified.

Fabulous.

* * *

Well, the fire ritual was a fucking disaster. What was meant to be some sort of profound, spiritual experience—writing down our fears and judgments, sharing them with the group, and ceremoniously burning them to let go—devolved into utter chaos. Gary couldn't even light the fire, Rose's speech made it sound like we were summoning gods, and Anna turned her moment into a full-blown self-love ode to her tits. To top it all off, the skies opened, drenching everything.

I'm surprised we didn't drink each other's blood or join hands and sing "Kumbaya."

Thank fuck we're going home tomorrow.

Chapter 12

April

Gemma's car rolls to a stop at the curb in front of my townhouse. We all hop out, and I hug each of them goodbye before they speed off down the street. As I turn and head for the door, my heart drums in my ears and a knot tightens in my stomach—I'm nervous to see James again. The state the house and I were in when we left. God, what must he have thought?

I really hope Basil didn't shit on the floor.

I rummage through my handbag, searching for my keys, but before I can find them, the front door swings open. James stands there in the doorway, dangling my keys in one hand, a playful grin on his face.

"Oh, right," I mumble, shaking my head, trying to appear nonchalant. Of course I didn't take them with me.

I follow him inside, heading to kick off my shoes—but am stopped dead in my tracks. I blink, taking in the room, struggling to make sense of what I'm seeing. The kitchen countertops are bare, free of the clutter of takeaway containers and used mugs. The coffee table is wiped clean, not a trace of the mess I left behind. The floors gleam, spotless and freshly mopped, and a subtle scent of mint lingers in the air.

He cleaned the *whole bloody house.*

I open my mouth, but nothing comes out. I take in his appearance. He's still in his work clothes. His vest is grimy, his chest sweaty—I assume from work and scrubbing this shit-heap—he's forgone his jacket today, showcasing his tattoos, winding from his left pectoral down to his wrist. I can't quite believe it. He worked all day, and then stopped by to not only feed Basil, but clean my entire townhouse.

"James, you cleaned? This . . . this is too much—" I start, but he cuts me off.

"It's not," he says with a simple shrug. "I just swung by after work each day to feed Basil and sort out his water and tray. I did a load of washing and cleaned the en suite too."

Shit. I hope there weren't any skid marks.

A lump rises in my throat. His unexpected kindness hits me harder than I thought possible.

Don't cry, don't cry, don't cry.

I start crying.

My bag slips from my shoulder, landing on the floor as I wipe my eyes. It's such a thoughtful gesture—so unlike the man I've known him to be. Quiet, reserved, broody. Lucas rarely cleaned anything, yet here James is, doing all of this without a word.

He steps closer. "Hey," he says. "Please don't cry."

He bends down until we're eye level, his hands moving over my shoulders in long, soothing strokes. The steady rhythm of his touch works its way through me, and slowly, the tears subside. Our gazes catch. His throat bobs as he swallows, his jaw tightening for just a second.

Up close, I take in more detail than ever before—the subtle gold and brown flecks scattered through his green eyes, like sunlight breaking through leaves. There's a tiny scar just above his left eyebrow, so faint it's almost invisible. His lips press into a thin line as he studies me. I don't know how long we stand there, staring at each other, before he whispers, "Hey, April."

"Hey, James," I whisper back.

His attention shifts from my eyes to my lips, then back again. His gaze feels gravitational, pulling me in. Instinctively, I shift closer. I'm not sure why; I just do. As if he's magnetic. Then, abruptly, he clears his throat and steps back, as though my touch might burn him.

My cheeks heat, unsure of what that was, self-conscious that I made him uncomfortable.

My thoughts are interrupted by the rapid pitter-patter of tiny paws as Basil bounds down the stairs, making his grand appearance. I swivel toward him with a smile. "Hey, baby!" I coo, squatting to meet him.

Trotting toward me, he leans into my hand, arching his back and purring like a little engine, the sound rumbling through him. I run my fingers along his soft fur, giving him all the scratches he demands. I glance up at James. "Thank you so much for looking after him. It really means a lot to me," I say.

He gives me a small smile. "I'm happy to. I'm glad the girls could take you away for a bit. Did you have fun?"

I huff out a laugh. "I'm not sure I'd call it *fun*, exactly. But it was . . . interesting." I try to inject positivity into my voice. "It was nice to get out of the house, at least. We had some laughs."

The room falls quiet, and I fidget nervously as he frowns.

"What?" I ask, unsure what to make of his reaction.

"You don't have to pretend with me," he says simply.

My brows knit in confusion and he adds quietly, "It's okay if you're not okay."

My eyes drift to the hall table, cluttered with framed photographs—pictures of Lucas and me, snapshots of happy moments I once thought we'd carry with us forever. I've avoided these photos since Lucas left. I can't bear the reminder that they represent a life I thought we'd still be living. Instead, James is here, looking after Basil and cleaning my house. It wasn't supposed to be like this.

The finality of it hits me like a punch to the chest.

"I'm not okay," I admit.

James's expression sharpens. He watches as if he's trying to read me, to figure out what's going on beneath the surface.

"Do you hate me?" I ask, the words slipping out before I can stop them.

"What? Why the fuck would I hate you?"

"Because I asked him to leave. I—" I swallow hard. "I told him to go."

James's jaw tightens. "I think we both know he deserved it. He didn't have to walk out that door, but he did," he says, his voice even and firm.

I shift on my feet. "He told you everything?"

James scoffs, the sound dry, tinged with bitterness. "Mum did. But we both know he didn't tell her the whole story. I'm sure I can fill in the blanks."

"Oh," I murmur, unsure what else to say.

He gives a small nod.

"How do you know?" I ask, almost afraid of the answer.

His expression hardens. "I just know."

I want to ask more, but his tone tells me not to push, so I leave it be.

"I should probably get going," James says, moving toward the front door.

"Right, of course. Thanks again." I pause, rocking back on my heels. "I'm sorry the girls dragged you into this. You didn't have to come, but...I'm glad you did." I offer him a grateful smile.

James glances back at me, softening just enough to stir something in my chest. "It was no trouble," he replies with a wave of dismissal, followed by a quick kiss to my cheek before turning to leave.

The gesture surprises me, leaving me stunned.

He's never so much as hugged me before.

I grip the door-frame as he descends the front steps. When he reaches the pavement, he turns, tucking his hands into his front pockets, his shoulders hitching slightly in the cool air. He gives me one last sharp nod.

"Bye, April," he says.

"Bye, James," I reply softly.

I watch as he retreats down the footpath. My eyes trail after him until he reaches his car and disappears from sight. Only then do my shoulders deflate, and I let out a long, shaky breath.

Closing the door behind me, exhaustion finally settles in, and I drag myself upstairs. I kick off my shoes by the bed, pull back the covers, and slip beneath the fresh, cool sheets. Reaching for my phone, I open Instagram and type Lucas's name into the search bar.

User not found.

The realization hits and it feels like I've torn stitches—Lucas blocked me. He actually blocked me. *He's only been gone a week.* I drop the phone onto the bedside table with a hollow thud as grief takes hold.

Just when I thought I couldn't feel worse, he's landed one final blow.

Curling into a ball underneath the duvet, I squeeze my eyes shut, mute and numb as the darkness creeps in, taking hold and pulling me under.

Chapter 13

James

By the time I get home, my mood is soured, tainted by thoughts of Lucas. If only other people could see him the way I did—beyond the smooth, practiced façade he wears so well.

I'll never forget that bank holiday when he was completing his final year of university. I was still finishing my A-levels and had been letting off some steam by playing guitar. He couldn't hide his irritation. Storming upstairs, he burst into my bedroom, seething.

"It doesn't matter how much you practice; you're never going to make it. No one will ever take you seriously."

Then, he twisted a peg on my guitar so violently that the string snapped.

I was devastated. Mum saw my distress and felt so bad, she quietly replaced the string the next day. At the time, she didn't mention it, but I later found out that she'd skipped her weekly coffee with friends to afford that string. It's a small sacrifice, but it matters.

After that moment, I made myself a promise: I would earn enough money playing music—something Lucas despised—to ensure Mum could have anything she wanted without hesitation. She'd never have to skip a cup of coffee, or sacrifice the little joys that made her smile, again.

Without a second thought, I head straight for my bass. She's a beauty—a rare Spector, her body carved from spalted buckeye in the U.S., one of only thirty ever made. I saved every penny I earned as a barista after finishing school, knowing she had to be mine.

Grabbing her off the stand, I sling the strap over my shoulder and let my fingers find the strings. Her smooth neck feels like a natural extension of me, and muscle memory takes over as I slide my fingers along the frets, plucking out a familiar melody.

There's something visceral about the bass compared to other instruments—it reverberates through my entire body, even when I play it without an amp. It's heavy and gives immediate feedback—you know right away if you've nailed it or missed the mark. Beethoven composed music without the ability to hear it; he felt every note through the vibrations. That's how I feel about the bass. It isn't just heard—it's experienced. You don't just listen to it; you *feel* it, deep in your bones.

And when I plug in and play onstage, the experience is out of this world. The sound pours out and fills the room, overpowering everything else, until there's nothing left but me and the music. When I play, the rest of the world disappears.

Although I *can* sing, singing isn't really my thing— that's Tom's job—but when I'm alone, I enjoy writing the occasional song. For me, music is like a journal. Every note carries a memory, every chord captures a feeling, and together they tell the stories I struggle to put into words. Music has always been my greatest refuge. When the world feels too heavy, the notes act as an anchor, pulling me back to solid ground. Words? They've failed me more often than not over the years. But music? Music never lets me down. It's always been my preferred language.

The melody of my song pulls me deeper, and I'm lost in it. The notes become my emotions, vulnerable and bare. And suddenly, I realize—I'm playing the way I heard *her*. She says she's fine, but it's what she doesn't say that screams the loudest. The truth is in her quiet tone, the way her voice wavers in the middle of a sentence. I wonder if she realizes how much she's revealing without saying anything at all.

I wonder if Lucas could ever hear it.

I've never spent much time alone with April—funny how that only happens now, after she's finally rid of my brother. Lucas never deserved her. She was always too good for him. I knew that from the start.

From the moment I saw the worried expression on April's face at their engagement party, I knew Lucas was hiding something. I could see it in the way he was constantly checking his phone, sneaking glances like a kid who'd just discovered his own dick for the first time.

It's weird for a man his age to be on his phone that much.

But that's Lucas. Always chasing more. Nothing's ever enough—jobs, friends, relationships. He gets comfortable for a while, then it's as if stability starts to itch. The second things feel settled, he bolts, always searching for something better, shinier, like it'll somehow fix what's broken inside him.

And the worst part? I think deep down he knew April was the best thing that ever happened to him. But his ego wouldn't let him see it through, so he let her slip right through his fingers, like a whisper in a breeze.

Lucas and I were never close growing up. The five-year age gap didn't help—we were in different worlds. When I started secondary school, he was already off to university. While I was learning algebra, he was drinking pints and studying. By the time I wanted to close the gap between us, too much distance had already settled in. We were too different.

We did spend a bit more time together in my early twenties, mainly during long weekends and bank holidays. I'd stay with Mum and Dad and bring Abigail, my girlfriend at the time, along. But outside of those trips, we stayed in our own lanes and kept to ourselves.

He always called me the Golden Child, but it was never really like that. When Lucas left for university, it was just me at home with our parents, and I always made more of an effort with Mum and Dad—something he never bothered with.

Mum struggled with her mental health while we were growing up. Some days she'd shut down, isolate herself and hide away from everything. Dad always tried his best, which was never great, so I'd try to step in and help her out.

Being the youngest, I noticed when Mum's mood began to shift. I was more reliant on them, so I saw when Mum needed support. I spent more time with her, played music for her when she was down. She'd take me to my guitar lessons and would stay to watch when I asked—that always made her happy. We had a bond. Not because I was placed on a pedestal or because I was the youngest, but because I cared—something Lucas never had time for.

He proved my point when he betrayed my trust and let me down harder than anyone ever had. It was the kind of betrayal you don't come back from. Honestly, he's lucky I still fucking talk to him.

When my hands finally grow tired and my fingertips sting from the strings, I set my bass back on the stand. I pull out my phone and shoot a message to the lads.

Me: *We all good for practice tomorrow?*
Oliver replies immediately.
Oliver: *Absolutely. See you boys then.*
Will: *Yup.*
Tom: *All good. See you tomorrow.*

Settling into my usual spot on the sofa, I drop my phone beside me and flick on the TV. I select my favorite show with the intention of distracting myself, but I can't stop thinking about April—how sad she looked. Meek and tired.

When Anna told me April hadn't been going to work, guilt gnawed at me. And when I saw her—when I took one look at her—I knew how defeated she was. My heart fucking broke for her.

The skin around her eyes appeared bruised with exhaustion, her skin pale and lifeless, missing that glow she always seemed to carry. Even her hair was undone, like she didn't have the energy to care. April's the kind of woman who takes pride in herself—always effortlessly beautiful. But when I saw her, her spark was gone. The woman I saw wasn't the April I know.

My own flesh and blood did that to her.

And I can't fucking let it go.

* * *

"Again!" Oliver shouts, clicking his drumsticks together overhead. I dive straight into the bass line. My fingers work on autopilot as they glide over the frets and my pick finds the strings.

Practice has been ramped up to multiple times a week, on top of the gigs we've already got locked in. It's tiring, but that's part of music.

We run through a few more sets, and by the time we're done, we're drenched in sweat and our bodies are heavy from exhaustion. Tom, our singer, grabs a water bottle and downs it in one go, wiping his mouth with the back of his hand as he catches his breath.

We start packing up, winding our cables and unplugging amps, my ears still buzzing from the music. As I coil my bass lead, Oliver asks, "So, how was your weekend, mate?"

I casually detail April and Lucas's breakup, and how I spent my weekend caring for Basil and tidying up April's townhouse, brushing it off as if it was no big deal, even though it was anything but.

Oliver chuckles, shaking his head. "You're way too noble for your own good, mate."

"Shit. I'm surprised," Tom says, scratching the back of his head. "I didn't think they'd ever break up—I thought they were, like, *grossly in love.*"

"Can't say I am," Will chimes in, folding a cable. "He's an absolute twat. Never deserved her."

Tom isn't finished, though. "Why'd they break up?"

I exhale through my nose. "Apparently, he wouldn't open up to her. Said he couldn't be honest, and she figured if they couldn't even have a proper conversation, there wasn't much hope for the relationship."

Tom wrinkles his nose. "Bullshit."

"I know," I reply flatly.

Will opens his mouth, his expression sly. "Do you think he—"

"No idea, don't care," I cut him off before he can even finish the thought. "All I know is he fucked up."

Will grins, the mischief in his eyes obvious. "Well, if you didn't shag her, you're a better man than me. She's fit as fuck."

My jaw tightens at Will's comment, and I have to bite down the urge to react. Instead, I focus on pulling the strap off my bass, slinging it into the case with more force than necessary. I keep my tone flat as I say, "Can't imagine why I'm still single, with you lot as role models."

Oliver walks over and gives me a light-hearted clap on the back, the slap making my sweat-soaked shirt cling even tighter to my skin. Excellent.

Oliver's my best mate—we've had each other's backs since primary school. He's been more of a brother to me than Lucas. There's nothing I keep from him, and he always knows when something's off.

"You good, mate?" he asks, his voice low.

"Yeah, man. I'm fine. Why?"

He shrugs, giving me that familiar, concerned look I've never liked. "Just checking in. I know Lucas—"

"Oliver, it's fine," I cut him off, my tone sharper than intended.

He holds my gaze for a second, then nods slowly, accepting my boundary. "All right, all right. See you at the gig."

"Sounds good," I say, giving him a quick fist bump.

And just like that, he drops it. That's the thing about Oliver—he knows when to push, and when to let me be.

I wipe down the strings and then close my guitar case. "I'll see you guys at the Mayfair Lounge on Friday," I say, giving them a quick nod before turning toward the door. Slinging my bag over my shoulder, I head out without another word.

I need to focus on the music.

Chapter 14

April

Three months later...

After a long day at work, I slap on a hydrating face mask and open my laptop. After months of neglect, I decide to log into my Pinterest account. As I scroll through Pinterest, I begin deleting the vision boards I'd made for the wedding—thankfully, one we hadn't planned yet. A task I'd been avoiding. One by one, images of idyllic garden ceremonies, lace dresses, and white rose floral arrangements disappear.

I've always loved roses, especially yellow ones; they were my mum's favorite flower. Lucas, however, always brought me white roses while we were dating. I never had the heart to tell him that white roses felt lifeless to me, as though their stark color drained the personality from the bloom. What's the point of a white rose? Roses are far too fragrant and beautiful to look so sterile.

With my mother in mind, I feel a surge of determination to start fresh and create a new board. One for myself, with things that make me happy. One brimming with vibrant roses, cats, ceramics and pastries. As I piece together my collage of cheerful images, I flutter around the kitchen, gathering a small teapot, a mug, and some milk before setting the tea to brew.

It's Friday night, and lately, weekends have started to haunt me. As time has passed, I've grown to dread them. Other than hitting up Portobello Market on Saturday mornings, I don't do much else. I usually keep to myself and read or watch TV. To be honest, it gets lonely. Even with the support of my wonderful friends, there are moments when the silence feels heavy, and I find myself wishing there was someone else—someone who could fill the space Lucas left behind.

Perhaps a hobby would be helpful.

A photo of a delicate, hand-thrown vase catches my eye, and I start to wonder if I could get back into ceramics. The thought feels both daunting and exciting.

Could I do it again?

Would it bring me the peace and happiness it used to when I would shape clay with my mother?

A knock on the front door pulls me from my daze. Pushing my tea aside, I swing the door open to find Anna and Gemma grinning on the stoop.

"Oh my God!" I exclaim, throwing my arms around them. "I wasn't expecting you!"

Gemma lifts a bottle of red wine with a smirk. "We thought girl time was in order."

"Perfect! Let me grab some glasses."

They follow me into the kitchen, gathering around the island while I reach into the cupboard for three long-stemmed glasses. Gemma uncorks the bottle with a sharp twist and pours us each a generous amount.

"Cheers," Anna says as we clink our glasses together. We bring the wine to our lips, and the first sip is nothing short of heavenly. "Mmmm," we all groan in unison.

As I lift the glass to my lips for a second helping, I notice Anna carrying a large paper bag. I raise an eyebrow and gesture toward it with my glass. "What's in the bag?"

"Well," she says, dragging out the word. "That's sort of why we're here."

"What?"

Anna places the bag gently on the counter, sliding it toward me with a cheeky grin.

"Okay, now I'm worried," I say, narrowing my eyes.

"Just open it!" Gemma urges, practically bouncing on her toes.

Lowering my glass to the counter, I grab the bag and pull it open with both hands. Inside, I spot a long rectangular box nestled amongst the tissue paper.

"You guys got me a gift?" I say, glancing between them. "You didn't need to do that."

"Oh, I think we did," Anna replies, her grin widening.

Curiosity gets the better of me, and one-handed, I pull the box from the bag. Flipping off the lid, I freeze, staring at the contents with wide eyes. My fingers curl around the wineglass as embarrassment sweeps over me.

"You bought me a sex toy?" I blurt, my voice catching somewhere between shock and utter horror.

Gemma beams, practically glowing with pride as I lift the toy to inspect it. "Not just any old toy—a *deluxe* one. Look! It's got a part for your G-spot *and* a suction bit for your clit. This baby is top of the line."

"Okay, Dildo Baggins," I say, holding it up between my thumb and forefinger, dangling it between us.

"It's a vibrator, actually," Anna chimes in, her grin widening. *"One Toy to Rule Them All!"*

We burst into laughter. "I honestly don't know whether to be thankful or mortified that my best friends bought me a sex toy."

"Thankful. Definitely thankful," Gemma says, shooting me a wink.

We spend the rest of the evening indulging in wine and picking at the small cheese board I've thrown together, catching up on our workweeks and laughing over Gemma's latest dating disaster.

"And then he sent me a photo of his finger shoved up his ass—in his work bathroom, no less," she finishes explaining. Anna and I cringe so hard it feels like our faces might get stuck that way.

"So," Gemma says, changing the subject as she swirls the last of her wine, "what are you both up to tomorrow?"

"It's me we're talking about," I say with a shrug. "I'll probably be drowning my sorrows in a bottle of red and binge-watching Netflix with Basil."

"As delightful as that sounds," Anna chimes in, "Mason has a work dinner tomorrow night, and I say we make the most of my free evening."

"It's like you read my mind," Gemma says, pressing a hand to her heart.

"Girls' night?" I ask, glancing between them.

"I'm thinking the Mayfair Lounge," Anna says, smirking.

"Absolutely," Gemma and I reply, raising our drinks.

With grins all around, we clink our glasses together.

* * *

It's Saturday morning, and the sun pours in through the windows, filling the room with a comfortable warmth. I stretch my tired arms and rise from bed to get ready for the day. Saturdays have become my favorite since Gemma and I became friends. They're somewhat of a ritual where we grab a takeaway coffee and stroll through the busy Portobello Market.

I usually did this while Lucas was out on his morning hike. Afterward, we would often meet to do something together, whether it was lunch, a movie, a drive through the countryside, hunting for books in charity shops, or exploring new exhibitions at galleries. Although my afternoons now look entirely different, I've still got my special mornings with Gemma, which I'm incredibly grateful for.

I have a little more spring in my step this morning after spending a night sifting through images of pottery and ceramics. Perhaps today I'll stumble across some ceramics that spark inspiration and rekindle that old flame.

After a quick shower, I brush my teeth, spray dry shampoo into my hair, and run my fingers through it. I slap on some color corrector and a layer of black mascara to try to hide my under-eye bags, which are definitely not Chanel.

Next, I put on my baggy jeans and black sweater, slip into my sneakers, feed Basil, and head out the door. I jump in the car and fire off a text to Gemma, letting her know I'm on my way.

I try to make the most of the sunshine when it dares to grace us, this hasn't been the warmest spring. So, I wind down my window and let the breeze kiss my skin while I crank up the music, singing along at the top of my lungs. Wild weekend, I know.

I pull up to Gemma's flat and find her waiting on the stoop, bundled in her cozy puffer coat. When she spots me, she leaps to her feet and jogs to the passenger side before swinging the door open and dropping into the seat.

"It's freezing! Why is your window down?"

"Because it's spring. The sun is shining!"

"So? It's still cold. Put it up!"

I shake my head but roll the window up as Gemma fiddles with the temperature dials on my dashboard, blasting warm air through the vents.

"I need coffee so badly. I had the worst night."

"What happened?"

"Okay, so remember that Kevin guy I met on that kink app?"

"Yes . . ."

"Well, he came over last night, and we ended up having sex."

"Classic."

"No, that's not it," she says, shaking her head before dropping her head into her hands.

"I was hoping it wouldn't be." I smirk, giving her a side-eye.

Catching up with Gemma is never dull. She leads the most interesting, fun life, exuding a confidence and dominance I can only admire from afar.

"He asked me to stick a mini vibrator up his ass," she mumbles from behind her hands. I quickly turn my head to face her, wondering if I'd misheard.

She sighs. "It got stuck and wouldn't come out, so I had to take him to the emergency room at 1:00 a.m."

I definitely heard correctly.

"No!" I gasp.

"Yes! It was so fucking awkward!"

"What did you do?"

"I didn't know whether to stay with him. We literally hadn't met before, so I kind of just dropped him off in reception and said goodbye. He went for a hug when I leaned in for a kiss on the cheek. All the while, he's still buzzing from the vibrator in his ass. It was a total disaster. I ended up just giving him a pat on the shoulder and walking out."

And for the first time in months, I laugh. I really laugh. Tears stream down my face, and my stomach muscles ache as I gasp for air, trying to steer. Gemma joins in, filling the car with a joyous sound. It's a moment of pure, unfiltered happiness that I hadn't realized I so desperately needed.

I squeak out, "It's all for the plot, Gem."

"I don't think I'll see him again," she says through her gasps.

"No," I say, wiping the tears from my eyes. "I don't think so."

She turns to me, scanning my face intently.

"What?" I ask.

"Nothing. It's just . . . nice to see you smile," she says, the corners of her mouth curling up.

I glance at her, feeling a warmth spread through me. "It feels good."

We spend a beautiful morning together laughing and shopping. We leave the market with a bag of goodies each, happy with our small treasures. Gemma stocked up on incense, candles, and crystals, and I walked away with a pair of handmade clay mugs.

I feel so inspired after our visit to the markets that, once I drop Gemma home, I pull my old pottery wheel and materials out of the shed. Dusting off the surface, I clear away years of debris and spiderwebs before setting myself up in the courtyard. I'd expected a wave of grief or guilt to hit me as I revisited my love for ceramics. But instead, I only feel comfort. The hum and thud of the wheel is soothing as it spins, and the clay is cool between my fingers. My foot works in sync with my hands, almost on autopilot, and I press and pull on the clay. It's messy and imperfect, a product of being out of practice for so long, but for the first time in years, it feels like a step toward healing. It's been a good day.

Eventually, I head upstairs for a hot shower, letting the water wash away the mess of clay before getting ready for the evening ahead.

Chapter 15

James

We're so close—*so* damn close to getting this set just right. Tonight, we're playing a gig at the Mayfair Lounge, one of my favorite bars in Central London. The atmosphere there is incredible, and they've always been good to us, hiring us regularly and giving us a chance when other places wouldn't.

This venue has become our home base, where we've built a solid following from the ground up. Any chance to play here is a no-brainer—we take every gig we're offered, and we treat every performance as another step closer to perfecting our songs for the big audition.

Tonight, we're playing a mix of covers and originals. We figure it's best to keep things balanced—if we only play our own stuff, the crowd might not connect as easily. Mixing in some well-loved covers keeps the energy up and the audience engaged. Plus, it gives us the perfect opportunity to showcase our versatility and let people see what we're really about as a band. Seeing the crowd react to our music will never get old.

My arms ache from a long day of setting up scaffolding and wrestling with wet concrete, but the exhaustion doesn't keep me from picking up my bass and playing. I'm completely lost in the rhythm, plucking away at the strings of my bass when the intercom buzzes, cutting through my focus. I lift the strap over my head and carefully place the bass in its stand before heading over to buzz the guys in.

Swinging the door open, I'm greeted with claps on the shoulder and nods from Will, Tom, and Oliver as they step inside.

"You lads want a drink?" I offer.

"Yeah, mate. Just a lager," Tom replies.

I glance at Will and Oliver, and they both nod. Heading into the kitchen, I open the fridge and grab a few beers before returning to the lounge, offering one to each of them.

We clink our bottles together in cheers, then lift them to our lips, taking long pulls of the cold beer.

"So, how are you guys feeling?" Tom asks as I drop onto the sofa, leaning back into the cushions and spreading my legs to get comfortable.

Will wanders over to the bookshelf along the far wall opposite the sofa and TV.

"Feeling great," he replies over his shoulder as he begins thumbing through the rows of books. "James, do you actually read all this shit?"

"That *shit*," I say with a smirk, "is called philosophy. And yes, I've read every one of them."

Oliver strolls over, pointing his bottle at Will. "You ever read a book, mate?"

"Of course I have," Will says, sounding defensive.

"*Spot Goes to the Zoo* doesn't count," I deadpan.

Oliver snorts, spitting out a mouthful of beer as he and Tom burst into laughter.

"Fuck you guys," Will mutters, raising his drink to his lips, draining what's left.

"Calm down," Oliver says, clapping him on the shoulder. "You've got a guitar to play, mate."

"I'll be fine," Will says sharply.

"Don't get sloshed, Will. This is a paid gig—don't fuck it up," I say, pointing at him in warning.

"All right, all right," he grumbles, making his way over to the coffee table to drop the empty bottle onto it.

My phone buzzes on the sofa next to me, and Tom and Will lean in to see who the notification is from.

"*Blonde from Pret*," Tom says, scoffing.

I roll my eyes. Yesterday morning, I met her at the local Pret while grabbing a coffee and a slice of banana bread. She was hot and struck up some small talk. One thing led to another, and she talked me into meeting her for a glass of wine last night—which quickly turned into three. Before I knew it, I had her bent over my sofa, fucking her from behind. Now, she's been double-texting and blowing up my phone all day.

I don't have time for dating or the drama that comes with it—not with the big audition coming up. I just needed to blow off a little steam before tonight's gig. We had a good time. She was fun, and I enjoyed her company for what it was. But there's only ever been one woman I'd actually consider making an effort for.

Fuck, that's the first time I've admitted it.

I push the thought away before it takes root. I don't need the distraction. Not now. Focusing on our music is too important. I can't keep working as a laborer forever—it'll never give Mum the life she truly deserves. Music runs in my veins, and that's where I belong.

"Just ignore it," I say, waving it off. I look over at Oliver, who responds with a smirk, but doesn't say anything.

We finish our beers, and I gather my bass and gear. The guys help me haul everything out to the van, loading it up like clockwork, like we've done a thousand times before. As Oliver turns the key and the engine rumbles to life, music blasts through the speakers, rattling the windows. Butterflies stir in my stomach, restless wings beating faster with every passing second. Tom taps my knee, sensing my nerves, and I shoot him a grateful nod.

I'll never get used to the feeling that hits me right before we play. It doesn't matter if we're at home rehearsing or standing in front of an audience. Whether there are five people watching or a packed room, it always hits the same way—settling deep in my bones, thrumming in my veins like a second heartbeat. It's a fire under my skin that I burn for.

This is what I was meant to do. The nerves, the rush, the music. And no matter how many gigs we play, I know I'll never stop chasing this feeling.

We pull into the alley behind the venue, loading through the back entrance. The place is quiet as we haul our gear onto the stage, getting everything set up before the patrons arrive. It's only 8:00 p.m., and we know the crowd won't start filtering in until closer to 9:00.

The quiet, early evening chatter from lingering afternoon patrons is welcome—it gives us a chance to focus, adjust, and fine-tune without distraction. And once everything's in place, it leaves us with just enough time to kick back with a drink. It's a ritual we all love—the calm before the storm.

Once everything's set up, the bar manager, Victoria, hands each of us a cold beer. Lugging in speakers, running cables, tuning our gear, and testing the sound takes time—and a lot of energy. We often work up a sweat by the time everything's ready.

As the bubbles pop on my tongue and the cold liquid slides down my throat, I feel my shoulders loosen as the chill eases the tension from my muscles.

"Good luck tonight, guys. You'll smash it—you always do," Victoria says, turning to Tom and flashing him a wink before slinking down the hall, her hips swaying with deliberate force.

"Well, well," Will says, grinning mischievously as he nudges Tom. "Looks like *someone's* getting lucky tonight."

"As long as she keeps hiring us, I'll keep shagging her," Tom says with a wicked grin.

"That's so wrong," Oliver mutters, shaking his head.

We hover backstage as people trickle in, the room gradually filling with the hum of chatter and the buzz of bodies swaying to the DJ's music. The energy builds with each passing moment, and I feel the excitement radiating from the guys—it's infectious. I pull my pick from my pocket and nibble on it, waiting.

Will peeks his head around the curtain separating us from the main bar, his eyes widening before he ducks back with a grin. "James, mate, you're not gonna believe who's here."

"Who?" I ask.

"April. And she looks incredible."

Fuck.

Chapter 16

April

I buzz Gemma's flat and impatiently wait for her to let me in. With my hands occupied fluffing my hair, I bounce slightly to keep warm, surprisingly cheerful to be here. After weeks spent wallowing in my sorrows, a fun girls' night out seems the perfect thing to distract me from the current shitstorm that is my personal life.

A buzz sounds before Gemma's voice spills through the intercom.

"The hot girl evening has officially commenced. I made margaritas!"

I swear that woman is a walking cocktail.

I chuckle under my breath and step inside. Anna flings the door of Gemma's flat open, and her eyes slide over me from head to toe, a low, appreciative whistle escaping her lips.

"Bloody hell. You ought to be careful tonight," she says.

"What? Why?" I ask, looking down to inspect my outfit.

"I'm a straight married woman, and even I'm tempted to shag you."

I'm drawn instantly to her stunning rose gold wedding ring adorning her finger. The pear-shaped diamond sparkles under the hallway lights, and a fleeting pang of envy washes over me, serving as a blunt reminder of what I lost. I dismiss the thought before it drenches me with misery.

I give her a playful twirl, showcasing my new Sophia Webster winged butterfly shoes and leather miniskirt, which I've paired with a baby pink cropped silk shirt, fully embracing the Taylor Swift "Lover" aesthetic. My straightened hair flows down, reaching my waist. To complete the look, I've added thick gold hoop earrings and cherry-red lips.

I must admit, retail therapy has become a favorite pastime since the breakup. The loud colors and luxurious fabrics I've added to my wardrobe have brought a semblance of joy and happiness back into my home. I love running my fingers over the soft material because I find that, when everything else feels sad and gloomy, my clothes brighten my day.

"Knowing my abysmal luck with the male species, I might just take you up on that offer," I joke, sharing a laugh with Anna. Inside, music fills the kitchen and Gemma stands, armed with margaritas.

"This is 98 percent alcohol," she states, passing me a glass.

My brows pinch. "What's the other 2 percent?"

"Lime."

"At least it's fruit," Anna replies, shrugging while she accepts her own glass and takes a healthy swig.

Gemma studies me for a moment, and I give her an insecure look. "What?"

"You look like you stepped out of a YouTube channel made for toddlers."

Anna chokes on her margarita, pounding her fist against her chest to stifle the coughing.

I look down to inspect my outfit, unable to keep from laughing. "Uh, rude! I figured if I dress in happy colors, it will make me feel happy."

"Don't get me wrong, I love the bright colors. They're much more your style, but I got so used to seeing you in black. I'm just surprised, that's all. It's like the first time you see your favorite Disney child actor all grown up at thirty," Gemma says with a chuckle.

Anna chimes in, "She was in mourning, Gemma."

"I wore black way before I found out my fiancé was an online predator," I reply.

Anna nods. "That was your subconscious speaking. It knew he was a shady subspecies."

I shake my head and bring the drink to my lips, delighting in the tangy flavors as they dance across my tongue. Lowering my drink, I check out my best friends in appreciation.

Anna is stunning in a tight, short-sleeved, black midi dress with nude heels, and Gemma is confidently rocking her signature ensemble: a sleek black leather skirt paired with a black see-through top, her maroon lacy bodysuit on display underneath.

It dawns on me that this is the first time in months I've gone out for drinks with my girlfriends without Lucas by my side. And now, I'm single. I've never been one to relish attention from men, or anyone, for that matter. In the past, I never had to worry about it because I always had an arm draped over my shoulders and a ring on my finger. But now, it's not just the absence of that anchor that hits me; it's the awareness that I've never really experienced being single. I met Lucas less than a year after breaking up with my ex, who I had been with since I was twenty-one. I wasn't really interested in partying during that time, let alone entertaining the idea of a one-night stand because the wounds from losing my parents were still healing. I was low for a long time.

I take a long pull from my glass, hoping the alcohol will provide the courage I don't possess.

"You good?" Gemma checks in.

I exhale deeply. "Yeah, just a little nervous. I've never really gone out as a single woman before."

Gemma smirks and wiggles her eyebrows suggestively. "You're gonna love it."

Anna joins in. "Tonight is all about *us*. Girl time. There's no pressure to do anything except have a few drinks, a bit of a dance, and let go. You need and deserve this. Tonight isn't attached to any expectations . . . and if Gemma *does* happen to leave with someone, well, I'll be next to you, cheering her on."

"This is why you're my best friends," Gemma says, clinking her glass with ours.

"That was oddly insightful, thanks," I say, surprised.

"Plus, I hear the live music on Saturday nights is amazing," Anna says.

For the next hour, we continue to blend and enjoy fresh margaritas, sing along to the music, and chat about our days before leaving for the bar.

* * *

Mayfair gleams under the city lights, pulsating with energy. Saturday nights out on the town have always been my favorite. The atmosphere is electric as the city comes to life. *This* is truly living.

I love nothing more than dressing up and indulging in beautiful food and delicious drinks. I can't imagine ever leaving London; I'm in love with this place.

The Uber stops outside the Mayfair Lounge, and we tumble out of the car as elegantly as we can in our tight skirts. Given our scant clothing, high heels, and alcohol, the tube wasn't an option this evening.

The streets bustle with people dressed up for all occasions, and music and voices fill the cool air.

The Mayfair Lounge is situated in a tall, three-story building on Regent Street. The ground floor features the main club, the second floor is exclusively for VIP members, and the third level, with its own entrance, hosts an exclusive sex club. Although I haven't experienced the atmosphere of the sex club firsthand, I've heard it's luxurious and sensual. My confidence in this information stems from my trusted source, Gemma.

I link arms with Anna as we step inside. Despite the bar's spaciousness, it's teeming with people dancing, toasting with clinking glasses, mingling in the booths, and ordering drinks at the bar. Exposed beams span the length of the ceiling, and the cocktail bar extends across the entire back wall. Shelves, illuminated by vibrant LED lights, are filled with every imaginable spirit, lining the wall from top to bottom. Professional bartenders are busy shaking, mixing, and pouring drinks while patrons bark out orders. Black leather booths stretch along the right side of the club, while a dance floor sits beside the stage on the left, where live bands perform every Saturday.

We push through the throng of people to the bar. As I survey my surroundings, I wonder which band will take the stage tonight. I love live music—the pulsating beat of the bass and drums echoes through my body, sparking it to life.

As we reach the front of the bar, Gemma waves down a bartender and orders a round of tequila shots. We each sprinkle a line of salt on the backs of our hands before licking it off, then downing the shot and chasing it with a wedge of lime.

"Another!" Anna exclaims, slamming her empty shot glass on the bar like a Viking.

"If I want to walk out of here tonight, I think it's best we don't go balls-to-the-wall on tequila," I say.

"I'll be pissed as a fart," Gemma agrees.

"You need to work on your fitness," Anna retorts.

"What does my fitness have to do with drinking?" I ask.

"Not exercise fitness, you tit. I mean, being piss-fit. A woman who can hold her alcohol," Anna says, turning toward the bartender. "Fine, three espresso martinis, please."

"Oh God," Gemma says.

Anna waves her hand dismissively. "Trust me, you'll love it."

The bartender gets to work shaking up our cocktails. We each take a glass and head to the booths, scooting in. Just as we settle, the music cuts, and we look over to the stage in anticipation of who will be playing tonight. Bright lights illuminate the performing area, and cheers ring through the room as the band makes their way out. The dance floor is packed tonight, forcing us to bob our heads to catch a glimpse.

"Oh, shit," Gemma says, turning to me with a concerned look.

"What?" I ask.

Then I see what she's talking about.

A tall man occupies the front, adjusting the height of the microphone. He runs his hand through his long, black hair and wets his lips before his gravelly voice filters through the room.

"How are we all doing tonight?" he asks.

I immediately recognize him.

His muscular arms are inked with tattoos, covering his golden skin. His nails are painted black, and he wears two large silver rings on his index and middle fingers. A charcoal T-shirt reading "Comfortably uncomfortable" stretches across his broad chest.

Anna winces, looking at me. "Is that—"

"Tom."

"Then where's . . ." Anna's voice trails off as three other men step onto the stage. My attention focuses on a tall, blond man in a leather jacket, who is casually slinging a guitar strap over his shoulder and retrieving a pick from his front pocket. I take him in as he tunes his guitar. I watch his biceps flex, how the bright lights accentuate his high cheekbones and sharp jaw, dusted in stubble. He's wearing dark jeans and his usual black combat boots. Jesus Christ, he looks *good*. His large hands grasp the neck of the bass as he begins picking the strings.

"James," I whisper before taking a large pull from my cocktail. At that moment, as if he heard me, James lifts his eyes, immediately finding me, and pauses his movements. I freeze. His brows furrow before he quickly looks away, dragging a hand over his stubble.

"Are you okay?" Gemma questions, placing her hand over mine.

"Yeah . . . Yeah, I'm fine." I wave her off, feigning indifference.

Fine. A simple but damaging word. The use of which completely contradicts its meaning.

But inside, my heart catapults into my throat. Why didn't he wave?

Why did he look away so quickly?

I'm trying to compose myself, I rub my forehead and down the rest of my cocktail. I feel panicky seeing him here after months of no contact. The thought of running into him didn't even cross my mind. Well, that's not entirely true—I still think about James.

It's hard not to.

But I didn't expect to run into him tonight.

"We're Atlas Veil! I'm Tom. Holding down the bass we've got James, my man Oliver's tearing it up on the drums, and Will's shredding on guitar! Hopefully, you'll recognize some of these songs."

The room is alive with excitement as the first few chords float through the air, and my head snaps in James's direction. I watch as he immerses himself in the song, his fingers gliding over the strings, eyes closed, tapping his foot to the beat.

"We can go if you aren't comfortable," Anna says.

"It's okay, really. Plus, I love this song." I smile, and it seems to put them at ease.

We settle into light-hearted conversation as the band plays their set and Gemma fetches another round of espresso martinis. Anna was right: She is loving them.

As the evening progresses, I forget the brooding man on-stage and focus on my girls. After our second martini, we switch to water and head to the dance floor.

I smile and throw my hands in the air, singing along to the music as a soft sheen of sweat coats my body. Without thought, I glance toward the stage and instantly lock eyes with James. He almost looks . . . angry?

I snap out of my trance as two hands land on my hips, and a firm chest presses against my back. I whirl around and find myself face-to-face with a tall, dark, and handsome stranger, whose friend seems quite taken with Gemma. Glancing to my left, I catch Anna waving her ring finger in another guy's face. Poor bloke, he doesn't stand a chance.

Leaning in, the stranger says, "I'm sorry to interrupt, but you ladies looked like you were having so much fun, we had to join in."

I swivel my head to find James still staring at me, his nostrils flared and jaw tense, still not missing a single note as he watches this exchange. Looking back at the stranger, I shout over the loud music, "We're having a girls' night."

He raises his eyebrows and says, "Your mate over there looks rather happy making a new friend." I flick my gaze to assess Gemma and his friend. He's right: she's already dancing, giggling, and batting her lashes at her new companion.

"Yes, well, Gemma's single," I clip.

"And you are not?"

I'm not prepared for this. I can't flirt or make small talk. Honestly, I'm terrible at it. Before Lucas, the last man who attempted to flirt with me was mortified when my "small talk" included asking for his star sign and deepest mother wound.

Surface-level conversations are boring. Knowing someone's job or where they went to university doesn't define who they are. It doesn't reveal why they think the way they do, or what genuinely makes them happy.

I crave deeper connections and conversations that uncover what drives a person, their passions, fears, and the moments that shaped them. I want to understand what brings them joy and what keeps them up at night.

At least with Lucas, our introduction was organic. There was a build-up of angst and anticipation before he asked me out on our first date. Perhaps his being an academic and poet made it seem easier; they generally explore deeper meanings instead of the usual "*How are you?*" and "*What do you do for work?"* Then again, all Lucas wanted to explore was other women's bodies.

I press my lips into a line as he regards me patiently, waiting.

"I am." I nod, and he smirks, like the cat who got the cream.

"I'm George," he replies, extending his hand. I take it for a shake.

"April."

"It's a bit crowded here, don't you think? Can I get you a drink?"

I'd rather shit in my hands and clap, thanks, George.

I look down at my empty glass and sigh in defeat as Anna sidles up to me, leaning into my ear. "Gemma's made a new friend," she says. George smiles and turns to shuffle to the bar, Anna and I in tow.

I can't help but chance another look at James, only to find him still watching me.

I'm so confused. *Why is he staring?*

George interrupts my thoughts, handing me a vodka, lime, and soda. I don't want to make a spectacle, so I accept the drink.

"Thanks," I say.

"You're welcome."

Lifting the glass to my lips, I take a tentative sip. The mixture of bubbles and lime coats my mouth, cooling me down. I exhale. "Look, I appreciate the drink, but I've just got out of a long-term relationship, and I'm really not looking for anything. I just came here tonight to have a good time with my friends."

"That's perfectly fine, April. I only wanted to buy a beautiful woman a drink. There are no expectations attached to the vodka soda," he says with a warm smile, and

I'm taken aback by the sincerity in his voice. Perhaps he's not as boring as I thought he might be.

"So, April, what do you do for work?" he asks.

Oh God. Kill me now.

* * *

After George realized he wasn't getting anywhere with me, and his mate didn't have a chance with Anna, they left. The band has finished their set, and a DJ has taken over. I scan the room, unable to spot James. He must have left. Gemma is happily dancing with her new friend, so Anna and I have left her to take a seat in a booth. Anna is filling me in on her latest work drama while we sip mojitos. I've almost had enough alcohol to make texting Lucas seem like a great idea, but I also know I'll regret it tomorrow morning, so I push the impulse aside and try to focus on listening to Anna.

"Honestly, she's so difficult to work with. She challenges every suggestion Daniel and I make. It makes planning the rest of term so difficult," Anna vents.

Anna is a primary school teacher who works tirelessly. She's incredibly devoted to her students and loves what she does; they are the luckiest kids to have her as their teacher. Anna has a heart of gold.

I continue to listen and provide as much support and advice as I can before her eyes suddenly bulge. I follow her line of sight to where it lands on Lucas.

At the bar.

With a woman.

My stomach does a nauseating flip, and I work harder for air.

"Shit. April, are you okay?" she asks, her face etched with concern as she lowers her voice.

I sit frozen in shock, my mind a whirlwind of jumbled thoughts. Like someone tipped over a Scrabble board, scattering the pieces, and I can't seem to find my words.

My attention is immediately captured by the woman beside him. Her dainty, pink-tipped fingers rest on his forearm as he leans in to whisper something. A coy smile graces her lips as she looks down, bashful. She's wearing a short, flowing sage-green dress, accentuating her ample cleavage and showcasing her tan, toned legs. Dark, curly locks fall just below her shoulders, highlighting her petite frame. She's undeniably stunning.

I don't recognize her from any of his Instagram messages, so I figure she must be new, and the knowledge that he's putting himself out there, already dating and exploring new women, sends an awful chill through me.

As I observe them, a pang of insecurity creeps in. I can't help but compare myself. I feel inadequate with my pale complexion, tall stature, smaller chest and curves. It's totally irrational, but I can't help but notice that she embodies everything I am not. She is beautiful in ways that I can't seem to match.

The questions pour through my mind, quick and fast.

Is that what he wanted?

Am I not pretty enough?

Am I too tall?

Was he not attracted to me anymore?

"April?" Anna questions, bringing her hand to rest atop mine.

"Sorry, I'm just . . . surprised," I respond, my voice tinged with disbelief. "I just . . . He's on a date." I look at Anna with watery eyes. "I didn't . . . I didn't think he would move on so quickly." I swallow the lump in my throat. "She's so beautiful," I whisper.

"He's a moron. I know it's tough to see beyond the hurt, but he won't find happiness in what he's doing. He won't find it anywhere until he addresses his own issues. This happened because he was unwilling to confront his problems. All these women he's finding are just feeding him the validation he craves until he moves on to the next. He'll likely repeat the same pattern with her and the next woman after that unless he sorts himself out. So don't feel jealous of her and don't feel sad. Feel sorry for both of them. He has to carry that heavy burden around with him forever. Can you imagine how unhappy he must be?"

This is why she makes such a wonderful teacher. As hilarious and fun as she is, she also has a knack for seeing things logically when it's hard to do so yourself.

I know she's right, but it's hard not to wonder if there's something wrong with me.

"You have to stop holding on to who he pretended to be, April." She gives my hand a squeeze, and I return a small smile.

"I really loved him."

"I know you did, hon." She takes a sip of her drink before squaring her shoulders. "I wasn't going to say anything, but now that you aren't together and I've seen him, I'm furious. I feel like it needs to be said."

"What?" I brace myself, preparing for the worst.

"There's no easy way to tell you this," she starts.

"Oh, for God's sake, just spit it out already."

"Lucas is a fug."

I blink. "Sorry." I shake my head, trying to understand. "What?"

"I said he's a fug. A fuggo. Fugly. He's fucking ugly—"

I raise my hand to stop her. "No, I got that part. I mean, why didn't you ever tell me?"

"It was too late by the time he wooed you with his 'amazing personality.'" She air-quotes *amazing personality*.

"What do you mean? He *is* handsome, and he's so charming!" I say.

"Please," Anna scoffs. "I've met urinal cakes with better personalities and more charm than that man. Lucky for James, he got all the looks in that family."

I sit frozen, stunned.

"I hope that makes you feel better," she finishes, shooting me an empathetic smile.

"Actually, I think that just made it worse." I release her hand and bring my drink to my lips.

"Fine," she says. "But I'm just being honest. For the record, you're absolutely gorgeous and *way* too good for him. I think he was batting well above his average with you, and it inflated his already giant, ugly head. He'll get a rude awakening when he realizes what he fumbled. Just you wait," she says, lifting her glass to knock it against mine in cheers.

As I lower my glass, Lucas sees me. It feels as though time slows to a crawl as my heartbeat pounds behind my rib cage. I feel my chest flush with nervousness, and my hands begin to shake. I suck in a breath and allow myself three more seconds to look before turning away.

"I think I'd like to go home now," I say to Anna, shifting to peek at Lucas once again, who has returned to his date, acting as though he never saw me.

How is it that you can get to know someone so intimately, and then act as if they never existed? To behave as though the person you once cared for so deeply no longer matters, as if you want nothing to do with them? It leaves a hole in my heart that begs to be filled.

"Yeah, let's go," Anna agrees, rising from her seat. "Wait here, I'll just make sure Gemma is okay."

I nod and wait for her to return, and when she does, it's with a sly grin. "She's going home with him. She's turned on her location so I can check in," she states, waggling her eyebrows. I manage a smile in return. The music fades as we step outside.

The evening air has cooled slightly as we wait at the curb. I retrieve my phone from my handbag and open the Uber app.

"Do you want to come back to mine? You're welcome to stay," Anna offers, her tone sympathetic.

Before I can respond, a gruff voice interrupts.

"I'll take her home," James says, catching us both off guard. I turn to look at him, finding his eyes already trained on me.

"Hey, James," I say softly.

"Hey, April," he replies, his voice tinged with concern.

A car pulls up to the curb.

We all stand in uncomfortable silence before Anna finally speaks up. "Okay. Well, this is me. Are you sure? April, you good?" she double-checks.

I look to James. "What about your stuff? Don't you need your bass?"

He shrugs. "Oliver can take it home for me." His gaze is as penetrating as it is devastating.

"Are you sure?" I ask.

He grunts.

Surprised by his offer, I swing to look at Anna and stammer, "Y-yeah. You go ahead."

"Okay, I'll come by tomorrow," Anna replies before leaning in to kiss my cheek, shooting James a wary glance, and then hopping into her Uber.

As the car pulls away, I turn to James.

"You don't have to do that," I say.

"I want to."

"Why?"

"I saw what happened in there, and you looked..."
He trails off, and I raise my eyebrows, waiting for him to
continue. He runs a hand through his hair. "You looked
upset."

This isn't the place to discuss this topic, so I swiftly
change the subject. "I couldn't find you after your set."

Now it's his turn to raise an eyebrow. "You keeping tabs
on me, April?"

"No...I just—"

"I'm kidding."

"Oh."

"I saw my brother."

I nod, saying nothing. The mere mention of Lucas sends
my heart plummeting and my stomach churns. I don't utter
a word as I resume booking the Uber on my phone. James
interrupts by reaching out, his hand gently covering mine.

"Let me get the Uber."

"Okay," I reply quietly, stealing a glance at him while
he's occupied with his phone. I take in his presence, realizing
just how different he is from his brother.

"You were really good out there tonight," I say, offering
a small smile.

"Thanks," he replies, a faint twitch at the corner of his
lip.

We lapse into silence once more before James hesitantly
says, "I'm sorry you had to see that."

I cast a brief look at him, feeling the pressure of tears
welling up behind my eyes. I turn my head away, refusing
to meet his sympathetic gaze. I know that if I say anything,
I'll break.

Luckily, the Uber pulls up to the curb a moment later.

Chapter 17

James

We slide into the back seat, and the smell of cheap air freshener shrouds us. I shoot Oliver a text asking him to drop my gear off at home, seeing as he has a spare key to my flat. I release a weary sigh and turn to stare out the window, doing everything I can to avoid looking at April. A somber song from the radio fills the car with melancholy.

I try to shake off my frustration after witnessing that idiot hitting on April on the dance floor. I swear, the moment he put his hands on her, I saw red. I'm not usually a jealous or possessive man, but for whatever reason, she manages to bring out a side of me no one else has.

But what made me even madder was seeing how April reacted to Lucas and his date tonight. I never expected him to show up to a gig; he's never shown any interest in my music, let alone with a date. Even though April was out with her friends, I could see it—I hated the sadness I caught on her face when she didn't know anyone was watching. I saw her so clearly in that moment, the hurt and the brokenness.

I've always had a soft spot for her. I wonder if Lucas ever told her why we aren't close.

I doubt it.

I'm furious with my brother. Furious that April's upset, furious that she's in pain, furious at him for refusing to take any accountability. I think back to when I looked after Basil that weekend after their breakup, when April came downstairs, she looked... *haunted.* Tired. I saw her left hand, her finger empty of his ring, and I felt sorry for her.

I'll call a spade a spade; my brother is a piece of shit. He may seem charming and gentlemanly on the surface, but deep down, he's always treated women like objects—mere entertainment, offering nothing in return.

We were raised in a relatively stable environment, save for Mum's mental health, which she struggled with on occasion. But for the most part, we were a happy household, so I never understood where his behavior stemmed from.

Who broke him?

I know he was bullied in high school. He was tall, skinny, and clever, making him an easy target for tormentors. Yet, his past struggles should have little to do with how he behaves as a thirty-four-year-old man.

Perhaps he sought external validation to fill a void fueled by his own insecurities. Who knows? I was surprised when the relationship with April became serious; I didn't think Lucas would ever be content with the idea of settling down.

I hear a quiet sniffle, which pulls me back to the present. I turn my gaze to April. Taking her in from head to toe, she's so fucking beautiful, even in her heartbreak. Her auburn hair spills over her shoulders and down her back. Her maroon-tipped fingers fall limp in her lap. Her long, dark eyelashes flutter and fan against her cheekbones. She's resting her head against the cold passenger window, eyes closed, defeated.

"I was doing okay. I was seeing my friends and *doing* things. I thought I was getting better . . . But seeing him just brought everything back." Her nose scrunches. "For him, today was just another ordinary day. I won't even be a thought. But for me, every day has been a struggle. It feels like there's a weight pressing down on my chest. I just want to reach out to him, to hear his voice." Tears streak her cheeks as she speaks. "He was my best friend." She turns to look out the window again, her lower lip wobbling. "Everyone who was supposed to love me has left me . . . He didn't want me," she whispers.

"April, that's not true—" I start, reaching for her hand. I entwine our fingers to provide some comfort when she interrupts me so softly that I barely hear it.

"Mourning someone who is still alive is a pain no one can prepare you for."

My heart aches for her.

I pull our joined hands into my lap and rub my thumb in circles over her knuckles, offering what little comfort I can. It feels inappropriate, but right now, her pain outweighs anything else. She looks like she's lost everything.

"Did Lucas tell you I had a serious relationship a few years ago?" I ask. "It ended just before you two met."

She looks at me. "Abi?"

I nod.

"Yeah, he told me about her."

"Did he tell you what happened?"

"Not really."

I respond after a beat. "She cheated."

"Oh, James, I'm so—"

I interrupt. "April, it's fine. I'm fine," I assure her. "I didn't exactly find out the same way you did, but..." I look at her, wincing. She rolls her eyes, a slight smile tugging at the corners of her lips.

I hate revisiting this day, but I sense she craves someone who can empathize, someone willing to share their own story to help her feel less alone. Clearing my throat, I continue. "We were on our way to dinner. It was our anniversary, and I had planned the whole night. As you can probably tell, I'm not much of a romantic, but I wanted it to be perfect. I made reservations at our favorite Italian restaurant. I even had Oliver light tea candles in my flat while we were out." I scoff, comprehending how foolish I was. "I had a ring..." I look up, trying to gauge her reaction. Her glassy eyes widen.

"What happened?" she whispers.

"She forgot her phone was connected to my Apple Play. A text message popped up on the dash... It read, 'I can't wait to taste you again.'"

April covers her mouth with her other hand. "Oh my God."

I blow out a breath and nod. "She had been going out a lot, and I hadn't seen much of her, but I assumed it was just due to her being busy. We all go through busy periods, right? Well, it turned out she *was* busy..." I shrug. "She was just busy fucking Matt from work."

"I had no idea. Lucas never told me. I'm so sorry," she says softly. Now, it's her turn to rub her thumb over my knuckles. I look down at our joined hands.

How is it that this woman, despite being wholly broken, finds the strength to comfort me over something that happened years ago while I'm trying to ease her pain?

I open my mouth to respond when the driver cuts us off. Neither of us realized that the car has slowed to a stop.

"Number 85? We're here."

We thank the driver as April grabs her phone and we step out of the Uber.

April turns toward me on the sidewalk, surprised when I step around the retreating car. Her cheeks heat when it registers that I got out with her.

"Oh, you're not . . . you're not going home?" she questions, fingers fidgeting.

"I will. But I want to make sure you're all right first. I'm not leaving you alone like this."

With a sharp inhale, she says, "Okay." Then, she turns and strides toward the front steps, fumbling around in her clutch for her key. Once she's opened the door, I peel off my jacket and follow her inside.

The house looks the same as it did a few months ago. You wouldn't know Lucas didn't live here anymore. Photographs of their happiest memories together still fill the hall table in the foyer, and the same paintings hang on the walls. Although the plants have withered, everything remains the same. Blankets are strewn across the couch, and the wooden floors are littered with crumbs and miscellaneous debris. Old mugs, empty plates, and takeaway containers clutter the coffee table, left uncleaned.

I see the house didn't stay tidy after my last visit.

April kicks off her heels, walking to the kitchen barefoot, and flips on the light.

My eyes are drawn to her hourglass silhouette and the way her hips move with every step.

I chastise myself. I'm not here for that.

I toss my jacket over the back of her sofa and follow her into the kitchen. I hear a scratchy crowlike sound before a furry dash of gray catches my attention in my periphery.

Basil emerges from behind the kitchen counter and slinks past my feet, darting away before I get to greet him.

"He's usually friendly," I say, staring after him.

"You won't get any love out of him at the moment unless you have chicken," April says. I casually rest my forearms on the island counter.

"Hmmph," I grunt.

"He's fifteen. Leave him alone," she teases. "Would you like a drink?"

"Sure."

She fetches a bottle of red and two glasses, setting them on the island before rummaging through the top drawer, eventually locating a bottle opener. I approach her as she continues twisting the screw into the cork to pry open the bottle. Stepping closer, I gently place my hand over hers before the cork releases, pausing her. My pulse pounds and my skin heats where we touch, creating a spark that sends a fiery path up my arm.

She halts upon contact, tipping her head to meet my eyes. Her lips part.

Without her heels on, I tower over her.

We stare for a few beats. My hand still covers hers when she whispers, "Abi was a fool to let you go."

I don't know where it comes from, but my response is automatic. "Lucas was a fool to let *you* go."

Her brows crease. "Why were you always so quiet around me?"

"I never knew what to say."

"I thought you didn't like me."

"I like you."

"Really?"

"Plenty."

"Oh."

We keep staring. Her blue eyes hold mine, and it's impossible to look away. The tip of her nose and cheeks are flushed pink from the cold, and her red lips look impossibly soft. I shouldn't, but I can't help but imagine running my fingers through her hair, tugging her close, and kissing her.

The things I imagine those lips doing to me.

Resisting the urge to reach out and touch this woman is proving fucking impossible.

How could Lucas mess this up so badly?

Blinking, I snap out of the trance. I quickly remove my hand from hers, as if her touch scorches. She releases her grip on the bottle. Looking away, I run my fingers through my hair. April releases the bottle and drops her hand to the counter.

"I don't think wine is a good idea," I say. Not because I don't want any—believe me, I do. But I know if we share a few glasses together, there isn't a chance in hell I'll be able to keep my hands to myself.

Her eyes drop to the floor, sad.

"How about tea instead?" I ask.

She clears her throat. "Yes, of course. Is breakfast fine?"

"Yeah." I rub the back of my neck.

"Take a seat, and I'll bring it over."

"Sure."

As April prepares the tea, I can't shake the tension hovering in the air. I glance around the room, my mind reeling after what the fuck just happened. Surely, I can't be the only one who felt it—that charged energy every time we lock eyes or touch.

As I wait, I notice how much of Lucas still remains in this room. I didn't notice it when I checked on Basil. But now, my attention snags on one of his favorite books, *Wolf Hall* by Hilary Mantel, sitting on the entertainment unit next to a potted peace lily that looks worse for wear. His old red scarf and leather work satchel still hang on the wooden coatrack by the front door. I can't help but wonder why he left those things behind if he never planned to return—and why she hasn't moved them since.

I shake my head and mutter to myself, "*Fuck.* Why am I here?"

April returns with the tea and hands it to me. We sit wordlessly, the only sound our soft sips and swallows as we drink.

"I need to thank you," she begins, "for bringing me home. For listening . . . for everything. I'm sorry you got caught up in all of this." She circles her finger in the air. "I know it puts you in an awkward spot. He's your brother—you probably shouldn't even be talking to me."

I place my mug on the coffee table, cupping both knees. I don't understand why she feels the need to apologize.

I'm the one who insisted on taking her home when she could have easily slid into an Uber with Anna.

I'm the one who got out of the Uber and insisted on coming inside. She's done nothing wrong. If anything, *I'm* the one behaving inappropriately.

But I can't deny I'm relieved that she felt comfortable enough to confide in me.

"You look nothing like him, you know?" she says, her eyes still trained on mine.

"No?"

"No." She shakes her head slightly, as if she wasn't entirely sure why those words escaped her lips. Her hands fidget nervously in her lap. I cover them with my own once more to stop her from feeling embarrassed.

"I'm here because I want to be, April. I want you to be okay."

"Why?" she whispers.

"Because I care," I say. "I want to help. Sometimes you just have to accept that things aren't meant to be and start living again, letting go of those who no longer need you. To stop waiting for the one who will never come back. To realize that loving hopelessly is not enough. You need and deserve to be loved in return. This is only the start of a new chapter. Try to embrace what it can bring. I was absent after Abi and I broke up, and I struggled with things. But it got better . . . It's all changed now. My life started up again."

A lone tear traces a path down her cheek. "I wish I'd been enough for him," she whispers.

I duck my head, level with hers. "You are enough, April. You're more than enough," I say.

She sniffles, looking down.

"Just you wait," I tell her. "Some lucky prick is going to find you and have enough sense to not let you go. Can you imagine being loved the way *you* love?"

I instinctively raise my hand to sweep away her tear. Time stands still as she swallows and locks her watery gaze with mine. I don't know why I do it, but hesitation doesn't stir. My fingertips graze her cheek, tracing the soft skin before tangling in her hair. Drawn by an invisible force, she leans closer, and I close my eyes briefly. She smells so fucking good, like coconut and vanilla.

I watch as she brings one of her hands to encircle my wrist, holding me in place. I focus on her parted lips.

She looks like sin.

I mirror her actions, leaning in closer until we're only an inch or two apart. With her eyes closed, she presses her forehead against mine, her hand trailing over my leg as she draws lazy circles. I fight back a groan as she moves her hand closer to my zipper, inch by inch, and my dick hardens.

I keep our foreheads pressed together as I tentatively lift my other hand, letting my fingertips trail down the nape of her neck before slowly descending over her shoulder. I move lower over the silk fabric until I reach her breast. Cupping it in my hand, I run my thumb over her nipple. It hardens under my touch, and she gasps.

My hand drifts from her breast to her legs, and our knees bump before I slide my hand between her thighs.

"Open."

She parts her legs without hesitation, and I press forward until my hand cups her heat. Slowly, I press the heel of my palm into her. A loud, desperate moan spills from her lips and I freeze.

April's eyes fly open, meeting mine. She stares at me with a dazed expression.

I pull away abruptly and stand, putting much-needed distance between us.

What the fuck am I doing? Stupid. Fucking stupid.

April gradually rises from the sofa with a look of horror on her face.

"James . . . I—"

"I should go." I look down and take in the obvious erection straining against my jeans before I clear my throat. "Thank you for the tea."

"That's okay," she says softly, frowning as I march to the front door.

I stop, glancing over my shoulder at her. "We're friends, right, April?"

The question slips out more to ease the guilt nagging at me for touching her, especially after she let her guard down.

"Friends," she repeats, her shoulders slumping. Her voice is somewhere between uncertainty and something more . . . Maybe hurt.

I yank open the door and leave without a second glance. I continue walking briskly until I reach the end of her street. Only then do I stop and order a car.

What am I doing? She's heartbroken and pining over my *brother.*

What might have happened if I hadn't walked out?

I wouldn't have stopped.

I didn't want to stop.

I am totally fucked.

Chapter 18

James

As soon as the Uber slows to a stop, I fling the door open and make a beeline for my flat. Once inside, I grab a beer from the fridge, taking a large gulp before setting it down on the counter. The rush of cold bubbles slides down my throat, cooling me. The icy sensation offers a fleeting reprieve, but it does nothing to drown the guilt clawing its way up my throat. I storm to the bathroom and turn the shower on full blast. I swivel on my feet and brace my hands on the vanity, staring at my reflection.

The desire on April's face is frozen in my mind as both remorse and need eat away at me. There was something about the haunted look in her eyes as she spilled her feelings like ink on paper. The way they turned from dark and tortured to heated as I shifted closer. I can't forget the way she felt after cracking herself open and letting me see her rawest parts. I saw her shattered pieces, but still, her beauty outshone everything.

Usually, after wrapping up a gig, I wind down by sharing a pint with the boys before heading home with whoever's attached themselves to my arm that night. Women like musicians; I learned that young. Ever since my relationship with Abi went up in flames, I've become accustomed to living alone, sleeping alone, and waking up alone. I like the freedom of doing whatever I want, whenever I want. I like the luxury of fucking whoever I want, whenever I want, with no strings attached.

I don't, however, typically escort my brother's ex-fiancée home, feel her up, and nearly fucking kiss her. But after seeing her face when she realized Lucas was at the Mayfair, on a date, no less, I couldn't just let her go home to solitude.

Her hurt was palpable, and she looked as though she needed someone—someone who wasn't going to take her home to sleep in a guest room while they hopped into bed with their own husband. The last thing she needed was the stark reminder of her failed engagement after seeing Lucas with a new woman. A woman I've heard nothing about, but that honestly isn't a surprise.

I should know.

"Fuck!" I push away and step into the shower, letting out a breath of relief as the hot water pelts my skin.

Too far. I took it too far.

Closing my eyes, I try to convince myself that nothing happened. I need the lie right now to shield myself from the truth.

I never catch feelings, *never*.

I haven't let myself; I haven't wanted to. Not after Abi.

But I can't fucking help it. April is alluring.

I've always envied my brother for having her, knowing she deserved better. She's good—*too good for me*, I tell myself.

I come to two conclusions:

Number one: I'm undoubtedly attracted to April.

Number two: I can't have her.

I need to wring this frustration out.

I grasp my hard cock and begin to pump my hand up and down. Closing my eyes, I picture her little leather skirt. The way her hips swayed as she danced, her heels elongating her creamy legs, and how sexy she looked moving to the music *I* was playing. I wish I could wrap her legs around me and fuck her.

I replay the way her body reacted to my touch when I ran my thumb over her hard nipple and cupped her pussy. The needy little noises she made.

Fuck.

I imagine my hand traveling underneath her tiny skirt, sliding up her thigh, teasing her until I reach the thin, drenched fabric covering her sweet pussy.

I envision pushing aside the flimsy material and running my fingers through her wetness, anticipating the sounds she would make as she arches back, pleading for more.

Finally pushing two fingers inside her. She'd be tight and hot. My thumb slowly circling her swollen clit as her hips rock, drenching me as she grinds against my hand. I imagine leaning in to kiss my way up the exposed column of her neck, and the tropical scent of her shampoo overwhelming my senses. I visualize sucking and nipping her supple skin while she runs her hands through my hair, urging me closer. And then, when she's finally wet and greedy enough, I would withdraw my fingers before adding a third, gently rubbing over her sensitive spot until she shudders violently, coating my hand in her release.

That does it.

With a grunt, I release long ropes of cum before collapsing against the tiled wall. That was all it could be now: a fleeting fantasy that never came to fruition and would never hold any real significance in the long run, because she wouldn't go for me. She wants *him*.

I lather up with body wash, rinse, then step out and dry off.

After throwing on pajama bottoms, I sink into bed and let the evening fade away.

I finally surrender to sleep, seeking solace in the darkness.

Chapter 19

April

A scratchy, tickling sensation rouses me from my sleep. Slowly, I open my groggy eyes and lift my head to discover Basil licking my fingers, which are dangling off the sofa's edge. The courtyard glistens with dampness and buttery sunshine spills through the large windows, casting a glow that makes me squint against the daylight. I spy an empty red wine bottle on the coffee table, faintly recalling pouring myself a generous glass after James dashed out last night, which probably explains my pounding headache.

"Hey, buddy," I coo at Basil, running my hands over his silky fur.

Sitting up, I drape a fluffy woolen blanket over my shoulders. "Fuck, it's cold this morning."

Confused and dazed, I look down at my bare legs and realize I fell asleep in my miniskirt.

On the couch.

After almost rubbing off my ex-fiancé's brother.

One minute I'm crying over Lucas, and the next I'm drawn to James.

Letting him *touch* me.

I know it wasn't right, but it felt good.

His warm touch. The deep, dulcet tones of his smooth voice.

He must have felt it too. It's what made him run.

"Ugh," I mutter, covering my eyes and cringing at the vivid memory of him slamming the door.

I'm struck by the memory of his large, calloused hands, the way they felt running over the thin fabric of my shirt, and how the pressure of his palm against my core set me on fire, igniting my insides and leaving me wanting more. The sharp contour of his jawline, and the intensity of his mossy eyes.

James showed me a side of himself I haven't seen before, a rare vulnerability, and it drew me in like honey. Well, that and he's one of the most beautiful men I've ever laid eyes on.

Even though he has that classic bad-boy look going for him, James also possesses a captivating beauty in his imperfections. There's a rugged kind of charm to him—the small scar by his eyebrow, his ever-present facial hair, and that singular dimple? *God*, that dimple. My mother once told me that dimples were kisses from angels, and that thought makes me smile. There's nothing angelic about James. He looks as sinful as they come—temptation personified. His wavy hair always sits perfectly, as if all it takes each morning is a quick run of his fingers through the strands to make them fall flawlessly into place.

He's gorgeous.

Reprimanding myself for the thoughts swirling in my mind, I reluctantly pull myself off the couch, padding barefoot to the kitchen to feed Basil, and then drag myself upstairs for a much-needed shower.

Flicking on the en suite light, I'm immediately confronted with my disheveled reflection. I fell asleep in last night's makeup, so my foundation has worn off unevenly. Thanks to my emotional outburst, mascara tracks streak my cheeks, and my hair is a mess.

Yes, I've certainly seen better days.

Rifling through the bathroom cabinets, I finally lay hands on my hairbrush and face wipes. I strip away the remnants of foundation and eyeshadow, and untangle the knots in my hair. With a determined twist, I turn the shower tap, opting for scorching hot to wash away the messy evidence of last night.

I'm stepping out of my skirt when the sight of the vibrator Anna and Gemma gifted me catches my attention. Deciding not to overthink it, I snatch it from my bedside table and return to the shower. I step under the spray, place the vibrator in the caddy, and tilt my head back, letting the heat soothe my sore head. Once I've shampooed and conditioned my hair, I lather my face wash before scrubbing my skin clean.

The longer I stand under the water, the more I fixate on James. The comfort that I felt with his touch. I'm still reeling from the revelation that he was on the brink of proposing to his ex-girlfriend. Lucas never mentioned their relationship being that serious. Then again, I suppose there are many things Lucas didn't share with me.

I think of James's sculpted arms and muscular legs as he sat inches from me on the sofa, and my cheeks flush.

I honestly don't think I would have stopped if he hadn't.

It felt *good* being that close to someone again.

I didn't realize how much I missed a man's touch until I felt *his*.

I wondered if I had imagined it, but he was hard, so I know he was as turned on as I was. His mouth was so close to mine I could taste him. I press my back against the cool tiles and reach for the vibrator.

I trail my empty hand down my stomach until I reach my wet center. With slow, deliberate movements, I part myself and begin circling my clit with two fingers. I imagine James's rough hands running over my skin and kneading my breasts. I picture him sucking a nipple into his mouth before biting down on my soft flesh. A whimper escapes my lips as I grow slicker.

A low hum echoes off the tiled walls as I click the vibrator on. Pressing it against my clit, I slide two fingers inside myself, relishing the sensation of fullness as I satisfy my craving for James from last night. I can almost feel his eyes on me, spurring me on as I indulge in the fantasy.

My chest rises and falls. The pressure sparks a surge of heat deep within me, spreading through my body and building toward my orgasm.

In my mind, I'm gripping his hair and tugging at the golden strands as I ride his hand. His tongue traces and teases every sensitive part of me. The pressure builds until I can't hold back, releasing a soft moan as the dam breaks. My body trembles, and I slow my movements, prolonging the pleasure.

Fuck.

I just got off to the thought of James.

After brushing my teeth and blow-drying my hair, I collapse onto my bed and bury my face in my hands.

A swell of shame funnels through me, and before I know it, tears begin to fall.

But I can't give in to self-pity. I can push through this.

I wipe my freshly scrubbed cheeks and head to the kitchen to make myself a cup of coffee. Cradling the hot mug, I lean against the counter and take calming sips.

My phone rings, snapping me out of my relaxed state.

Setting my drink down, I cross the room to the coffee table, grabbing my discarded clutch and fishing out my phone. A smile tugs at my lips when Gemma's name flashes on the screen.

"Hey!" I answer.

"Are you awake?" she asks.

I laugh under my breath. "Obviously."

"Okay, great. Can you open the door?"

"What? Are you here?"

"No, I'm hanging out with Rose and Gary," she says sarcastically. "Yes, I'm here."

I end the call with a soft chuckle, slipping my phone into my pocket as I head to the door. When I open it, I find Gemma standing there, balancing a tray of three coffees in one hand and a takeaway bag in the other. "Let me in, my nipples are threatening to cut cloth!"

I step aside and reach for the tray of coffees. "Here, let me."

"No, no, I'm all good," she insists.

"Three coffees?" I ask as she follows me into the kitchen, the fresh brew filling the room with a delicious aroma.

"Anna's on her way," she shoots back, hobbling behind me. I look at her ankle, wondering about the story behind the limp, but I hold back the question and instead turn my attention to setting plates on the counter.

"I was just making a drink. I could've offered you a coffee," I tell her.

Gemma sets the tray on the kitchen island, sliding a paper cup in my direction. "Ew, no thanks. You drink that instant crap—I'm not poisoning myself with that."

"Let's be real. You've let much worse things inside your body," I retort, raising a brow. "You're a total coffee snob. But thank you for the cappuccino. You're my hero."

"First of all, that was research—you know this," she fires back. "I went on those awful dates and let those men into my body *for the plot*." She jabs a finger at her chest. "And second, former barista, remember? I have standards."

Her grin turns sly as she leans against the counter. "Also, I'm not the hero here. Word is that title belongs to James."

I sigh. "I'm guessing Anna filled you in on last night?"

Gemma wiggles her eyebrows suggestively.

"Nothing happened."

Gemma slaps her palms on the bench, rolling her eyes. "Boring!"

I zero in on the takeaway bag. "What's in there?"

We both smirk and exclaim in unison, "Croissants!"

Anna doesn't bother knocking as she lets herself inside. Shrugging off her jacket and slipping out of her shoes, she looks over, eyes snagging on the takeaway bag. "Gemma, if that isn't a bag of fresh croissants, I will fucking riot."

"She brought coffee too," I say.

Anna looks to the ceiling and mutters, "There is a God."

Gemma extends her hand, offering Anna the cup of liquid gold, which she gratefully accepts. At my first bite, the crispy pastry coats my mouth with sweet, buttery goodness, and I release a long moan.

"That good, eh?" Anna asks, taking a bite of her own.

I give her a sidelong glance, my words muffled by a mouthful of croissant as I reply flatly, "It's been a while."

I quickly chew and swallow before shifting my focus to Gemma. "Now that we're all here"—I gesture toward her ankle—"what happened? Why are you limping?"

"So, remember that guy from last night?" Gemma begins, catching both Anna's and my attention. "Well, he took me back to the hotel he was staying at. He accidentally fell on my ankle when he tried to move me mid-intercourse. I'm pretty sure he sprained it." She calmly takes a large bite out of her croissant.

My eyes widen before Anna and I burst into laughter.

"That's almost as good as the vibrator story," Anna says.

"Would you like some frozen peas?" I offer.

"You can stick your peas, smart-ass. Laugh all you want, I'm not the one who left the bar with my *ex-fiancé's brother*," she replies, pinning me with an accusatory glare.

I side-eye Anna—damn her for telling Gemma. "Nothing happened!"

Anna pops her hip and purses her lips. "I call bullshit."

Letting out a sigh, I run my fingers through my still-damp hair, gathering my thoughts before speaking. "Okay, fine . . . something happened."

"I KNEW IT!" Gemma yells, rubbing her hands together. "Start from the beginning."

I take a steadying breath and recount the details of Lucas turning up with a date and how James ended up bringing me home. Their eyes just about fall out of their sockets when I tell them about James brushing my boob, cupping my core, and getting hard before he bailed.

Frowning, I cast my gaze downward, consumed with guilt as my body buzzes from the memory.

Gemma places a comforting arm around me. "What do I do?" I whisper.

I stand in the middle of the kitchen, confused and exposed. It's clear James and Lucas aren't close, but if anything had happened last night—and if I'm being honest, I would've let it—would I have made things worse between them? The question picks away at me. I never meant to come between them or cause pain, yet here I am, feeling like my actions and words confessed to James can do only that.

"I think it would be best to pretend that the incident never occurred. You won't have to see James again. I'm sure neither of you anticipated that happening, and he's probably feeling just as guilty as you are. It's normal to seek comfort from someone familiar, especially when you're hurting. And, in reality, nothing *actually* happened between the two of you," Gemma says, always the voice of reason.

"Gemma," Anna says firmly, "you know I love you, but I disagree." She turns to me, her expression earnest. "I think there's something between you two. I've seen the way he looks at you," she adds, covering my hand with hers and giving me a reassuring smile.

"What?" I ask, shocked. "He doesn't *look* at me."

"He does. He always has," Gemma says.

What? Have I really been that oblivious this entire time?

Anna nods. "And anyway, Lucas can't be angry even if something did happen."

"He's Lucas's younger brother, Anna," I say in a small voice, looking down. "It's too close to home. Sure, he's good-looking, but—"

Anna scoffs. "Good-looking? April, a blind lesbian would be attracted to that man."

Gemma laughs. "You already know what I think of him."

I narrow my eyes and point at her. "Don't even go there."

She presses her lips together, clearly fighting the grin threatening to break free.

"Ugh," I say, frustrated. "It doesn't make any sense."

Gemma shoots me a sympathetic smile. "That's completely understandable. Emotions aren't exclusive. You're allowed to feel a range of things simultaneously. It's normal to find James attractive while acknowledging Lucas's shortcomings. They're different people, and one feeling doesn't cancel out the other."

"Oh my God," I state, dropping my head into my hands. "I'm such a mess!"

"Maybe this thing with James will be good for you," Anna chimes in.

I look up, my brows pinched. "What do you mean?"

"Well, Lucas and James aren't close, right?" she asks.

"Right..." I start, unsure of where she's going with this.

"So, have you considered maybe seeing where things could go with James?"

"Anna, they're *related*," I say.

"So? And you were Lucas's *fiancée*. It didn't stop him from doing whatever the fuck he wanted." I wince before she continues. "Why should Lucas's opinion stop you from seeking happiness?"

"I'm not even sure James sees me that way," I say.

"April, please." She looks at me in disbelief. "No one's buying that crap. The man had his hands on your tit and your minge less than twenty-four hours ago."

I feel my cheeks pinken. "I think I'll send him a message. Just a quick thank-you for bringing me home...and I'll apologize for what happened."

"I don't think you need to say anything, but if it will help you, then I don't see anything wrong with it," Gemma says.

"Agreed. If it makes you feel better, then I think it could help," Anna adds, nodding.

It's a good idea.

It will clear the air.

I pull out my phone and begin typing a message.

Me: *I'm really sorry about last night. I apologize if I made you feel uncomfortable. I wasn't myself. But I appreciate you seeing me home, thank you.*

I blow out a breath and drop my phone on the counter, anxiously awaiting a reply.

Chapter 20

James

I barely slept a wink the rest of the evening, which is no surprise. I feel like death warmed over. Once I woke up, there no was no chance of getting back to sleep. I spent the night tossing and turning, unable to keep my mind off *her*.

I release a groan and pull myself out of bed. Shrugging on a sweater and gray track pants, I shuffle to the kitchen on tired legs to turn on the kettle.

While it boils, I retrieve my phone from where I tossed it onto the hall stand last night, opening it to find a message from Tom in our group chat.

Tom: *Did I see you get into an Uber with April?*

Great.

I tap out a reply, divulging just enough to satisfy the group without giving too much away. I know full well they're going to give me shit for last night, but I hit send anyway, bracing for the inevitable.

Oliver: *James. My boy. What did you do?*

I can hear Oliver's taunting tone through his message, and I scratch at the bristles on my chin, frustrated. Giving in, my thumbs fly across the screen.

Me: *I took her home.*

Oliver: *Well, this just got a lot more interesting.*

Tom: *I saw this coming from a mile away.*

Me: *What are you talking about?*

Tom: *I have a sense for this kind of shit. I know longing when I see it.*

Will: *It's true, he does.*

Ping.

A notification pops up from April and my heart thunders erratically in my chest.

April: *I'm really sorry about last night. I apologize if I made you feel uncomfortable. I wasn't myself. But I appreciate you seeing me home, thank you.*

Unsure of what to say, I switch back to the boys.

Me: *She just messaged me.*

Will: *I knew she would.*

I roll my eyes.

Tom: *What did she say?*

Me: *She apologized for last night and thanked me for taking her home.*

Will: *Ah, to be young and in love.*

Oliver: *Will, you're actually a moron.*

Me: *Are you guys free to come round?*

Tom: *Yeah, mate, see you in 20.*

Oliver: *Sure. See you soon.*

Will: *I did just settle in with Vaseline and tissues, but I'll see you soon.*

Oliver: *Please wash your hands.*

I move to the sofa and sit down, impatiently drumming my fingers on my leg. To distract myself, I open Instagram and scroll. It proves futile when I stumble upon a story from April.

Unable to resist, I click on it.

It's a mirror selfie of April in her tiny skirt, a glass of wine in hand. Her body looks incredible, toned with curves in all the right places.

God, she's sexy.

I tap to the next story.

It's a video of April, Gemma, and Anna clinking shot glasses filled with amber liquid. They cheers, then *fuck*, April's tongue darts out to lick a line of salt off the back of her hand, before throwing back the shot and sucking on a wedge of lime.

I swipe to the next story, which is a selfie of the three of them, grins spread across their faces.

Catching myself smiling at the image, I quickly exit Instagram and toss my phone onto the coffee table. Leaning back, I nestle into the sofa cushions and close my eyes.

I shouldn't be thinking about my brother's ex like this.

I never want anyone.

But there's something about April. Yes, she's attractive; that much is obvious. But it's her laughter, her smile, her innocence, the way she lights up a room—she's captivating.

I unwillingly revisit the way her face fell when she saw Lucas. We had finished our set, and I was grabbing water from the end of the bar when I saw her notice him. And he did nothing. He acted like he hadn't seen her at all. That's his superpower, acting as if nothing affects him. Whether he actually feels anything is another question. He's always been too much of a coward to face his emotions. It's easier for him to drop out and detach completely.

She deserves so much more than indifference.

I shake my head, trying to clear the thoughts.

I can't let myself go down this road—the one that leads to *her*.

If we land this gig with Bound to Oblivion, I'll be on the road for seven months. Even if something *did* happen between us, would it survive the distance? Could I really ask someone to wait that long, just to see if it might work? The thought feels selfish, and I hate myself for considering it.

With a sigh, I pick up my bass. As I pluck the strings, a familiar sense of calm washes over me.

I'm lost in the music when the buzzer rings. I gently place my bass back on its stand and head to the door, swinging it open to find Tom, Will, and Oliver standing at the threshold. I'm immediately drawn to Will's stupid amused expression. As Oliver passes, he gives my shoulder a comforting pat and I clap him on the back. We all make for the living room and settle into the sofas.

"So, did you write back?" Tom asks, leaning forward and rubbing his hands over his thighs in anticipation.

"Not yet," I reply, pulling my guitar pick from my pocket. I absently nibble the edge while my knee bounces as I consider my response.

"You did the right thing by waiting for us," Tom says, nodding like a moron.

"Can I see the message?" Oliver asks, and I lift my chin. He grabs my phone from the coffee table. I watch him as he swipes to unlock the screen and taps into my messages, reading April's text out loud.

"'I'm really sorry about last night. I apologize if I made you feel uncomfortable. I wasn't myself. But I appreciate you seeing me home, thank you.'" His brows press together in confusion. "James?" he questions, looking at me suspiciously.

"Mmmph," I mumble around the guitar pick.

"Did you *only* take April home last night?" he asks, cocking an eyebrow.

I slip the pick back into my pocket and blow out a breath, opting to chew the inside of my cheek instead.

"Something fucking happened!" Will exclaims, jumping to his feet.

"Sit down, you muppet," Oliver says, pulling Will back down to his seat.

I look over at Tom, staring back at me with a smug look on his face.

"Fine. Something might have happened," I admit.

"I knew it," Tom says, slapping his thigh.

"Of course you fucking did," I say, averting my eyes. I take a deep breath. "I saw how upset she was when she noticed Lucas, so I offered to take her home."

Oliver nods, scratching his stubble.

"She started opening up to me in the car, so I let her talk. I tried to offer whatever advice I could. I've been there. I know how it feels to love someone and then find out they've betrayed you. It's like your whole world shatters. And the fact that it was my *brother* who did that to her . . ." I trail off, shaking my head in disbelief that my own flesh and blood could behave like such a piece of shit. *Again.*

Tom and Oliver exchange glances, and their expressions soften.

"And?" Tom prompts, leaning in.

"And . . . I couldn't help it. Seeing her so vulnerable stirred something in me. I didn't want to leave her alone to deal with it. So, I went home with her."

"You didn't . . . ? You know . . ." Oliver asks warily.

"Fuck her," Will finishes for him.

I shake my head. "Christ, no, I didn't fuck her."

Oliver nods in understanding.

"You said you almost kissed?" Tom asks.

I scrub my face with my hands, unsure of what to make of last night. "We sat on her sofa. She made tea. She got upset and started crying, and I didn't know how to respond. I felt so bad, I wanted to comfort her . . ."

"What did you do, James?" Oliver asks, his tone serious.

"I touched her," I admit.

"You touched her," Oliver deadpans.

When I look over at Will, he's pumping his eyebrows. I love the man, but sometimes I worry that one day, he'll procreate.

"Mate, we need more details than that," Tom interjects, waving his hand for me to continue.

"Well, you're not getting more than that. I touched her, and I almost kissed her, and I shouldn't have. That's all you need to know. She's not mine."

"James, you realize she isn't Lucas's anymore either, right?" Tom asks.

I fall silent. Of course I know she isn't his anymore, but if anything had happened last night, it would've complicated matters even more. April is different. I know that much. She's not the type of woman you sleep with and forget. She's not a one-night stand. She's the kind of woman who changes everything.

"Right, so what happened after you touched her?" Oliver presses.

"I pulled away before anything else happened, and then I left."

"What do you mean *you left?*" Oliver repeats, his tone flat.

"Did you say anything before you left?" Tom asks, narrowing his eyes.

"I thanked her for the tea?"

Silence.

"What?" I glance between the three of them, confused.

Oliver sighs, shaking his head. "Mate, I get you felt guilty. But how do you think *she* felt after you touched her, then bailed?"

Fuck.

He's right.

She must have felt like shit.

She was being vulnerable, and I bailed on her.

"You need to reply," Tom says, nodding toward my phone, still in Oliver's hand.

"Here, give it to me," Will says, reaching to snatch it from Oliver.

"No!" Oliver and I yell at the same time. Before I can react, Will dives at Oliver. Oliver grunts as Will maneuvers behind him, putting him in a chokehold and quickly swiping the device from his grasp. Will shoves Oliver forward and leaps over the back of the sofa, standing triumphantly. He thrusts out his arm, holding it aloft.

"I know what I'm doing, James. I've done this before," he announces, pulling the phone down from mid-air as he begins to type away, pacing back and forth.

"You'd better not, Will. I swear to God," I warn, pointing at him.

"Just trust me," he insists, his head down as he continues tapping away.

"Mate, I'd sooner trust a priest in a playground than trust you with messaging a woman," Tom retorts.

I pull the back of my hair. "What the fuck are you saying? Why are you typing so much?"

"I have to get it right," Will replies.

Oliver remains seated, rubbing his temples as if trying to stay calm.

Will steps around to stand in front of the sofa, a proud look on his face as he hands me my phone. I tap the screen, lighting up the text he sent, and read it.

"Oh, Jesus," Tom says.

"Will," I say sternly.

"Mmm?"

"I'm going to fucking kill you."

"What did he say?" Oliver asks, turning toward me.

I thrust the phone in Oliver's direction, and he takes it from my hand, squinting to read the message.

His eyes widen. "You're a fucking idiot."

"What? What did he say?" Tom asks.

* * *

April

I wring my hands, nervous for James's message, when my phone lights up.

"He's written back," I say, glancing nervously at Anna and Gemma.

Gemma reaches out and places her hand gently on my forearm to steady my nerves. My heart pounds as I swipe up to unlock the screen and open the message. As soon as I do, my face falls.

What.

The.

Fuck.

"Well?" Anna asks, her eyebrows lifted in anticipation.

I turn the phone around, revealing the screen to them. The look of surprise and disbelief on their faces mirrors my own as they lean in to read the message.

James: *So, can I see what those incredible breasts look like without the clothes?*

We all exchange puzzled looks. Suddenly, Anna throws her head back and releases a deep belly laugh.

"I know Lucas is clever, but surely he didn't rob James of all the intelligent genes floating around his father's ball bag," she says. Gemma chuckles.

"Surely that's not him," I say, shaking my head in confusion.

* * *

James

I thrust out my arm, pointing at my phone. "This is your idea of helping me?" I say, locking eyes with Will. He shoots me a wink, and despite my frustration, I can't help but roll my eyes and huff out a laugh.

"I didn't think it was that bad," he replies, and I think he's being serious.

The tension breaks, and soon we're all laughing at his futile endeavor to help. Tom reaches over to give Will a sympathetic pat on the back.

Oliver leans in and hands my phone back to me. Accepting it, I type furiously, attempting damage control.

"What are you saying?" Tom asks.

"I'm letting her know that Will is a dumbass," I say, my eyes fixed on the screen as I figure out what to say next.

"You really want our help?" Oliver asks. "My advice would be to make her feel better. You don't want her to feel guilty about what happened last night, right? And you want her to know that you're sorry for leaving, instead of talking about it like a big boy."

"Right," I reply.

Fuck, I messed up. I can't imagine how my walking out so suddenly would have made her feel after everything she shared with me.

I feel bloody terrible.

She was so hurt, and I just left her.

"Just be honest," I mutter to myself.

"Just be sincere," Oliver says. "She'll appreciate that you're taking responsibility."

Nodding, I press send.

* * *

April

My phone buzzes as another message comes through.

James: *I'm so sorry, that was my mate Will. He shares DNA with a banana. Please ignore him.*

As soon as I read the message, three dots appear on the screen to indicate he's typing again. Gemma, Anna, and I all lean over the counter together, our eyes fixed on the screen, waiting in anticipation.

James: *You have nothing to apologize for. I wanted to make sure you got home safely. Thank you for opening up to me. It means a lot that you trusted me. And I'm sorry for leaving so abruptly—there's no excuse. I haven't stopped thinking about it.*

I lift my hand to my chest, my shoulders sagging with relief.

"See, I knew it would be fine," Anna says.

"That's really sweet," Gemma says, giving me a tender look.

"He is really sweet." I crook a smile, rubbing my finger over the screen. I twist my mouth to the side, contemplating my next message.

Me: *It was really nice opening up to you, so thank you for listening. And you don't need to apologize for leaving—I understand.*

I put my phone down and continue sipping my coffee as Gemma fills us in on the unfortunate end to her evening. Just when I think I won't hear a reply from James, my phone chimes.

James: *To clarify, I didn't want to leave.*

My expression must be readable because Anna immediately notices. "What is it?" she asks, leaning closer.

I glance at her, a mix of emotions swirling inside me. "He said he didn't want to leave."

Gemma's eyes widen. "What?"

My face wrinkles, unsure of how to interpret his words.

"You're smiling!" Anna points at me excitedly, and I quickly change my expression to feign indifference, my cheeks searing.

Anna gently places her hand over mine. "Hey, if he makes you smile, that's a good thing."

But the moment those words leave her lips, my smile falters. "But Lucas . . ." I trail off, unsure of how to finish.

Gemma and Anna share a look before Anna reaches over, rubbing a soothing circle over my shoulder. "You have to let him go, honey. He let you go—it's time you do the same," she says, her voice soft and filled with a tenderness she rarely uses. "Some things aren't meant to be. You can't keep holding on to someone who isn't holding on to you."

Her words feel thick, but they're true. Hearing her say it somehow makes it easier to accept, simply because it's a truth I didn't have to say aloud myself.

She scoots forward, encasing me in a hug. "Don't let thoughts of Lucas or his feelings dictate your actions. Let yourself enjoy this," she says, nodding at my phone encouragingly.

I consider her advice. "I don't know what to say to him," I admit.

"You don't have to say anything. At least find some comfort knowing there's no need to feel embarrassed because James clearly cares about you too," Anna reassures me.

"Yeah," I reply. "You're right."

As the conversation shifts back to Gemma's story from last night, my mind remains preoccupied, replaying James's message. I roll my lips inward to hide the smile tugging at the corners of my mouth.

The words repeat in my head.

What did he mean by that?

Would he have kissed me?

Did he *want* to kiss me?

Because I can't deny that I certainly wanted him to.

I push the phone away, deciding to leave it at that.

Chapter 21

April

Two months later...

As I walk through Kensington Gardens, I take in the breathtaking sight. The summer air is fragrant, filled with the sweet scent of roses and freshly cut grass. Flowerbeds dot the manicured lawns in bursts of oranges, yellow, and purple, their petals catching in the breeze.

The sun filters through the lush greenery of the trees and shrubs, forming speckled shadows on the ground. The gardens come to life with the sound of birds chirping their morning songs as dogs bounce around their owners, chasing each other and fetching balls. Swans and ducks glide across the waters of the Round Pond while children, with animated smiles, laugh and play, stopping to point and watch the animals.

I tilt my head up, letting the warmth of the sun heat my skin. Walking amongst the rich colors makes Wednesday mornings before work far more tolerable. Nothing worse than setting out on the tube while it's dreary and drizzling.

It's been months since I've had the strength to return to my favorite café, the Daily Grind, fearing it would bring back painful memories of Lucas. It's where we met. I would come here every Wednesday morning for a coffee and almond croissant before work. One morning, the barista mixed up our coffee order, and when Lucas handed me my drink, he smiled in a way that could only be described as indecently charming. He had that whole movie-star thing going on. The moment I looked at him, I was a goner. I hadn't noticed him there before, but after that, he would turn up every Wednesday morning until I gathered the confidence to ask him to join me at my usual table.

Each time I considered returning here since the breakup, tears would prick my eyes, and I couldn't bring myself to face it. But now, I refuse to let his absence keep me from enjoying my Wednesday morning treat. I refuse to let his memory taint the place that once brought me peace and comfort. It might be where we first met and where our chapter began, but I get to decide how the story ends. I'm writing an entirely new book, and I won't let sadness in.

The bell above the threshold chimes as I enter the café. I head to the counter, where I can't help but ogle the display cabinet. I'm cloaked in the intoxicating scent of freshly baked pastries. The smell of buttery croissants, muffins, and Danishes fills the air, and my mouth waters.

I place my usual order and sit by the window, pastry in hand, to enjoy the lovely view of the gardens. After setting my handbag down, I pull out my latest romance novel and settle in to make the most of my morning.

I'm immersed in my book and sipping my coffee when the bell overhead sounds, and I naturally lift my head.

My eyes widen as I take in the striking figure entering the café. I watch as he strides over to the display cabinet, drawing the attention of every female in the room. My teaspoon rattles as I quickly drop my cup onto its saucer.

I look around and notice the other women in the café shamelessly ogling him, even those with partners. I can hardly blame them.

His blond waves have grown out and curl at the nape of his neck, just peeking out from underneath a gray woolen beanie. He's wearing dark jeans that hug his muscular thighs, Timberland boots, and a plain black T-shirt.

After placing his order, he pulls a guitar pick from his pocket and starts twirling it in his fingers before turning around to find a place to sit. I exhale, trying not to make a big deal of it as his eyes dart around the room before landing on me. My cheeks heat, and I shrink slightly in my chair. For a moment, I'm reminded of the first time I saw Lucas, except James's presence feels different—more intense, more magnetic.

It appears not seeing or hearing from him for two months has done nothing to curb my attraction and appetite for him.

Fucking great.

My traitorous body is practically purring at the sight of him, and I could slap myself.

It's so *wrong*. I never replied to his last message. I wasn't sure how to respond, so I figured ignoring it was my safest option.

His lips tip in a smile as he walks over to me, and his eyes bore into mine. When he finally stands in front of me, I have to tilt my head up to meet his stare.

"Hey, April," he says, slipping his guitar pick back into his pocket. Ugh, his deep, resonant voice sends shivers down my spine.

"Hey, James," I reply, doing everything I can to hide my emotions.

"Do you mind?" he asks, pointing toward the empty chair opposite me.

"Not at all," I say as I close my book, shifting my bag closer to make room.

He raps his knuckles on the table as he sits down. I wriggle in my seat, my gaze falling to my hands as they hug my warm coffee cup. He leans back in his chair, one arm stretched out on the table. I can feel his eyes still fixed on me.

He clears his throat before speaking. "I haven't seen you here."

I look up to meet his emerald stare. "I didn't know you came here."

"I never used to." He leans forward to cross both arms over the table.

"Oh."

He's not dressed in his usual work clothes, so it's hard to believe he's simply been on-site somewhere nearby.

"I always used to come here, every Wednesday morning," I say.

"I know."

The air rattles in my lungs, glancing up at him. "Have you been hoping to bump into me?"

He shrugs casually. "Figured it wouldn't be the worst thing, seeing you again."

I blush at his brazen honesty. His words touch me in a way Lucas's never did, and I can't figure out why. I'm *so* drawn to him.

"What are you reading?" he asks, nodding to my book on the table.

"Oh," I say, surprised by his question. "It's a romance."

"What's it about?" he asks, settling in.

"A single mum moving to Scotland and falling in love with a security guard."

"Sounds good," he says, shooting me a panty-melting grin.

"It is." I smile shyly, then take a bite of my croissant.

"Almond. Good choice."

"They're my favorite," I say around a mouthful, and he chuckles.

"I'm quite fond of them myself."

I lower my pastry, threading my fingers together in my lap. "How's your music going? Have you been playing many gigs?"

He shifts in his seat. "We have, actually. It's been good. The Mayfair Lounge has been great. They're hiring us weekly. It's nice to build a solid following and bring people to a local venue. It's a win-win."

"I don't blame them. You guys are great."

"Thanks."

"You're welcome. You have that audition, right?"

"Yeah," he says, licking his bottom lip. "It's not too far away now. We're getting excited."

"I bet. It's a big deal."

He nods and as we fall into silence, my mind can't shake the last words he wrote me.

I didn't want to leave.

With him sitting before me, all I can see are his strong hands moving over my body.

"I'm sorry if my last message made you feel uncomfortable," he says, breaking the silence.

I straighten up. Uncomfortable? *I'm* the one who should be embarrassed. I was a train wreck that night.

"You didn't make me uncomfortable at all," I assure him. "I felt *so* embarrassed for the way I behaved that night. And I'm sorry I didn't respond. I wasn't sure what to say."

"You really need to stop apologizing, April."

I'm about to reply when the waitress interrupts us. "Strong latte?" she asks sweetly, batting her long eyelashes at James.

"Thanks," James says with a polite smile. She lowers his cup to the table, making a show of dipping lower than necessary to showcase her prominent cleavage. He doesn't respond to her blatant flirtations, instead turning his attention back to me.

The waitress drops her arm and her smile falters, clearly frustrated by his lack of reaction. She quickly moves on, barely concealing her annoyance as she tends to other patrons.

He pushes his drink aside, leaning in. "So, how are you?"

"I'm good."

"Yeah?"

I laugh. "Yes. I promise. I've been doing well." And I have. Work's been great, so no complaints there, as usual—I love what I do. Anna and Gemma have been amazing, and I've been seeing them regularly. I've even started my weekly morning walks again. I used to enjoy them every week, but I stopped after Lucas and I broke up. Slowly but surely, I'm starting to feel like myself again. I've been diving into ceramics more these days, particularly after work. Painting my pieces in a kaleidoscope of colors and rediscovering the joy of sculpting and creating. I can already see a noticeable improvement in my technique. I'm starting to wonder if I could consider selling them at markets. Throwing clay ties me to Mum in a way that offers me solace.

Seemingly accepting my answer, he smiles softly, his eyes tender. "I'm really glad to hear it."

My face transforms as it hits me. "Wait, have you only been coming here because you've been worried about me?"

He fiddles with the handle of his mug. "I wanted to make sure you're all right."

I'm speechless.

Totally dumbfounded.

That night after the Mayfair, he looked at me like he *really* saw me. Having someone to talk to, someone who could relate to what I was going through outside of my usual circle, was refreshing in a way I haven't experienced. But I hadn't really allowed myself the indulgence of thinking much past the conversation we had that night, or even beyond what happened—or *almost* happened—between us.

I couldn't.

But the fact that he cares enough to go out of his way just to bump into me, and check that I'm okay, triggers a flurry of hot embers.

"You could have just messaged me," I whisper.

"I wanted to see you."

"Why?"

He shrugs. "Just did."

"Well, thank you. It means a lot."

"You're welcome."

I exhale sharply. This isn't something I'd ever thought would happen—I'm sitting in a café on an ordinary Wednesday morning, sipping coffee with James.

I peek at him over the rim of my mug. "Is this weird?" I ask.

I don't want him to feel like he has to talk to me just because we've finally crossed paths and he's not pulling me back from the edge, but I also can't deny that I don't want him to go. Despite the nerves I feel around him, I enjoy his company.

Although he doesn't always say much, it feels like each of his words matter.

I think he gets me, like he truly listens.

I see a side that's caring and attentive, and it makes me want more.

"Does it feel weird?" he replies.

"No," I say, shaking my head. "It doesn't."

"Good." He sips his coffee before setting the cup back on its saucer. Leaning forward, he drums his fingers on the table, gazing at me thoughtfully.

"What?" I ask, suddenly insecure.

"Come to my gig on Friday."

"This Friday?"

His eyes dance with amusement. "Yeah." He laughs. "This Friday. We're playing a set." He shrugs. "If you want to, I mean."

"What will people think?" I ask, ducking my chin.

"It's just a gig, April."

I watch him attentively; his jaw tenses and his knee bounces under the table.

Is he as nervous as I am right now?

I nod. "Okay."

Of course I was going to say yes.

He smiles, and it's breathtaking. He radiates sunshine, his whole face lighting up. "Good."

James reaches into his pocket and pulls out his phone to check the time. My heart races as I watch him type, because my mind leaps to a conclusion that sends a pang of unwarranted jealousy through me. *Is he texting a woman?*

The thought slices through me, reminding me of Lucas's lies and deceit, but I shake it off when his gaze meets mine. "I've got to get going. I'm meeting the guys for rehearsal," he says, standing. "But it was really good seeing you, April."

I have no right to feel jealous or assume he's seeing someone.

It's none of my business.

So why does my body react like this around him?

I nod, trying to push the irrational unease aside.

157

"You too," I say.

"I'll text you the details for Friday."

"Sounds good."

He smiles softly, and I blurt the words out before I can stop them. "I didn't want you to leave either."

He pauses. Fire floods my chest. It takes him a second to understand that I'm referring to his last text, and when it clicks, his features ease. He gives a sharp nod, his hands flexing nervously, before turning and walking out, leaving my heart ricocheting around my chest.

I shove my book into my bag and finish my pastry and coffee with jittery hands. Slinging my bag over my shoulder, I head home to get ready for work.

Chapter 22

April

Friday night arrives, and my mind spins as I get ready with the girls. Just as I expected, and as much as I hate to admit it, I'm on edge about seeing James tonight. He sent over the details about when Atlas Veil is starting their set, and we decided to arrive a bit later so we only catch their performance. After Gemma's disastrous one-night stand last time, she's in no hurry to arrive early and risk striking up a conversation with any men, only to end up with another dud shag.

"How are you feeling?" Gemma asks as she expertly swipes black liquid eyeliner across her eyelid.

"I'm fine. I don't know why you keep asking me that," I reply, twirling an auburn lock around my curling wand. I'm aiming for that clean, effortless look, which, in reality, takes me fucking ages and a boatload of products to achieve.

I rest the wand on the bathroom counter and sip my Brut Rosé champagne. Suddenly, I'm engulfed in a cloud of hairspray. My eyes dart to Anna, who's spraying the living daylights out of her up-do. Gemma and I cough dramatically.

"Are you right?!" Gemma says, frantically waving her hand in front of her face to swat away the spray.

"My hair sure as shit is—look at this masterpiece," Anna replies, turning her head side to side as she admires her handiwork. I huff a laugh, going back to styling my hair.

"So, do you think you'll get a chance to talk to James tonight?" Anna asks casually, adjusting a bobby pin.

"I have no idea what to expect. I guess, if we hang around long enough," I say, attempting to play it off as if I'm unaffected.

"CUTE!" Gemma squeals. I wince, closing an eye and turning away as her voice pierces the air.

"The other brother," Anna says longingly, her hand over her heart.

"What?" I reply, caught off guard.

"You want the other brother," she says matter-of-factly.

"I don't want anyone."

"You," Anna starts, pointing the can of hairspray at me, "are full of shite."

Thankfully, Gemma shifts the topic as we continue getting ready.

I slip into my ripped jeans, throw on a black silk shirt, and step into a pair of sparkly pink strappy stilettos. My hair tumbles over my shoulders in loose waves, grazing my ribs. I've opted for sheer, glowy, neutral makeup and have emphasized my lips with a pink glossy tint. I've accessorized with a sparkly bag, a thick gold chain around my neck, and matching small hoops.

I look at my reflection in the mirror, and I feel sexy in this outfit. It's been a long time since I've felt this confident about myself.

After polishing off our bubbly, we quickly down a shot of liquid courage before finally jumping on the Underground.

I'm nicely buzzed, the warmth from the alcohol rippling through my body.

Out of the tube, the streets teem with life as people eagerly head out for their Friday night adventures. When we arrive at the Mayfair Lounge, it's busier than I expected—hopefully, in part, because the crowd is here to see Atlas Veil. Lively chatter fills the space while groups of people dance and sing, swaying to the pulsing music on the dance floor.

We order a round of margaritas, enjoying sips of the sweet, tangy citrus as we find a free booth. Sliding in, I tap my fingers to the beat against my glass, trying to distract myself from the butterflies taking flight in my stomach.

Gemma's voice suddenly cuts through my daze. "How are you feeling?" she asks.

"For the hundredth time, I'm fine," I reply.

Anna scoffs, and I look at her, raising my eyebrows expectantly.

"What? We all know that when someone says they're *fine*, they're totally not fine."

Damn it. She has a point.

"What time is he playing again?" Gemma asks.

I shrug, checking the time on my phone. "They should be on any minute now."

The music abruptly cuts off, and partygoers turn their heads toward the main stage, now illuminated by spotlights. Anna nudges my knee with her own, playfully pumping her eyebrows. Gemma laughs, and I roll my eyes, unable to keep from smiling. These girls have been my lifeline these past few months—the sunshine after the rain.

Then, a voice booms through the speakers.

"Ladies and gentlemen, please give it up for our favorite band, Atlas Veil!"

The crowd erupts in cheers and applause as the band approaches the stage.

"There he is," Anna says, nudging my knee again.

"I have eyes, Anna—I can see," I reply as heat flushes my body.

"You're turning red," Gemma says, her eyes sparkling with amusement. She leans closer, pointing an accusatory finger at me. "It's so cute that you have a crush!"

I touch my hands to my cheeks, trying to hide the flush. "Shut up, it's the alcohol and my rosacea—you know this," I protest, though I can't help but smile at Gemma's teasing.

It's definitely *not* alcohol or a skin condition.

I turn back and watch as Tom occupies center stage, adjusting the microphone stand while he flicks his long, black hair out of his eyes. The other band members position themselves at their instruments, and my gaze fixes on James. He runs his fingers through his sandy waves, and I notice he's forgone his usual leather jacket tonight. Instead, he's wearing only dark jeans and a charcoal T-shirt that shows off his thick biceps and veiny forearms. The top stretches tightly across his strong-set shoulders, fitting him like a second skin.

Reaching into his front pocket, he retrieves his guitar pick, then slings the bass strap over his shoulder, ready to pluck the strings.

Holy shit. This man is a walking wet dream.

"Okay, April. I know he's your ex-fiancé's brother and I'm married, but it has to be said—the guy looks like he can fuck," Anna says.

"What?" I ask, taken aback.

"Just look at him. You can't deny the man is a total sex god," Anna says.

"I second that," Gemma chimes in.

"I guess I can see what you mean," I say, playing it cool, taking a long, thoughtful sip. As I lower my glass, James lifts his head and his eyes meet mine. The corner of his mouth twitches and his eyes light up. He shoots me a subtle nod before shifting his focus back to the bass.

Anna and Gemma exchange a knowing look. My best friends can see right through me. I can deny it until I'm blue in the face, but I can't argue the fact that he's gorgeous, or that I find him irresistible.

"Okay, fine. I agree. He's a total sex god."

Does that make me a bad person? Ever since we bumped into each other at the café, James has occupied my mind. It doesn't matter what I'm doing, my thoughts seek him out. The way I'm drawn to him terrifies me—it's magnetic, consuming, something totally unlike what I felt with Lucas.

And that's what scares me most.

If it didn't work out, if I was just another fleeting moment to him, another night easily discarded, could I handle it? He's never been in a relationship as long as I've known him. Could he break my heart just as deeply, just as carelessly?

My eyes flit over the stage as Oliver starts twirling his drumsticks while Will grips the neck of his guitar, opening and closing his hand in preparation to play.

Tom introduces the band, and the bar bursts with applause as Oliver launches into his drum intro before the rest of the guys step in.

The energy in the room surges, and I glance around, taking in the sight of everyone's beaming faces. James bobs his head slightly as he plucks the strings, the veins in his hands working as he skillfully runs his fingers along the bass frets.

We finish our margaritas and order a round of gin and tonics, and Gemma tugs me toward the dance floor. As the music pulses, I sway my hips and sing along, letting the rhythm take over. Anna throws her arms up and moves effortlessly with the beat. I tilt my head back and allow the music to consume me. My mind is free. I feel peace.

I seize the moment, embracing the sense of worthiness that comes from knowing I deserve real love and happiness—a love like my parents shared and the unwavering happiness my best friends bring into my life. Tonight, I let go of the past and allow myself to truly live again.

Sweat glistens on my skin as we dance. I face the stage and catch James's eyes watching me, strong as steel. His gaze roves over me with an intense, almost ravenous look that makes my heart murmur. I offer him a smile and lift my glass in a silent toast. The breath is nearly knocked out of me when he returns the gesture with a dazzling smile. I'm talking dimple-deepening, pulse-accelerating, megawatt smile.

"You are so screwed," Gemma says, shouting in my ear over the music, and I quickly turn my attention to her.

"What do you mean?" I ask.

"You two can't keep your eyes off each other."

"It's not like that," I say.

"April, the sexual tension between you is about as subtle as a boner at church," Anna yells over the music.

"We're not giving you a hard time," Gemma says, touching my forearm. "There's nothing wrong with it. In fact, it's lovely. I'm just saying you don't have to deny it anymore. There's clearly something between you two." Her gaze darts between James and me.

I glance back at James and find him still watching me. Mulling over their words, I step away.

"I'll be back," I tell them. I swing by the bar and catch the bartender's eye, ordering a tequila shot and downing it quickly before zipping to the bathroom to freshen up. After washing my hands, I reapply my gloss and tousle my hair until I'm satisfied with my reflection. Feeling sure of myself, I straighten, shoulders pulled back, push open the bathroom door, and step into the hallway, ready to return to the dance floor—only to slam right into what feels like a solid brick wall.

Scratch that—a chest.

A hard, sweaty chest.

"Ooft," I mutter on impact.

Two large hands grip my shoulders, steadying me.

"Sorry, I didn't mean to run into—" I look up, staring into pools of sea glass as James ducks his chin to read my expression. "I was just heading back to the girls," I say.

"Are you okay?"

Ah. That velvet-smooth, deep voice.

"I'm fine, thank you," I say, adjusting my shirt and necklace.

He nods, slipping his hands into his pockets. "I'm glad you came. You look . . ." He clears his throat. "You look great."

"Thank you," I say, casting my eyes down nervously.

"You're blushing," he says with a glint in his eyes, and I instinctively clap my hands over my cheeks.

"I am not blushing. I have rosacea. It's the tequila."

"Of course." He rolls his lip between his teeth to hide a smug smile.

"I thought you were playing," I say, throwing a thumb over my shoulder.

"We did. We're finished now."

"That was quick."

"Well, we played for three hours."

"Oh," I say, surprised. I was so caught up dancing that I hadn't even noticed how quickly the time had passed.

His eyes pierce mine. "You looked like you were having a good time out there."

My heart is beating like a drum. "It was fun. Thank you for inviting me tonight. It was just what I needed."

"I'm glad. It's good to see you enjoying yourself," he says, his voice softening before he nods toward a door at the end of the hallway. "Do you want to come out back while I pack up?"

The invitation hangs in the air.

Of course I'm fucking going.

"Sure, I'd love to."

Chapter 23

James

April follows me backstage, and I gesture toward a chair in the corner, offering for her to sit while I pack up.

"So, how did you enjoy the show?" I ask, bending down to wind up my cables.

"It was amazing. Everyone was having so much fun. You were so great out there," she says.

"Thanks," I respond, my voice gruff, and she nods.

God, she's stunning.

Those tight jeans make her legs look endless. Her silk shirt hugs her in all the right places, dipping in at her waist to show off those killer curves. She always looks incredible, but I couldn't take my eyes off her tonight. Every step she took, every glance she threw my way, pulled me deeper under her spell. I haven't seen that side of April in a long time, without cares and free, and I can't help but want to see more of it. I feel a little smug knowing I was the person playing the music that made her body move and sway.

And it was me she was stealing glances at.

They were *my* eyes she sought out across the room, and it sent sparks straight through me. It was impossible not to feel a surge of pride knowing I played a part in her happiness tonight.

I carefully place the rolled-up cables in a tub alongside the power boards and my pedals, making sure everything is organized. Then, I throw the covers over my amp and speaker box, securing them for the trip home. Finally, I slide my bass back into her case, clicking it shut.

I stand and rub the back of my neck. "So, are you staying a little longer?" I ask. I'm fucking exhausted. I always am after a gig, and I could really use a shower, but if she decides to stay, I could hang around a while longer.

Anything to be near her.

"I don't think so. I'm a little tired after a long week," she says.

"Ah. Well, thanks for making the trip. How's Basil doing?"

"He's great! Honestly, I don't know what I would have done without him and my girlfriends these past few months. They've been a wonderful distraction."

A *distraction*.

From my piece-of-shit brother.

She stands and approaches my equipment, peering into the tub of cables.

"You lug this stuff around with you every time you gig?" she asks.

"Yeah, you get used to it after a while. It becomes second nature—the more you do it, the quicker it is to pack up at the end."

I watch as she circles the room, her forefinger trailing lightly over my amp, speaker, and guitar case.

There's something about the way she touches my gear that I like.

She stops in front of my guitar case, thumbing the latches before lifting her gaze to mine. "May I?" she asks.

I raise my eyebrows. "Go for it."

Her whole face lights up—not just a polite grin, no. It's a full, beaming smile that catches me off guard. I watch as she clicks the latches, swings the lid open, and lifts my bass, sliding the strap over her shoulder.

"This thing is heavier than it looks," she says, her fingers brushing lightly over the strings. I slip my hands into my pockets, watching her with intrigue.

Honestly, I could watch her all bloody night.

"How's practice been this week?" She glances up at me.

"It's been good. We're getting there," I reply.

"Well, if you play anything like you did tonight, they'll love you," she says, looking at me with a sincere expression.

Her sparkling eyes hold mine. "Thank you."

"You're welcome," she says, her voice soft.

There's a pause as we watch each other, and I want to reach out and touch her more than ever. But then, the audition, the possibility of landing the gig, and the reality that I'd be away for seven months of the year if the audition is successful all come rushing to mind, and I stop myself.

"So," she says, breaking the stillness, "how old were you when you started playing?" Her fingers fumble over the strings. The notes are scattered, but I can't help the twitch tugging at my mouth as I watch her. There's something endearing about the way her fingers glide up and down the neck, pressing on the frets as if she's trying to figure it out by feel alone.

"I was twelve when my dad gave me my first guitar—an old Yamaha acoustic. I begged for a guitar for the longest time. We didn't have much money growing up, so I never expected it. But that Christmas, I came downstairs and spotted a guitar case poking out from under the tree. I couldn't believe it. I remember skipping the last two steps and rushing over to open it. It was the best gift I've ever received." I shrug. "From that moment on, I was hooked. I spent hours learning to play. I played until my fingers were raw, but I didn't care. It was everything to me. Years later, I picked up the bass."

I reach out, wrapping my hand around hers. "Here," I say, gently pressing her finger down on the fret. "Hold your finger there." Then I guide her other hand, trailing it down the fretboard. Still holding her hand, I move her fingers to demonstrate a walking bass line. I let go and begin to step away, noticing the way she watches me.

"I'm doing it," she says, looking up at me excitedly—and my heart almost bursts out of my chest.

I return her smile. "You're a pro."

She plays around, moving her hand up and down the neck of the bass, trying out different notes. "God, this hurts my fingers. How do you play for so long?"

"I mainly use my pick, but you do get used to it after a while." I shrug.

"Ouch." She drops the neck, inspecting her finger. Without thinking, I step forward and take her hand in mine, examining it closely.

"Does it burn?" I ask.

"Yes," she says.

Our eyes meet, and, without thought, I lift her hand to my mouth, gently sucking her finger and soothing it with my tongue. Her lips part slightly, and she sucks in a breath, but she doesn't pull away. I know this is entirely inappropriate, but at this point, I can't bring myself to care.

Her lashes flutter, and I slowly remove her finger from my mouth. She rubs the glistening tip with her thumb, her focus on me unwavering.

I lower my voice. "Better?"

She swallows. "Much."

Instinctively, she moves closer, dissolving the space between us, and the bass presses into my stomach. I tentatively reach out to brush the exposed column of her elegant neck, and she takes it as an invitation to rise onto her toes.

Fuck.

I know I'm treading a dangerous line with her, but I can't pull away now—not when I'm this close to her. She's temptation, and I can't resist.

I lower my head to meet hers and thread my fingers gently through her hair, tilting her head at just the right angle. She exhales softly, closing her eyes as I lean in. Her sweet gloss brushes against my lips when the door suddenly flies open, shattering the moment.

The heat evaporates like morning mist.

I drop my hand and turn toward the intruder with a jolt.

Tom stands in the doorway wearing a shit-eating grin. My pulse rages and bubbles to the surface, threatening to spill over and scorch everything in its path.

"Bloody hell, Tom. What is it?" I ask, irritated.

"Sorry, mate," he says, wincing. "Oliver's nearly done loading his drums into the van. I was going to offer a hand with your gear, but I'll...come back later," he says, gesturing over his shoulder.

"It's fine, Tom," April says, glancing at me. "I'll leave you to finish packing up. You've had a long night."

She swiftly removes the strap and hands me the bass, which I place back in its case. She presses a quick kiss to my cheek, leaving a glossy mark, before heading out.

I shoot Tom a murderous glare.

He raises an eyebrow, crossing his arms and leaning against the door-frame. "Interrupting something, was I?"

Smart-ass.

"If you want to help"—I lean down and grab my tub, walking over to Tom and shoving it into his arms with more force than necessary—"you can start with this," I say.

Chapter 24

April

I fling open my front door, slip off my heels, and head straight for the sofa. I collapse onto it with a sigh. Gemma follows me in, barefoot, and flops onto the floor, stretching out her legs. Her back leans against the arm of the sofa as she calls for Basil, who struts in, tail high. She extends her hand, and he nuzzles against it, purring contentedly.

Anna went home to Mason, so I told Gemma to stay with me.

"Tonight was so much fun," she says.

"It was, but my feet are killing me," I say, wincing.

"You had such a good time," she replies with a smile. "It was lovely to see you let loose."

I nod. "But I'm paying for it now." I reach down to rub the ball of my foot, which has gone totally numb. I press my thumbs into the pad of my foot and groan, relieving some of the tension as I coax the circulation back.

My eyes narrow when I notice something stuck to her dress. "Gemma, what's clipped to your chest?" I squint to read the text.

She looks down, bringing her hand up to inspect the badge pinned above her left boob.

"Does that say *Daniel*?"

"Huh," she says, surprised. "I think it's a Tesco employee badge."

"Where did you get that?"

"Probably from the twenty-one-year-old I made out with on the dance floor. Fuck if I know." The shit this woman gets up to when I'm not looking. She shrugs. "Where did you disappear to, anyway? One minute you were at the bar, and the next, you were gone. You didn't get the shits, did you? I told you not to eat those samosas before we left. I'm telling you, bubbles and curry don't mix."

I laugh. "Actually, if you must know, I bumped into James as I was coming out of the bathroom. He asked if I wanted to keep him company while he packed up his gear."

Gemma twists around, planting her hand firmly on the rug. "He took you out back?" she asks.

I nod, switching feet.

"So, you got a chance to speak to him? That's great! Did he have fun?"

"Yeah, he did. I can't believe how much stuff they have to pack and unpack for every gig. It's seriously impressive. I got to play his bass," I gloat, pumping my eyebrows. "You're looking at the next Paul McCartney."

"Ugh, there's something so sexy about musicians."

"Amen."

Ping.

I reach over to grab my phone from the coffee table, and my pulse kicks up as James's name flashes on the screen.

"Who is it?" Gemma narrows her eyes as she watches me intently.

"It's James."

"Oooh, what did he say?" she asks, leaning forward.

"I haven't opened it yet..." I trail off, staring at the message, my thumb hovering over the screen. "But I feel like I should tell you what happened tonight."

Her brows shoot up, and she air quotes, "What do you mean, 'What happened tonight'?"

I pull my knees to my chest and spill the whole story, starting with me walking out of the ladies' room, then James sucking my finger, and ending with Tom walking in just as we were about to kiss.

Her eyes bulge. "Read the bloody message, will you!"

I bite my lip, tapping the screen as his message illuminates.

James: *I can't stop thinking about how badly I want that kiss.*

I tilt the screen toward Gemma, letting her read the message. She lets out a low whistle. "Oh, he *definitely* wants you."

"You think?" I ask, my voice betraying the flicker of hope I'm attempting to hide.

"I *know.* If it were me, I'd go over there."

"What? I can't go over now. It's almost 1:30 a.m."

"Which is precisely why you *should* go over there."

I close my eyes, battling the truth that's itching to escape, but I lose the fight. "Gemma, we both know what's going to happen if I go over there."

"Exactly. That's the whole point."

Nibbling the inside of my cheek, I try to untangle the mess in my mind.

Do I want to sleep with James? Of course I do—I'm only human. James is gorgeous, charming, and the chemistry between us is undeniable. But he's *Lucas's brother.* We were engaged not that long ago. What Lucas did to me was unforgivable, but would sleeping with his brother make me just as bad?

Am I giving in to a fleeting desire that will only lead to more heartbreak? That night in the Uber changed things. Or, if I'm being honest, maybe this started earlier. But a few stolen glances here and there didn't mean anything—it was innocent, nothing serious. But my situation has changed.

I'm single now.

If I go down this road, it won't just be harmless or playful flirting.

It'll be real. Tangible.

And deep down, I know James and I could never have a meaningless fling.

With him, it's different. *He's* different.

If I let this happen, there's no turning back.

Oh, for fuck's sake, who am I kidding?

"I'm going over there," I state with as much confidence as I can muster.

Gemma hollers and hoots. "Yeah, you are, you dirty slag!" She pauses, then waves her hand in front of me. "But first, you need to sort out *this* situation. Go shower, freshen up, clean the minge and—oh!—don't forget to wear sexy underwear." She winks.

"Right." I nod. Before I know it, I'm on my feet, heading to the bathroom. I remove my makeup and jump in the shower for a quick rinse and shave before slipping into something casual and comfortable—a cute, gray lounge set made of soft fabric that drapes over my figure. I pull on a pair of trainers, and sweep my hair into a high ponytail, keeping it neatly out of my face. Underneath, I wear my most seductive black lace bra and thong set.

Before heading out, I spritz some perfume. The rich, sultry scent wraps around me with hints of vanilla and amber. I head downstairs to check on Gemma, ensuring she's settled before I leave.

As I expected, she's already fast asleep on the couch.

I gently drape a soft blanket over her, then lean down to plant a tender kiss on Basil's head.

With a final glance, I pull up the Uber app.

This is happening.

I'm going to sleep with the other brother.

Chapter 25

James

I'm wrecked by the time I've hauled my gear inside. My muscles scream at me. I've been working on a large-scale development in Canary Wharf, and the days have been grueling.

I manage a weary wave to the lads as they head off down the street, the music from the speakers fading into the night. Regardless of how exhausted I am after a gig, I always have a difficult time sleeping. My ears ring and adrenaline continues to course through my veins long after we finish playing. I'm also fucking ravenous. My stomach gurgles loudly at the mere thought of food, but I decide to freshen up before settling in for the night.

I head straight for the shower, stripping my sweaty top as I go.

As I step under the warm spray and lather up, my mind drifts to the auburn-haired beauty who's invaded my thoughts for months.

I close my eyes, letting the water beat down on me, and think about the way her body pressed against mine as she pulled up on her tiptoes to kiss me. Her sweet perfume lingers in my senses, I can almost taste it. I think of her plump, glossy lips and the way they barely brushed against mine, her sweet taste leaving me wanting more. God, *this woman*. I can't help but ache to finish what we started.

The way Tom barged in made my blood boil—I could've throttled him right then and there. The urge to pull her back in and claim her lips was almost unbearable the moment she stepped away. She was going to kiss me. And God help me, I would've met her halfway without hesitation. Was she as disappointed as I was?

I have to know what was going through her head. Or am I the only one who can't seem to let it go?

I reach for a towel, scrubbing myself dry with exaggerated force. I pull on a pair of sweatpants and a black hoodie before heading to the lounge, grabbing my phone and flopping onto the sofa. Opening our text thread, I start typing before I have time to overthink it, my thumbs tapping quickly over the screen. I keep it simple and honest, reading the message back once before hitting send.

Me: *I can't stop thinking about how badly I want that kiss.*

I drop the phone beside me and lean back, running my fingers through my damp hair.

There.

It's sent.

I've put it out there, now it's her move.

I haven't felt this uneasy about a woman since Abigail.

I don't usually send messages at this hour, especially not over a simple almost-kiss. My usual approach is straightforward—quick texts for a quick fuck. No strings attached—we each take our pleasure, then go our separate ways. So, what the hell is going on with me? April isn't someone you treat like a casual hookup. I *know* this. She's the kind of woman you take seriously, the kind of woman you date and build something lasting with. She's smart, interesting, loving, kind, and loyal. She's got a depth that goes way beyond casual.

But is this something that could last? I'm not sure.

I grunt, frustrated, sinking back into the sofa cushions. If we end up sleeping together, it will change everything. Am I ready for that? I'm not interested in adding her to the list of fleeting encounters in my phone, and I definitely don't want to start something that might not last if Atlas Veil ends up touring.

But I can't stop myself, no matter how hard I try.

I've thrown everything I have into my music, but she's always there, tucked away in the recesses of my mind.

Late nights are just part of the gig routine, and I'm used to them now. When I'm unable to sleep, I either tinker with writing music or settle in with a book until sleep claims me. I fix myself some tea and toast, taking a hearty bite, and head back to the sofa, ready to settle in with my book. I've just made myself comfortable when the jarring buzz of the doorbell blares through the quiet of my flat, making me jump.

"What the fuck?" I mutter as I walk over to the window and peer out, wondering who would be ringing my buzzer this early in the morning.

And there she is, standing on the stoop, her fingers twisting together nervously. My pulse quickens, and my eyes dart around the flat to ensure it looks halfway decent before I let her in. I hear the dull thud of footsteps as she approaches my door. I swing it open just as her hand is raised, ready to knock.

We both freeze, eyes locked.

Neither of us says a word, but we both know exactly what this means. The air between us thrums with tension.

I clear my throat. "Hey, April," I say with a low voice.

She hesitates momentarily. "Hey, James," she replies, quietly.

I step aside and gesture for her to come in. As she moves past me, her eyes sweep the room, as if she's searching for something. She's been here before, though only briefly, when Lucas needed to pick something up, so she's already seen my flat.

"I just boiled the kettle. Can I get you something?" I ask.

She's standing in the middle of the room, arms wrapped around herself like a protective shield.

"April?"

"You feel this, right?" she asks, whirling to face me, gesturing between us. "I'm not going crazy, am I?"

I blink because I'm caught off guard by her directness. Clenching my jaw, I take a careful, tentative step toward her, as if one wrong move might frighten her off.

"Right?" she repeats, her tone uncertain now.

I hold her eyes. "No, April. You're not going crazy."

"Good." She nods in affirmation, more to herself than me. "Good."

"April."

"Yes?"

"Why are you here?"

"What?" she asks, distracted by thoughts.

"Why. Are. You. Here?" I repeat, closing the distance between us.

I take her in as she stands before me. She glows without a hint of makeup, her porcelain skin flawless. Her auburn hair is pulled into a high ponytail, exposing the soft curves of her heart-shaped face and the delicate columns of her throat. In this light, her blue eyes shimmer, catching a silvery fleck I hadn't noticed before, and her dark, thick lashes flutter, kissing the tops of her cheekbones. My gaze lingers on her plush lips, desperate to taste them.

And before I can stop myself, images flash through my mind—those lips wrapped around my dick, her hair twisted in my fist as she takes me deep into her mouth. I really hope she's here for the reason I think she is.

"I . . ." she starts, then falters.

"You?" I ask, an eyebrow kicking up.

"I want—" She hesitates, breath shaky.

"What do you want, April?"

She lets out a slow breath, squaring her shoulders. "You. I want you, James."

"Finally," I growl, stepping closer.

"Wait," she whispers, raising her hands between us, and I halt.

Her turbulent eyes pierce into mine, and I lift my brows, waiting for her next words.

"Is this a bad idea? What about Lucas?" she asks, her voice so small I almost miss it.

The black cloud hovering over us is suffocating, but the pull toward her is irresistible, and I'm drawn into the impending storm.

Heat thrums between us, and the restraint I'd clung onto snaps.

"Fuck it," I grit out, grabbing her face in a fierce hold as our mouths crash together.

Chapter 26

James

The kiss is raw and frantic—full of pent-up desire and everything we've been holding back. It's ravenous, like we've both been starving for this moment. We're a tangle of hands and lips—desperate, unapologetic. She claws at my back, pulling me hard against her, and presses her body tightly to mine. Her lips are soft and pliable, and her subtle, sweet taste lures me in further. Our heavy breaths mingle as she opens to let me in.

I trace my tongue along hers, eliciting a moan that reverberates through me, sending a jolt of desire straight to my cock. I slide my hand around the back of her neck, up and into her hair. As I reach her scrunchie, I slowly pull her locks free, feeling the silky strands fall through my fingers. I wrap the tresses around my wrist and give them a firm tug, deepening the angle. My other hand trails down her neck, desperate to explore the warmth of her skin. I reach her breasts, grazing my fingers over the thin fabric of her top.

I stroke her nipple with my thumb, tugging it between my fingers until she gasps, and I repeat the motion.

Breaking the kiss, I pull back slightly to meet her heavy-lidded gaze.

"Is there lace under this?"

She nods.

This woman will be my undoing. My cock twitches as my fingers leisurely trace down the sides of her top, reaching the hem.

"Is this okay?"

"Yes," she says.

Slowly, I roll the fabric up, revealing her soft, ivory skin. Her breasts are held in place by the sexiest black lace. I groan, taking in the sight of her perfect tits and rosy nipples through the material. Not too big, not too small. *Perfect.*

I watch her hands as they trail down the front of her body at a maddeningly slow pace. When her fingers graze the waistband of her pants, she tugs them down over her hips before kicking them away. Standing before me, she's a vision. A natural flush spreads across her cheeks, and her lips are swollen and glistening from our kiss. Her long hair tumbles over her shoulders, disheveled and gorgeous.

Nothing has ever been so perfect.

She steps forward and reaches for the hem of my shirt. I watch in fascination as she begins to undress me. As she lifts the fabric, her fingertips graze my skin, leaving a trail of ashes in their wake. I lift my arms to help her, pulling the shirt over my head and dropping it behind me. Her fingers move with purpose as she loosens the drawstrings of my sweatpants. She pulls at the waistband, and they fall, my cock already straining under the fabric of my briefs.

We stand face-to-face, stripped down to our undergarments. I feel I'm studying something sacred—every inch of her is molded to perfection, like living artwork. I step forward and pull her in for another bruising kiss, pressing my erection against her stomach. She loops one arm around my neck, while the other hand trails down to my cock and begins rubbing me. I moan and my cock jerks against her touch, releasing a bead of precum.

"James," she says against my mouth.

A grunt is my only response.

"I need more," she pleads.

Without hesitation, I slide my hands behind her thighs to lift her. She gasps, clapping her legs around my torso. Her hips start to move, grinding feverishly against my cock. Her warm pussy presses into me, and I can feel how drenched she is through the fabric separating us.

I need to feel her, *taste* her.

I carry her to my bedroom and gently lower her onto the bed. She sprawls out, hair fanning across the sheets, her skin stained with a flush. She's stunning—like something out of a dream. Every curve of her body begs to be worshipped.

"You're so beautiful, it hurts," I tell her.

"So are you," she says.

I crawl toward her until I'm settled between her legs. Lowering myself, I take a lace-covered nipple into my mouth and swirl my tongue over the sensitive peak as I knead her plump flesh. She latches onto my hair, pinning me in place.

My free hand trails down her stomach until I reach the edge of her thong. I'm unbelievably hard. Her breathing hitches, and I release her nipple. Slowly, I slip my fingers beneath the lace, running them softly along the seam of her warm slit. She's completely bare and fucking soaked.

"Is this all for me?" I ask.

"Yes," she says on a breath.

Her hips push against my hand, a silent plea. I obey, gliding my fingers through her center to find her clit swollen and ready. Gently, I begin to circle it with my thumb. Her lips part, completely lost in the sensation as I continue the slow, teasing rhythm.

"Do you want more?"

"Yes," she says, fisting the sheets.

"What do you need, sweetheart?"

"I . . . I need . . ."

"Does this sweet pussy need my fingers?"

"Oh God, yes." Her voice trembles as her knuckles turn white, gripping the sheets. Her back arches and a low moan escapes her lips.

"Fuck, April. Look at you." The sight of her like this—so responsive, so lost in the pleasure—makes me fucking wild. My middle finger circles her entrance, eliciting another long moan from her. Slowly, I push into her wet heat until I'm knuckle-deep. Her eyes flutter shut as she tightens around me.

She's tight and hot.

"Open your eyes."

Her eyes snap open and her lips part as I slide another finger inside her, feeling her stretch and clench around me as I press firmly against that sweet spot, rubbing it in slow strokes.

I can't take it anymore.

Watching her body respond to my touch stirs something primal within me.

I need my mouth on her.

My hand hesitates before pulling away, her startled gaze landing on mine. I smirk, reaching for her panties, hooking my fingers under the elastic and sliding them down her shapely legs. I throw them over my shoulder and lower myself, dropping a kiss to her ankle. I take my time, nipping, licking, and sucking on her supple skin until I reach the tender juncture of her thighs. Her teeth sink into her plush lower lip as I part her, exposing her delicious pussy—wet, ready, and irresistible.

"So fucking pretty." A low groan rumbles from my chest.

I'm met with the overwhelming urge to claim her, mark her, so everyone knows she's *mine*. I want to fill this greedy little pussy with my seed, watch it spill out of her, then fill her up again.

I dip my head, ghosting my lips over her pussy without touching, teasing her with all the restraint I can muster.

"Please, James."

I drag my tongue in a firm, deliberate stroke from her entrance to her clit. Her head drops back, and a shuddering cry falls from her lips as I dive deeper into my ministrations. She tastes fucking incredible. My fingers join in, sliding through her folds as I flick my tongue back and forth. She mewls, grinding against me. I push three fingers inside, and she clasps her legs around my shoulders. Her body tightens.

She's close—I can feel it.

"Fuck," she gasps. "James."

I groan against her pussy as she shamelessly rides my mouth.

"Fuck, James. I'm gonna—"

I increase my pace and grind my hips into the mattress, hungry for friction. I wrap my lips around her clit and suck hard as I continue to drive my fingers into her. She falls apart. Her pussy soaks my hand. The sound of me slipping in and out of her is positively feral. She releases a long string of moans as her inner walls flutter and contract around me. I lap up her release as she comes all over my mouth, petering off my movements to wring every last tremor out of her.

Spent, she softens under my touch, sighing as I slide my fingers out.

My stubble is coated in her. She watches me, cheeks and chest rosy, as I lift my fingers to my mouth and suck her juices off.

"You taste so fucking good."

"You feel so good," she breathes.

I crawl up her body and flop down beside her, pulling her into the crook of my arm. She rolls onto her side so we're facing each other. Lifting her hand, she wipes my facial hair, giggling, before resting it over my racing heart. I pull her closer, reveling in the comfort of having her so near.

I lean in and press my forehead against hers. "How do you feel?" I ask softly.

"Amazing, thank you," she replies, obliterating any hesitation I had about the possibility of us before tonight. I've had one taste, and it's already an addiction.

Her eyelids drift closed as my thumb strokes back and forth gently over her shoulder. She looks so peaceful and serene, as if she's reciting a silent prayer.

"I've wanted you for so long," she says.

"Me too."

"Is it wrong? This? *Us?*" Her voice has an edge to it, as if she's hesitant to ask the question. I can understand why, because it's the same question that's occupied my mind for the last few months. Only now, I've decided that I don't care. I can't help but feel that if something comes so naturally and effortlessly, it can't possibly be wrong.

Tonight feels as if the universe somehow shifted everything into place, and this is where she is supposed to be. In my arms. Her skin against mine feels like a truth I can't argue with.

"I don't think anything has felt more right."

She lifts up and presses her lips to mine. I sweep my tongue against hers, and she opens for me, tasting herself.

Her hand slips between us, catching on the elastic of my briefs. I can't believe I'm still wearing these. I lift my hips to help her tug them off and my cock springs free. Her expression shifts, shocked or amazed, as she takes me in.

"James, that thing is huge."

I chuckle, pushing her hair from her face, then I groan as she fists my shaft and runs her thumb over my sensitive crown, smearing my precum before pumping firmly.

"Fuck, April."

"Does that feel good?"

"That feels *so* good."

She increases her pace. I snake my hand between her legs to find her sopping. I trace laps around her clit before she uses the hand resting on my chest to push me onto my back. In one swift motion, she kicks her leg over my thighs to straddle me.

I wrap my hands around her hips, squeezing her ass firmly before sliding them up the smooth curve of her back. With a quick, practiced motion, I snap open her bra, watching as the delicate lace fabric falls away. She briefly releases me to slip the straps off her. I cup her perfect, perky tits, weighing them in my hands. She lowers herself, rubbing and smearing her wetness over my erection. I take in her naked body on top of mine, totally awestruck. Her dips and curves make it seem as if she were carved by hand.

I sit up, and she instinctively adjusts, winding her legs around my torso and her arms around my neck, pulling us closer.

"Sweetheart, that feels so good. I'm not going to last much longer."

"I want you to come inside me." Her words almost make me fall apart. The thought of being inside her, feeling her squeezing my cock as I fill her, sets me on fire.

"Are you sure?"

She nods, full of intent.

"Are you on the pill?"

"I have an IUD."

"I'm clean," I assure her, needing her to know this is safe.

"So am I."

I gently shift her hips, guiding her as she positions my dick at her entrance. Our eyes lock as she pushes herself onto me. My tip slides in, and we both groan, the sensation of taking her bare overpowering. I can feel every muscle and ridge inside her tight channel stretch as she adjusts to my size. When I'm fully seated inside her, she releases a long sigh. I can only groan in response, intoxicated by how fucking good she feels—so warm, so wet. Perfect.

She rolls her hips in slow circles, becoming more urgent when she starts grinding, shifting her pelvis back and forth. The pleasure is almost too much, and I release one hand to lean back on my arm and thrust gently into her as she rocks. My other hand keeps her close, holding on to her as she rides me. Her little moans are frantic.

She quickly shifts her legs, adjusting her position to lift herself up on her knees. I lie back as she hovers just above the tip of my cock. Then, in one fluid motion, she drops back down. I moan as she whimpers. She leans down and I grip her hip, weaving my other hand through her silky hair, tugging her head to mine. Her touch is like breathing fire into my soul. Her thigh muscles tense as she bounces, and I plunder her mouth. A soft sheen of sweat coats our bodies as the sound of our skin slapping together echoes through the room.

"Fuck, April. You're so tight."

I move my hand from her hip and bring it to my mouth. She stares as I spit, massaging the saliva between my fingers, dropping my hand to where we're joined. I thrum her clit.

"Oh, fuck," she cries. I keep my fingers working as she bounces up and down on my cock. "It's too much." She gasps, but I press down harder, the rhythm of my fingers perfectly matching her movements.

"I want to fill you up. Do you want that? Does your cunt want to squeeze my cock while I come inside it?"

She mumbles something unintelligible, and her walls tighten around me. She's right there, close to the tipping point. "James!" she cries. I feel her pulse on my cock. Her pussy gushes, coating my groin. She snakes an arm behind her and begins to massage my balls as she circles her hips slowly, riding out her orgasm. She softly tugs them and pulls them away from my body, adding a whole other level of sensation.

"Fuck. Yes. Just like that," I encourage.

My balls tighten, and a warmth rushes through me as I spill inside her, rope after rope. She milks every last drop until, finally, she collapses on top of me, limp. I wrap my arms around her, holding her tight, feeling her heart beat against mine as we catch our breath.

I roll her onto her back, and she giggles softly. I smile at the sweet, playful sound and plant a kiss on the tip of her nose. She cants her hips toward me.

I can't get enough of this woman.

I push up onto my knees, spreading her legs apart, and lower myself until I'm eye level with her pussy, watching in awe as our liquid seeps out of her. I glance up to meet her hungry eyes. I run my finger through her slick, swollen folds, gathering our cum on my fingertip. "I love seeing you full of my cum." I bring my finger to my mouth and suck our mixture off.

She lets out a soft whimper.

"Does that feel good? Do you like it when I play with our cum on your cunt?"

"Yes," she breathes.

"Are you sore?"

"No, I feel good," she says. I slip three fingers inside her again, slowly pumping and rubbing against her inner walls. I can't get enough of the wet, animalistic sound our juices make as I press back inside her pussy. I gather saliva in my mouth. She's transfixed on me as I open my lips, letting my spit dribble out and pool on her pussy. I dive in, flicking my tongue back and forth, side to side over her clit. I watch her body undulate and shudder under my touch as she chases her orgasm. Her whimpers gradually fade as she comes down from her climax.

I ease my fingers out and lift them to her lips. "Open," I tell her. She leans forward and her tongue darts out as she wraps her lips around my fingers, sucking. Once she's finished, I place a soft kiss on her inner thigh. "I'll be back," I whisper.

"Me too," she murmurs, a hint of shyness in her voice before she slides off the bed. I track the thin trail of liquid that trickles down her thigh, catching the light as she walks to the en suite. The door clicks softly shut behind her.

While she freshens up, I head to the kitchen, retrieving my wheat bag from the cupboard and popping it in the microwave to heat. Once it's warm, I return to the bedroom to find April curled up beneath the sheets. The sight of her in my bed sends a pang through my chest—it feels so right having her here.

I slip under the covers beside her and place the warm wheat bag next to her, offering comfort as we settle in together.

She pushes up onto one elbow and looks down at me, dreamy. She doesn't say a word—she doesn't need to. It's all there in her expression: contentment. Her lips curve into a soft smile, and I can't help but reach up, running my fingers through her long red tresses. I pull her closer, sealing her mouth to mine. Unlike earlier, this kiss is unhurried. It speaks of everything we just shared.

Sex has never felt this intense or intimate before. Even with Abigail, it was different—it felt transactional, like something we did out of obligation rather than something we needed with each other. Usually, with other women, it's quick and meaningless—simply quenching a desire until we're equally spent and satiated.

This was so much *more*. It's as if every barrier between us has broken down and we've finally given ourselves permission to feel.

As we pull apart, I plant a quick kiss to her forehead and tip of her nose before rolling onto my side. I pull her against me so her back is to my chest and bury my head in her neck.

Selfishly, I know I'm not going to give this woman up.

Chapter 27

April

I wake with a dull throb between my legs. The sun casts soft rays which flitter through the room. I blink into focus and a slow smile spreads across my face as I reflect on last night, my skin tingling as I recall his touch. Rolling over, I reach for the other side of the bed, finding it empty. I stretch my hand, brushing my fingers against the cool sheets.

He must have got up a while ago.

Deciding to freshen up, I slip out of bed and into James's bathroom on wobbly legs—they worked hard last night.

I study myself in the mirror and find a woman I barely recognize staring back at me. I look alive. My skin is flushed with color, and my eyes are bright. It's as if he's magic, breathing life back into my lungs and reviving my body. Slowly, I bring my hand up, tracing my fingers over the tender skin where James bit and sucked at my flesh. The memory of his mouth on me sends a rush of heat straight to my core.

Turning on the tap, I test the water until it's tepid. I cup my hands under the stream, letting the water pool in my palms before splashing it onto my face. My hair is a mess, which isn't surprising. I comb my fingers through the tangled strands, trying to tame them into some semblance of order. God, we were thoroughly undone last night.

I find a tube of toothpaste on the counter and squeeze a bit onto my finger, rubbing it over my teeth—it's the best I can do, considering I didn't bring an overnight bag.

I hoped we'd have sex, but I didn't anticipate sleeping over. It wasn't even a question, not when he heated a wheat bag to warm me before pulling me into his chest. I haven't slept that soundly in a long time.

It felt so wonderful being held again. I was nervous, thinking I'd fall apart the first time I slept with someone who wasn't Lucas. But there's no sadness, not even a trace.

I do feel a touch guilty, because honestly, I can't help but compare the brothers. Yes, Lucas was big, but James... James is bigger. *Much* bigger. And he knows exactly what he's doing.

I twist the tap on once more. Lowering my mouth to the stream, I swish the water around before spitting. "That's as good as it's gonna get."

I quickly scan the bedroom in search of my clothes, suddenly remembering I undressed in the lounge. Standing at the threshold of his bedroom door, I poke my head out, scanning for any sign of James. Nothing. I hold my breath, listening carefully for any sound. But again, nothing. My brows knit together in a frown—where is he?

Straightening, I make a mad, naked dash to the lounge, spotting my clothes scattered across the floor. I quickly pluck them up and rush back into his room.

Dressed and somewhat decent, I head back to the lounge and grab my phone. My eyes widen when I see ten notifications. I open my inbox to find messages from Gemma, Anna, and—what the fuck?—*Lucas.*

My heart gallops as I stare at his name. Why is he messaging me? I haven't heard from him in months. He blocked me, for fuck's sake.

I take a deep breath in, count to four, and release it slowly.

My thumb hovers over the screen as I debate opening the message. I close my eyes and try to gather my thoughts.

It could be nothing.

Maybe it was an accident?

No. You don't block and unblock someone by accident.

But why now?

I was *finally* doing better.

I don't know what it is about men, but it's like they have some sort of radar that can sense when women are either struggling or doing just fine. And it's not until the needle lands on "fine" that they think *You know what? I'm going to ruin her day. Just for fun.*

I'm at a loss for what he wants, and right now is definitely not the appropriate time to find out. I just had his brother's dick inside me, for Christ's sake. Instead, for now, I choose to ignore it.

I open the text thread with Gemma and Anna, grinning as I read their messages. My fingers dance over the keyboard as I type out a response, then hit send.

Gemma: *You're out of litter, and Basil shat on the floor.*

Anna: *What? Where's April?*

Gemma: *She went to James's last night.*

Anna: *WTF? When? We all got an Uber together. I literally dropped you home!*

Gemma: *After we got home, he sent her a text because they almost kissed after the gig. After said text, she went to his house to seduce him. Judging by her suspicious silence, I think it's safe to assume he dipped his wick in her vag.*

Anna: 😨 *OMG!*

Me: *I'm going to have to miss the market this morning. Sorry, Gem. I'll grab litter on my way home. Thanks for letting me know.*

Gemma: *You're lucky you have a good excuse. Good idea, it was gross and I gagged. But worry not, I ordered you a new bag to be delivered.*

Me: *Ugh, you're amazing. I owe you. Thank you!*

Anna: **le sigh* No one cares about the cat turd. What you owe us is some details!*

Me: *Yes, I went to James's house. Yes, we had sex. I'll tell you about it later.*

Gemma: *Come to mine tonight for margs and we can discuss.*

Me: *See you then. X*

Anna: *See you then.* 💩 🖤

The sound of a key jingling the lock startles me, and I quickly drop my phone onto the coffee table just as James swings the door open. One hand balances a tray with two takeaway coffee cups, while the other clutches a brown paper bag. My core throbs as I watch him. He looks like he belongs in a museum. Seriously, who looks that good in the morning?

He's wearing a lightweight long-sleeved top that clings to his broad shoulders, loose joggers, and a pair of trainers. His sandy locks are tucked behind one ear, while the other side hangs loose, a stray strand falling over one eye as he juggles his keys and the takeaway. He glances at me with heat in his eyes. I drop my gaze to the floor, suddenly aware of how exposed I feel after last night.

"Hey, sweetheart," he says in a smooth rumble.

Sweetheart. I like it.

"Hi," I say, hiding my smile. He walks toward me, and I stand frozen, unsure of what to do.

Do I kiss him?

Tingles bubble inside me.

Fuck, why am I so nervous? This man has seen and tasted every inch of me—I was literally rubbing my vagina in his face last night.

Perhaps it's because I know just how good he looks *underneath* his clothes.

He closes the distance between us and leans in, planting a firm kiss on my lips, and his scent—a mix of cedarwood and something distinctly him—envelops me.

"I didn't want to wake you. I'm sorry you woke up to an empty flat," he says as he moves to the kitchen. I follow closely behind. "Did you sleep well?" he asks, setting the cups and bag on the counter.

"It's fine," I tell him. "And I did, thank you. I haven't slept that well in a long time."

I pull out a barstool and take a seat. James turns, giving me a soft smile that makes my pulse accelerate.

"Me too," he says gently. "I could get used to falling asleep with you in my arms."

"I certainly wouldn't protest," I tell him.

I turn to liquid at his smile. He swivels back to the counter, opening the paper bag and pulling out two freshly baked pastries.

His phone chimes, and my stomach twists as my eyes dart to his pocket. He pulls it out, swiping the screen to dismiss the notification before slipping it back. The quickness of his movements unsettles me, like how Lucas's did before I found—

I stop myself before I follow that train of thought, shifting in my seat.

He isn't Lucas.

Instead, I lean over to peek at the treat. The warm, buttery scent wafts through the room. I catch sight of the flaky, golden pastry dusted with icing sugar and speckled with almonds, and my mouth waters.

"That smells divine," I note, and my stomach grumbles loudly.

James laughs. "Here, you need to eat. I'm sure you worked up quite the appetite after last night."

He isn't wrong.

He sets a coffee cup and an almond croissant in front of me before taking a sip from his own. I wrap my hands around the cup so its warmth seeps into my fingers. I inhale deeply, breathing in the heavenly scent of freshly brewed coffee—it might just be the best smell in the world.

As I look down, my eyes catch the familiar stamp on the cup, one I hadn't noticed when he first arrived. A flurry whirls in my chest—he went to the Daily Grind.

I know it's just a simple coffee and croissant, but it's so incredibly thoughtful.

He remembered my order.

My gaze catches on his. "A cappuccino and almond croissant?"

He looks at me nervously. "They're your favorites, right?"

"Yes, thank you," I confirm, beaming from ear to ear.

"You're welcome," he says, his eyes warm.

He pulls out a stool and settles beside me, resting his hand on my thigh. He gives it a gentle squeeze and rubs back and forth over the fabric of my joggers. We sip our coffees and munch on our croissants in comfortable silence. The flaky pastry melts in my mouth, and I can't help but moan at the rich, decadent flavor.

"That good, eh?" he asks, cocking an eyebrow.

"It's orgasmic, thank you," I say around a mouthful.

"You're welcome." He chuckles, taking a generous bite. His eyebrows furrow before his head swivels in my direction. "Wow, this is incredible."

"I know. If it weren't for the risk of a heart attack, I'd live off these."

"Well, we definitely can't have that," he says, pulling my stool closer to his. "Not after last night. I'm far from finished with you yet."

"No," I agree. "That would be positively awful."

"Positively."

I smile. We continue to eat, and I sneak a glance at him out of the corner of my eye, noticing that he's watching me. Last night was incredible, but as I sit here and melt under his gaze, I can't help but wonder where we go from here.

We've crossed the line—we've slept together.

I slept with my ex-fiancé's brother.

This is real.

It happened.

But now what?

How do we navigate this?

Was it just a one-time thing?

There's a look on his face I can't quite decipher.

"What?" I ask, bringing my hand up to check if there's any icing sugar or coffee around my mouth.

"Nothing," he says, reaching up to push my hair over my shoulder. His hand hovers, and he slowly runs his knuckles along my collarbone. "You're just beautiful."

I look down, feeling my cheeks redden. "I look a mess." I laugh, my fingers fidgeting incessantly.

"You've never been more lovely."

Ugh, my heart. This man.

On the surface, he looks like a classic bad boy—playing bass in a band, covered in tattoos, the wayward hair. If you searched *trouble* in the dictionary, I'm sure you'd find his picture. He's the type of boy your mother warns you about. But underneath it all, he's unbelievably sweet. So attentive and observant—he's the kind of person who surprises you with how deeply he cares.

Lucas was always charming. He would easily win people over with his poetic words, but that's all they ever were—words. James is different. He's thoughtful, and doesn't just say the right things but takes action. He pours his whole heart into everything he does, chasing after what he wants with unwavering determination. James isn't the type to wait for you to ask for help—he gives it without prompting.

Shit. Lucas's message.

The reminder burns through me like a searing flame. I'm sitting here, having breakfast after being fucked by his little brother, completely distracted, and I haven't even opened his bloody message yet.

"I can see the cogs turning in your brain." James's gruff voice cuts through my spiraling thoughts.

"Huh?"

"What are you thinking about?"

"I suppose . . . I'm wondering what happens now."

He cocks his head. "What do you mean?"

"Well, we've slept together . . . I just don't know what it means," I say, searching his eyes for an answer.

"What it means?" he says. "Well, it was amazing. It doesn't have to *mean* anything right now. We enjoyed ourselves, right?"

I swallow a lump in my throat and nod.

"So, we'll figure it out. We don't need to rush anything."

I jerk my chin, unable to speak as panic unfurls in my chest.

"Hey," he says, shifting my stool to face him. "Sweetheart, look at me."

I can't.

I can't look at him.

I know he's right.

He's not putting any pressure on this situation; he's been nothing short of amazing. But I just sat here and compared sex with this beautiful man to sex with his *brother*.

I try to convince my nervous system that everything's fine. But Lucas's message wraps around me like tungsten chains.

What could he possibly have to say to me?

And why did he have to send it the morning after *I had sex with his brother?*

God. This is a mess.

I'm a mess.

Does this make me a terrible person?

My heart rate spikes, and a wave of panic crashes over me, panting as I near hyperventilation.

What have I done?

This isn't me—I don't sleep with people I don't love, let alone someone who was supposed to be my future brother-in-law.

I loved Lucas.

I was going to *marry* Lucas.

James has been single for years. I can't expect him to suddenly change because we slept together once. For all I know, that message he just received could have been from another woman, and I have no right to feel possessive.

I can't act like he owes me anything.

I cringe at my own actions, becoming consumed by shame. I abruptly stand from my stool, stepping back as if

202

creating distance could somehow erase what we did last night.

"April," James says, reaching for me.

I pull away, avoiding his touch.

"What just happened? What's wrong?" His voice is laced with concern as he stands, and his expression shifts from confused to worried.

Tears brim my eyes. "What did we do?" I whisper, bringing my hand to cover my mouth as the reality sinks in. "What did we *do*?" I repeat, my voice frayed.

I blink and a lone tear slips down my cheek.

I look at James, scanning his face for an answer, desperate to find a solution to my turmoil in the depths of his ivy-green eyes.

He just stands there, shocked. His throat works as he swallows.

"I should go," I say, turning to head for the front door.

"Go? What? April, you don't have to go—you haven't even finished your coffee. We can talk about this." His voice is anguished as he reaches for me again, but I dodge, moving past him.

I quickly pluck my phone off the table. My grip wavers as I swipe to unlock the screen and pull up the Uber app, punching in my address. I connect with a driver one minute away.

"What are you doing?" he asks, stepping forward cautiously.

"I'm leaving," I reply, eyes glued to my phone as the car icon moves closer.

"You don't have to leave. Can we please just talk about this?" His voice is so thick with hurt that I finally look up, meeting his eyes. "I don't want you to go." His voice is hollow and stripped of hope.

My phone vibrates with a notification: My Uber is here.

"This was a mistake. I'm sorry."

"A mistake," he echoes.

"Yes. A mistake."

His arms fall to his sides, defeated, his face painting a tortured picture. His jaw tenses as his eyes flicker to the unfinished food and drink on the counter before returning to meet mine, searching for something—anything—that might change my mind.

With one last look at James, I release a rattled breath. My hand rests on the door handle when his voice reaches me.

"April . . ." But the words die on his lips.

"Bye, James," I whisper, stepping through the door.

I slide into the Uber, dropping my head back against the headrest and close my eyes.

Fuck.

What did I just do?

Chapter 28

James

"Fuck!" I yell, returning to the kitchen and kicking the barstool under the counter. My breathing comes in ragged gasps as I struggle to get a grip, my hands clenched behind my head, tugging at my hair in frustration. What went wrong? We had an incredible night together—I've never had sex like that before. And then she just . . . ran.

I replay the morning over and over in my head, questioning everything.

Was the coffee and croissant too much?

Did I creep her out?

Was I too . . . relaxed about everything?

I don't know what to make of it.

She came to me, not the other way around.

She almost kissed me at the bar—not the other way around.

I pull my phone from my pocket and open my text thread with Oliver. I need to talk to someone, and God knows Will and Tom are fucking useless when it comes to women. I punch out a quick message.

Me: *Hey mate, are you free this morning? I think I fucked up.*

I watch the three little dots appear, and when Oliver's reply comes through moments later, I let out a breath of relief.

Oliver: *Yeah, mate, you okay? I was heading to Hyde Park for a coffee and a stroll in 20, if you want to meet around there?*

Me: *Sounds good. Meet at the Peter Pan statue?*

Oliver: *See you soon.*

I drop my phone on the counter and change out of my disheveled clothes. I quickly shove my legs into a pair of shorts, throwing on a gray T-shirt and slipping back into my sneakers in record time. I rush past the kitchen, my gaze landing on the breakfast we barely touched. I close my eyes as hurt floods through me.

I can't help but dissect every word April said this morning, hoping that by analyzing them closely enough, I'll uncover the truth.

This was a mistake.

She couldn't have meant that, right? Last night was many things, but a mistake certainly wasn't one of them. She told me there was something real between us. So, what happened this morning that made her change her mind?

What if I pushed her too hard in bed?

Perhaps I came on too strong and made her pull away?

The idea that this could be my fault coils uncomfortably inside me.

I mull over all the possible reasons, but no matter how many scenarios I consider, I keep circling back to the same answer.

My brother.

It has to be.

Shoving my phone and wallet into my back pocket, I snatch up my keys and head out the door, quickening my steps.

It's half past eight on a weekend and the streets are already alive, even at this early hour. Couples and friends huddle together, coffee cups in hand. People walk their dogs, leads tugging as the dogs sniff out every scent the city has to offer. Everyone goes about their morning as if it's all so normal—so *easy*—yet I feel anything but.

My legs move on autopilot, and I make it to Hyde Park in record time. I try to calm myself by watching the birds peck at the grass, and a squirrel scurries across the path in front of me, disappearing into a bed of dense shrubbery.

I've always loved London in the summer—there's a quiet beauty to it—the buildings, the gardens, the people. I spot Oliver weaving through a crowd of joggers, two coffee cups in hand. Like me, he's tall, towering over most people, making him easy to pick out in the busy park. He grins as he hands me a cup.

"Cheers, mate," I say, raising the cup in thanks.

He gives me a solid pat on the back and nods ahead, and we start strolling. "All right, tell me," he says, nudging me. "What's going on?"

"April came over last night."

"April came over, did she?" He barely conceals his smirk. "Go on, then."

I spend a few minutes recounting everything to Oliver, starting from the moment April walked in, right up to when she stormed out. "And then she said, '*This was a mistake,*'" I finish.

Oliver winces, sucking in a breath. "Ouch."

"I need some advice. It's fucking eating me alive."

Oliver bites his cheek as he mulls over my words. I stay quiet, letting him think.

"Right," he says after a beat. "Did you catch her on her phone or anything?"

"Nope."

"Well, what about the sex? Did she give off any vibe that she wasn't into it, or didn't fancy staying over?"

"Mate, considering the *multiple* orgasms, I'd say she was pretty into it," I reply, huffing in frustration. "She seemed happy staying over—curled up in my arms all night. Everything was fine, great, in fact, until this morning. Then she just . . . freaked out and legged it."

"I'm going to throw this out there, in case you haven't thought of it," he says, and I give him a nod to continue. "Lucas."

"Yeah, I've considered that." My jaw clenches as I try to rein in the anger that flares at the mention of his name.

"Do you reckon there's a chance she bailed *because* she loved the sex and how it made her feel this morning?" he asks, raising an eyebrow.

His question makes me pause; I hadn't considered that.

"Like, she isn't actually upset with *me*?" I ask.

"Exactly. I don't think she's upset with you, mate. You've not done anything wrong. My guess? She's upset about the situation. I mean, the girl was engaged to your brother. She's probably feeling a right mess—she was supposed to marry him, and now she's in your bed." He shrugs. "I reckon she's feeling guilty."

"Guilty," I repeat, weighing his words.

"Yeah, but not because she feels bad for Lucas—he's a wanker. She probably feels guilty because, after everything he put her through, maybe part of her thinks she shouldn't be allowed to find happiness with *you*."

The ball drops.

I hadn't even considered that possibility.

I'd been so wrapped up in thinking Lucas was the issue—wondering if maybe she still had feelings for him, or worse, that she might want him back after everything. But it never crossed my mind that she could be feeling guilty for finding happiness . . . with *me*.

It all makes sense now—the way she shut down this morning after asking me what last night meant.

It wasn't about Lucas, not really—it was about her, about being caught between the pain he caused and the fear of letting herself move on with me. And honestly, I don't give a fuck about what that sod thinks. Lucas made his choice, and he chose to lose her.

Suddenly, the weight eases off my chest.

Good. This is good.

I might still be in with a chance.

"Fuck. Do you think I should call her?"

Oliver pauses for a moment, thinking it through. "I wouldn't push her. Not now—it's all a bit fresh. Give her the day."

"Okay." I nod, trying to steady my thoughts. "I'll give her some time . . . and then what?"

"Do you *want* her?"

"Of course I want her."

"Then do what Lucas didn't—*chase her.*"

Chapter 29

April

I rest my head against the cool leather of the headrest, squeezing my eyes shut as the Uber speeds off down the road. I can't get James's tortured expression out of my mind.

This was a mistake.

He looked devastated.

I stare out the window, lost in thought as the city blurs into streaks of white, green, and red.

I take a few deep, shaky breaths, trying to quell the storm building inside me. Lucas couldn't have chosen a worse time to send his stupid message.

Why would he unblock me now?

What could he want to say to me after all this time?

I wonder if he found out about James and me somehow. Surely not.

Of course the first time I hear from him in months is the morning after his brother was buried balls deep inside me. Just my bloody luck.

There's no point putting off reading the message. Might as well do it now, like ripping off a Band-Aid. My finger hovers over the conversation with Lucas—the one that's been dead silent for months. I open the thread, and my eyes fix on his three simple words.

A wave of nausea rolls through me and my palms start to sweat.

I'm panicking.

I know this isn't a typical or healthy way to respond to a message from someone I once loved, but the truth is, I'm powerless against it.

I reread his message over and over.

Lucas: *Can we talk?*

Can we talk?

Is he serious?

This is the guy who was hiding behind a fucking Instagram account, messaging dozens of women, and sending voice notes and dick pics. Who fell out of love with me to pursue women online, broke my heart, and then ghosted me without so much as a word. *Now* he suddenly wants to talk?

The questions pour in thick and fast, stealing the breath from my lungs.

I'm anxious.

I'm anxious and I'm pissed. It feels like fire is erupting beneath my skin.

A couple of months ago, I would have done anything to receive a message like this from him. I would have clung to every word, desperate for any sort of connection. I was so consumed by the hope of us getting back together that I would imagine him showing up on my doorstep out of the blue, pleading for my forgiveness, confessing that he still loves me, that he wants me, that he misses me as much as I miss him, that he chooses me.

That he made a mistake.

But he never did.

His message just proves that everything is always on his terms.

It always was.

I was just too enamored with love to see it.

The more time has passed, the more I've realized how obvious the signs were. I was so ignorant.

I place my phone in my lap, deciding not to respond. I need to calm down and clear my head after the shitshow performance I pulled this morning. I'll hold off on figuring out what to do next until I'm with the girls for margaritas later. As I wipe my cheeks with the back of my hand, I'm surprised to find them wet. I hadn't even realized I was crying.

God, how did I mess everything up so spectacularly?

The Uber pulls up to the curb in front of my townhouse. As soon as I step through the entrance, I rush upstairs to my bedroom. The moment I enter, Basil wanders in, greeting me with a soft squawk.

"Hey, buddy," I murmur, bending down to scratch his ears. His purrs and quiet trills warm my heart, and I scoop him up, cradling him like a baby. With him nestled securely in one arm, I gently rub under his chin, watching as his eyes slow blink at me—what I call his "love eyes." I pepper kisses over his tiny forehead and snout before placing him gently back on the carpet, watching as he slinks away.

I freshen up and head downstairs, feeling somewhat revived, to flick on the kettle. I make a conscious decision to leave my phone untouched—I don't want to be accessible to anyone right now, and I refuse to be drawn back into rereading old messages from Lucas.

Messages that are largely one-sided.

I can't go back to that place.

I've come so far, thanks to the strength and comfort my

best friends have given me, I won't allow myself to be drawn back into the black hole.

It's not worth it. *He* isn't worth it.

Instead, I make a pot of breakfast tea, curl up on the sofa with Basil, and turn on my favorite film. It's still early morning, and I won't be seeing the girls until tonight, so I decide to switch off from the outside world.

These are the moments when it's so easy to feel alone. I love my space, but when everything around me is quiet, the solitude and loneliness drowns me.

What I wouldn't give for the warmth of my mother's arms and the wisdom of my father's words. I miss them so much it hurts. A mother's hug has the magical ability to stop the world from spinning, if only for a moment. I feel so lost without her.

And just briefly, Caroline creeps into my thoughts. I miss her too. When Lucas and I broke up, it wasn't just him I was grieving—I lost his parents too. They showered me with love and made me feel at home. Birthdays and holidays became something to look forward to again. I hope she's doing well. She adored Basil; we'd always bring him along when we stayed over, and he seemed to offer her comfort during her darker days.

Not having my own mum around anymore made me appreciate Caroline even more. Because Caroline struggles with depression, Lucas often called to check on her, and she would always mention that James had been to visit her most weeks. Even though I miss her terribly, it's a comfort knowing she has James.

She's in the best possible hands.

I lean back on the sofa, closing my eyes as the film plays in the background, and before I know it, darkness swallows me.

* * *

I wake to the sound of my vibrating phone. Groggily, I peel my eyes open, realizing it must be late afternoon.

How long was I out?

Slowly, I lift myself off the sofa and head toward the phone, noticing I've missed a couple of calls from Gemma. I hit the call button, and she answers almost immediately.

"Hello?"

"Hey, I'm sorry I missed the market this morning," I say, stifling a yawn.

She chuckles. "It's totally fine. I'd miss the market too if it meant I had the opportunity to shag a modern-day Apollo. Did I wake you?"

"It's fine, I didn't mean to fall asleep."

"Tired from last night?" she teases, and I can picture her wiggling her eyebrows on the other end of the line.

"Oh God," I mutter, cringing as I run a hand down my face.

"What's wrong?"

I blow out a breath, wincing. "It's easier if I tell you tonight. What time is it?" I ask, pulling the phone away from my ear to check the time. Six. "Shit, I slept all day."

"Come round now. I'm not doing anything. We can have a quick cuppa together before Anna arrives."

"Ugh, you're a lifesaver. I'll be there soon."

"Love you."

"Love you."

I hang up and bolt upstairs. I throw my hair up into a messy claw clip, and make sure Basil has enough food to last through the evening in case I end up crashing at Gemma's. As I check everything, I sigh in relief, thankful Gemma had a fresh bag of litter delivered. I spot Basil and plant a kiss on his head. "Please don't crap on the floor."

I dash out the door, popping my AirPods in as I rush to the tube.

I arrive at Gemma's flat fifteen minutes later and, as usual, I start skimming over her bookshelf, trying to distract myself from the clusterfuck I'm about to unload on her.

I pull out her latest purchase, a smutty monster romance, and flip it over to read the blurb. I shelve it, laughing after I spot the word *milking*.

I love Gemma, but our mutual love for romance novels starts and ends with hockey.

"I loaded up on Oreos."

I jump, startled as Gemma strolls into the lounge carrying a tray with two steaming mugs of tea and a packet of biscuits.

"You're an angel."

I join her on the sofa and pluck an Oreo from the tray. I dunk it into my tea before taking a bite, the chocolatey flavor melting on my tongue.

Gemma's phone lights up, and she takes a long sip of her tea before setting it down and leaning over to read the message. "It's Anna. She'll be here in five."

"Fab," I say, nodding toward her bookshelf. "When did you get the new monster romance?"

"Last weekend. I was on a date with a guy from that kink app, Evan. We met at Green Park, so I dragged him into Waterstones. He was totally smitten, obviously—I was wearing that off-the-shoulder top that makes my tits look lush, and he insisted on buying it for me. It was a great date, actually. We walked around St. James's Park, had a coffee by the lake, and watched the birds. Then we headed over to Soho for a drink. I brought him back to mine and . . ." She trails off.

"Oh God, what happened?" I ask, chuckling. I will never tire of hearing her dating horror stories.

"Your imagination couldn't even conjure this," she says.

My brows knit together, and I turn to face her fully. "Try me."

She closes her eyes dramatically, blowing out a long breath. "We came back to mine, and things escalated pretty quickly. We started making out—you know how much I love making out." She gives me a pointed look, and I nod as she continues. "I was in his lap on the couch, and he asked if he could suck on my tits. So, I called him a good boy. You know how I've been wanting to explore my Mommy Dom side."

Of course I didn't know, but I nod all the same.

"Well, I pulled his dick out and went down on him. Then told him to bend over my lap so I could spank him."

My eyes widen and I almost spit out my tea.

"After that, I told him to wait while I grabbed some lube."

I have no fucking clue where this is headed, but I tell her to keep going.

"When I came back, he was on all fours on the couch, ass up like a bitch in heat." She pauses, shutting her eyes for a moment.

"Oh God," I whisper.

"I know. I told him I wasn't into eating ass."

"I don't think that's an unreasonable boundary to set."

"He looked so disappointed, but I just couldn't do it, you know? So, we had sex instead, and just when I thought it couldn't get any worse—"

"Please stop—"

"—the condom came off inside me."

"Jesus Christ."

"It was the worst sex I've ever had. I was left fishing the condom out of my cervix."

"How far up was it?"

"Much farther than I expected his mediocre dick could reach."

That's an image I could've lived without.

Her shoulders slump. "Anyway, at least I got the book out of it."

"Silver linings."

The intercom buzzes and Gemma leaps up, rushing to let Anna in. She sweeps into Gemma's flat, tote bag swinging on her shoulder. "Hiiiii!" she says, rushing toward me. She drops her bag beside the sofa and pulls me into a tight embrace, nearly crushing me in her arms.

"Hi, love," I say with a smile, hugging her back.

Gemma eyes Anna's bag. "You got the goods?"

"Yep, *so* many limes," Anna replies with a grin.

Gemma grabs the tote and heads toward the kitchen, where I can only assume she's about to make margaritas. Anna plops down on the sofa beside me, and I lean close to whisper, "Did she tell you about Evan?"

Anna throws her head back in a snorting laugh. "Ahh, yes, *Ass-to-the-Wind Evan*," she says, shaking her head. "It's one of her better stories."

"It sounded fucking awful."

"Ah well. You live and you learn. Speaking of—I can't wait to hear about your evening, you promiscuous thing, you," she says, giving my arm a playful poke.

"I'm going to need a drink for that."

Her face falls. "Oh shit. What happened?"

"Let's give Gemma a hand. I'll fill you in once we're all settled."

Anna nods, and we join Gemma in the kitchen, slicing limes, salting glasses, and blending tequila with Cointreau, perfecting the margarita as we chat and catch up. We clink our glasses and take a sip. I fill a bowl with kettle crisps while Anna grabs hummus and crackers. With snacks in hand, we reconvene on the sofa. Gemma fiddles with her phone, tapping away until music flows through the portable speaker.

Both sets of eyes settle on me.

Excellent. I'm up.

I take a generous gulp of liquid courage, the tequila burning slightly as it goes down, before crossing my legs. I clear my throat.

"I'll start off by saying that last night was, hands down, the best sex I've ever had in my life."

"Way to rub it in," Gemma huffs.

Anna slaps my thigh with a grin. "Attagirl."

I clench my jaw, and the smile slips from her face.

"All right," she says, her eyes narrowing. "Tell us. Start from the beginning."

I fill Anna in from the moment Gemma and I got home last night, all the way to waking up in James's flat this morning. They nod, giggle, and laugh at all the right moments, fully engaged in the story. I can tell they're both thinking the same thing—that James is adorable, thoughtful, and sweet. And he is, which makes me hesitate to share what comes next.

I suck in a breath and push forward. "But then . . ."

"Oh, for fuck's sake, just spit it out already!" Anna says.

"Lucas messaged me."

The silence is heavy.

I wait, expecting one of them to say something, anything,

but they just stare at me, stunned. Finally, Gemma gently places her hand on my thigh. "What did he say?"

"It said, '*Can we talk?*'"

"That's it?" Anna asks, frowning.

"Yup," I reply, popping the *p*.

"Did you reply?" Gemma asks. I shake my head. I'm so, *so* happy about what happened with James, but Lucas reaching out has me torn. I can't determine how I feel. I'm so frustrated. The whole situation is fucked.

"Oh, honey," Gemma says, rubbing my thigh gently.

"James and I had an unforgettable evening. It was everything I'd hoped it would be. But then, I woke up to a text from Lucas, and suddenly I felt . . . Guilty? Angry? A bit of both? I can't quite pinpoint it. James had been so kind, so considerate, and I froze. Panic took over. I shut myself off. I didn't know how to react, so I pushed him away, and before I could stop myself, I bolted," I say.

"I'm sure he'll understand you were just overwhelmed," Anna says.

"I told him it was a mistake," I whisper, as my lip starts to tremble. I feel so terrible. I quickly catch a stray tear with the sleeve of my shirt, wiping it away. "Why did Lucas have to ruin everything?"

Gemma moves closer, wrapping her arms around me while Anna rubs my back in soothing circles.

"He ignored me and walked away like I never existed. Like he never *loved* me. I'm so mad at him. So why do I feel guilty? It's not fair."

"You feel guilty because it's not just about sex with James," Anna says. "It's not some meaningless hookup. You have real feelings for him, and that's where the guilt is coming from. You care, and that makes this messy and complicated. You're kind, maybe even *too* kind sometimes, and that's why it's weighing on you." She pauses for a moment, making sure I'm still with her. "But listen, it's okay to feel conflicted. You're not a robot—you can't just switch off your emotions. You didn't sleep with James to get back at Lucas or to prove a point. You did it because you *like* him. Because there's something between you two that you couldn't ignore. And that's fine. Lucas doesn't get to have power over that." She continues, her voice a little firmer now. "You're human, and humans don't choose who they fall for or when. You deserve to be with someone who cares about you, who treats you right. You're allowed to find happiness with someone who values you—without Lucas looming over your decision."

I know she's right. I agree with everything she's saying, but the guilt is suffocating.

Yes, I have every right to move on, but does that right extend to James?

Is it different because he's Lucas's brother?

I'm terrified that pursuing James makes me just as bad as Lucas. Isn't sleeping with your ex's brother just as much of a betrayal?

Isn't it just as cruel?

Are the two comparable?

Lucas was having emotional affairs, but I actually slept with James.

Dick in vagina.

This is physical, tangible.

"But he's his brother...Doesn't that make me just as bad?"

Anna shakes her head. "No, it doesn't. Lucas made a promise and lied, deceived you, and hurt you repeatedly. You haven't done that. You aren't playing some twisted game. This isn't about getting attention, and what you have with James isn't about Lucas. This happened naturally, after all the damage Lucas left behind. You shouldn't feel guilty for finding something amidst the wreckage he caused. The only person Lucas ever considered in his actions was himself. Quit thinking about everyone else—you need to think about *you* now."

Gemma nods, and I shift my gaze to her, her eyes meeting mine with intensity. "I'm gonna be real with you right now," she begins. "Fuck Lucas. He didn't think twice about how his actions would make you feel, and even if he did, he clearly didn't give a shit. Why should his opinion dictate how you live your life? It's none of his damn business. Why should he hold any part of you hostage?"

She grips my hand, giving it a squeeze. "This guilt isn't yours to carry. It belongs to Lucas. *He's* the one who should be ashamed for what he did, not you. You don't owe him anything. You deserve to make your own choices without worrying about what *he* thinks. Don't let him hold that kind of power over you anymore."

My eyes dart between Anna and Gemma. Slowly, I nod. Perhaps they're right. I can't keep carrying the weight of someone who never bothered to consider my feelings. I'm not responsible for Lucas anymore.

I'm exhausted.

He's been the source of my sadness for far too long.

I square my shoulders. "You're right. Both of you. Honestly, I don't know what I'd do without you. I was on the verge of losing it this morning—like, I'm talking a full-on meltdown. I acted like such an idiot." I sigh. "I haven't heard from James since, and I can't say I blame him. I just . . . I hope I haven't scared him off." I drop my gaze. "I hate that I might have hurt him."

Anna immediately jumps in. "Babe, we all have moments where we freak out. Don't beat yourself up. If James really cares about you—and it sounds like he does—he'll understand. You just both need to give each other some time to process everything."

Gemma nods encouragingly. "Exactly. You had a vulnerable moment, and he needs to see that. If he's worth it—and I really think he is—he's not going to run just because things got a little messy. He's not Lucas, remember? I've seen the way he looks at you, and trust me, you couldn't have scared him away. You probably caught him off guard. Give it a little time, and I'm sure he'll come around."

Once my anxiety subsides and I've calmed down, Anna shoots me a smile. "So, you really like him, huh?"

"Yeah," I say. "I really do."

Her eyes twinkle as she grabs my and Gemma's drinks, handing them to us. She clinks our glasses together with a grin before taking a big gulp. Then, she snatches Gemma's phone off the couch, her fingers tapping rapidly on the screen until a familiar beat fills the room.

Gemma shoots to her feet, raising her glass high above her head, a wide smile spreading across her face. Anna stands up too, joining Gemma in the toast. Both of them look down at me, their expressions full of excitement and solidarity. I can't help but return their smiles as I rise to join them.

"To April!" Anna says. "Our resident brother fucker. May you fuck that brother to your heart's content." She waves her glass around wildly, liquid spilling over the rim, and we all burst into laughter.

"To being a brother fucker," I say, clinking my glass with theirs.

I can do this.

I deserve to be happy.

James deserves to be happy.

Now, I suppose it's only a matter of time until Lucas finds out about us.

Chapter 30

April

We called it a night after the alcohol caught up with us. Anna was fast asleep on the sofa before I crawled into Gemma's bed.

The screech of the milk foamer echoes around the flat. I'm a foul mess without my morning caffeine fix. Anna and I are seated at Gemma's small table pushed up against the kitchen wall as she makes us coffee.

"Here, love," Gemma says, handing me a freshly brewed cup. I raise an eyebrow as I glance down at the foam art.

"It's a penis," she says.

"I can see that."

She points. "See? That's the semen."

"Lovely."

Her face lights up, clearly pleased with her artwork.

Gemma used to work as a barista at Caffè Nero when she was studying, and her foam art is always a wild card.

Anna lifts her cup to mine, shaking her head. "What the fuck, Gemma? She gets a penis, and I get a vagina that looks like a dropped sandwich?"

She's not wrong—it really does look a bit tragic. I lean

224

forward, peering into Gemma's cup. "And what about you? What masterpiece have you got?" I ask.

Anna leans over to inspect it too. "A leaf," Gemma replies.

Anna raises an eyebrow before muttering, "Of course you give yourself something pretty."

After a few gulps of coffee, I head to the fridge and pull out eggs and bacon. Grabbing a loaf of sourdough, I slice three thick pieces and pop them in the toaster. I reach for two pans, drizzling each with a bit of oil before cracking the eggs and tossing in the bacon. The sizzling sound fills the kitchen, and the smell of crispy bacon hits us hard.

We're all practically salivating. There's nothing quite like a full English fry-up after a night getting loaded.

We're deep in chatter after our breakfast, laughing when the sound of my phone buzzing from the lounge grabs my attention. I pluck it off the table where I left it last night, swiping to open the message.

"Ugh." I roll my eyes.

Anna notices and follows me to the sofa. "What is it?"

I spin my phone to show her the screen. *Lucas.*

I never replied to his message.

My heart stutters. Why does my body react like this? It's like I've been conditioned to fall into disarray whenever his name pops up.

It's pissing me off.

Anna reaches out, taking my free hand and rubbing her thumb gently over my knuckles.

"Hey," she says, pulling me back to the present. "It's all right. We're both here. You don't have to read anything you don't want to, and if you *do* open the text, we'll be right here next to you, yeah?"

"Thank you."

Gemma strolls in and kneels in front of me while we sit on the sofa, her eyes flicking between Anna and me. "Lucas?" she asks, and Anna dips her chin in confirmation. Gemma's gaze shifts to mine. "Would it make you feel better if we read the text for you?" she asks.

I nod. "Yes, please. I don't think I can read it. I'm too jittery."

"That's completely fine," Gemma reassures me, holding out her hand. I place the phone in her palm. Her eyes scan the message briefly before she reads aloud. "*Are you free today? I'd love to grab a coffee and have a chat.*"

"Do you want to see him?" Anna asks. I pause.

As confused and pissed off as I am, there's a part of me, as much as I hate to admit it, that wants to hear what he has to say.

I haven't seen him since his date at the Mayfair Lounge— where he had the balls to act as though I didn't exist. I can't imagine he's looking to get back together.

Maybe it's something else, something unrelated.

Could it be he's missing Basil? My thoughts are in overdrive as I reach another possible conclusion—Caroline.

A pit forms in my stomach at the thought that something could be wrong with her. But if that were true, surely James would have known about it and told me.

"I don't *want* to see him, not really," I say. "But this is the second text he's sent in two days. If he's going to be persistent, I'd rather just get it over with than have this hanging over me." I pause, bobbing my knees up and down. "But I'm terrified. If this is how my body reacts to a bloody text, I can't even imagine how I'll handle seeing him in person. What if I completely fall apart?"

My pulse spikes at the possibility of facing him again. The idea I might break down in front of him—of showing him that kind of vulnerability after everything—feels humiliating.

Gemma leans forward with a serious look on her face. "Of course you feel anxious. But, *if* you decide to meet him, don't think about how *he* might see you—think about what *you* want to get out of it. If you cry, so what? He's lucky you're even giving him the time of day. He deserves a kick in the dick."

"Yeah," Anna says, jumping in. "Who gives a fuck what he thinks? If you cry, you cry. If you shit your pants, you shit your pants. But you're seriously not giving yourself enough credit. You're so much stronger than you think, April. And at the end of the day, it's just a conversation. You don't have to talk to him ever again after this if you don't want to. But if hearing him out gives you closure, especially if you're serious about James, then maybe it's worth it. It's a hurdle the two of you will have to jump sooner or later."

She gives me a reassuring look, and I press my lips together, evaluating my options. She's right. They both are. I *definitely* want to see James again. I need to make it right with him. As much as it's awful that James and Lucas can barely stand each other, their strained relationship actually works in James's and my favor. It's not like I'll have to deal with Lucas much if things move forward with James.

I comb my fingers through my tangled hair, smoothing out the kinks. I silently count down in my head, matching my breath to the rhythm, and slowly my heartbeat returns to its usual pace. I feel calmer now, more in control.

"I know it's ridiculous, but if I'm going to see him today, I want to look good. He sought attention from so many beautiful women online, and it really messed with me . . . I want him to know what he lost, you know?"

"Gemma," Anna says, her tone sharp with determination. "Hand me the phone." She holds out her arm expectantly.

"What are you doing?" I ask, my voice rising with panic.

"I'm telling Fuggo that you'll meet him today," Anna replies. Gemma smirks knowingly at her as Anna takes the phone and starts typing. "And we're going to help you look hot as shit."

* * *

I've showered, spritzed dry shampoo for volume, and now Anna is curling my hair while I sit, trying not to fidget.

Gemma's in her room, sifting through her wardrobe to find me an outfit. I'm just hoping she doesn't come out with lingerie.

I'm meeting Lucas in an hour at the Daily Grind. If there's one good thing that's going to come out of this, it's that I'll at least get an almond croissant.

I'm focusing on the positives.

Months ago, the thought of meeting him would've had me buzzing with excitement. But now? I just want to get this over with. There's no anticipation left, only a heavy feeling in my chest and a desire to move past whatever this is once and for all.

"Ah ha!" Gemma shouts excitedly from her room.

"You know she's going to dress you like a hooker, right?" Anna says as she curls the last section of my hair.

I press my lips together to stop my laugh.

"I heard that!" Gemma calls out before marching into the bathroom, holding two sets of hangers aloft. "All right, we've got two options. Option one: cute skirt and cropped top combo. Personally, I think your waist is *killer*, and this silk skirt is going to show it off. Plus, it'll look super chic with the white trainers you wore here last night. Now, I don't have much to work with in the footwear department because your feet are the size of surfboards, but I think it'll do."

She pauses, then lifts the second outfit. "Option two: this skintight midi. Again, all about that waist, and this one has the bonus of showing off that ass. Honestly, April, you could bounce a penny off that thing. I don't know why you don't show it off more. You could throw a denim jacket over it and wear the same shoes. Personally, I think they're both solid choices."

Anna narrows her eyes suspiciously, peering around Gemma's arm. "What's behind the dress?"

"Oh, this?" Gemma says with mock innocence, pulling out something black and lacy. "In case you were feeling frisky, I've also got this lace bodysuit and mini school skirt. You know, just throwing it out there. Could be a fun backup plan." She shrugs.

"I'm not wearing lingerie to coffee with my ex-fiancé after sleeping with his brother," I deadpan.

"*Slag*," Anna says, coughing into her hand.

My mouth drops open, and I place a hand over my heart, feigning offense. "How *dare* you!" I say dramatically, but we all burst out laughing. I cut in with a mischievous grin. "Lucas was an ass guy. I think I'll go with the dress and denim jacket . . . Anna, what do you think?"

She smirks, already knowing where I'm going with this. "Hell yeah, flaunt that ass and remind him exactly what he's lost."

Chapter 31

April

It's not until I round the corner to the café that my stomach stirs, but I raise my chin and tell the pesky nerves to fuck right off. I can do this.

I opted for the skintight black midi dress and my white trainers. I've folded a cropped denim jacket over my arm, just in case. The sun is shining, so I want to take advantage of the warmth and show off as much of my figure as I can. My hair is curled into relaxed beach waves, which bounce lightly against my ribs with every step, and I've slathered my skin in cocoa and shea butter lotion. I smell fantastic.

My makeup is simple but pretty. I've dusted soft pink blush across my cheeks for a hint of color and added a thin coat of mascara to make my blue eyes pop. A pink glossy lip ties it all together. I feel *really* good about how I look.

The bell above the door chimes as I step inside, and the usual barista glances up, doing a double take before flashing me a wide, beaming smile. "Hi," he says, his eyes sweeping me from head to toe, appreciatively. "You look great, April!"

He's handsome, but in a more understated way.

I blush under his gaze, feeling a bit self-conscious. "Hi," I manage, giving a small wave.

I scan the room, my stomach flipping when I find Lucas. The moment he sees me, he swallows hard, his jaw clenching as he adjusts the lapels of his jacket before standing to greet me. Instead of giving him a hug, I drop into the chair opposite his.

He's clearly made an effort. I smell his usual Ted Baker cologne—citrus and black pepper. His cropped chestnut hair is tousled perfectly with just the right amount of product. He's dressed in a simple yellow T-shirt under a casual gray jacket, which he's paired with blue jeans and beige trainers. As always, he looks neat, polished, and completely put together. The total opposite of his brother.

He's so proper, it almost seems staged. But instead of nerves and nostalgia, there's a strange sense of distance, like I'm looking at someone I used to know rather than the man who was once my home.

Maybe Anna was right—there's nothing remarkable about him at all. It's almost as if the shine and magic I once saw in him were never his; they'd always come from me. From the hope that we could build something spectacular together.

But after spending time with James, being here with Lucas now feels so ... wrong. So lacking. There's nothing staged about James—no calculated effort to impress or mold himself into some perfect image. James is unfiltered. There's something about him, something honest and unpretentious, and it's there for everyone to see.

Maybe, deep down, it's always been about finding something we've been searching for within ourselves. James has it, and for the first time, I think I've finally found it too.

Lucas rolls his shoulders and clears his throat at my dismissal, taking a seat. "April," he says softly, his voice as smooth as ever, "thank you for meeting me."

I offer a forced smile. "Sure."

A heavy silence settles between us, and I blink, waiting for him to say something, anything. I'm unsure whether he expects me to start the conversation, so I just dive in. "You asked to see me," I say, keeping my tone flat.

"Yes, I did," he replies, resting his hands on the table. "Honestly, I didn't know if you'd even respond, so I'm glad you came."

"How are you?" I ask, forcing kindness into my voice.

"I'm well, a little overwhelmed with work, so naturally I feel a bit withdrawn, but I'm good. How are you?" he asks.

"I'm good. Basil is good. Still shitting on the floor, but that's Basil," I say, shrugging.

He smiles at the mention of the cat. He always loved him. "I'm glad you're both well. I'm happy you have him," he says.

"Me too."

"How's work?" he asks.

I hate this, I've never been great at playing the surface game. I wish he'd get to the point.

"Works been fine, just the same. I've taken up ceramics again. I heard you were back with your parents in Toton?"

He nods. "I was there for a few weeks after we split, yes. But I found myself a flat in Battersea a couple of months ago. That's wonderful to hear about your ceramics. I've managed to run some small study groups at the university, which I've been enjoying."

Ah. That explains why I saw him at the Mayfair Lounge.

"That's great, Lucas," I say, annoyed. This conversation feels like wasted air, so I cut to the chase. "What did you want to talk to me about?" My voice comes out sharper than I intended.

He looks momentarily taken aback but quickly recovers. "Look, April, I know things didn't end well between us. But you're still one of the kindest, funniest, most soulful, and sympathetic people I've ever had in my life. Not to mention, the most beautiful. You were the best thing that ever happened to me—a diamond among the rubbish." He reaches out, resting his hand over mine. "A beautiful blood-red diamond," he adds softly.

Has Hell frozen over? Did I hear him correctly?

This isn't at all what I was expecting. I blink. "I don't understand what you're trying to say," I reply, confused.

"I made a mistake," he says, his eyes softening in a way I can only describe as pleading.

A mistake.

I whisper his words, weighing them up as I speak them aloud.

A mistake?

Is he serious?

Suddenly, a wave of fire rips through me, but I temper the anger to keep my composure.

"A mistake? It didn't seem like a mistake when you were messaging those women for months. When you blocked and ghosted me. When you acted like we never even happened," I snap.

He rubs his thumb over my knuckles, but I pull my hand away, watching the expression on his face drop. "I messaged other people occasionally, but it was just light-hearted—mostly meaningless, not even flirty all the time. I couldn't get this intense"—he gestures between us with his other hand—"with anyone else, because they didn't mean anything."

"Really?" I raise an eyebrow, sarcastically, but he barrels on, totally oblivious.

"April, I could never have what we had with anyone else. We shared so much, and yeah, parts of that I've shared with others—like the occasional picture or chat about...steamy stuff. But you're the only person I've ever been with who I could consider... *more*. It was casual with the others when it happened, which wasn't all that often." He pauses for effect. "You're the only one who has my heart."

I honestly don't even know how to respond to that. It's strange—hearing him spout his usual charm doesn't affect me anymore. It's quite the opposite. This is his pattern, what he's always done. He did it with me, with those women online, and probably countless others. I'm starting to see it for what it really is—manipulation to get what he wants.

"Get to the point, Lucas. What do you want?" I ask, my patience thinning.

"I want you back, if you'll have me."

I clench my fists under the table, grounding myself. I try to tame the myriad of thoughts whirling in my mind before speaking.

"Lucas, what you did was disgusting. It was deceitful, disloyal, and it destroyed my trust in you. Not to mention fucking weird behavior for a thirty-four-year-old man. You lied to me. You had my whole heart, and you shattered it." My voice gains strength as the anger rises. "You don't get to just waltz back into my life and expect everything to return to the way it was. I haven't heard from you in *months*. You blocked me, dated other people—you *moved on*. And now, so have I."

His face hardens as he sits up straighter. "Wait, you've moved on? You've met someone?"

I can feel the shift in his demeanor, but I don't back down. "This isn't about that, Lucas. This is about you thinking you can just turn up when it suits you. Life doesn't work like that."

I watch his shoulders sag as my words sink in.

It's tragic, really. After all the heartbreak he put me through, he's only just now realized what he's lost. But it's far too late. The hurt in his eyes is unmistakable.

But I won't sway.

Not this time.

All I can think of is James.

He's the one who saw my broken pieces and helped me put them back together. He saw me slipping under and dove into the depths to help me. I replay the look on his face when I told him what we did was a mistake, and my stomach sours.

He's the one I want. The one I care about.

I sit up straight, take a deep breath, and after a long pause, reach over and take Lucas's hand in mine. His skin feels familiar, but foreign, like I'm touching a memory rather than a person. I meet his gaze—those dark obsidian eyes that once held every promise I ever dreamed of. But they're just blank now. Windows to a place I no longer belong. I've already moved toward James. Lucas may have realized he still wants me, but James makes me feel like I deserve to be wanted.

"Lucas, you were everything to me. I'll always be grateful for the time we shared. You became my family when I had no one else. We built a beautiful life together, and I'm so thankful that I met you. We supported each other and brought joy into each other's lives. You were my safe place, the one I cherished and looked forward to coming home to every evening..." I trail off.

"But you don't want to try again," he says, nodding in understanding. "I feel so incredibly awful for how I treated you, for what I did. Hurting you was the last thing I ever wanted. You're so positive, and I think so highly of you. I hate the idea that I ended up having the opposite effect on you. It's been on my mind every day."

I shrug, offering him a small smile of my own. He continues, "I want you to know that nobody else has come along, and I don't think anybody could."

I close my eyes, his words slicing through me more sharply than I expected. If no one else could ever come along, then why did he do it? What was the point of it all? What was I missing?

And then it finally clicks—no amount of questioning will ever bring me the answers I was once searching for. I could spend the rest of my life trying to untangle the web of his choices, trying to make sense of why he threw us away, but the truth is, I'll never understand. It doesn't matter anymore. Because the fact is, he wanted other women. He's a liar. It's that simple. It doesn't need to be deeper or more complicated. I've learned to accept that some things are just that—messy, senseless, and hurtful. And even if I could understand, it wouldn't change the past.

It wouldn't undo the pain, wouldn't rewrite the nights I cried myself to sleep, or erase the self-doubt I've carried since.

Understanding won't change the fact that he made a choice, and I was left to deal with the fallout. I can't change what happened, but I can choose how I respond. Moving on doesn't require forgiveness or forgetting—I can move on without either of those things. But at least now, he sees the damage. At least now, he's sorry. And maybe, just maybe, that's enough to give me some peace.

I squeeze his hand gently, and he goes on. "I've always had this feeling . . . that we walked into each other's lives at exactly the right moment, when we both needed someone to remind us we were worth something."

I smile softly. "Yeah," I say, nodding. "I like the sound of that."

I look at him before leaving. *Really* look at him. For someone who exudes such confidence, I can't help but wonder how lost he must feel inside. It must be a constant battle, fighting the need for external validation. I almost feel sorry for him.

I truly hope he finds what he's looking for. But it's not my place to see that it happens.

As I step out of the café, another truth settles in.

This isn't over—not yet.

No matter how relieved I am to put the betrayal behind me, it's only a matter of time before he finds out about James and me.

And when that happens, everything could fall apart.

Chapter 32

James

I haven't heard from April. I've just returned home from practice with the lads, and it's late. I played like shit. My mind is all over the place, and the guys noticed. Tom was obviously pissed at me, and I can't blame him. I was missing notes and out of rhythm, so it fucked up his timing with vocals. Oliver shot me a few knowing glances, which pierced straight through me. I haven't told Will and Tom about April and me, because frankly, I don't want to. We're getting too close to the audition, and the last thing I want to do is encumber them with worries about my personal life. Not until I know where April and I stand.

Every part of me aches. My stomach growls, and all I crave is a hot shower to wash away the exhaustion. I stride to the bathroom. Dark circles hang under my eyes, and my hair is a mess. I look as wrecked as I feel.

I step under the spray, tipping my head back to let the hot water pound against my skin. I close my eyes, but no matter how hard I try to shut my thoughts out, she's there—her face, her laugh, her voice, haunting me. Her absence makes me feel sick, the kind of sick that no amount of distraction can shake.

Is she thinking about *him?*

Does she regret what we did? Or worse—is she even thinking about me at all?

This is exactly the kind of distraction I didn't want.

It's why I buried my feelings and pushed my desires to the side.

If one night with her affects me this much, what happens if we're on tour next year?

I shut off the tap and feel uncomfortable with the sudden silence. I can't stay here trapped with my own thoughts for another second. I need to get this off my mind—I need to see her. Stepping out, I towel off quickly, my skin still semi-damp as I pull on a pair of joggers. The fabric clings to me, and I shove my feet into trainers, tugging on a band T-shirt. I grab my gray beanie, its worn, floppy edges covering my ears as I pull it down snug over my wet hair.

The not-knowing claws at me like an itch I can't reach. Oliver's words repeat in my mind.

Then do what Lucas didn't—chase her.

I shake off the exhaustion and force my limbs into motion. Snatching my keys from the counter, I shove them into my pocket and head out. I can't be fucked navigating London traffic or the stifling Underground, so I wave down a black cab, sliding into the back seat. My heart pounds in my chest, and all I can think is that I need to get to April.

Right fucking now.

Chapter 33

April

Basil hops up beside me on the bed, headbutting my face as I bury it into the pillows. His soft fur brushes against my cheek and I give him a scratch underneath his chin. He leans into me and I kiss his chubby little cheeks.

I release a long sigh. Thinking back to the woman I was months ago, I can't help but mourn the version of myself I used to be. That woman was so broken. If only I could go back and tell her everything would be okay—that things would get better, that she would heal and move on. That there's a light at the end of the tunnel.

Sometimes life steers you in a new direction, but it's better to view it as an opportunity to step onto a different path.

And I like where this one has led me.

Seeing Lucas again today stirred something completely unexpected: pride. I'm proud that I made it through such a dark, uncertain time, when the future felt overwhelming and intimidating. Proud that I faced it head-on and kept going. And above all, I'm grateful—for the incredible friends who stood by me, who never gave up on me, and who nurtured my light when I couldn't see it myself.

I roll over and stretch my arms out. I close my eyes for a moment, processing everything that's happened over the last couple of days.

I feel like I've broken through the water's surface and I can breathe again.

I peel myself off the bed and traipse to the kitchen drawer to grab a lighter. One by one, I light the scented candles dotting various surfaces, casting the room in a soft, ambient glow as the flickering flames dance across the walls. The warm, comforting scents of vanilla, chai, tobacco, and caramel weave through the air, wrapping around me in a warm hug.

Then, I turn to the photographs still sitting on the hall table, their frames holding snapshots of a life I'm finally ready to leave in the past. Memories of a person who once was but isn't anymore. One by one, I slide the pictures free, leaving the frames empty. I stack the photos in a pile before plucking his worn work satchel and old red scarf off the coat stand, exactly where he left them. With my arms full, I head outside to the wheelie bin, toss them in, and shut the lid.

Finally, once inside, I grab the last of his books from the entertainment unit and stack them by the front door, ready to donate to a charity shop.

I feel nothing.

They're nothing.

For the longest time, I thought getting rid of these things would mean losing a part of myself, like tearing out the final chapter of a story I believed shaped me. But as I stand here now, throwing away the remnants of a life that no longer fits, I realize it's not the end of my story. Not anymore.

It's just the beginning of something new.

Something exciting.

James.

I draw the blinds, shutting out the rest of the world. I trudge upstairs to my bathroom, pausing briefly to run my fingers through my hair. Anna's handiwork is flawless. I love the curls, so I make the executive decision to gather them into a silk scrunchie on top of my head, preserving the style and skipping the shampoo.

I freshen up and release my waves, watching them bounce perfectly back into place. I change into a pair of fluffy bed socks, tartan pajama pants, and a plain top. Basil scampers after me downstairs, the sound of his little paws quick on the steps. I almost drool when I reach the lounge, encased with all the glorious scents.

I'm poking through the pantry in search of crisps when my phone pings. I spin and I grab it off the counter, glancing at the messages.

Gemma: *Well? How did it go?*

Anna: *Are you okay?*

I smile widely upon seeing their names and quickly type a reply: *Surprisingly well. I feel so much better. I'll tell you guys about it when I see you this week. I'm wrecked. Thanks so much for last night. Love you both xx*

Setting my phone back on the counter, I pluck my crisps from the cupboard and tear the packet open. I'm tits-deep in a new TV series when the doorbell rings. Reluctantly, I toss my crisp packet aside and, with a groan, I stand to open the door.

"Swear to God, if this is some Jehovah's Witness bullshit..." I mutter under my breath as I shuffle toward the front door. I swing it open and freeze.

James swallows, shifting on his feet, raising a hand to rub the back of his neck. *Fuck*, he looks so good my ovaries almost explode.

He's in plain black joggers that cling to his thick thighs, his top stretching across his broad chest. And—Jesus Christ—a beanie.

A fucking beanie.

If there's one thing in the world that could bring me to my knees, it's a man in a beanie. His sandy waves peek out from underneath, just enough to make me weak.

Tears well in my eyes before I can stop them as shame barrels through me, reminding me of my behavior from yesterday morning.

"James," I say, my voice desperate. He lifts a hand to my cheek, brushing his thumb back and forth in a soothing motion. The warmth of his touch makes my breath catch.

"Hey, sweetheart," he says, a small smile tugging at the corner of his lips, his left dimple deepening.

"I'm so sorry . . ." My voice cracks.

He cradles my head in his hands. "Hey, hey . . ." He bends so we're eye-to-eye. "You have nothing to be sorry for," he whispers, leaning in to rest his forehead against mine. He kisses the tip of my nose, and butterflies erupt wildly in my stomach.

"Is it okay that I'm here?" he asks gently, and I nod.

"Good," he says. "Because it would have been extremely humiliating if you rejected me," he adds with a smirk.

I close my eyes with a chuckle, stepping aside to let him in. He slips past me, and even with the candles burning, I catch the scent of him drifting through the room.

I follow him to the sofa and plop down, crossing my legs underneath me. James casually throws his arm over the back of the sofa as he sinks into the cushions. Basil jumps up, nuzzling against James's arm. James gives him a gentle pat, a smile ghosting over his lips as Basil purrs madly.

He turns his gaze to me, his expression tender. "I'm sorry I didn't call or text yesterday or this morning. I thought you might have wanted some space."

This thoughtful, beautiful man.

"It wasn't a mistake," I whisper, leaning in to place my hand gently on his thigh.

I need him to understand. His gaze falls to where my fingers rest, and I can't resist the urge to study him. The dancing candlelight contrasts the sharp angle of his jaw, his plump, kissable mouth, and the shadow of stubble on his face.

His green eyes connect with mine, covering my hand with his own.

"I know you didn't mean to hurt me."

He's so kind, which is far more than I deserve after what I said.

I need to tell him why I freaked out, why I pushed him away. I need to tell him about Lucas's message, and that I'm ready to move on. With him. He deserves to know everything. "I have a lot to say, if that's all right?" I ask.

"Of course," he says, gesturing between us. "This only works if we communicate."

And he's right. I nod in agreement before continuing.

"Lucas messaged me," I say, watching as James's brows crease. His expression shifts and I rush to ease whatever worry might be stirring.

"Yesterday morning, before you got home. I woke up to a text from him."

His nostrils flare. "What did he say?"

"He said he wanted to talk."

James glances away, his lips pressing into a thin line before he turns back to me. "Did you talk to him? Is that why you left?" he asks, his tone worried.

"I did talk to him, yes." I squeeze his hand. "But I didn't talk to him before I left." I let out a frustrated sigh, trying to find the right words. "However, I did meet with him this morning."

His jaw tenses, and I rush to clarify. "It's not what you think. I promise. Nothing happened. We met for a coffee." I pause, taking a deep breath before revealing the next part. "He wanted to get back together. He said he made a mistake and that he wanted to try again."

"I see," he says, dropping his gaze.

"I don't want him back, James ... I want *you*," I tell him. His eyes dart to mine.

"We had the most amazing night together." I thread my fingers through his. "Truly, I've never enjoyed or *wanted* something more." He gives me a reluctant smile, and his eyes fill with a mix of hope and hurt. "I freaked out because I opened the message, and I panicked. I didn't know what he wanted, and it caught me off guard. Then you came back with breakfast from my favorite café, which was so thoughtful. It made me realize how much I care about you. But I felt guilty. I kept thinking, 'Does this make me no better than Lucas? Sleeping with you, his brother ... am I a terrible person?'" His expression softens as he processes my words, and I continue. "I was thinking about Lucas's feelings when I should've been thinking about yours—about *us*. I don't want to hurt anyone, least of all you."

He gently cups my face, kissing each cheek. His fingers weave through my hair, cradling the back of my head and drawing me closer. His touch sends my heart into a wild dance.

"I understand," he says. "It's natural to worry. We're not in an easy situation. But, April," he says, his eyes searching mine, "you're not alone in this. I'm right here with you. I'm sorry I didn't give you what you needed when you asked me what spending the night together meant for us. It meant everything. When I said there's something between us, I meant it. We're not imagining this. It's real, and I want to explore that with you. I think we deserve to explore it, don't you?"

"Yes," I whisper.

"Okay, that's good," he says. "While we're laying everything on the line... There is something else that we need to talk about..."

"What is it?"

"I need to know that you're okay with this... with us," he says, rubbing my hand with his own. "Even if Atlas Veil ends up touring next year. It's not a quick thing, April—it'd be seven months that I'm gone. I just—I need you to be sure."

My brow furrows. "Are you asking if I can handle it? Or are you asking whether I'll wait for you?"

"Both," he replies. "I don't want to drag you into something that might ruin what we have. I want to land that tour. But I also want you. Seven months is a long time, and I can't ask you to put your life on hold for me. But at the same time, I'm selfish enough to want you to."

So am I. It hadn't even crossed my mind to frame his potential tour as a reason to question whether we should let ourselves enjoy this, to see where it goes. I want him to win this audition—I want the world to see the man in front of me. And if this does continue, then seven months isn't that long in the scheme of things. If he's brave enough to face his brother for us, then the least I can do is stand by him through this.

I tilt my head. "James, if you think touring is going to scare me off, you don't know me as well as you think you do."

"It'll be hard. The distance, the schedules. It's not just about missing each other—it's about wondering if this thing we're building can survive that kind of pressure."

I kiss his hand. "I'm not saying it won't be hard. But what's the alternative? Walking away now, before we've even tried? I'm not willing to do that. Not now. Are you?"

He shakes his head. "No. God, no. But I also don't want you to feel like you have to—"

"Stop," I interrupt. "You don't get to decide what I can or can't handle. I'm in this, James. And I'm willing to try, if you are."

He pulls me closer, resting his forehead against mine. "I am. I'm all in, April. I just . . . I needed to hear it from you."

"I'm all in."

"Good," he says, dissolving the space between us.

Chapter 34

April

My mouth brushes against his, the touch feather-light at first. When I part my lips, our breaths mingle, and he sweeps his tongue against mine. His movements remain slow but fervent. Compared to our first kiss, this isn't rushed. We take our time to savor it, like we're exploring each other in an entirely new way.

His other hand slides to my waist, anchoring me closer, and I melt into him. As the kiss deepens, my mind quiets. There's only James—his taste, his touch—and the overwhelming realization that this is more than I ever expected.

I reach up and slowly pull off his beanie, letting it fall to the floor as my fingers weave through his damp hair. He groans against my lips, and a surge of heat spirals down to my core.

I lower my hands to the hem of his top, gripping the fabric and tugging it up over his head. He helps me by threading his arms out and discarding it. My pupils dilate as I take in the expanse of his chest, the way his muscles shift beneath his skin. My eyes catch on his cock, straining against his joggers. My teeth graze my lower lip, and I reach for the elastic. His hands quickly join mine to strip them off.

I sit back once he's naked. He looks different in the candlelight. Ethereal, like Adonis. Slowly, almost lazily, I run my hands down his veiny, tattooed arms, charting the inky lines that bend and twirl with my fingertips, as if I'm committing every inch of him to memory.

"April," he growls, licking his lips as he grips my hips firmly, fingering the waistband of my pajama bottoms. I lift my hips to give him better access. Slowly, almost agonizingly, he unties the knot and begins peeling my pajamas down my legs.

I don't waste time, lifting my shirt over my head and tossing it onto the floor beside his. The air hits my exposed skin, causing it to pebble, and my nipples harden in response. He pauses, nostrils flaring as his gaze rakes over me.

I lie down, slowly parting my legs for him. His eyes lock on mine for a moment before they trail down my body, lingering on the sight of my naked, glistening sex. A low, animalistic groan escapes him.

He leans over me, bracing his hands on either side of my head as he settles between my thighs. He kisses me, and I give it all back to him. I feel his hard cock pressing against my stomach, and I reach between us to grip him.

He bites and tugs at my lip as I smear his precum over his crown.

"Fuck, sweetheart, your hand feels so good wrapped around my cock."

I turn liquid.

I pump him slowly, relishing the feel of him as he pulses in my hand, knowing exactly what he wants but making him wait for it.

He ducks his head, his lips brushing my ear as his hips begin to move in sync with my hand, the pace between us quickening. "I want you so fucking bad, April," he growls. "I want to come all over those perfect tits, then flip you over and fuck you from behind. I'll bury my cock deep in your sweet cunt while I finger fuck your ass."

His words are feral, my body writhing beneath him. I'm growing wetter with every second. My arm begins to tire, but I don't stop.

"I want you to come," I say.

He groans in response, the sound sharp and rough. "Yeah? You want me to come on your tits? Or do you want me to come all over that sweet pussy and lick it off?"

Jesus-fucking-Christ. His dirty talk was good two nights ago, but tonight—it's on another level. And I'm not mad about it. Not even a little.

"I want you to come on my pussy," I say. "I need your cum on me, James."

His mouth drops open in a silent moan, and I feel him tense before he spills, rubbing his hard cock over my pussy as he comes, coating me in warmth.

He captures my mouth in a possessive kiss, lowering his body so we press together.

"I need you, James."

"Yeah?" he rasps. I nod eagerly. "Tell me what you need." His eyes darken.

"I need your mouth on me."

"Where, sweetheart? Where do you need my mouth?"

"On my pussy."

"Good girl."

Fuck. Me.

He slides down my body, worshipping me. His lips and hands explore every inch, touching and kissing my skin like

250

it's sacred. When he reaches my lower abdomen, he places his hand over my uterus. "Here," he murmurs, his voice low, "I'm going to fill you up here."

Oh God. A rush of heat floods through me. Why is the thought of him filling me with his cum so unbearably hot?

I nod, biting my bottom lip. "Yeah," I say, breathless.

He smirks before lowering his head. My fingers thread through his hair and I'm rewarded with a long, languid lick. His tongue flattens against my center as he glides up and down. He circles my clit, brushing over it with just enough pressure to make my hips buck.

Then he devours, his tongue plunging into me. I moan, yanking at his hair. I clamp my legs over his shoulders, and his grip on my thighs tightens in response.

"More," I beg. "James, I need more."

Without warning, he slips three fingers knuckle-deep inside me, the sudden intrusion making my back arch. I gasp, and he curls his fingers, rubbing against my inner wall.

"Fuck," I cry out. His stubble scratches at my skin, and I love the idea that he'll leave me marked. He doesn't let up, his mouth still working over me as his fingers thrust inside, fucking me with steady, unyielding precision. Each curl of his fingers sends shockwaves through my body.

I release his hair and grip the sofa cushions as the tension coils tighter in my core. I throw my head back as he drives me higher.

"James, ohgodohgodohgod!"

"Eyes on me, April," he says. "Look at me when you come on my tongue."

I meet his gaze just as I unravel, piece by piece. A wave rushes through me, surging along every nerve.

I fall apart, turning to dust and floating away.

He slows his tongue and fingers, easing their pace.

When I finish, he gradually withdraws, placing a gentle kiss on my inner thigh. He glances up at me with a satisfied glint in his eyes and wipes the back of his hand over his mouth. Then, he brings his fingers to my lips. I lean forward and dart my tongue out before wrapping my lips around them, sucking them clean.

He crawls up my body to capture my lips. I pour everything I can't put into words into that kiss. I show him exactly how much I feel, how much I want, with each pass. "Thank you," I whisper softly.

He smiles and rubs the tip of his nose against mine, making my heart swell.

"I'm all sticky," I say, glancing down between my legs.

"Hmm." His eyes flick over me with a glint of mischief. "Guess I'll just have to take care of that, won't I?"

I smile up at him. He stands to his full height. Every inch of him is taut, golden, and defined. In one smooth motion, he scoops me into his arms, lifting me effortlessly, bridal style. Then, he turns and walks us upstairs. His muscles barely strain as he holds me, as if I'm not five foot nine; I weigh nothing in his arms. I love seeing this playful side of him. The thought of being the person he reveals this part of himself to makes me feel so incredibly lucky.

When we reach the bathroom, he sets me down carefully, making sure I'm steady on my feet. He opens the shower door, turning on the tap. Whirling back to me, he effortlessly lifts me onto the vanity and positions himself between my legs. His strong arms cage me, setting his hands flat on either side of me against the countertop.

"You're too good to be true," he says, his voice full of sincerity. My cheeks flush, and I duck my head. But he gently tips my chin up, bending down until we're eye-to-eye.

"I feel the same way about you," I whisper.

"Let's get you cleaned up," he says, lifting me off the counter.

"I have legs, you know," I tease, but he smirks, testing the water with his foot before carrying me into the shower.

"You have no idea how many times I've thought about you in the shower," he says.

"Yeah?"

"Yeah."

His gaze darkens as he presses me against the tile wall. He's hard and ready as he rubs his cock through my folds, lubricating himself and teasing me.

"What did you think about?" I ask.

"You, spread out like this." His hands dip down to the tops of my thighs, where he runs his fingertips tentatively over my skin. "Your body wet, pressed up against me. The way you'd feel . . . the way you'd sound when I finally take you."

"How did I sound?" I ask, breathless.

He responds with a low grunt, lifting one of my legs and hooking it over his forearm. I pull myself up to stand on tiptoes as he holds me. His cock nudges against my entrance. My breath catches as I watch him slide in, inch by delicious inch, filling me completely. A shudder runs through both of us, and the way he looks at me—hungry, possessive—makes my heart gallop. I release a long, keening whimper.

"You sounded just like that," he says, pumping into me. The sound of skin slapping fills the bathroom. I can't hold back my moans as he fucks me at a brutal pace. My body is a live wire, and each thrust sends waves of electricity rippling through me. His eyes latch onto my tits, watching them bounce with every thrust. He shifts, kicking a leg up beneath my thigh to support my weight, angling himself even deeper inside me. His now free hand snakes between us, finding my clit, rubbing it in slow, deliberate circles.

"I fucking love your cunt."

"*James,*" I gasp, raking my fingernails down his biceps.

"Are you gonna let me come in this pussy?"

I can feel him getting closer, his movements more urgent, and I'm right there with him, teetering on the edge.

"Yes. I want you to give me all of it. Fill me up."

A harsh moan escapes him as he hastens his movements, driving into me harder.

"Fuck, April."

"I'm so close."

"Come with me."

With one final, deep thrust, I feel him pulse, unloading inside me. The feeling undoes me, my body shaking with the force of it.

He drops a firm kiss to my lips before slowly pulling out after we catch our breath. His cum trickles down my thigh, and he captures the stream with two fingers before sliding his hand up and pushing his fingers back inside me.

"I can't get enough of you," he breathes.

"Please stay."

He smiles against my lips. "I wouldn't dream of leaving."

Chapter 35

James

A honeyed flush of sunlight filters through the edges of the curtain. I wake to the soft, steady rhythm of April's breath, deep and peaceful in sleep. The relief when she said she'd be willing to wait if I tour next year was immediate, almost overwhelming. I felt like a selfish bastard—wanting her to say those words, because I know it isn't a small ask. On top of dealing with her emotions about us, it's a lot.

I hope I've made it clear that this isn't just some casual fling for me. And seven months . . . seven months is a long time. A lot can happen. People change. Feelings fade. The thought of being gone, of not being here to hold on to whatever it is we're building, picks away at me. And yet, when she looked at me and said she was happy to try, it felt like she offered me a lifeline. One I wasn't sure I deserved but am willing to cling to.

I press a kiss to her head and gently loosen my arms from around her. She murmurs something incoherent, shifting onto her back without waking. A smug smirk tugs at my lips as I slide down her naked body, my hands trailing lightly over her skin. When I reach her thighs, she parts them, welcoming me even in her sleep. Her pussy still glistens with evidence of last night, and my cock twitches at the sight. I part her with two fingers, watching as she opens for me.

Leaning in, I drag my tongue in a slow, hard line from her entrance to her clit, sucking gently before swirling my tongue around the sensitive nub. A soft moan escapes her lips, and her body shivers as she stirs awake. She threads her fingers into my hair, tugging at the strands with a sleepy urgency.

"James," she whispers, her voice husky as she shifts her hips, pressing herself closer to my mouth, asking me to continue, and I do.

I get to work, lapping eagerly at her center. She tastes divine as I indulge. Teasing her entrance with two fingers, I feel her body tense beneath me. When she lets out a needy whimper, I slowly slip them inside, feeling her clench around me to pull me deeper. She's tender, her body arching as I work her with my hand and tongue, coaxing her toward the edge, only to slow my movements, making her whimper. I'd do anything to draw that delicious sound from her.

"Does that feel good?"

"Uh-huh."

"More?"

She hums.

I withdraw my fingers and push the covers off us, exposing our bodies. My hands glide up her smooth calves before I lift her legs over my shoulders, settling her perfectly beneath me, like my own personal feast. At this angle, I can see every inch of her delicious pussy—pink, pretty, and swollen with her arousal.

"Look at you, sweetheart," I murmur, eyes trailing over her flushed cheeks and the rise and fall of her chest. "Look at how that tight little pussy weeps for me."

I drag my aching cock through her slickness and her hips shift back and forth, rubbing herself against me.

"Please, James," she says, her voice a whisper. "I need you inside me."

That's all the invitation I need. Lowering my head, I spit onto her pussy and start rubbing my thumb over her clit. Her head falls back, hands gripping the sheets. Lining myself up with her, I push in slowly with a low hiss. Her mouth falls open as she accommodates me. I drag myself out slowly, right to the tip, before driving back in to the hilt, reveling in the way she squeezes me, hot and tight as I start pumping.

"I want you on your hands and knees," I say.

Pulling out, I grip her hips and flip her onto all fours. With a firm hand, I press her head down into the mattress, arching her back just right, before jamming into her again.

I slide my hand down to where we're joined, running my fingers through her pussy and coating them. Then, I trail them back to her ass, spreading the moisture around her tight hole in careful preparation.

She gasps, her breath hitching. "James..."

"Do you like that?" I say, my tone low and thick.

"I've never done that before," she says, timidly.

"Do you want me to fuck this tight little hole? Do you want my cock to be the first inside your hot, perfect ass?"

She mewls and nods eagerly in response, rocking her hips back and forth as I coat her asshole. I raise one hand and bring it down with a sharp slap, watching as her flawless skin shifts from pale to a warm, flushed red. I rub the spot tenderly, feeling the heat bloom beneath my palm before striking her again, each slap drawing a needy gasp from her lips. I repeat the motion, over and over, until she's writhing beneath me, urgent and dripping, her body begging for more.

"Top drawer," she says, panting.

With my cock still buried inside her, I lean over, sliding the drawer open. A grin spreads across my face as I spot what she's referring to. I pull out the toy, inspecting it— one arm designed to fill her pussy, the other with a suction attachment for her clit.

"You want me to play with this?"

"Yes," she says on a breath.

She gasps as I suddenly pull out and flip her back over, lifting her hips to slide a pillow beneath her lower back, giving us both a deeper angle. She hooks her legs over my shoulders, and I admire the perfect view of her milky body.

We lock eyes as I push the long arm inside her hot channel. Her head falls to the side, and a shuddering moan spills from her lips as her eyes squeeze shut, lost in euphoria.

I press the button, and the toy hums to life. I keep it on the lowest setting, vibrating inside her and sucking her clit. I work it steadily, thrusting the toy in and out so it rubs against her walls. I almost blow my load watching her twist her hips, fucking the toy deeper. When I feel her relax further beneath me, I shift, positioning my cock at her tight hole and ever so slowly slip my tip inside.

"Oh God," she gasps, her breath coming in harder.

"Are you sure?" I murmur, giving her one last chance to change her mind.

"Yes. I need to feel you everywhere, James. Please. I want everything."

I nudge forward, easing myself further into her. "Relax, sweetheart. I'll be gentle, I promise."

She nods, her gaze meets mine. I watch as her body opens for me, inch by inch as I disappear further inside her. A low, keening moan slips from her lips just as a groan rumbles from my chest. "I'm in," I grunt, my voice thick with praise. "You did so well, sweetheart. Taking my cock so perfectly."

I synchronize myself with the movements of the toy while the suction teases her clit. She rocks in tandem beneath me, meeting every bit of what I give her. I watch as her stomach muscles tense, her breathing hitches, and tears gather at the corners of her eyes, overwhelmed by the intensity.

"I'm so close."

"I know, honey. Me too," I grit out, feeling her clench tighter around me.

I keep my tempo steady, driving my hips as I take her ass. A gush of wetness spills from her pussy, coating my hand, sliding past where I'm buried deep, and dripping onto the sheets as she untethers beneath me. Her voice breaks into a delicious chant. "Oh fuck, I'm coming, I'm coming, I'm coming!"

Just as she shatters beneath me, I let go, groaning deep and low. With a few final thrusts—once, twice—I unload inside her, my release surging through me in waves as I bury myself deep.

I click the toy off when she begins convulsing and extract it from her pussy. The suction lets go with a raw, slick sound as it detaches from her sopping clit. Dropping the toy beside us, I lean forward, pressing my forehead against hers as we catch our breath, our bodies still trembling from the aftershocks.

Her arms wind around my neck, drawing me in and sealing our mouths together. When she finally releases me, I pull back, eyes locked on hers as I slowly withdraw from her ass. I watch, mesmerized, as my cum leaks out of her ass, dripping down between her cheeks.

"*God,* that's a beautiful sight," I say, my voice low and thick. "Do you know how much of a turn-on it is knowing that I'm the only man who's ever taken your tight little ass?"

Her cheeks stain with color as her eyes hood.

She's fucking amazing.

Her hair fans out across the pillow like a halo, framing her beautiful face. Her creamy skin glows, tinged with the blush of her orgasm. I watch her chest rise and fall with each breath, entranced by the subtle movement of her breasts.

She's *mine.*

"You feel so perfect. You are perfect," I say, dropping down beside her. I pepper kisses over her shoulders and across her collarbone before wrapping my arms around her. I pull her tight against my chest, our bodies fitting together seamlessly.

"I had no idea sex could be like that," she says, sounding shy. "James, that was . . ."

"I know, sweetheart. I know."

I gently cup her chin, tipping her head back and capturing her mouth with mine. It's the only way I know how to communicate right now, letting her feel what words can't express—that I feel it too.

Words fall short of conveying what this moment with her means to me.

So, instead, I show her.

Chapter 36

April

We've spent every free moment together these past two weeks, alternating between each other's places. After work, we gravitate toward each other, escaping the outside world and losing ourselves in the other's arms.

I love seeing James in his usual work clothes. There's something undeniably hot and primal about the dirt and sweat that cling to him. It only gets sexier when I'm the one helping him lather up and wash the grime away.

Every night together feels brand-new—fingers and tongues tracing untouched paths, lips documenting every curve and edge of each other's bodies. I've never felt more alive. It feels like a dream—one long, happy dream where nothing exists but us.

But it's not just the sex, though that is incredible—it's the way we lie together in silent heartbeats, we talk in the quiet moments afterward, the soul-nourishing conversations, sharing things we never expected to with each other. I tell him about my parents and my childhood, and about the car accident. I share stories about how I met Anna and Gemma, and

James laughs along with me, especially at Gemma's horror dates.

In turn, he opens up about the band and how they came together. He's known Oliver for as long as I've known Anna. It's fun learning about his friends; it helps me understand him a little more. I've only ever met the guys in passing, so hearing about their music and the effort they've put into auditioning is exciting.

He tells me about his mum and the struggles she faced raising them. I can't begin to imagine how hard it must have been for James—being just a kid and wearing the responsibility of constantly checking in on her. He's a remarkable man.

He shares things Lucas never did—parts of his life I never even knew existed. Our friendship has blossomed so naturally, to the point where it feels as though we've known each other for years. There was a hole inside me, and James has managed to fill it. It's the way he pulls me closer in his sleep, like being apart isn't an option, even unconsciously. The way we laugh together over late-night wine and takeaway.

With James, everything just *is*.

He's softened my splintered edges.

We've become addicted to each other. By the weekend, our routine seems set in stone—meeting up after he finishes work, talking, exploring each other until the early hours of the morning, and waking wrapped up together.

He's been so supportive of my ceramics, always offering just the right words when my hands falter or my confidence wavers. It's the kind of assurance that makes me believe I might actually be able to approach some of the small businesses around the markets to see if they'd consider stocking my pieces. I floated the idea by Gemma and Anna, who both responded enthusiastically.

When James isn't offering his thoughts, he's playing his bass, fingers gliding over the strings as I shape my clay. Words aren't even necessary. We simply just exist, lost in the beauty of our own creations, together.

But there's this persistent voice in the back of my mind reminding me that we can't stay hidden forever. What we're doing isn't just fleeting: It's growing and taking shape into something deeper and more substantial. Though we agreed that we wouldn't rush into anything, we both know that eventually Lucas will find out about what we're doing. And when he does, I can't shake the fear that it'll be like setting off a bomb.

What will happen when our bubble bursts?

When the safety of this little world we've created together is ripped away?

I glance over at James as he sleeps beside me. I care about this man so much, it makes my chest ache. He doesn't seem to feel the ticking clock like I do, or maybe he just does a better job at ignoring it. I wish I could do the same, but I know the fallout is inevitable, and I can't stop wondering whether we'll survive it. I trust James implicitly, but will the beauty of what we have between us break under the pressure?

I want to believe that we can make it through, that we're strong enough to face whatever comes. It feels like we're bound by the same thread, something unbreakable. No matter the distance, time, or directions our lives took, it feels like life was always meant to lead us to each other.

It feels real.

It's worth the risk.

* * *

The soft patter of water fills the room as James steps into my en suite shower, and I can't stop the smile spreading across my face. I'm floating on cloud nine.

It's early Sunday morning, and we woke the way we usually do. Well, usually, I'm rolled onto my back, and James slides inside me. This morning, however, I took control, pushing him onto his back and sinking down onto his hard, rigid length.

I moved over him, slow and steady until we couldn't last any longer, his release spurting deep inside me. Afterward, James insisted on cleaning me up. He ran a cloth under warm water before returning to my side and gently wiping me down. His touch was tender, and between the soft strokes, he pressed gentle kisses on my lips, my forehead, and my temples.

Grabbing the robe from the back of my door, I slip it on and wrap it snuggly around myself, pulling the belt tight at my waist. I let him shower in peace, though it's hard to resist the urge to join him, and I head downstairs.

I make a beeline for the coffee machine. Grabbing two of my own handmade mugs from the cupboard and my beloved coffee pods, I fetch the milk from the fridge. I pour the milk into the frother, the quiet thrum filling the kitchen as the milk spins and thickens into a creamy foam. I watch as the rich, dark liquid flows, infusing the air with my favorite scent. I take a deep breath in, inhaling the rich aroma, and close my eyes. I lean back against the counter. My mind is still, and my heart is steady. This is peace and happiness.

We haven't discussed our plans for the rest of the day, but I'm happy to play it by ear. I'd love for James to stay, but I'd understand if he needs to head out—his audition is coming up fast, and I know how much every moment counts.

Over the past few months, I've noticed a real shift in the way the band plays compared to when I first heard them. I'd like to think I might have contributed to James's passion onstage, but I know I can't take all the credit. Watching the guys perform, they've become a single, cohesive unit—completely in sync and feeding off one another's energy. Their chemistry as a band is undeniable, and it's electric to witness.

There's something incredibly sexy about a man with drive. In the mornings, he softly taps his fingers on the countertops, thumping his foot in sync with the rhythm. I can almost hear the melody running through his head as he moves.

As much as the idea of not seeing him for months will be difficult, I know how amazing this opportunity would be for him. It could be career-defining—opening doors to endless possibilities and finally giving the band the recognition they've worked so hard for. And who knows? They might even score a record deal. If anyone deserves it, it's James. A swell of emotion and pride rises in my chest at the thought of it, and I can't help but buzz with excitement.

I'm pouring the last of the frothed milk into the second mug when a knock sounds at the door. My brows crease in confusion; I wasn't expecting anyone.

Maybe it's a delivery.

Wiping my hands over the front of my robe, I walk to the door and swing it open. The moment I see who's standing there, a cold paralysis takes over, leaving my body heavy as stone.

Lucas.

"Hey," he says.

I blink, caught off guard, before my gaze drops to his hand. He's holding a bouquet of white roses.

"Hey . . . ," I say.

"These are for you," he says, extending the flowers toward me. Confused, I reach out and take them. He gives me a small, hopeful smile.

"May I come in?"

I exhale, gripping the bouquet a little tighter. "What are you doing here?"

"I wanted to see you. I thought perhaps we could talk . . . and, well, maybe I could see Basil," he says, his voice trailing off.

"I would have appreciated a call or text," I lower the bouquet. "Look, Lucas, I don't—"

"I know I fucked up. The thought that I hurt you— it's been eating at me every single day. I'd do anything for another chance. Please." His voice cracks and his eyes shimmer with hope. The hurt in his voice stings. I haven't thought about him at all since I last saw him. I've been so wrapped up in James, literally and figuratively—the two of us like a pair of horny teenagers.

I knew our paths were bound to cross at some point, but I certainly wasn't ready now.

Not like this.

"Please," he whispers, "can I come in?"

"Now really isn't a good time."

I hear James behind me and startle as his footsteps thud heavily on the staircase.

Fuck.

"Is someone here?" His expression drops and his voice turns serious as he looks over my shoulder.

"Lucas, it's—"

"Lucas?" James's voice interrupts us, and I squeeze my eyes shut, wishing, just for a moment, that this was all some twisted dream. When I turn around, James's focus falls to the bouquet in my hands. His expression shifts and the color drains from his face as his eyes flick between me and Lucas. His jaw twitches.

He stands with only a towel slung low around his hips, his chest bare and glistening, the sharp V of his hips leading to places I know far too well. The fact that his skin and hair are still damp from the shower makes it painfully obvious he didn't just drop by for tea.

"I didn't know he was coming," I say.

James's eyes narrow as they lock on Lucas, and I can feel the tension rolling off him in waves.

"What the fuck is he doing here?" Lucas asks. I watch helplessly as Lucas's gaze sweeps over James—from the damp strands of his hair down to his bare feet.

This doesn't look good.

"Are you two shagging?"

Silence.

Lucas steps over the threshold, and I instinctively retreat, caught off guard.

"I said," Lucas seethes through gritted teeth, "Are. You. Fucking. Her?"

"Yes," I whisper in response, the word slipping out before I can stop it.

"April—" James moves toward me.

"No, James, it's fine." I lift my hand to stop him. I turn back to Lucas, squaring my shoulders to feign a confidence I absolutely do not have. "We've been seeing each other. And before you ask again—yes, we are sleeping together."

Lucas's face twists in disbelief, as if the words physically wound him. "You . . . with *him*? He's my *brother*. How could you do this?"

The look he shoots me feels like a bullet, and I swallow the lump rising in my throat, forcing the tears to stay at bay. "Me? Are you serious? How could *I* do this? We were *engaged*." I emphasize my words. "You hurt me in ways I can't even explain. You *broke* me." My voice cracks. "And James was . . . It just happened. You *told* me you couldn't return the depths of my affections."

Lucas's nostrils flare. "I made mistakes, April, but I *never* stopped loving you. I was wrong." His voice strains. "We could've fixed this. I wanted to fix this . . . We could've had everything."

James shifts, subtly positioning himself between us. "You need to leave, Lucas." His voice is steady and cold. Protective.

Lucas's eyes flick to James. "Of course *you'd* swoop in, wouldn't you?"

"Oh, you are so full of shit and you know it," James says. His hand grazes mine, a faint reminder that he's right here with me.

"So, what's this about then, James? Payback? You wanted revenge, so you decided to fuck my *fiancée*?"

"*Ex*-fiancée."

My eyes flick between them, because I have absolutely no idea what Lucas means.

"Payback?" I ask, completely lost.

James's jaw tightens, the muscle in his cheek twitching. His eyes bore holes into Lucas's. "Stop it, Lucas," he warns, his voice full of venom.

But Lucas doesn't stop. He steps closer, invading James's space, their faces just inches apart.

"Oh no, I think I'll continue. You couldn't handle the fact that your girlfriend wanted *me*."

"What?" My voice trembles as I turn to James. "What is he talking about?"

James's jaw ticks and his expression darkens.

"James," I whisper, placing a hand over his heart, feeling it hammer beneath my palm.

He swallows hard, avoiding my gaze. "Remember when I told you Abigail cheated on me with her colleague, Matt?" he says.

Oh God. I think I know where this is going. My stomach plummets.

"Yes," I answer, already dreading what's coming next.

"It wasn't Matt," he says, his voice stripped of emotion. "It was Lucas."

"What do you mean?"

"Lucas fucked Abigail." James's voice is razor sharp. "He was shagging her the *entire time.*"

I bring a hand to my mouth, completely stunned.

Lucas stands firm, but his charming and polite facade cracks, revealing a truth I'm now awake enough to see. I barely recognize him. My heart shatters for James, breaking apart at the reality that Lucas ruined his future too.

And it all makes sense.

Tears pool in my eyes as I glance between them, disbelief and hurt burning through me. "How could you do that to him, Lucas? How could you hurt your own brother like that?"

Lucas's gaze drops, and I swear I see shame flickering across his face for the briefest second, before his jaw tightens again, a steel wall sliding back into place. "It was a mistake. I tried to end it with her, but she wouldn't have it," he mutters defensively.

"Really? Is that why *your* messages were popping up on her phone?" James says.

Lucas scoffs. "Believe what you want."

"Lucas, I really think you should leave. Please," I say, my voice shaky.

Lucas frowns. James steps closer to me, his hand curling protectively around my waist. "It's okay, sweetheart," he murmurs, brushing his thumb over my hip. He looks at Lucas. "Get out."

Lucas's eyes dart to me, then the hand holding the bouquet one last time. He looks regretful and resentful, but I don't flinch. I won't dare give him the satisfaction.

"I really did love you," he says quietly, as if those words could somehow undo the damage. With a final, vicious glance at James, he storms out, shutting the door behind him with a loud crack. The silence that follows feels suffocating. I stand there, totally stunned.

James steps closer, his hand rubbing slow, soothing circles on my back. "Are you okay?" he asks.

I nod, though the tears still burn at the edges of my eyes. "Me? Are *you* okay?"

He presses a kiss to my temple. "I've got you," he says against my ear. "As long as I have you, I'm good. And I'm not going anywhere."

Chapter 37

James

I'd wondered how to approach the subject with April—if I even wanted to bring it up at all. My relationship with Lucas is my issue, and I don't want it to influence how anyone else feels about him. He did a shitty thing, no doubt, but in the end, it was my choice to keep him in my life, however distant that relationship might be. I could choose to dwell on the past and let it eat me alive, or I could choose to accept it and find peace somewhere else. It was just easier that way. I didn't have to like him, but I could be civil, for everyone else's sake. Not that the prick deserved it.

This was never how I wanted April to find out about Lucas and Abigail. It's not that I intended on keeping it from her forever, I just felt that it wasn't the right time, and it's a subject I hate revisiting. The woman I thought I loved—the woman I thought I wanted to *marry*—was shagging my fucking brother.

Had I not found out, I don't know if it would've ever stopped, or if they would've just kept going, my ring on her finger or not.

When I heard that April and Lucas had called off their engagement, the alarm bells instantly began ringing. Even though I hadn't spent much time getting to know her while she was with Lucas, we communicated enough for me to figure out that she was a kind person and far too good for him. It was clear he didn't deserve her.

April wouldn't end a relationship over something as trivial as lack of communication. I can tell she's the kind of person who is all in, that she would try everything to make it work. She's loyal. And when she told me about finding the messages on his hidden account, I wasn't surprised in the slightest. Not after witnessing his appalling behavior at their engagement party.

I wrap my arms around April, squeezing her tight, and press a kiss to her temple. Her touch is like a gentle wave washing over the shore, and everything from the past evaporates. She's all I want to focus on.

"James, I'm so sorry," she whispers.

Gently, I cradle her face in my hands, tilting her head so our eyes meet. "Don't be sorry for me," I murmur, brushing my thumbs lightly across her cheeks. "I'm okay. It was a long time ago now."

As I lower my hands, she turns toward the kitchen, and I watch as she opens the bin and tosses the bouquet inside. Releasing a huff, she drifts toward the sofa, and I trail behind, sinking into the cushions beside her. I shift closer to pull her into me, securing my arms around her. She leans back into my chest, and I take a deep inhale, soaking in the smell of her sweet shampoo.

"Who else knows?"

"The guys know," I say.

"And your parents?"

I exhale, shaking my head. "No, not my parents. I can handle a fractured relationship with my brother. I can pretend we're fine for Mum's sake, because I don't think she could handle the truth. It would crush her, and I just... I can't do that to her." I press my lips to April's hair. "She already hates that we aren't close. She knows things are fragile between us and assumes it's just because we're so different, but if she ever found out the real reason... I can't even imagine what it would do to her."

April stays silent, her head tilted back and her light blue eyes locked on mine.

"I'm sorry you have to pretend," she says, drawing languid circles across my forearm with her delicate fingertips.

"I've accepted it now," I say, giving her a squeeze. "I don't think I'll ever forgive him, but I've learned to let it go— for my own sake. I don't want to be the reason there's tension in the family, and I don't need the constant reminder of what he did. She wasn't worth the fight, and neither is he. Losing me as a brother? That's his punishment. He'll have to live with that every day—and now, with what he's done to you as well."

She shakes her head slowly. "It's not the same, James. He's your brother."

"Isn't it, though?" I ask. "Whether he's my brother or not, he was about to be your family too."

She hesitates, her eyes searching mine. "And what about us?"

"What about us, sweetheart?"

"This... what's happening with you and me." She gestures between us. "What will your mum think about it?"

I blow out a breath, leaning my head back against the cushions. "Mum loves you, April. Did you know that? I could see it in the way she would look at you, the way she still talks about you. She was devastated when you and Lucas broke up. She doesn't know the real reason—"

"I'm not sure I'd want her to know," April murmurs.

I nod in understanding. "But us..." I say. "I think she could come around to it. I think she could be happy for us. It might be a bit strange at first, especially during holidays with Lucas."

"Are we spending the holidays together?"

"Yes," I reply without a second thought.

"How would it work? What would it look like?" she asks, worrying her brows.

I shrug. "We always have Christmas at Mum and Dad's, so I don't think this year would be any different."

She rolls her lips. "Won't Lucas be staying there?"

"Yeah, he will." She shoots me a nervous look, and I rub her shoulder. "And the first time, it'll be weird. But it's not like we can hide forever. I want you in my life, April. He'll need to get used to it. We're going to have to face them at some point."

"What if they don't want me there?" she whispers, not sounding entirely convinced.

I give her a small smile. "Of course they'd want you there."

She shifts in my arms, twisting her body to face me. "What if they think this is wrong? That *we're* wrong?"

I trace my hand down her arm. "We're grown adults. I won't let their opinion affect what we decide to do... as a couple."

The words slip out before I have a chance to consider them. But when it comes to her, I don't want to wait. I know what I want. My family can accept it, or not. It's their choice. But this is mine. *She* is mine. And I'm not letting her go.

"A couple?"

"If you're okay with that?" My heart pounds and I feel ridiculous—like a nervous teenager asking their crush out for the first time.

She grins and her eyes warm. "I'm okay with that."

"Good."

April's face mirrors what I feel in my chest, her face whimsical as she waves her hand between us. "So . . . this is really happening?"

Fuck, yes, this is really happening. I brush my nose against her head. "You're in my blood now, April. Every song I play, I hear you in it. I feel you in the spaces between every word I speak. No one's ever affected me like this. Being around you, feeling this way . . . it's as natural as breathing. I can't close my eyes without seeing your face or hearing your voice. You're under my skin, April. So, yeah. This is really happening."

I squeeze her tighter as her deep blue eyes lock on mine. That look. Right there. The happiness, the softness, the joy and utter delight in her eyes. I wish I could capture it, frame it, and hold on to it forever.

The rest of the world falls away as I pull her closer, my hands eager to worship all of her.

Chapter 38

April

"Our coffee's getting cold." I giggle, watching James's hands glide down the front of my bathrobe, his fingers gently tugging at the belt around my waist, slowly unraveling it.

"We can always make more."

He eases the soft fabric apart, exposing my naked body. My nipples harden into taut peaks. My back bows, seeking his touch. His rough fingers trace over my bare breasts, teasing the sensitive skin before clamping my nipples between his thumb and forefinger, drawing a cry from my lips. A rush of heat pools at my core. I'm already wet and aching for him.

He takes his time, pinching and kneading my breasts, and I squirm against him, desperate for relief. For *more*. My breath comes in shallow and uneven pants.

"Fuck, James."

His voice drops to a low, gravelly murmur. "Do you like that?"

"Yes," I breathe, grinding my hips, seeking friction.

I feel him smile against my ear. One of his hands drifts lower, gliding down my abdomen until he reaches my slick center, and I feel him harden against my back. He runs a finger through my slit, and I hear his rough exhale. "Fuck, sweetheart," he says as he raises his hand to study his glistening fingers. "You have no idea what you do to me."

"What do I do?" I whisper, knowing full well what I do to him.

He presses his erection into me. "This."

I catch his wrist, lowering it to my center again, and he rewards me with a slow, teasing stroke from my entrance to my clit, where he stops to circle. A low whimper escapes me, and I'm relieved to feel his touch exactly where I need it most.

"Yes," I coax him on, and he obliges.

"Is this what you do to yourself? When you're alone? When you think about me?" His other hand trails down to dip two thick fingers inside me, curling them to find that perfect spot.

"Yes," I moan loudly, completely shameless, and he groans in response when he feels my sex clench around him. "Just like that."

"Fuck, you're such a sexy little thing," he says.

He keeps working me, thrusting and curling his fingers just right while his other hand teases my clit. I pant as the heat gathers low in my belly, but he doesn't let up. He continues edging me. The wet sounds of his fingers working me only spur me on, and I can feel my juices seeping into the fabric of the sofa beneath me. I whimper, hips rocking, desperately chasing my release.

Stars dance across my vision as I shatter, waves of warmth crashing through me in rough pulses. My body shakes under his touch, shuddering as my orgasm tears through me. I grip his forearms, desperate to hold on to something as cries spill from my lips. His fingers slow, matching the pulse of my release, ringing out every last tremor until I feel completely spent.

He slowly pulls his wet fingers from me. I turn in his arms, wide-eyed as I watch him lift those slick fingers to his mouth, sucking them clean. His pupils dilate, and a low, guttural groan escapes him.

"Fuck, April," he murmurs. "You taste so fucking good."

I push myself off the couch, my heart pounding in my chest as I drop to my knees before him. My robe hangs open and the air brushes over my wet center. I nudge his legs apart, settling into the space between them. He watches as I untuck the towel from his waist and part it.

His hard, thick cock springs free, standing proudly. I admire him—his perfect olive skin, the intricate tattoos I've traced with my fingers and tongue, inch by inch, and that mussed blond hair that begs to be pulled. His broad shoulders, defined abs, and bulging biceps that make him appear as if he were carved from marble. I'll never get over his cock. It's the prettiest I've seen—long, thick, and perfectly cut.

I wrap my fingers around the base, and he rewards me with a deep rumble. I smirk to myself, because I've done this. I've made him *this* hard. Lowering my head, I lap my tongue over the bead of precum at his tip, and we both moan. His salty, musky flavor coats my tongue, and the taste makes me hungry for more. Flattening my tongue along his length, I lick long, slow strokes from base to crown, my hand following in rhythm as I begin to pump him.

"That's it," he says, his voice dripping with praise. "Look at you. So fucking perfect with your lips wrapped around my cock." His head falls back against the sofa. "Deeper, honey. You can take it."

His filthy words encourage me, and I'm aching to unravel him. His large hands knot in my hair, guiding my head up and down his length, each thrust tapping the back of my throat. Tears spill from the corners of my eyes but I don't care—I relax my throat, breathe through my nose, and take everything he gives me.

I gently begin to massage his balls with my free hand, and his breath grows choppy and ragged, his grip in my hair punishing as he moves me faster and harder, greedily fucking my mouth. I hum around him, sucking eagerly, and hollowing my cheeks, determined to give him everything I have.

"Fuck, I can't last much longer," he says through ragged pants.

I keep going, licking, sucking, and massaging, loving the way he responds to me. The muscles in his thighs tense beneath my palms. He's close, and I want nothing more than to tip him over the edge.

"I'm going to come, April . . . Do you want my cum?" he asks.

I hum around him in agreement. He moans deeply as he unloads in my mouth, hot cum lashing the back of my throat.

Leaning forward, he meets me at eye level, gently cradling my jaw in his hand. I open my mouth, showing him his seed. "I want to see you swallow it," he says, his thumb tugging at my bottom lip. Holding his gaze, I obediently gulp, swallowing every drop. A small, satisfied smile curls his lips as I open my mouth to show him it's all gone. "Good girl." He grips my waist and pulls me up to straddle him. I wrap my arms around his neck and plant my knees on either side of his thighs, feeling him harden underneath me.

I pull away and cock my eyebrow playfully. "Again?"

"I can't get enough of you," he replies. He slowly slides the belt from my robe, nodding toward the seat next to him. "Lie back."

Obeying, I slip off his lap and lean against the sofa cushions.

"Arms above your head." He leans over me, and I feel my heart leap into my throat as he slowly wraps the belt around my wrists, tying it in a secure knot. "Tug," he instructs, and I test it, finding myself unable to move. His eyes simmer with heat, as he takes in the sight of me. "Keep them there." I nod silently. "Let me look at you."

I drop my knees, and my legs fall open to expose my wet center. He draws in a sharp breath. "God, you drive me wild, April. Every inch of you." He trails his fingers lightly over my skin, making me shiver. I feel myself growing slicker with every touch.

My eyes drift down his body, full of admiration and appreciation, until they land on his cock—angry for attention. He runs his cock through the wetness, lubricating himself. I rock my hips as he pushes into me. My eyes roll back, and my mouth falls open in a silent O as I lift my hips, urging him deeper.

"Fuuuuuuck," he groans, pushing in until he's fully seated.

"Yes," I whimper.

His thumb presses against my lips, and I part them, swirling my tongue around it as I suck. His pupils dilate as he watches me. He starts moving. He pulls out, just to the tip before ramming back into me. The force of his repeated thrusts makes me gasp, my tits bouncing, and his thumb slips from my lips to my jaw.

"Open wide," he murmurs, and I obey, opening my mouth for him. Holding my jaw, he leans forward and spits into my mouth. I moan louder than I care to admit, closing my lips to swallow. I move my hips, matching his thrusts.

My wrists strain against the robe's belt as he jams into me over and over. I'm savage.

Fire blooms under my skin as waves of electricity ripple through my body, teetering on the edge. I clap my legs around his waist, tilting my hips so he hits the perfect spot with every stroke.

"Ah!" I shout, yanking against the tie.

"That's it," he says. His hand lowers and his fingers start strumming my clit. "Come for me, baby." I unravel when he picks up his pace, fucking me with fervor.

"I'm coming," I manage, my voice straining. I feel a rush of wetness leave me, coating him just as he swells and pulses inside me.

"*Jesus*, April." His groan is low and deep as he reaches his release, filling me.

He drops to his elbows, caging me in. He dusts his thumb across my jaw before his hands move to untie the robe belt from my wrists. Once undone, he discards the fabric and rubs slow, soothing circles over my skin. A gentle smile tugs at his lips as he lifts one of my hands to his mouth, peppering feather-light kisses over my knuckles.

I squeeze my eyes shut as my lower lip begins to tremble. The prick of tears builds behind my eyelids as emotion, too big to contain, swells inside me. I can feel myself becoming consumed by him.

"Sweetheart," he whispers. "What's wrong?"

Steadying myself, I open my eyes to meet his waiting gaze. "I'm terrified."

His brows pull together as he cups my cheek. "Terrified of what?"

"Of the way I feel for you."

He drops his forehead to mine. "You don't have to be scared," he murmurs, "because I'm right here. I feel it too, just as deeply." He brushes away a tear that slips free. "Okay?"

I nod.

"You're mine," he whispers, and my heart explodes.

"I'm yours."

He pulls out slowly, and I feel his liquid trickle between my cheeks. Standing, he offers a hand to help me to my feet. Just as I turn to head upstairs, his fingers curl around my elbow, spinning me to face him. I giggle in surprise, my hands landing softly against his hard chest. Slipping a finger under my chin, he tilts my head, pressing a delicate kiss to my lips before pulling back.

That's when he leaves his mark, carving himself into my heart.

He gives my bottom a playful tap. "I'll make us some food."

I watch as he walks toward the fridge, in all his naked glory, and I decide that I could very easily get used to having James in my kitchen every morning.

Chapter 39

James

After an eventful morning, one that fortunately ended peacefully, I head home to play my bass. The last few weeks with April have been euphoric. It's been *so* great, I almost feel like I'm living in a dream I half expect to wake from at any moment. Whatever time's not spent working or practicing has been spent with her, and it's bliss.

As hard as the last few years have been, after all the shit my brother put me through, I've finally found a place where my life is starting back up again. Every day April and I spend together, getting to know each other more deeply, I feel myself falling further. It's happened faster than I ever imagined. She is so unexpected. It's this strange, exhilarating kind of freedom, like we're both free-falling, yet somehow, together, we'll land safely.

She's gorgeous, intelligent, and funny, and every little thing I discover about her only makes me want to hold on tighter. The way she dances around the house singing when she's happy. The way she steals glances and smiles shyly. The way her face glows when she's excited. The way she speaks to Basil in hushed tones when she thinks no one can hear her. She awakens thoughts and emotions in me that I've never had about anybody before.

I finish up prepping some meals for the week ahead before picking up my guitar and running my fingers across the strings.

After a few minutes of tuning, I set into one of the harder songs we've been perfecting. I'm lost in a musical trance when inspiration suddenly hits me, and I pause. Walking to my bookshelf, I pull out my notebook, then head back to the sofa with my bass. I drop into the cushion, setting the notebook on the coffee table and flip it open to a blank page. Reaching into the coffee table drawer, I sift around until I find a pen. I pull the cap off with my teeth, spit it aside, and dive in.

I jot down notes and lyrics, spilling the melody from my mind onto the paper. I alternate between singing, playing, and writing, scribbling and crossing out notes until I'm satisfied with the sound.

Hours must pass until I come up for air. It's dark out and my stomach grumbles in protest as I glance down at my notebook. Pages full of emotion and raw vulnerability that I needed to expose. A sense of pride swells in my gut and a smile spreads across my face.

I just wrote a whole damn song.

* * *

I wake the next morning feeling energized. The audition is next Friday, and it'll run like a mini festival. The competition spans two days, with each band assigned a day and time to perform one set—ideally of their own music, and we're playing day two. Bound to Oblivion and their management will be there, so we've decided to stick with our usual progressive rock sound. It's our favorite, and it's what the crowd will connect with. Only one of our songs requires a little more fine-tuning, but I think we're ready to show just how far we've come. We're up against some impressive talent, but I'm feeling good. And no matter the outcome, we'll know we gave it our all.

I get ready for the day, load my gear into my car and head to Oliver's.

Oliver's place is out in Richmond. It's lush, with sprawling greenery and paths along the Thames, not to mention some excellent pubs. It's a great place to be in the warmer months. The lucky bastard had it made with a solid finance background; both his mum and dad were investment bankers, so they're not short of a quid. They were gutted when he chose not to pursue law after earning his degree, and instead, chose to pursue a career in music. They got over it after seeing how happy music made him and witnessing the dedication he's poured into the band. He's an incredible drummer, and I couldn't imagine playing without him.

I pull up, switch off the engine, and round the trunk. The front door swings open, and Oliver strides out to help with the gear. He claps me on the back, greeting me with a quick "Hey."

"Hey. The other guys here?"

"We're just waiting on Will."

We carry the equipment through the house, navigating our way to the garage next to the utility room, where I begin to set everything up.

Tom saunters into the garage with a sly look on his face. "How you doing, mate?"

I narrow my eyes at him. "Good, Tommy," I drawl. "You?"

"Not as good as you, apparently," he says, leaning against the brick wall and crossing one leg over the other, fixing me with a pointed look. I can't contain the smirk tugging at the corner of my mouth as I focus on untangling a cord.

"Oh, you've got it bad, huh?" Tom teases in a playful tone.

Oliver walks past me, clapping me on the shoulder. "Give him a break, yeah, Tom?"

Tom grins. "So," he says, pushing off the wall and stepping closer. I drop the cord on the floor.

"Yes, Tom," I say, opening my arms wide. "What is it you'd like to know? Just ask me."

He cocks his head. "You and April?" He lets the question hang in the air.

"Yes," I confirm, holding his gaze. "Me and April."

He cocks an eyebrow, curious. "Does Lucas know?"

"Yes."

"Shit," he says, clearly not expecting that answer.

"Yes," I repeat, nodding.

Oliver's gaze darts between us, a look of amusement spreading across his face.

"How?" Tom asks.

"Well, he figured it out pretty quickly when he showed up on April's doorstep and found me coming down her staircase in a towel," I say, a smug grin breaking through.

"Oh, *shit!*" Tom shouts, pressing a fist to his mouth to stifle his laughter. Even Oliver's trying to contain his delight. He can't stand Lucas, so I know this is music to his ears. I can't help but feel a small sense of satisfaction at the memory.

Was his unplanned, unannounced arrival at April's awkward? Definitely. But seeing the look on Lucas's face . . . I have to admit, it felt pretty good.

"What did I miss?" Will bursts into the garage, sweaty and out of breath, clutching his guitar case—no amp, no cords.

Oliver raises an eyebrow. "What the hell happened to you?"

Will grins, waggling his eyebrows. "Stayed over at Victoria's place last night," he says between pants.

I eye him suspiciously. "Why are you so sweaty?"

"Had to leg it from the station," he replies, dropping his guitar to the floor.

I shake my head. "I would've picked you up, mate."

"Well, maybe you could have mentioned that!" he shoots back, irritated.

"And how the fuck was I supposed to know? I'm not a bloody mind-reader," I reply.

Before he can answer, Tom cuts in. "Lucas knows James is shagging April."

Will's head snaps to me so fast I'm surprised it doesn't fall off. "You're shagging April?"

"Yup," Tom says, smiling. I roll my eyes.

"I'm *dating* April," I clarify. Tom wiggles his eyebrows.

"Well done, my man," Will replies, walking over and clapping me on the shoulder. "So, how'd *brother dearest* find out?" he asks, wide-eyed.

I open my mouth to answer, but Tom beats me to it. Again. "Caught James at April's place in nothing but a towel."

Will's gaze swings to me, and I just shrug.

He beams. "That's amazing."

"Serves him right," Tom says.

I crook a small smile and get to work plugging in my cables.

"Do you think he'll say something to your parents?" Will asks.

I straighten up. "Doubt it. He's not exactly in a position to start airing my shit."

Oliver chimes in, more serious now. "Does April know? About Lucas and Abi?"

I let out a sigh, running a hand through my hair. "Yeah, she does."

Whenever the guys used to bring up Lucas and Abi, I'd cringe and quickly change the subject. But now...I don't feel anything about either of them. And it feels like I've broken free from the chain.

Oliver nods, understanding. "How did she take it?"

"As well as I'd expected," I say. "She was surprised, hurt...worried."

Oliver nods, and Tom tilts his head. "So, what's the plan?"

"Nothing changes," I say. "We want to be together, and Lucas will just have to live with it." I take a steadying breath. "I'm going to have to tell Mum."

"What do you think she'll say?" Oliver asks.

It's a question that's been weighing on my mind for weeks. From the moment this thing with April began, I knew it would eventually lead to this conversation. It won't be comfortable, and I have no idea how Dad's going to respond, but it's inevitable. One thing is certain—nothing will keep me from her. Not Lucas. Not Mum or Dad. Not even the possibility of touring, not anymore.

"I honestly have no idea. But there's only one way to find out," I say. Walking over to Oliver, I pull my notebook from my back pocket and hand it to him. He flips it open and begins scanning over the chords I scribbled down yesterday.

His brow pinches as he turns to me. "What's this?"

"I wrote something. I know it's late notice, but I thought maybe we could try it out," I say, suddenly nervous. It's been a while since I've written a song, let alone sung, but this one *feels* right. I opened myself completely, like I took a dagger to my heart and spilled my blood onto the pages.

He nods, a grin tugging at the corners of his mouth. "Yeah, all right, I reckon we can give it a shot." He holds up the notebook. "Let me scan a few copies and we can get started."

When he returns, Tom steps aside, giving me the mic, and we dive straight into it. We work through my song bit by bit, making adjustments until it blends perfectly. A current buzzes through me as we play, and I can tell the guys are loving every moment.

That's what I love most about this band—we feed off one another's energy and offer unwavering support.

After a few run-throughs, we're all in agreement—if we can nail it by next week, we'll add it to the set. The thought alone sends my pulse racing, and I can't help but imagine what it would feel like performing something so personal, sharing that moment with my best friends.

By the time we're done, the sun has sunk, and we're completely exhausted, especially Oliver—drumming's no joke and practice takes it out of him more than the rest of us. Not that he ever complains. The bloke is jacked. We exchange a few tired goodbyes, and I load my gear into the car, drop Will off at his flat, then finally head home.

With Lucas out of the way and the band on track, there's just one final hurdle to clear.

I'll tell Mum about April and me tomorrow.

Chapter 40

April

I push open the café door, my gaze flicking between wooden tables and mismatched chairs until it lands on Anna by the window. She's already tucked in with her drink, standing and smiling for a hug as I walk over. The girls and I decided to meet for an impromptu Sunday breakfast stop at the Daily Grind before we head off for a stroll through Kensington Gardens. It's a gorgeous morning here, and we want to take full advantage of the sunshine while we have it.

I lean down to kiss Anna's cheek before taking the seat across from her.

"Well," Anna says, leaning forward with a sly grin, her arms crossed over the table. "Aren't you glowing?"

I feel my cheeks heat. "It's amazing what a few orgasms can do for the skin."

"Well done, you," she says. "I already ordered your usual."

"Thanks." The waiter delivers my pastry and cappuccino, which I waste no time tucking into. The bell above the café door jingles again, followed by a ripple of gasps from fellow patrons. I glance over my shoulder and my jaw practically hits the floor. Anna scoffs, choking on her hot chocolate between coughs. Gemma strides in like she owns the place, rocking thigh-high patent black boots, a navy-blue pleated skirt, and a barely there lace bodysuit with a mesh top held together by a few thin strings. It's 8:00 a.m.

Her makeup is rubbed off and her blond hair brushes her shoulders in tousled waves, with that unmistakable "freshly fucked" look.

I usher a waiter over, ordering an apricot Danish for Gemma as she takes a seat.

Anna cocks a brow. "Whose hole have you just emerged from?"

"Ugh," she groans, pulling her seat forward. "You guys, I had the worst date."

"Did you come straight from his?" I ask.

"Yes."

"Why did you stay over if the date was so terrible?"

"He has a cat."

"Point taken."

"Enlighten us," Anna says, taking a sip of her hot chocolate.

"So, I met this guy called Richard." Anna and I glance at each other, trying hard to contain our laughter. Gemma rolls her eyes before continuing. "Anyway, we went for dinner at a pizza bar—fine, great. He turns up and he's shorter than me. He told me he was six foot!" Gemma stands at an easy five five, five six at most.

"Tell me more about this tiny Dick," Anna says, gesturing for her to continue.

"So, the chat was fine, whatever. Food was decent. But then the bill comes, and he actually has the nerve to suggest we split it."

"The audacity!" Anna says, shaking her head, and I smother a laugh.

"Right? Anyway, I agree to go halves, and he invites me back to his place. Apparently, he has a cat. And I think, *screw it, I've come this far.*"

"Naturally," I say.

"So, we get to his flat. Then he starts making out with me, leads me to his bedroom, and—with no warning—shoves his fat, filthy sausage fingers into my mouth. His hand tasted like cottage cheese."

Well, that's fucking revolting.

"—and he's got the smallest penis. I think it's a micro. I'd never seen one in the flesh until now. Thank God he was done in two pumps, and then he just rolled over and fell asleep. He was still passed out when I snuck away this morning." She shivers, traumatized.

Anna scrunches her nose. "*Jesus Christ.*"

"I know," Gemma says.

"I was referring to the micro penis. I can't believe you haven't come across one till now. You churn through dicks like an Amish with butter," Anna says.

Gemma shrugs, casually picking up her Danish and taking a big bite.

I've kept the news to myself about Lucas discovering James and me, deciding it's best to tell the girls in person rather than over the phone, and now's the time. Deciding there's no way to ease into the conversation, I blurt it out, sparing no details.

"Damn right, girl!" Anna says when I finish, holding up her hand for a high five.

I laugh, clapping her hand before my expression shifts. "There's something else..." I hesitate, feeling a twinge of uncertainty about sharing the next part. "Please don't repeat this to anyone," I say, looking between them.

Anna and Gemma exchange a quick glance, then turn back to me, both nodding. "Of course," they reply.

I exhale slowly. "I found out Lucas was shagging James's ex while they were still together. For months."

Their expressions morph into a mixture of horror and pure outrage. Anna brings her hand to her mouth, eyes wide with disbelief. "That prick!" she hisses. "To his own brother?"

I shift in my seat. "I can't believe it...I don't *want* to believe it. How could I not see the real him sooner? I feel like I never really knew Lucas at all. How could someone do that?"

Anna leans closer, her voice firm. "People like him... they're experts at showing only what they want others to see."

I nod, still reeling from it all. As difficult and dark as those months were following our breakup, I'm finally at a place where I feel like I can look back with a sense of gratitude. I'm grateful I discovered that account, grateful I had the chance to end things before we were legally tied to each other. In some fucked-up way, Lucas's betrayal was a gift.

If he hadn't left his phone at home that day, I would have committed myself to a life with him built on a foundation of lies. If I hadn't endured the heartache, it wouldn't have led me to James. So, standing where I am now, I'm not sure I can resent Lucas for what he did. To either of us.

"Is James okay?" Gemma asks.

"Yeah, surprisingly, he seems fine. It happened a long time ago. But it explains why they aren't close. I just assumed it was due to their age difference."

"I'm surprised he still speaks to the tosser," Anna says.

"Caroline has struggled with her mental health, and he knows the truth would break her, so he puts up with him for her sake," I explain.

"That's . . . actually quite decent of him," Anna says. "I mean, I'd have told him to fuck off."

"I'm with you on that one," I say.

"And how are things between you and James?" Gemma asks.

I smile. "Really good. I like him. A lot."

Anna reaches across the table, taking my hand in hers. "I can tell. You two deserve to be happy."

"It's so nice seeing you like this," Gemma says, smiling.

"Like what?" I ask.

"Yourself."

Chapter 41

James

I set off early to visit my parents in Toton, where I grew up on the outskirts of Nottingham in the Midlands. It's surrounded by trails and nature reserves, where Lucas first discovered his love of hiking. He sought peace out amongst nature anytime the weather permitted, as I was holed up in my room immersing myself in music, moving my fingers along my guitar as I practiced endlessly.

Growing up, we didn't have much, but Toton offered a good school and access to after-school programs and hobbies, like my music lessons. It's a welcoming community. Knowing Mum would be well cared for after we left made it easier to move to a new city after finishing my A-levels. She's active in local clubs, has made great friends, and finds purpose in the social circles that keep her happily engaged and out of the house.

Dad, on the other hand, isn't one for change. He sticks to what he knows, finding comfort in familiarity, which has suited Mum well enough.

Their marriage has always seemed steady but lacking the open affection I witnessed between my friends' parents.

Lucas and I, despite being grateful for all our parents provided, never felt we could open up to Dad as easily as we could with Mum. He's stiffer. More serious.

Growing up in Toton provided a great start, but Lucas and I both longed to experience big-city life, so we made our way to London as soon as we could, only returning home during the holidays and long weekends. Lucas moved back to Toton for a brief period after he and April split, but according to Mum, he recently set himself up in a small flat in Battersea, so I can't deny that I'm relieved he won't be home for the conversation I'm about to have with Mum and Dad.

The guitar solo blasts through the car, and I tap my fingers against the steering wheel. It's about a two-and-a-half-hour drive from London to Toton, giving me plenty of time to crank the volume and lose myself in music without complaint from the neighbors. And I'm making the most of it, blaring the latest release from Bound to Oblivion.

I pull up in front of Mum and Dad's brown brick, semi-detached and turn off the ignition. It's been ten years since I've lived here, and the street hasn't changed a bit.

Mum swings open the door, beaming as she rushes toward me. She's in her usual trousers and white shirt, with that soft maroon cardigan she always wears. Her chestnut hair is cut into a bob, and her tortoiseshell glasses perch on her small nose. She's so cute.

"Peter!" she calls over her shoulder. "James is here!"

I lean down, letting her eager arms wrap around me as I lift her off the ground. She squeals, laughing as I spin her around, then set her gently back down. She swats at my chest, still giggling, and I return her bright smile.

I really need to make more of an effort to see her. I've become slack since amping up with band practice. I call her a few times a week to check in but seeing her face light up in person stirs warmth in my chest.

Dad appears in the doorway. "Son," he says, giving me a sharp nod.

"Dad," I reply, clapping him firmly on the shoulder as I step inside. The furniture dotted throughout the home is sparse but decent, most having previously belonged to my grandparents. I follow Mum into the family room, where a cup of tea and a plate of her homemade gingerbread biscuits sit waiting on the table.

She knows they're my favorite, the angel.

Mum and Dad settle on the sofa, while I sink into a floral armchair across from them. Leaning forward, I snatch a cookie off the plate. They're still warm.

Dunking it into my tea, I take a generous bite. An ungentlemanly groan escapes me—nothing beats Mum's homemade gingerbread. I glance at Mum, her eyes gleaming. She loves feeding people. It's her love language—you only have to look at Dad's potbelly to see the proof.

Dad murmurs around a mouthful of gingerbread. "So, what's new, son?"

I swallow before answering. "Same as always—practicing. The audition's next week. I got you both tickets, just in case you're able to make it. It'd mean the world to me if you were there. I know it's a long trip for you both, but—"

Mum waves her hand dismissively. "Oh, don't be silly. We wouldn't miss it for the world, love."

"We'll be there," Dad says.

Pride unfurls inside me. They haven't seen me play in years, and the thought of them witnessing how much I've grown as a musician excites me. When I first chose to pursue music after forming the band, their concern was only natural. I understand how few musicians land deals or make enough to live comfortably—it was a risk. But I was never cut out for a life of desk jobs, shirt and tie, or buried in textbooks—*sucking the corporate cock*, as I call it. I hated school and studying. That was always Lucas's path, never mine. It was never going to be. Once they understood how dedicated I was to music, their support became steadfast. After seeing Oliver struggle with his own parents' acceptance, I recognize how fortunate I am.

"Thanks, that means a lot," I say, and Mum's lips tug into a soft smile.

Dad takes a sip of his tea. "Have you seen your brother since he moved back?"

I let out a long breath, brushing crumbs off my leg. I knew this was coming.

"Uh, no. I haven't," I say, rubbing at the nape of my neck. Might as well get this over with—like pulling a loose tooth. "Actually, speaking of Lucas, that's kind of why I'm here."

"Oh?" Mum leans forward, and she shares a quick glance with Dad.

"Yeah." I take a steadying breath. "There's really no easy way to say this, so I'm just going to come out with it." I close my eyes and say a silent prayer that they won't bite my head off. Dad is known to be ... unpredictable at the best of times.

I hadn't expected to feel this nervous.

"What's wrong?" Mum asks.

I open my eyes and meet hers. "I'm seeing April."

Mum freezes, her mug halfway to her mouth as silence settles over the room. Her expression shifts from concern to something illegible, and Dad just stares with a frown.

It feels an eternity before anyone speaks.

Shit.

"Dad—" I begin.

He holds up his hand, stopping me. "I heard you, son. Just . . . give me a minute."

Mum looks at me with surprise and curiosity. "You and April," she says. "As in, you and April are . . ."

"Together. Yes," I finish for her.

"Right," she says, lifting her eyebrows as she nods to herself.

"How long has this been going on?" Dad asks, sitting up straight.

"A few weeks now," I confess, rubbing my hands over my thighs.

"And your brother . . . he knows?" Mum asks, wincing slightly as she grinds the words out.

"He knows." I nod.

The room falls silent again, the only sound the loud tick of the creepy old grandfather clock echoing from the entryway.

"Well," Mum finally says, "I always thought you held a candle for her."

"What?" I ask, genuinely surprised.

She nods. "I noticed the way you used to look at her."

"No, I didn't," I say.

"You did, son," Dad says.

Well, fuck. How was it so obvious to everybody except me?

"You're not mad?" I ask.

Dad shoots me a lopsided grin. "Son, you're twenty-nine years old. You're an adult. Of course we aren't mad at you. Surprised, sure." He shrugs. "I can't say the same for your brother, of course."

I scrub a hand down my face and my shoulders sag with relief.

"Honey . . ." Mum leans forward, placing her mug gently on the coffee table. "All a loving parent ever wants is for their children to be happy. So, are you happy?"

I think of April and my heart swells. "Yeah. I am. She makes me happy."

She gives me a small, understanding smile. "I know you and your brother don't exactly see eye to eye," she starts, lifting a hand to stop me before I can jump in, "and I don't need to know the ins and outs of it all—that's between you two. You're grown men now, and I can't make you do anything. But I do care about April—deeply. And I'm not so daft as to think their breakup was only about 'communication issues.'" She looks at me with a mix of sadness and knowing. "All I ask, James, is that you're honest with him."

I nod, understanding.

"Good," she says, reaching for her mug.

"How did Lucas react when he found out?" Dad asks, his tone serious.

"He was livid," I say.

Dad blows out a breath and shakes his head. "Give it time. He'll come round."

Jesus. There is so much I could say, but I bite back my words. I decided I wouldn't share the truth behind my and Abigail's breakup, and I'll stick to my word. Instead, I force a smile and bite into a fresh piece of gingerbread.

"How is she?" Mum asks, her voice soft.

"She's good. Really good, actually."

"Is it serious, this thing between you and her?" she asks.

"Yeah, Mum. It's serious." The corner of her eyes crinkle as she smiles. She always had a soft spot for April. "I plan on bringing her here for Christmas . . . If you're happy to have us both?"

Mum's face lights up as she claps her hands together in excitement. "Oh, that would be wonderful!" She looks at Dad. "Wouldn't it, Peter?"

Dad inhales deeply, wary—I can only assume because of Lucas's impending reaction—before his shoulders droop. "It would be wonderful." He clears his throat. "But perhaps we'll break that news to your brother, yes?"

I couldn't agree more. I can't even imagine how awkward that would be. And, as much as I dislike him, I don't want to rub it in his face. "I'd appreciate that, thank you," I say, shooting him a grateful smile.

Mum looks between us, her excitement still bubbling. She stands, brushing down her trousers before walking over to me. Leaning close, she presses her cheek to mine, holding my shoulders with both hands. I cover one of her hands with my own as she says, "It's about time you found someone who sees you as we do, James. You're a brilliant man, and April is a delight. I'm pleased for you, love. I really am."

We spend the next couple of hours chatting. Mum fills me in on her latest book club read, something a little more scandalous than the ladies in Toton are used to, apparently, and I can't help but laugh, trying to picture her reading and discussing steamy romance novels. Good for her. She seems happy.

I fill them in on the songs we've selected for the audition and give them a rundown on how the day is expected to unfold.

I hug each of them as we say our goodbyes. Mum squeezes me, planting a firm kiss on my cheek and I laugh, lifting my hand to rub off the smudged lipstick. Just as I'm about to leave, Dad hurries into the kitchen and returns holding an unlabeled bottle of red wine.

"What's this?" I ask, studying the bottle.

Pride flashes in his eyes. "I've started making my own wine. Rob from down the road got me set up with a home kit. It's a Spanish variety, Rioja. It's turned out pretty decent. Here," he says, extending the bottle toward me. "Share it with April."

I accept it, reading the subtle changes in his expression. He looks relaxed, almost content. I lift the bottle in salute. "Will do, Dad. Cheers." I'm just about to step out the door when Mum's small fingers wrap around my biceps. I stop in my tracks.

Mum considers me, her voice firm. "She's a beautiful woman, James. You treat her well. She's been through enough."

"I will," I promise, bending down to plant a kiss on her head.

On the way home, I belt out the lyrics to my favorite song. I'm so relieved we managed to have that conversation without anyone losing their shit. It feels like a monumental weight has been lifted from my shoulders.

No more secrets.

No more sneaking around.

I step on the accelerator, eager to get back home to my girl.

Chapter 42

April

James returned home from visiting his parents yesterday afternoon, and he told them everything about us. My heart raced with nerves until he assured me they are happy for us. The relief that washed over me was indescribable. They've always been so kind and supportive, welcoming me into their family with open arms when I was with Lucas.

Despite her own internal struggles, Caroline always goes the extra mile. She has a special motherly way of making the people around her feel heard and loved. She's a beautiful soul, with a heart so tender, and knowing she's given us her blessing is elating. They'll be at the audition next week, which will be the first time I've seen them since the engagement party. Standing by them while I cheer James on will be quite the juxtaposition, but I'm excited to see them again.

I step through James's flat, wearing nothing but his T-shirt. My hair is tied in a messy topknot, and a dull, delicious ache throbs between my thighs from last night. I peer through the doorway to his kitchen and watch as he cracks two eggs into a bowl. He's shirtless, wearing only gray tracksuit bottoms, and I salivate as I study the muscles in his back working while he whisks. He flings a tea towel over his shoulder before seasoning the egg mixture with salt and pepper. I smile to myself as the smell of bacon sizzling and coffee brewing fills the flat.

I bypass the kitchen, go to his bookshelf and begin thumbing through the titles—Dante, Dickens, Freud, and de Beauvoir. Classics spanning literature to philosophy are arranged neatly by genre. This, right here, is him. The softness beneath the hard exterior.

"Coffee?" he says, and I jump, whirling around to face him.

"You gave me a fright," I say, holding my hand over my heart, and he smirks. Extending his arm toward me, I accept the mug and bring it to my lips. "Mmm," I moan. "You make the best coffee."

"Breakfast's ready too. You need to eat. Your stomach has been grumbling for the last hour." He chuckles. I follow him to the small table nestled against the kitchen wall. Setting my mug down, I pull out a chair and settle in. He grabs two plates from the counter, placing one for each of us before taking a seat. I sneak a glance, catching a glimpse of his abs tightening as he scoots his chair forward and reaches for his cutlery. I almost drool on the table.

A thick slice of buttered sourdough is topped with creamy scrambled eggs, crispy rashers of bacon, sautéed mushrooms, wilted spinach, and a plump pork sausage.

"Thank you. This looks incredible," I say, picking up my knife and fork to dig in.

"You're welcome, sweetheart," he replies, giving me a soft smile as he slices into his bacon. The sound of utensils hitting porcelain fills the air as we eat.

"So," I manage around a bite of bread, "have you read all those books on your shelf?"

He swallows a large mouthful. "Most of them, yes."

"I didn't really take you for the philosophy type."

He smirks. "Then I guess you shouldn't judge a book by its cover."

Cheeky.

"Touché," I say, pointing at him with my knife. "When did you start reading philosophy?" I ask.

"When I was eighteen, one of my old school friends from Toton gave me a book by Jean-Paul Sartre called *The Age of Reason*. I picked it up one day when I was bored after moving to London. Since then, I've just accumulated more. I love it."

I raise my eyebrows, a smile tugging at my lips. Music and philosophy—this man just keeps impressing me. "A little different from my romance novels," I tease.

He chuckles. "Just a little. But if you ever asked me to read one, I would. For you."

Happiness tickles my heart, and I swear it doubles in size.

A phone notification chimes, and James ignores it, focusing on his meal.

Ping. Another notification. He glances at his phone briefly but continues eating. When his phone chimes again, I lock up. My gaze shifts nervously between my plate and his phone on the counter before flicking to James, and I catch him watching me curiously, his brows pressed together in concern before he quickly smooths his expression.

"It'll be one of the guys," he says, and I nod, cutting into my toast, pushing the sinking feeling in my gut aside.

After finishing our meal, we get dressed and head out to spend a lovely morning strolling through Hyde Park. We sip our takeaway coffee as we wander, pausing to watch the birds glide across the pond. We spot an empty park bench and take a seat, nestling in to watch the world go by. Children dance and play on the grass. Families fly kites that dip and flutter in the breeze, while packs of runners dash by in a blur, their loud footfalls slapping against the pavement. James drapes an arm over my shoulders, pulling me into his side. I lean my head against him and close my eyes. These are the precious moments I love sharing with him. This city is so busy, so *alive*, but with him, I feel calm. He wraps both arms around me and the bustling city noise fades into the background.

I trust James. Really, I do. But, for whatever reason, hearing his phone ping this morning set me on edge, triggering a surge of panic. That tight, squeezing sensation that grips my lungs and lights a fire in my chest. When it sets in, it's hard to focus or catch my breath. It's the second time I've felt this way since finding Lucas's secret persona, and to be honest, it scares me. I don't want it to get to me, because I know, deep down, that James would never act with self-serving intentions. I try to push the thoughts and feelings aside to enjoy the rest of the afternoon with James. I can't let my fears intrude on my happiness. He's been nothing short of perfect.

James places his hand under my chin tenderly, tipping my head back. He regards me, and I shoot him a small smile.

"I can practically *hear* you thinking, gorgeous. What's on your mind?" he asks as he scans my face.

I close my eyes, mulling over my thoughts to find the right words without making me sound psychotic. I don't want to be the woman with trust issues. The woman who feels like she needs to check her partner's phone or worry about what he's up to. I never used to be that person.

I worry my lip in contemplation. His hand squeezes my shoulder affectionately before he pulls back, a flicker of concern crossing his face.

"Baby, what's wrong?" he asks.

I think back to the conversation we had after I met with Lucas. *This only works if we communicate.* "You're going to think I'm crazy." I huff out a laugh. "I felt this wave of anxiety when your phone kept going off this morning. I don't even know why . . . my mind just flashed back to when I found Lucas's phone, and . . ." I trail off, letting the words hang in the air.

James's eyes fill with understanding, and he strokes my jaw softly. "April, you're not crazy. What you went through with Lucas . . . I get why that would stay with you." He pauses, his thumb brushing over my bottom lip. "But I need you to know that I will never hide anything from you. If there's ever something that makes you feel uneasy, just tell me." He holds my gaze. "I want us to have complete trust. You don't have to worry about anything like that with me. I promise."

A small, grateful smile lifts my lips.

I reach up, placing my hand over his and lean into his touch. "Thank you," I murmur. "I know I don't say it enough, but I really do trust you. It's just . . . sometimes old fears sneak up on me."

"I get it," he says. "After how badly he hurt you, it's only natural. Thank you for telling me." He kisses me. "And if those fears ever come up again, just talk to me, okay? I'd rather know what's on your mind than have you be alone and in pain."

I give his hand a light squeeze. "Thank you."

* * *

I'm relaxing on the sofa after work, an exfoliating mask working its magic to brighten my skin as I watch my show and sip a glass of Peter's homemade Rioja. Basil is curled up beside me, purring away happily. I'm running my fingers through his lush coat when my phone on the sofa arm lights up with a message. I reach over and swipe the screen to read James's text.

It's a mixture of random words and numbers that I can't make sense of. My brows furrow in confusion as I try to decipher the message. I type out a reply.

Me: *What's this?*

The three little dots appear before he shoots through a response.

James: *It's all my passwords.*

My breath catches.

Me: *Why are you sending me all your passwords?*

James: *I never want you to feel like I'm hiding anything from you. I'm sorry someone betrayed your trust before. Having yours means everything to me. I promise, I'll work every day to prove I'm worthy of it.*

My eyes shimmer with unshed tears as I read his message over and over. My lip trembles as I press the call button, needing to hear him. His phone rings twice before his smooth voice fills the line.

"Hey, April."

"Hey, James," I whisper back, my voice cracking. "I'm so sorry."

"Hey," he soothes. "You have to stop apologizing. You have nothing to be sorry for."

A wave of humiliation crashes over me, and I pull in a shaky breath. "I feel so embarrassed. You shouldn't have to give me your passwords."

"April, I want to give you everything, because it's yours by choice. My thoughts, my heart, every piece of me—they belong to you. Anything you want, consider it yours."

A broken sound escapes me, and he's quick to respond. "Sweetheart, why are you crying?"

I drop my hand to my lap and fidget nervously with the faux fur blanket. "Because I really like you."

He chuckles. "I really like you too. I'll let you get back to your night. I'm just playing around with some songs, but I'll see you before I leave for the audition tomorrow, yeah?"

"Absolutely. I'll see you tomorrow."

"Goodnight, gorgeous."

"'Night, James."

I hang up the phone and release a little sob, pulling Basil in close.

He's starting to show me what it truly means to be cared for—the way my parents cared for each other.

He's shown me that it's not only in the words, but the little things. It's in the way he brings me coffee in bed every morning. It's in the way he only plays my favorite songs in the car, instead of his own. It's in the way he washes my hair for me when I'm tired and heats my wheat bag when I'm cold.

James has accepted me despite knowing that his brother and I share a past. A past that in ways, I'm still recovering from. Even so, he's taken the time to know me, let his feelings for me grow, and shown just how much he wants this—wants us, fully aware that his brother will always be part of our lives.

And *still*, he chose me.

I know there are a lot of uncertainties in this life, but it brings me a little comfort knowing that I'm certain about *him*.

Chapter 43

April

The next day—the audition

I lean forward over my bathroom counter, dusting a light layer of shimmery eye shadow across my lids. I step back, scrutinizing my makeup in the mirror. I drop my makeup brush and shake out my hands, trying to calm my nerves. I'm so jittery, I can barely contain my excitement for James.

Today is the day.

Atlas Veil's big audition.

James's silky voice makes me freeze. "I've got to get going now, sweetheart. I'm meeting the boys at Will's before heading to the venue. We want to watch the other auditioning bands before we play."

I spin around to face James, my breath catching as I take him in, and my stomach flutters in response.

His sandy blond hair is tousled, curling just slightly under his ears, a wavy strand falling over his eye. He's wearing black jeans and a loose-fitting vest, exposing his muscular shoulders and tattooed arms, with his worn leather jacket folded over his forearm, and combat boots. He looks good enough to eat.

I step forward, tugging my robe tighter. He throws his jacket on the counter beside me, pulling me in so we're chest to chest, pelvis to pelvis, and wraps his arms around me tightly. I crane my head back, drinking in the delicious sight of him.

"Hey, April."

"Hey, James," I whisper. He rocks us gently from side to side, giving me a heart-stopping smile, and I melt.

"How are you feeling?" I ask, locking my hands behind his neck.

"Nervous. Excited." He runs his knuckles gently down my cheek. "Hard to believe the day is actually here."

"You've worked so hard for it. You'll be great," I say, and he drops his forehead to mine.

"I'm happy you're here," he murmurs.

"I'll always be here," I promise, rising onto my tiptoes to kiss him. His tongue grazes my lips, and I open for him. Our tongues move together in a slow dance, and I feel myself growing wet. His hands slide down my back, gripping my waist before dropping lower to squeeze my bum, and I whimper, feeling him grow hard against me. I instinctively rock my hips, desperate to feel him.

He pulls back, breaking the kiss. "Fuck. I want you so badly, but I have to go."

A small smile tugs at the corners of my lips, and he groans, guiding me back toward the bathroom counter.

"What are you doing?" I ask, my tone playful as he lifts me up, setting me down beside the sink. I brace my hands behind me, knocking products over as I lean back.

He pushes my robe apart, revealing my naked body underneath. He draws in a sharp breath. "I think the boys can wait a few more minutes," he says, nudging my thighs. "Show me."

I part my legs, exposing my core to him.

"Fuck," he says. I watch, breathless and wide-eyed, as he drops to his knees before me, running his nose through my wetness. His gaze doesn't waver as he slowly pushes three fingers inside me, sending a jolt through my body, and my head falls back on a low moan. "Watch me, April," he demands, and my eyes snap to him, obediently holding his gaze. He rubs his fingers back and forth over my most sensitive spot, the slick sounds of my arousal filling the quiet room, blending with my heavy breaths.

He teases my slit before latching onto my clit and I cry out. Sitting up, I thread my fingers through his hair, tugging him closer as I move against him wantonly, fucking his face.

"You have the sweetest pussy, April," he says, the vibration of his rough voice adding to the building sensation.

"Fuck me," I breathe.

He withdraws, and I snatch his wrist, lifting his hand to my mouth. I wrap my lips around his fingers, hollow out my cheeks and swirl my tongue, sucking my juices off him. He looks at me adoringly as he lowers his free hand to fumble with his jeans, popping the button and dragging the zipper down. Releasing his fingers, he pulls back from my pussy before standing to push his jeans and briefs down. His thick, throbbing cock springs free, and I swallow a whimper, desperate to feel him.

This is his show, so I sit back and let him take full control. His hands firmly seize my waist as he pulls me closer, hovering my ass over the edge of the counter. Wrapping his large hand around the base of his shaft, he slides his tip through my slick folds, saturating his cock, before pressing inside. His lips crush down on mine as he fills me.

We don't take our time. This isn't slow, sensual lovemaking. No. He fucks me hard and fast, thrusting with furious rhythm, and I rock my hips to meet him. The room spins as we desperately chase release. The sound of wet skin colliding echoes through the room, mingling with our moans as the pressure in my core builds. It's pure fucking bliss.

"Fuck. You're so wet," he grits out, slamming into me. "You were *made* for me."

I squeeze my eyes shut, the pressure overwhelming. "James," I breathe.

He grunts. "Keep making those sounds and I'm going to blow my load."

"More," I cry. My fingers dig into his shoulders as he continues to fuck me. He snakes a free hand up to my throat, his other hand clasping my hip with a bruising intensity. His fingers press firmly around my neck, applying just enough pressure to make my pulse flutter. I coil my legs around his waist as he ruts into me.

Waves of warm ripples begin to spread through me, igniting every nerve as my orgasm builds. "Are you going to come, April? You want me to fill this pussy up?" he growls.

My body molds to his. I need this. *He* needs this. I can only manage a breathless moan, my eyes rolling back as he releases my throat. The tidal wave hits, my body igniting as my orgasm crashes over me, and I shudder.

My pussy clenches, contracting around his cock as he pumps into me. "Fuck, April, I'm going to come," he says, voice ragged.

"Please," I beg, needing more. I feel his body jerk as he lets out a low sound, and a moment later, he spills his heat inside me.

I soften against him as my body comes down from the high.

"You're fucking beautiful." He pants, catching his breath.

I study his face, cheeks flushed from his release, and my eyes gloss over as overwhelming affection washes through me. All my senses are heightened. I've never felt so connected to someone before, mind, body, and soul. He owns me. My body speaks to his. A lump forms in my throat and I swallow it down, unsure whether to lay my cards on the table and show him just how vulnerable I feel.

He pulls out, my thighs sticky from his release, and tucks himself back into his pants. The scent of sex and sweat hovers in the air. Leaning forward, he presses his mouth against mine, and I savor the taste of our mixture. A rough thumb brushes my cheek, and I take a ragged breath, his touch so tender.

"You have my heart completely," he says against my lips, and I close my eyes, soaking in his words. He takes my hand in his and presses it flat against his chest, where his heartbeat matches the erratic thumping of mine.

"I've tried to guard my heart, but with you, every wall just falls away." My voice cracks.

He places a soft kiss on my knuckles. "Your heart is precious to me. I promise to treat it with the care it deserves."

My lips tremble as I process his words, and I sniffle, shifting to gently cradle his face. "It's yours," I whisper. I manage a watery smile and nod toward the door. "You shouldn't keep the guys waiting."

He falls still, a delicate tenderness floating between us. "I wish I could stay and clean you up."

I chuckle. "Go. I'll see you there," I say, and he shoots me a wink, giving my hand a squeeze and snatching his jacket off the counter before he pulls away.

As he steps toward the door, he pauses to look at me over his shoulder. "It makes the whole thing easier, knowing you'll be there today." With a grin that makes my heart skip, he disappears through the doorway.

This man has salvaged my heart.

As I listen to his footsteps down the staircase, that's when it hits me.

I'm utterly in love with James.

Chapter 44

James

We rock up to the stadium, and the sheer size of the place nearly knocks the wind out of me. It's massive. Nerves and adrenaline surge through me as I take it in. It looks even bigger at this time of day. The car park is mostly empty, save for a few other bands unloading their gear.

Oliver claps a hand on my shoulder. "Mate," he says, nodding toward the stadium. "This is it. How are you feeling?"

I huff out a laugh. "Ask me once it's done," I tell him.

Tom grunts as he jumps out of the van. "I'm proper shitting myself."

"Well, hold off, will ya? I haven't got any toilet paper on me," Will says, sliding the other van door open.

Oliver and I laugh as he barrels out with his guitar case in hand. "Well, lads. Let's go give 'em a show," Oliver says.

With a silent nod, we grab our things and make our way to the rear entrance where we're met by two burly security guards with crossed arms and stoic expressions, standing next to a striking brunette in a tailored skirt suit and heels, clipboard in hand. They carefully check our IDs, then cross our names off a list.

"Just follow the signs and my colleague Rachel will meet you at the other end. Good luck, gentlemen," the woman instructs. A nod lets us know we're good to go, and we step inside.

The security is intense—way more than any club or small venue we're used to. We're directed through metal detectors and our bags are inspected.

Once we're cleared, we follow a sign that leads us to the backstage hallways, opening into a labyrinth. Painted concrete walls with posters of past tours and bands who've made it big follow us as we make our way through.

At the end of the passage, a raven-haired woman waits. She's petite but her face is fierce. She's wearing a headset, barking orders into it. "No! I don't care if they say they signed up. If their name isn't on the list, they aren't fucking coming in!" She pauses, listening to whoever's speaking on the other end. "I said *no*, Jeremy," she hisses. With a sharp sigh, she raises a hand to click the side of her headset, switching it off before turning to address us.

We exchange uneasy glances. Jesus. She might be small, but she's fucking terrifying.

"Hi, boys! Welcome, welcome! You made it in okay?" she asks, her tone so friendly that I whip my head back, caught off guard.

"I'm Rachel, the event coordinator," she continues, flashing us a quick smile. "Follow me, and I'll show you to your dressing room. I'll give you some time to settle in before taking you to the main stage. Your guests have their electronic tickets?"

"Yes," I reply. "They all confirmed they were emailed and texted to them."

"Fab. As long as none of your guests' names have changed, they shouldn't have any issues entering via the VIP entrance." She brandishes four lanyards as she walks and talks, passing one back to each of us. "These will give you full backstage access. Just try not to go wandering. We've had musicians get lost back here right before a show—and they missed out on performing."

"Right," Oliver says, nodding, and we all look at Will.

"What?" he says, looking offended. He holds up his free hand in surrender. "Fine, I won't go wandering, *jeez*."

"Right this way, boys," Rachel says, her heels clicking against the polished concrete floors. "You're in one of our larger dressing rooms, so you should have plenty of space to spread out. We've set up a drum kit, amps, and a mic, so rehearse as much as you need, and don't hesitate to contact one of the staff if you need anything else."

We follow her until she stops in front of a set of worn black double doors, swinging them open. "Feel free to settle in. I'll come fetch you when it's time for the stage walk-through. There's a bathroom through there"—she points to an adjoining door—"and if you need anything, just press the button on the wall." She gestures toward a small intercom panel by the entrance.

"Thanks," I say.

"Right. I'll leave you to it." She shoots me a wink before disappearing down the hallway.

As soon as she's gone, Oliver lets out a low whistle, dropping into an armchair. "Can you believe this? We're actually here."

I flop onto the leather sofa. "Here we are," I say, a

wide grin spreading across my face. The nerves are there, yeah, but they're nothing compared to the thrill of what's coming next.

* * *

An hour later, a stage manager appears and gives us a tour of the main stage before setting us up for the sound check. I glance over at the guys, and I can tell they're feeling it too—the adrenaline. The stadium is empty, so it appears huge. Rows of seats stretch out into the distance, waiting to be filled. My pulse races as we take the stage, the black flooring bending lightly as we set up our instruments and adjust levels. The sound techs swarm around us, checking each piece of equipment thoroughly to ensure everything runs smoothly.

Tom steps up to the mic, while Will, Oliver, and I stand in our places.

Once we're given the thumbs-up, we run through a couple of tracks. The depth of the bass vibrating underfoot as it echoes through the empty stalls propels my pulse into the stratosphere.

When sound check wraps up, we're led back to our dressing room. We pass a few other bands in the hallway. Even though this is a competition, the rock and metal community's support runs deep, and I spot a few familiar faces from past gigs. We exchange quick greetings, wishing each other luck, and head back to our room.

Now it's just a waiting game until we're called to perform. We go through our set list, running over each song to keep busy when we're interrupted by a light knock on the door.

Will jumps up and swings the door open, then freezes in place.

"Will, my boy," Oliver asks across the room. "What is it?"

"Uh . . ." Will trails off, which catches our attention. We look up, only to find Atticus Shore, the lead singer of Bound to Oblivion, standing in the doorway.

Oliver's drumsticks slip from his hands, clattering to the floor as silence sweeps through the room.

"You all right, mate?" Atticus asks, giving Will a friendly pat on the chest as he steps inside. Behind him, the rest of Bound to Oblivion files in. I blink hard, trying to convince myself I'm not dreaming. My mind scrambles for words, but I'm completely speechless.

Rachel pops her head around the doorway, chuckling at our stunned faces. "Thought you boys might want to meet some friends of mine," she says, grinning.

Heart pounding, I spring to my feet and stride over to Atticus, extending my hand. "I'm James. Bass guitarist."

Atticus clasps my hand with a firm shake. "Atticus. Great to meet you, mate."

One by one, the rest of the band steps forward. Phoenix Riley, their bass guitarist, gives a nod of recognition. Knox Turner, the electric guitarist, offers a quick grin, and Tony Jensen, their drummer, lifts his hand in a casual wave.

This. Is. Fucked. We're standing face-to-face with the band we've admired for years.

"I heard one of you is from Beeston?" Knox says.

Tom raises his hand. "Yeah, man. That's me."

"It's pretty cool seeing talent come out of my small hometown. I'm excited to see what you guys have for us tonight."

"We're excited to show you," Tom replies.

Musicians always hold a soft spot for others who come

from their hometown. There's a sense of familiarity. We recognize that we've all started in the same place, whether it's playing in the same dingy bars, working at the same music shop, or learning to play at the same music school. Our hometowns and their crowds are what shaped us. In most areas of music, that connection can fade, but rock is different. We understand what it's like to work our way up from the bottom. That's something you don't forget.

Tom and Knox get lost in conversation about Beeston, and I watch Phoenix's eyes land on my Spector bass, his brows furrowing as he takes it in. His gaze flicks to mine. "Is that yours?" he asks.

"Yeah," I say, feeling a surge of pride. "Rare as hens' teeth."

He lets out a low whistle, stepping closer. "She's beautiful, mate," he says, and I lift the bass off its stand, holding it out to him.

"Go on. Give her a go."

Phoenix's face lights up as he takes it, slinging the strap over his shoulder. He weighs the instrument in his hands, and I watch as his fingers settle on the neck before he starts plucking the strings.

A lump forms in my throat.

I think I might fucking cry.

Phoenix Riley is playing *my* bass.

I watch in awe as his fingers dance over the strings and frets, playing the bass line of one of their classics in front of me. I'm completely entranced.

"Right, well, great to meet you lads. Looking forward to seeing you out there," Tony says, giving us all a nod as their crew wraps up. We exchange quick nods and handshakes, saying our goodbyes as they file out of the dressing room. As soon as the door clicks shut, we all glance at one another, trying to process the last ten minutes.

"What. The. Fuck," Will says.

"Did that actually just happen?" Oliver finally blurts out, jerking a thumb over his shoulder.

"I think so," I say, overwhelmed and awestruck.

"I didn't think they were actually going to meet the bands," Tom throws in.

"Me neither," Oliver says, shaking his head in disbelief.

* * *

The crowds start pouring into the stadium, grabbing drinks from kiosks and chatting among themselves as they find their seats. The space grows louder by the minute. We're the second-to-last band up for the night, so we have the chance to watch the others perform first. I'm relieved we're on late—it would be brutal going up as the first cab off the rank. Now we just have to keep our nerves steady, pull it together, and hope we play better than the rest.

April's out there somewhere, and I let that knowledge ground me.

Once everyone's found their seats, the first band of the night takes the stage, and the crowd roars to life. We're tucked in the wings where we can see everything. The energy vibrating through the stadium is intoxicating and electric.

The guitarist starts off with a slow prelude, before the intensity builds and the drummer joins in.

They get stuck into the first song when Tom nudges me, his eyes glued to the band out front. "They're good," he mutters.

"Yeah," I reply. "But we're better."

Oliver laughs, clapping me on the back. "That's the spirit. Just remember to breathe, all right?"

Easier said than done. I feel like the wind has been knocked out of me.

The first band finishes their set, and we stay where we are, watching each group work through their songs. They all play incredibly well; there's no doubt about their talent. We exchange a few nods and murmurs with the bands as they file offstage, which just amps us up even more.

By the time we're down to the final three performances, almost two hours have passed and my fingers itch to play. I want to stand out there and feel the stage under my feet, the lights heat my skin, and my bass vibrate through my body.

Rachel appears next to us, capturing our attention as she flashes a smile. "Five minutes till it's your turn. Get ready."

Finally, the band wraps up, and the crowd's cheers echo through the stadium as the performers exit. The lead singer catches my eye and acknowledges me, sweat dripping down his face. "Break a leg out there," he says, his voice hoarse, and the crew moves in to reset the stage for our act. I clap him on the shoulder as he passes. "Will do."

Rachel appears with her clipboard. "All right, lads, this is it," she says, throwing a quick grin. "You're up."

I blow out a long, heavy breath.

Fuck. I can see why people get addicted to this feeling.

The crowd explodes with excitement as we take our positions.

The lights dim and the crowd quiets, and then Tom's voice booms through the stadium as he announces our name. "I hope you don't mind, but my friend here, James, is going to start us off. How do you feel about that?"

Nerves erupt through me as I stride toward the microphone. I quickly adjust the stand, and Tom gives me an encouraging slap on the back. "You'll kill it," he says.

This is it.

I inhale and ready my hands over my bass strings. Oliver raises his drumsticks in the air and clicks them together, counting us in: "One, two, three, four!"

Releasing my breath, I start singing.

Chapter 45

April

Gemma, Anna, Mason, and I arrive at the stadium together, weaving through the crowd toward the VIP entrance.

"Mason, I'm so glad you're tagging along!" Gemma says.

He chuckles. "I know, it's nice to spend some time with my wife," he says, flinging his arm around Anna and pulling her in.

"What are you crapping on about?" Anna retorts.

"I feel like I hardly see you on weekends, my love."

"Bollocks," she says, teasingly.

"I don't think so, you're always busy having a sleepover with this lot," he says, flashing us a playful smile.

I shoot him a smirk.

"I'm thirty-one, Mason. I'm not dead. Just because we're married doesn't mean I lose my independence."

Gemma turns to me, a mischievous glint in her eye. "Uh-oh, I think we're in the middle of a lovers' tiff." I laugh along with her.

"No, no," Mason says, planting a kiss on Anna's head as we approach the door, "I could never be mad at this one." He squeezes her shoulder, and she pinches his waist.

"Oh, by the way, Gemma," Anna says, turning to her, "Max is going to be leading some big, flashy marketing campaign that your agency's been hired for."

Max is Anna's older brother. He's forty and has been working in some impressive leadership role in New York for the last ten years. I've hardly seen him, he's so busy. He used to give us real grief when we were growing up, but he's a lot of fun.

"Oh? It'll be nice to finally meet him," she says, wiggling her eyebrows, "I've rather enjoyed the photos you've posted with him."

Anna stops dead in her tracks and points an accusatory finger at her. "Don't you fucking dare even think about shagging my brother."

"Me?" Gemma says, fluttering her lashes as she holds a hand over her chest. "Why, I would never!"

"Fuck sake," Anna says, storming off to join the line.

I spot Caroline and Peter up ahead.

"Caroline!" I shout, and she spins around. Before I know it, she sweeps me into her arms, pulling me into a bruising hug. I let out a relieved breath. It feels so wonderful to see her again. She squeezes a little too tight, as she always does, and I smile.

"Oh, honey," she says, her eyes watery. She cradles my face in her small hands. "It's so good to see you." The comforting, familiar scent of her floral perfume invades my senses, and pressure builds behind my eyes. Her arms feel like home.

We pull apart and my gaze shifts to Peter, standing awkwardly beside Caroline watching the whole exchange. My expression softens as I lock eyes with him. "Hi, Peter," I say, my voice small.

He rolls his eyes. "Come here, love," he says, and I step into his embrace.

Caroline and Peter greet the rest of the gang as we wait in line.

She gives my shoulders a gentle shake. "Are you ready for this?"

I nod enthusiastically, barely able to speak. I am *so* pumped for James, and so proud of him. Caroline's eyes light with what I know is the same thrill I'm feeling. I turn to glance back at the others to find them also grinning.

I can already tell tonight will be unforgettable.

* * *

"Do you think they'll let you backstage?" Gemma shouts in my ear over the waves of screams and cheers around us.

"I don't know. Should I give it a shot?" I yell back, cupping my hands around my mouth to be heard.

She shrugs. "I don't see why not!"

Good point.

"I'll message you if I run into any issues," I say before I start moving. Caroline and Peter watch with curiosity as I thread through the row, and Gemma fills them in on my plan. When I look back, I catch Caroline's gaze. She gives me a very enthusiastic thumbs-up.

Unsure of where to go, I start walking through the stadium hallways until I spot a small woman with a clipboard, shouting into a headpiece.

Bloody hell. I wouldn't want to be on the receiving end of her wrath.

Squaring my shoulders, I approach her. "Excuse me, my boyfriend is playing tonight, and I was wondering if there's any chance I could get backstage to see him?"

If this doesn't work, I'll be devastated. The crowd erupts in another wave of whoops and cheers as the current band finishes up.

She scoffs, giving me a once-over. "All right, love. Sure, he is," she says, rolling her eyes.

"No, I'm serious," I insist. "He's with Atlas Veil. He's the bassist—James. My name's April," I say as I lift the VIP lanyard.

I shift on my feet, anxiety building in my chest. I can't miss him playing.

Her expression shifts, a flicker of recognition flashing in her eyes. She presses a hand to her headset, speaking into it—probably with security. After a moment, she gives a sharp nod, then looks back at me.

"He's on next. Follow me. Quickly," she says, gliding through the hallways far more gracefully than I'd expect on those four-inch stilettos. We wind through the maze of hallways before reaching a set of black metal stairs. I follow her up until, finally, we reach the landing.

Sound equipment is everywhere. Massive speakers and lights hang from the ceiling, and webs of cables snake along the floor and walls. Racks of controls with blinking lights line the walls, humming with activity. There are about ten stagehands stationed around the area, all dressed in black and wearing headsets. They move with efficiency, pressing buttons, speaking into their mics, and adjusting settings as they keep the chaos under control.

The woman walks me to the wings, stopping just short of the stage entrance. She spins on her heel. "He'll be out any second now. Just stay here, and you'll see him as soon as he comes off."

"Thank you," I tell her, giving her an appreciative look.

She nods before sauntering off down the stairs, heels clicking as she yells aggressively into her headpiece.

I focus my gaze on the stage, and my heart leaps into my throat as I watch James. My brows pinch in confusion as he strides over to the microphone, exchanging a quick word with Tom. Then, to my surprise, Tom steps back, handing the mic over to James.

What's he doing?

The audience is eerily quiet as the guys get into position.

Finally, Oliver counts the band in, and they start to play. James's voice booms through the microphone, filling the enormous space with a husky, powerful tone that takes my breath away.

My jaw drops.

What. The. Fuck.

I had no idea he could sing like this.

I watch in wonderment.

His fingers work deftly over the neck of his bass, coaxing each note as he pours his heart out to the audience. I'm completely captivated, unable to look away. It might be night, but the sun rises inside me.

Tears fall, gathering at the corners of my lips as I catch them in a smile. He sings about stolen glances, longing, and waiting. He sings about hope, forgiveness, and new beginnings.

And just when he reaches the final verse, he sings about finding love in unexpected places, and that's when it hits me.

My stomach bottoms out and I float away.

He's singing about *me*. About us.

Chapter 46

James

"We're Atlas Veil. Thank you, London!" Tom belts into the microphone. We finish the set, and my ears ring as the crowd ignites— screams, cheers, and whistles rattle around the stadium like thunder. I'm riding a high I've never felt before, and after experiencing it, I don't want to come back down. *This* is nirvana. *This* is my purpose. *This* is what I am meant to do.

I've never experienced anything like it.

We give the audience a final wave, soaking in the energy one last time before stepping offstage. As I reach the wings, I spot April waiting. She's frozen, her eyes wide and cheeks splotchy with tears, her face a mix of disbelief and awe.

She's wearing tight jeans tucked into heeled knee-high boots. A skintight bodysuit hugs her torso with a knitted cardigan draped over her shoulders. Her red hair falls in soft curls, cascading to her ribs, catching the light. Under the bright stage, her eyelids shimmer with a hint of sparkle, giving her an ethereal glow.

I wish I could capture this moment, this blip, and keep it forever.

I cross over to her, my own heart pounding, and lift her into my arms. She wraps her legs around my waist as I take her mouth in a deep, hungry kiss.

"Attaboy," Will says, giving me a hearty smack on the back as he walks past. I laugh into April's mouth, and she smiles against my lips. Gently, I lower her to the ground, pulling her close as I tangle my fingers in her soft curls.

"Sweetheart," I murmur, cradling her cheeks.

"I love you," she blurts out.

The words scorch themselves into my brain, and my heart stops. I swear it actually stops.

I move my hands to her neck, pulling her in closer, and place a tender kiss along her jawline. "Tell me it's true," I say, my voice barely above a whisper.

"It's true," she says.

A tear slips over her lashes, and I gently kiss it away, tracing a path down her cheek. I kiss her forehead, then her nose, and finally, her mouth.

"I love you too. So fucking much."

I wrap her tightly in my arms, breathing her in, feeling her heartbeat against mine. This memory is already etched into my mind, a moment I'll replay forever. I'm so certain of this woman, of us. I feel it, deep down, right to the marrow of my bones.

Chapter 47

April

Three months later...

Basil lets out a long, mournful howl from the back seat and I turn, reaching an arm around to settle him. I poke my fingers through his carrier, scratching his chin through the bars.

"It's all right, buddy. We're almost there," I reassure him. He looks up at me with those wide, adorable eyes, thumping his tail against his plastic prison.

"What's that god-awful smell?" James asks, steering the car with one hand while covering his nose with the other.

"Oh no." I squint, trying to peek inside Basil's carrier. "I think he's done a poo."

James groans, his eyes narrowing as he glares in the rearview mirror. "I swear, that cat has a serious shitting problem."

"He's sensitive," I say, defending Basil's honor. I swivel in my seat, laughing at James as he gags, winding down his window.

"It's freezing, James! Don't put the window down!"

We're currently en route to Caroline and Peter's home in Toton for Christmas. We decided to head over on Christmas

Eve so we can wake up together on Christmas morning, instead of spending most of the holiday stuck in horrendous traffic. Caroline is completely obsessed with Basil, so I can't wait to reunite them—he stayed with her and Peter often when Lucas and I went on holiday. Speaking of Lucas, I believe he'll be there when we arrive.

As awkward as it might be, it's time to face things head-on and get it over with. James and I are in love, and we're together. That won't change, and Lucas will just have to get used to it. He made his decision, and now he has to live with the consequences.

He's alone.

At his parents' house.

On Christmas.

"But it stinks!" James fires back.

"We're almost there. It'll be over soon," I say. After a beat of silence, we give in to the laughter. James is laughing so hard he almost steers the car off the bloody road. I pull my sleeve over my hand and rest it against my nose, breathing the sweet scent of my perfume clinging to the fibers.

After a half hour of basking in shite, we arrive.

Fairy lights line the windowsills, and giant candy canes protrude from the garden beds, making the house look warm and inviting with holiday cheer. James pulls up to the curb, and we both race to unbuckle our seat belts, eager to get out of the car. I swing my door open, taking in a deep breath of the fresh, crisp winter air.

James rounds the car, opening the back door and carefully lifting Basil's carrier. Raising it to eye level, he shakes his head, grinning. "You dirty bastard," he says, and Basil lets out a low meow in response.

The front door swings open, and Caroline hurries out, arms wide. I beam, unable to hold back my excitement. "Caroline!"

"Merry Christmas, honey!" she exclaims, enveloping me in one of her firm hugs.

"Merry Christmas," I return, rubbing her back affectionately before stepping away. James moves toward her, bending slightly to kiss her hello as she reaches for Basil's carrier. A distinct, unpleasant odor wafts through the air, making us all pause.

"Oh!" Caroline cries, wrinkling her nose and waving a hand in front of her face. "What's that god-awful smell?"

I giggle, sharing a glance with James. "Basil pooed in his carrier."

She clicks her tongue, peering down at Basil's guilty little face. "You're lucky you're cute!" she scolds before tottering back toward the house. We follow her inside where we're immediately wrapped in comforting warmth. The scent of roast chicken, potatoes, and gingerbread fills the air, creating a delightfully cozy atmosphere.

As I shrug off my coat, heavy footsteps fall from the staircase. We're staying for three nights before heading back home, so I cross my fingers, hoping for a miracle. I hang up my coat and turn, finding myself face-to-face with Lucas. I have to crane my neck to look up at him. A flicker of hurt crosses his face before it's quickly replaced with indifference.

With a steadying breath, I decide to be the bigger person and step forward, opening my arms for him. I'm shaking from the nerves; our last encounter was less than amicable, so I can't deny that seeing him in this setting puts me a little on edge.

"Hi, Lucas. Happy Christmas," I say.

He hesitates for a second before stepping into the embrace. I catch the familiar scent of citrus and pepper. It's nostalgic. For a moment, it feels as if I've traveled back to another time.

The feel and smell of him are still comforting in a small way, like an old song that evokes memories of a time once filled with happiness and love. It's a part of me that won't ever disappear—I might revisit it sometimes, but it will never feel quite the same as it did the first time I heard it.

"Merry Christmas, April," he replies calmly. But I know him well enough to detect a hint of sadness and maybe . . . resignation?

Someone clears their throat behind us, and I spin on my heels to find James standing there. I freeze, rooted to the spot, my gaze darting between the two brothers. James moves first, exhaling a heavy breath before stepping forward and extending his hand. I watch as Lucas's jaw tightens, a flicker of something unreadable crossing his face, before he gives a small nod and accepts the handshake.

"Lucas," James says, measured and serious.

"James," Lucas stiffly replies.

And that's it.

James places a possessive hand on the small of my back before guiding me toward the kitchen where Caroline's fussing about with gravy and Peter is carving the chicken.

The kitchen spans the entire rear of the small house. It opens into a cozy glass sunroom where an oakwood dining table sits nestled beside expansive French doors. The doors open out to the backyard, filling the space with natural light. The kitchen itself exudes a charming, well-kept 1990s feel, with dark wooden cabinets and cream laminate countertops. It's dated but comfortable and welcoming, fitting Caroline and Peter perfectly.

The kitchen counter overflows with beautiful food—crispy roast potatoes cooked in succulent duck fat, a creamy broccoli and cauliflower bake, and perfectly golden, homemade Yorkshire puddings. Roasted Dutch carrots are tossed with fresh coriander, sultanas, and crumbles of goat cheese, alongside a rich chestnut stuffing that fills the air with a delicious nutty aroma.

"This looks fantastic, Caroline. Is there anything I can do to help?" I offer, practically salivating over the spread.

She waves her tea towel in the air dismissively. "Oh no, honey. We're almost done here. Please"—she gestures to the dining table—"have a seat and make yourselves comfortable. You've traveled a long way. Peter can fix you a drink."

I watch as Peter strolls over to the small wine rack by the fridge, pulling out an unlabeled bottle. Turning to us with a smile, he extends the bottle. "I made some Mourvèdre. Would either of you fancy a glass?"

"Yes, please," James and I say in unison.

James slings an arm around my shoulders, pulling me in close.

Looking out the window, I spot Basil's carrier—thankfully placed outside—and Basil, happily making himself at home in the garden. He sniffs the plants, then flops down, rolling around in the garden bed.

I catch sight of Lucas gliding by, heading straight for Basil. A soft smile spreads across my face as I watch their little exchange. Basil rolls onto his chubby legs and trots over to Lucas's outstretched hand, rubbing against him affectionately. I'm happy they'll still have the chance to see each other, I know how much Lucas loved Basil.

Early dinner is served, and we settle into comfortable conversation, though Lucas remains largely silent. He's seated directly opposite and is too busy watching James's hand when he touches me, eyes narrowed and posture tense.

"So, James, what date do you set off on tour?" Peter inquires.

I turn to James, who's absolutely beaming. Atlas Veil won the audition, landing the opening act for Bound to Oblivion's European and UK tour. James quit his laboring job immediately. I'm so incredibly proud of and excited for him. He talks animatedly about the cities they'll visit, the venues, the chance to perform on a massive stage night after night. James's entire face lights up, and it brings me so much joy and happiness seeing him like this.

Lucas fiddles with his cutlery as Caroline and Peter fire question after question at James, sharing in his achievements.

This is his moment.

* * *

The sun retreats and the evening passes easily, aside from a few terse glares and quiet brooding from Lucas, which James and I do our best to ignore. We stay focused on enjoying the night instead, especially as we have three to get through. I curl up on the sofa with a book as Peter gets the fireplace in the lounge going, the flames roaring to life and filling the room with cozy heat. The fire crackles and pops, bathing the room in an amber glow.

Lucas disappeared to his room as soon as I settled on the sofa, which is perfectly fine with me. Basil is curled up on the blanket draped across James's lap next to me, my cat's eyes fixed on James as he enjoys a piece of Caroline's gingerbread.

I reach a particularly spicy scene in my book and feel my cheeks pinken. James notices, leaning to read the page

I'm clearly blushing over. With a devious smirk, he scoops up Basil and sets him gently on the blanket, then extends a hand to me, pulling me out of my seat with a heated look.

"We're going to bed," he announces.

"Right, love. Night, night! We'll see you lot in the morning," Caroline calls out from the kitchen. James wastes no time, practically dragging me upstairs. When we reach the landing, he scoops me up and pushes open the guest bedroom door, striding toward the bed. He sets me down on top of the covers, his pupils dilated. I drop my gaze to the obvious tent in his trousers and lean back on both hands.

"We have to be quiet. Lucas is right next door!" I whisper-shout.

James smirks in response and locks the door. Cheeky.

"Clothes. Off," he says, his voice low and firm. I obey, making a show of it, trailing my hands slowly down my shirt to the hem. I lift it over my head and let it fall aside before reaching back to unclasp my bra, slipping it off and tossing it to the floor. My breasts fall free, and James's eyes darken as he rubs a hand over his erection.

Biting my lip, I pop the button on my jeans, dragging the zipper down slowly, then shimmy out. He hums his approval, pulling his own jumper over his head, his gaze never leaving mine. I watch hungrily, the veins in his forearms rippling and the muscles in his legs flexing as he undresses.

He stands in his briefs. If sex had a humanoid form, it would be James.

"Spread your legs."

I drop my knees.

"Touch yourself."

"James." My eyes dart to the wall separating us from Lucas. "Your brother, he's—"

"Ignore him," he says.

I part myself with two fingers, showing him everything. Sliding my fingers through my slickness, I begin rubbing slow, tantalizing circles over my clit, my breath hitching as I work myself over. He grunts his approval.

I feel so exposed—I've never done this in front of anyone before—but the thought of getting myself off in front of him, combined with the scandalous possibility of my ex hearing, only increases my excitement. It makes me wetter.

I moan. "I want you to touch me."

"Not yet," he says, his voice low.

I continue circling my clit before slowly pushing two fingers in my pussy, one hand working outside, the other plunging inside, fucking myself. I pick up my pace, and my head falls back against the pillows as a long, needy whimper escapes me.

Okay. Lucas *definitely* would have heard that.

"Who owns the pussy you're touching, April?" James asks, my eyes snap to his as he slides his briefs down.

"You," I breathe out, pumping and rubbing my fingers.

His cock stands thick and proud, and he fists the base, giving a slow, deliberate pump, precum glistening at the head. The sight drives me even wilder. He watches me with a feral gaze.

"That's right," he says, climbing on top of me. "You're fucking beautiful, April."

I continue to rub my G-spot. "Please."

"Lie back, sweetheart," he orders. I pull my fingers away, letting my arms fall back over my head as I grip the sheets. He lowers himself onto his elbows, bracing on either side of my head, shifting his hips until he's perfectly lined up with my entrance. His cock rubs through my slit and I rock my hips. I wrap my legs around his waist, digging my heels into his buttocks, urging him forward.

He chuckles. "Is this what you want?"

"Yes. Please. I need you," I whimper.

"How do you want me?" he growls. I hum in response, barely able to form words. "Do you want it hard, sweetheart?"

"Yes." I pant.

He slides into me. His eyes hood as he begins to move, hard and fast, pumping a rhythm that leaves me arching beneath him, a helpless sound escaping my lips. A soft sheen of sweat glistens on our bodies as we move in sync.

"God, I'll never get over how tight you are," he says.

"Don't stop, don't stop," I whisper, my voice breathless as I feel the hot build of my orgasm. The bed creaks with each thrust, and I drape my arms around his shoulders, pulling him down to crush his lips against mine. My orgasm begins to swell, and I dig my fingers into his shoulders.

"Are you gonna come, April? Right here with my brother next door? Do you want him to hear me fucking you?"

Good God. That's all it takes to send me over the edge. I grip his biceps tightly as my climax crashes over me and I spasm around his cock.

When the waves finally subside, he flips us over so he's on his back, guiding me to straddle his thighs. My skin is flushed from the orgasm. I grip his cock, lowering myself onto him once more. We both grunt as I sink down, taking him fully.

I plant my hands on his broad chest as I start rocking my hips and bouncing up and down on top of him, his thick cock hitting that sensitive spot inside me with every thrust. He grips my hips in a bruising hold as I gyrate on top of him. He slides a hand down, his fingers dipping into the wetness where we're joined. Then, he brings those calloused fingers up to my clit, circling it slowly. I gasp as I ride him, feeling the muscles in his thighs tense beneath me.

The sensation of him filling me is too good.

He grunts, his breathing ragged. "I'm close, baby. So close."

"Me too." I pant, the tension coiling tightly in my stomach. He continues drawing circles over me. I arch my back, climaxing again. Lifting my hips, he ruts into me, hard and fast, chasing his own release. With a long, guttural groan, he shudders, emptying himself inside me.

Once we're both fully spent, I drape myself over him, chest to chest, and bury my face in the curve of his neck. His hands trail slowly up and down my back, causing me to shiver. He kisses my temple, then whispers, "I love you so much."

I pull back slightly, studying his face, taking in every detail of him in all his masculine glory. "I love you too," I whisper.

He brushes a stray lock of hair from my face, his eyes soft. "Merry Christmas, sweetheart."

Smiling, I place a gentle kiss on his lips. "Merry Christmas, James."

Epilogue

April

Seven months later...

I change into the outfit I've been planning for the past month—a casual cream cashmere lounge set paired with intricate lace lingerie in James's favorite color on me—ivory. I tousle my hair, teasing volume into the roots, and swipe on a layer of black mascara, finishing the look with a coat of pink lip balm. I decide to keep my skin bare and natural. I spritz my new perfume over my neck and in my hair, and do a final sweep through the house, ensuring everything is just right.

Basil is curled up on the sofa, purring away. Scented candles flicker across the room, filling the space with aromas of vanilla, popcorn, and cinnamon. Once-empty photo frames now hold snapshots of my new life—me with Anna and Gemma, photos of Basil, and, of course, James. I pause in front of my favorite: James smiling wide as he shakes hands with Phoenix Riley onstage. Yes, *the* Phoenix Riley from Bound to Oblivion. Since the tour started, they've become close friends, and having that moment captured is an ode to how hard he's worked, and how wonderfully talented he is.

The bookshelf is now overflowing with more classic titles, thanks to James, and my wardrobe houses variants of his oversized T-shirts and ripped jeans. We decided that he would move in when he returns from tour, and Caroline has been helping shift his belongings while he's been away. I understand why some people might think it's too soon, but that phrase *when you know, you know* has never felt truer. I've missed him with the same desperation as needing air to breathe.

Why waste time when you know exactly what you want?

Between my work and his overwhelming schedule, we only managed to spend one incredible week together in Vienna back in April. We ate our weight in apple strudel, and toured old concert halls and opera houses, immersing ourselves in the city's impressive history and music. James couldn't believe he was standing in the same buildings where composers like Mozart and Beethoven once performed.

After that, we decided we didn't want to waste a single moment. I can hardly believe he's finally coming home.

No more late-night FaceTime calls or rushed texts squeezed in between work hours and shows.

No more waking up in the middle of the night clutching his pillow, or coming home to a dark, empty house after a long day.

I can't wait to hear the rumble of his bass as he plays or walk downstairs to the mouthwatering smell of bacon and eggs frying on the stovetop.

I dart outside to bring in my latest clay creations— fruit bowls, vases, and a set of matching coffee mugs. When James left, I decided to take my ceramics seriously. I opened an Etsy shop, created an Instagram, and started sharing my work. The girls got behind me, posting about my pieces, which led to an influx of custom orders. I reached out to a few of the market stalls Gemma and I frequent, and they agreed to stock my work. We started with just a handful of pieces, but word spread and it took off. Now, I'm scouting small spaces to rent, with plans to open my own shop.

Mum would be so proud and excited. She always believed in my skills before I even did. She used to say that ceramics are beautiful in all their imperfections, that no two pieces could ever be the same. If the last year taught me anything, it's that our imperfections are what make us unique. Whether it's a dent in a bowl, a curve you perceive as too large, or a scar on your skin, they set us apart from everyone else.

I hope I've made her proud.

I quickly check the utility room before leaving and, as always, spot a stray poop right next to the tray. "Bad Basil," I mutter, grabbing paper towel and disinfectant spray to clean it up. Nothing says "welcome home" after months on the road quite like a fresh turd waiting on the floor.

Once everything's cleaned up, I race upstairs to the bathroom to check on the surprise I've been keeping to myself for twelve weeks. I can't wait to see the look on James's face when he sees what I've been hiding.

Confident that everything is as it should be, I snatch my keys off the kitchen counter and head to Heathrow Airport. It's late, so thankfully the traffic isn't too congested. My heart thumps erratically in my chest as my excitement builds. The velvety voices of the narrators fill the car as I crank up my latest audiobook, hoping to make the time pass faster.

Twenty-five minutes and two chapters later, I pull into

the car park. My hands shake as I lock the car, and my legs are jelly as I head toward arrivals. My fingers twist anxiously as I watch person after person pass through the gate.

When a pair of worn combat boots appear, my stomach drops, and I freeze. I watch, motionless, as James wheels his suitcase beside him. He's wearing a gray beanie, a Bound to Oblivion concert T-shirt, and dark jeans. He's nibbling on his guitar pick, his eyes scanning the crowd until they land on me.

My lip trembles and tears begin to spill. He smiles, a megawatt grin, and his left dimple pops as his entire face lights up. Before I can fully process it, I'm moving toward him. He stops, bending slightly as I leap into his arms and wrap my legs around his waist. I bury my face into his neck, inhaling a deep, shaky breath. One hand supports me under my bottom, while the other tangles through my hair to hold me close.

"Hi, sweetheart," he says, his warm breath lighting a spark inside me. I cry harder, holding on to him as if he might float away if I let go. I pull back to look at him, releasing his neck as I gently cradle his face in my hands. His eyes still hold the same sincerity and warmth they always did. His hair is longer now, falling just above his shoulders, the ends curling beneath his beanie.

"Did you miss me?" he whispers. I lean forward, crushing my lips to his. Slowly, I pull his beanie off to run my fingers through his waves, tugging gently at the ends. He chuckles when I finally release him. "I'm taking that as a yes," he says.

"So, so much."

* * *

James

"I love you," I say, holding her close and breathing her in, jasmine and something else, something sweet.

"I love you too."

Right here, this is where she belongs—in my arms. The smell of her perfume is the only thing tethering me to the reality that this is happening—she's really here.

I'm home.

I slide my hands from her soft hair and slowly lower her to the floor. People passing are smiling, a few even crying, at our reunion. I'm having a hard time keeping my emotions at bay myself. I hold her at arm's length to take her in. My eyes sweep from her trainers to her cute lounge set, the waves in her hair, and finally, her porcelain face. The one that's occupied all my dreams. She's barefaced, which is my favorite look.

I grab my suitcase with one hand, threading her fingers through the other as we head toward the car park. Once we're loaded, I buckle in, and as soon as she starts the car, we're met with the sound of two raspy, breathy narrators going into detail about a shower sex scene. I roll my lips inward to keep from laughing. April's face flushes the sweetest pink as she quickly hits the off button.

"That was good timing," she mutters.

"I'd say."

"How was your flight?"

I exhale, sinking into the seat. "Long, but good. Very smooth. I had plenty of legroom, which made all the difference," I say.

The record company booked business class. I'm used to curling into myself and enduring cramped seats and screaming kids, but this return trip, after months on the road, was total bliss. Kicking back, enjoying a film, and snacking on everything they offered.

"That's great! I've never flown business before," she says.

"Well, when we have a holiday, I'll make sure we fly business."

Her smile is radiant as she bounces up and down excitedly in her seat. "Really?!"

"Of course," I say, placing my hand over her thigh, giving it an affectionate squeeze. Fuck, I've missed her. I've missed her beautiful mind, her gorgeous body. After spending seven months having phone sex and masturbating, I never want to wank myself off again.

"This is so exciting!" She wiggles her eyebrows. "So. Tell me. How does it feel?"

I drop my gaze to my hand, inching higher and higher up her thigh. "Just as good as I remember," I say.

She smacks my hand playfully. "I meant finally being signed. You guys have a record deal!"

It's true. I can hardly believe it. Four months into the tour, Bound to Oblivion's manager approached us and asked if they could add us to their portfolio. The obvious answer was yes. Shortly after being listed under their management, Star Records, the biggest rock record label in the UK, contacted us after a show and wanted to sign us. We have eight weeks off before we hit the studios and start recording our debut album.

I'm determined to spoil her rotten. I've already gone ahead and bought Mum a new car. It feels good being able to provide for the two most important people in my life.

I spend the rest of the short trip home talking about the various countries we visited and the crowds we performed in front of, while April fills me in on everything at home.

Mum and Dad have been visiting her quite often, which they all enjoy. I've spoken to my parents here and there while I've been away, and they've been so excited to have April back in their lives. She's a ray of sunshine, spreading light everywhere she goes. Her happiness and joy for life are infectious.

She's spent a lot of free time with Gemma, Anna and Mason, and her ceramics work has been keeping her busy. She's extremely talented, and I'm so fucking proud of her. I'm excited to see what she does with her own shop. She has such a unique vision, so I have no doubt she'll succeed. Now that we have the means for her to leave her job as a personal assistant, I can't wait to support her as she nurtures her passion.

We pull up to the curb outside April's townhouse. Sorry—*our* townhouse. That's going to take some getting used to. I'm so excited about living together. It never made sense to keep packing bags and traveling back and forth between each other's places when we could just share a home. She's it for me. I know she is. So, the moment she suggested it, there was no hesitation—I said yes without a second thought.

The door clicks open, and as I step inside, I'm instantly enveloped by the warm, comforting scent of vanilla and cinnamon. The place looks incredible. She's replaced the old photographs with new ones, and my heart flutters as I scan the images. She looks so happy, so at ease.

This is the April I knew—her laughter in every snapshot, her eyes shining with that same spark that first captivated me the moment she walked through my parents' door all those years ago. That woman, the one who stole my heart without even trying, is still here, and I can't believe I get to be a part of her life now.

The sight of my books next to hers makes something inside me shift. She's transformed this place into a home—*our* home—and I can't wait to wake up beside her every morning and return from the studio to her each night. I'm a lucky bastard.

"Home sweet home," April says, flashing me a bright smile. I wheel my suitcase in, discarding it at the door before pulling her into me. I rock us side to side in a slow dance, unable to wipe the grin off my face.

"What?" she asks.

I shrug. "I'm just so lucky that I get to come home to you. I don't know what I did to deserve you, sweetheart."

The corners of her lips tip up. "I feel exactly the same way." At once, her eyes widen, and she takes a quick step back, waving her hands in front of her. "Oh my gosh! Your surprise! Stay here, okay?"

"Surprise? Baby, you didn't need to get me a surprise."

She's already halfway up the stairs when she calls over her shoulder. "Trust me, you'll love it!" I stay frozen, listening to the sound of her footsteps hurriedly moving around upstairs. A door creaks open, then shuts, and she shouts, "Okay, close your eyes!"

I do as she says.

"Keep them closed," she adds, her footsteps drawing nearer. I can feel her presence before she speaks again. "Okay," she whispers. "Open them."

I open my eyes to find what might be the cutest thing I've ever fucking seen in my life.

She's holding a puppy.

A chocolate Labrador puppy.

My mouth pops open, and I instinctively reach out to take the puppy from her hands, cradling him against my chest. "And who's this?" I ask, scratching his ear.

"This is Loki," she says, stroking his velvety coat. "He's eight weeks old. I signed the paperwork twelve weeks ago . . . I'm sorry I kept it a secret, but I really wanted to surprise you. Isn't he divine?" she says, brushing his soft fur affectionately.

"Loki, the God of Mischief," I say, looking into his pale green eyes. He excitedly licks my face. "I can already tell you're going to be trouble." I laugh as he paws at my chest. "Does he get on well with Basil?"

"They love each other."

We sit on the floor together while Loki bounces between us. "This is perfect," I say, barely believing it, as I look at her, feeling more at home than I ever have before.

* * *

April

We settle Loki in the utility room for the night before heading upstairs.

As I pull back the duvet, James steps closer, wrapping his arms around me from behind. His fingers sweep my hair aside, baring the curve of my neck. His lips dust lightly across my skin, which pebbles at the contact. My breath catches, and I reach back, threading my fingers through his hair to pull him closer. He grazes his teeth along my earlobe, nipping softly before peppering feather-light kisses across my jaw.

My hands move to the buttons of my top, one by one, slipping it off my shoulders and letting it glide down my arms until it falls away. Turning in his embrace, I meet his jade gaze.

The corner of his mouth tips up and he gently brushes his knuckles over my collarbone.

"Did you wear this for me?" he asks, tracing the line of my bra strap.

I nod.

He drops his hands to the elastic of my lounge bottoms. "And under here. These too?"

I nod again.

"Show me."

I tug the bottoms firmly, letting the fabric pool at my feet before stepping out and kicking them aside. His jaw tightens, a muscle ticking as he swallows thickly.

"Sweetheart," he says, "look at you."

His gaze sweeps over me appreciatively, and I press my thighs together, desperate for friction.

"I want this," I whisper. "I want you."

He leans down as I rise onto my tiptoes, our lips pressing together. I sigh into his mouth as his hands trail around my back, unhooking my bra. His palms find me, weighing my breasts in both hands.

"April," he murmurs, his voice strained.

"Don't stop."

Reaching forward, I grab the hem of his shirt and tug it upward. It catches around his head, and we chuckle as we work to tug it free. Once it's off, I make quick work popping the button on his jeans and dragging the zipper down. He takes over from there, leaning back to shove his jeans off. The bulge straining against his briefs begs to be touched.

I lean in, running my hand over his length, earning a deep groan. He quickly tugs the briefs off, tossing them without hesitation. He hooks his fingers under my thong, dragging the lace over my legs until nothing is left between us. I settle back, and he adjusts between my legs. I push my hips up, grinding myself against him. He hisses, reaching down to grip his cock and guide it to my entrance. I'm already slick with anticipation and need.

"I've wanted this for so long," he says.

"Me too."

He captures my lips at the same time he presses into me. Leaning on one elbow, he lifts a hand to caress my cheek. We lock eyes as he starts to move, rolling his hips and thrusting into me. I've thought about this moment for seven months, and now that it's finally here, the ache of his absence evaporates. Every nerve comes to life and heat floods my veins, filling me with a new kind of love I didn't know was possible. The kind that reaches into my soul and awakens the deepest parts of me. The kind that paints my world in a kaleidoscope of colors and a haze of emotions. Emotions I haven't confronted since the passing of my parents. Emotions I'd forgotten were real.

Until him.

We take our time. Cherishing every touch, every kiss, his movements matching our heavy pants. I can't look away as we lose ourselves in each other.

He picks up his pace, and I drop a hand to where we're joined, rubbing myself as he drives into me.

"Faster, James."

"You want more?" he asks.

"Yes," I say, breathless.

He picks up speed, fucking me hard, and our moans deepen. He sucks a nipple into his mouth, pulling and nipping and suckling, and my core clenches. Sweat breaks out across his forehead as he pumps, and I clap my legs around him, urging him deeper.

"Fuck, that's good," he says, groaning as my climax builds low in my belly. I bow my back to press our bodies closer, feeling the beat of his heart against mine. I lift my hips as our bodies slap together, meeting his tempo.

"Say you're mine," he groans.

"I'm yours."

His mouth crushes mine as we come undone. His body tenses before he grunts, releasing inside me just as I clench and quiver.

We collapse together, and he pulls me close, scooping me into his arms. His hand comes up to brush my jaw, and I comb my fingers through his hair as we catch our breath.

I don't know how long we lie there, watching each other, kissing, touching, feeling. But it's perfect. *He's* perfect.

This man is it. He's my home.

My forever.

"Always?" I ask.

He presses a kiss to the tip of my nose. "Always."

THE END

Afterword

Thank you so much for reading. I hope you enjoyed April and James's story as much as I loved writing it. Your support means everything to me, and I'm so grateful you chose to spend your time with these characters.

I hope you found joy amongst the pages.

Acknowledgments

To my incredible readers and followers, thank you for all your support and encouragement over the years. Without you, I wouldn't have ever had the courage to pursue this dream. To my family and friends, your love, patience, and belief in me have got me through the difficult late nights and moments of reservation.

To my talented team—Emily, Anna, and Jennifer—thank you for your expertise, dedication, and assistance in making this book the best it could possibly be.

A special mention goes to Sara, who has been an extraordinary friend and mentor over the past twelve months. Your wisdom, support, and belief in me have shaped so much of my journey. If I can even be half the author you are, I'll consider it a success. Thank you for everything you've taught me. I appreciate you and our friendship more than words could ever express.

I'm forever thankful to each and every one of you for being part of this journey.

About the Author

Tierney Page is a contemporary romance author and content creator based in Melbourne, Australia. She crafts stories filled with relatable characters, swoon-worthy MMCs, heartfelt connections, and spice that keeps readers turning pages late into the night.

When she's not writing, Tierney enjoys traveling, doting on her fur babies, and indulging in a good book. Most days, you'll find her curled up on the sofa in cozy, fluffy socks, a steaming cup of coffee in hand, a cat on her lap, and a spicy romance novel keeping her company.

To learn more, visit her at:
Instagram @tierney.reads
TikTok @tierney.reads